Dedication

This book is for Tammie, my beautiful wife, the love of my life. Her hard work, dedication, love and inspiration turned an idea into a reality.

Also in loving memory of my "best Bud" ever, Wayne Wadsworth, who was always there with the answers to my many questions about growing up in an Alabama "coal camp" in the 1940s.

For nothing is secret, that shall not be made manifest; neither anything hid, that shall not be known and come abroad.

—*Luke 8:17*

When thou vowest a vow unto God, defer not to pay it; for he hath no pleasure in fools: pay that which thou hast vowed.

—*Ecclesiastes 5:4*

Author's Note

ONCE UPON A TIME, IN A WORLD MUCH DIFFERENT than today, two young boys shared a secret—a secret they concluded must ultimately be revealed. These were not ordinary boys and it was certainly no ordinary secret.

The two boys realized that other lives would be affected when the secret was disclosed, since others were involved. They also knew that a catalog of involvement would undoubtedly show them on the cover.

Both boys were egotistical and cocky by nature, which served to produce a tendency towards selfishness in their demeanor. It was a combination that induced plotting and scheming, so together they contrived a ploy for their revelation and a plan for its inception. A plan each considered foolproof.

It would be an act of contrition for everyone involved and would also, to their delight, guarantee abundant self-preservation.

Be advised that it was a very sad day for the two, but after developing their ingenious plan, they became giddy. They laughed and joked about their accomplishment; about the good of it and the bad of it, but especially the good of it for the two of them.

Their jubilant mood camouflaged the passing day. Too soon twilight was near and it was time for them to part. Once again they became disconsolate, both realizing that this would be an uncommon goodbye.

The years passed and the secret remained intact. However, from time to time, from right out of the blue, one or the other of them would recall memories of their friendship. They would remember the guts and imagination they had shared as kids and they would also remember how these two attributes had saved their lives.

And so time marched on and the two young boys became two

old men and by then, when the memories would come, they would pretend it never really happened—probably just something they fantasized, something they imagined. But still, deep down inside, both knew these memories were true and that no matter how hard they had tried, the reality of the past was hard to forget. But then, as always, they would wipe it from their minds, filing it as far back into the brain as possible, so as to delay the time it would emerge again.

Time raced on. Over half a century passed before the inevitable happened—before time stopped. At least, it did for one of them.

Bad news travels fast and when the one heard of the other's death, he was sad and perplexed and this time when the memory came, a sense of reality set in. He knew that time had not only run out for his friend, it had also in a sense run out for him. For now the contract must be fulfilled and the secret finally revealed.

TO THE READER

MY NAME IS KERRY COPELAND SMITH...

I was born on March 6, 1936, at 6:00 P.M. It was on a Friday, the sixth day of the week and it was also the 66th day of the year.

I weighed 6 lbs. 6 ozs. And if you can believe anything a doctor says, I was the sixth baby he had delivered that day. And... just to put the icing on the cake, I became the sixth member of my family.

Everyone laughed about it and teased my mother, said she had given birth to a little "Boogieman."

Much to my mother's dismay, the name stuck and I was known as "BOOGIE" from that day forward.

In May of 2008, I started writing this book. It was something I was totally unprepared to do. Having no formal training in writing and having never written anything significant, it proved to be a most arduous task—by far the most difficult I have ever undertaken.

First and foremost in this was the fact that I'm lazy and simply did not want to do it, which will serve to dispel any notion that a 72-year-old man awoke one morning with an uncontrollable desire to write a book...far from it.

As a matter of fact, not only did I not want to do it, I conjured up a multitude of reasons as to why I shouldn't even try. They all seemed sound and for a while I was relieved, but then the memories came flooding back to me.

Memories of a promise made almost sixty years ago. And... I had made that promise. I just didn't have the guts to keep it.... that was it. I was a coward at 72 years of age, something I had never been—a bona fide, yellow stripe down the back, coward. I finally came to realize it.

That did it! None of the excuses could offset my haunting obligation. I was bound by my promise and now, completely unanticipated, a chain of events had happened in my life that convinced me beyond a shadow of a doubt that this book must be written to finally complete the story.

So I said, "To hell with it," and undertook the task. I have written it the only way I know how, to share it with readers in the tone and verbiage of that period. I want them to live it and feel it as it actually happened and so, I feel it is necessary for me to apologize in advance for any vulgar or distasteful language and/or any racial overtones I have had to use to make the story complete. It is direct and to the point, exactly as I remember it on that day. And, to further enlighten the reader, I have also told the story of the strange events that began to happen in my life that led to convince me that I must keep my vow.

It has taken many reflective hours and gallons of stored-up tears to complete this project, but even now that my visit to the past has been finally completed, I ask myself once again—was it really a necessity or was it just an old man grasping for a straw of redemption, who gave way to his imagination?

I'll let you, the readers, decide.

Kerry Copeland Smith
April 2011

— CHAPTER 1 —
UNFORESEEN

Friday – May 2, 2008
Tampa, Florida

A BLACK CAT RAN DIRECTLY IN FRONT OF ME TODAY, just as I walked out of the post office. It stopped, turned, looked straight at me for a few moments, and then ran in front of me again. I watched it as it disappeared around the side of the building.

I sized the critter up good both ways. Its fur was a glossy coal-black and believe me, I looked really close, hoping to see at least a smidgen of white—something I think we all do when a black cat crosses our path.

It was fat and appeared well-cared for, so I determined immediately that it wasn't a stray, it was eating too well. It was also collared, which led me to believe that it was more than likely a pet, one that had zipped out someone's door without being seen, a feat cats are famous for.

For some unexplainable reason, I knew it was a male. Don't ask me how. Maybe I'm getting psychic in my old age.

His collar was very odd, but also very pretty—just a small red-velvet rope that hung loosely around his neck. It was tied off with a wraparound knot, a sort of lanyard I guess, but strangely it reminded me of a noose the way it swung to and fro as he ran.

Unlike most black cats, his eyes were a brilliant dark blue, like a swimming pool looks when it's shadowed. The pupils were black and dilated and they sat low and mournful when he turned to stare at me.

His actions and demeanor had peaked my interest, so I walked to the corner of the building and looked across the parking area, gazing in all directions, but no sign of him at all.

The parking lot is long and wide, with no places to hide, and he hadn't the time to cross it. I wondered if I was starting to imagine things.

There was only one car other than mine in the lot and as I looked, it began to pull away. It was a new red Corvette, with shiny chrome wheels and dark-tinted windows—the car every guy dreams about… but still, no sign of the cat.

As I walked towards my car, I hesitated, then turned back once more to check the front of the building, thinking he may have circled and was back at the front door hoping to hex someone else…but still, nothing. He had disappeared into thin air, so I gave up the search and headed for home.

As I pulled out on Tampa Road, the traffic was heavier than normal. A beautiful May day, everyone vacating their offices, cruising out for lunch.

As I thought of eating, my stomach began to growl. I looked down at my watch for the time, but was unable to see the face. It had flipped around to the side of my wrist and I was unable to see it clearly. I used my chin to worm it back and then realized I didn't have my magnifiers on, so all the gyrations were for nothing.

My watch is one of those big gold things, a "status symbol" with a flexible band. My wife bought it for me several years ago for Christmas. It used to fit snug to my arm, but in the process of aging, I seem to have contacted a dose of the "shrinks" and now it constantly spins around my arm like a hula-hoop. I'm not shrinking in my gut where I need it, but in my arms and legs and another place I won't mention.

I fished my magnifiers from the breast pocket of my coat and put them on, all the while trying to concentrate on my driving. My efforts, however, must have been lacking, for no sooner discovering that it was 12:15, I also discovered that I was apparently not moving fast enough for a dump truck hanging right on my tail, the driver playing "Get the hell out of my way" on his horn. I would have changed lanes and moved out of his way, but I was positioned in the far left lane for a left-hand turn about a block away, so I sped up a tad and stayed where I was.

Apparently pissed, the driver of the truck swerved quickly to his right, passed me, and then cut back in front of me so close he almost hit my car. Not to be outdone, I immediately give him an "up yours, too" honk and fell back a couple of car lengths just in case he decided to suddenly stop, remembering also to hit my door lock switch for security.

Today hadn't started well. I had just picked up a registered letter informing me of a code violation on a house I was remodeling to "flip." I had no desire to top that off by getting the shit beat out of me by a dump truck driver, but my precaution was for nil—he was in too much of a hurry to care about me. He zipped into the left turn only lane, honked at another car in front of him and proceeded to ride its bumper through the turn, yours truly right behind him, taking the light on amber.

Dump truck drivers don't fuck around. They know how to move through traffic. I've often thought how nice it would be just to have one to precede you every time you have to drive.

I continued to follow him as he zoomed up Racetrack Road, vastly exceeding the speed limit. As he blew through the crosswalk at the Racetrack he almost snared two old men for hood ornaments. He had to have seen them, but made no effort to stop. I must admit, however, that he did have the Rebel flag flying on his antenna and an "eat me" sticker on his bumper, signaling his concern. Shortly after that, I lost him when he veered to the shoulder of the road to pass a line of slow-moving cars that were gawking at a new restaurant that was being built. I'm hoping it's going to be a Bob Evans. Anyway, I didn't have the guts to follow him, so by the time "gawking time" was over, he was long gone.

Remembering I needed to gas up, I passed up my turn at Nine Eagles Drive, took a right into 7-11, and headed toward the pumps. That's when I saw him again.

He was parked at the air and vacuum center, just off to my right, standing outside his chariot with a cell phone to his ear. I slid by him fast, hoping he hadn't noticed my car and pulled up to the pump farthest from him, the one at the south end, which by the way is the fastest pump of the lot, if you were to ever buy gas here. As I pumped my gas, I took note of his appearance: he looked familiar, reminding me of someone I knew or had seen before, but I couldn't place him in my mind. Probably mid-forties, big and burley, heavy, without being fat—not the type of guy you want to mess around with. With long, graying, black shabby hair, covered with a grimy, faded, red baseball cap turned backwards, it looked like he hadn't shaved in several days.

He was dressed in ratty, faded denim, worn-out cowboy jeans with the jacket to match. Under it was a gray thermal sweatshirt, torn and frayed at the collar. Their condition looked self-induced, not bought that way. I pegged him as mean and dirty, wrinkled and stained— "Redneck" for sure.

He paced to and fro as he talked on the phone, randomly kicking at the tires on the truck, something he did frequently from the looks of the scuffed brogans on his feet. I couldn't hear the conversation, but a series of loud expletives alternating between "fuck you" and "screw you" periodically floated my way.

Just as I'm telling the pump I wanted no receipt, I heard him fire up his engine. I turned and watched as he wheeled my way and got a cold chill as he pulled up and stopped beside me.

He rolled the window down and without saying a word, he just sat there looking at me and smiling. And then with no seeming animosity, he calmly shot me a "bird," then, just as calmly, rolled his window up and pulled away. And as strange as it may seem, throughout the whole scenario, the one thing that registered foremost in my mind was the fact that he was missing his two front teeth.

My gas tank was full, but my stomach was empty. The thought of food drove all else from my mind until that is, just before I'm pulling into my garage, when it hit me—a weird, sick, somewhat humorous remembrance from the past. I shook my head and chuckled. *God, you are getting old,* I thought.

It's always nice to come home on a weekday and see my beautiful wife Tammie's car in the garage. Still out fighting the "old rat race," she's rarely home other than nights or weekends. Her being home, however, destroys any illusion I might have had of a big, fat Dagwood sandwich for lunch, since she has recently decreed bread my number one enemy and banned it from the house. Unfortunately in the purge, she missed a loaf of squished-up sourdough hidden deep in the bowels of the freezer, conveniently used by yours truly in emergency situations, which I might add, usually only occur when she's not around.

As I entered the house, I caroled my usual salutation, "Honey, your hard-working husband's home." I got no reply. I searched through the house, but no sign of her was evident. Out for a walk I surmised, probably strolling the cat. I looked at the entrance to the front door. Sure enough, the stroller was missing.

Yes, you heard it right! Strange as it seems, our cat, Bubbles, has a stroller, a gift from Santa this past Christmas. Can you believe it? I couldn't! In fact, when told of the impending purchase, I thought Tammie had gone nuts! "You gotta be kidding," I told her. "She'll never get in it, cats hate to ride," remembering how the little shits always cry and moan when you have to take them to the vet.

"You don't think she'll love it?" I remember Tammie asking and me saying, "Honey, whatever you wanna do is fine with me. You can go down to the Scooter Store and buy her a Hoveround if you want, I just don't think she'll ride in it."

And, of course, Santa brought the stroller. And, of course, the old Grinch was wrong. The little shit loved it. Five minutes after Tammie finally pushed me aside and assembled the contraption, Bubbles was sitting in it like a privileged princess waiting for her chauffer. Now she wants to be strolled constantly and to make matters even worse, the other two cats who allow us to live here, Buster and BoBo, they love it, too. BoBo's fat and lazy and loves to be pushed around, so as not to have to walk, and Buster, Mr. Alpha cat, who's a real prick, just loves to sit or nap in it just to piss the other two cats off.

Tammie's suggested that I might want to take them for a daily stroll. "Enjoyment for the cats, exercise for you," was the way I think she put it. But in an effort to convince the neighbors that at least one of us is sane, I have so far refrained. Although I have to admit, I did scoot Bubbles around the block late one night when everyone was asleep and I have to also admit, it was somewhat enjoyable.

Wondering how long she had been gone, I quickly headed to the kitchen, thinking maybe there was still time for a sandwich if I hurried. I had no more opened the freezer door before I heard the front door do the same. Foiled again, I closed the freezer, opened the frig and pulled out the cheese.

Bubbles came running into the kitchen, Tammie following suit, all flushed and beautiful from her midday jaunt. Bubbles went right to the dry cat food bowl and Tammie asked me, "What was the registered letter about?"

"Just some stupid nonsense about some code violation or something," I told her, unwrapping the cheese.

"On that last house you bought?" I think was her question. "That very one," I answered.

"Well, you said you should have never bought it," she said.

"Wonder what I could have with this cheese?" I asked her, trying not to think about my "fuck up" on buying the house.

"There's some sliced roast beef in the meat drawer." Roll a pickle and the cheese in it with a little mayo. It's really good that way. You won't even miss the bread," she said.

Wanna bet, I think, but I asked, "How was your stroll?" still debating the suggestion of the rollup.

"Bubbles fell in love," she said.

"Really? When did this happen," I asked her.

"Just a short time ago, right up the street where the house is for sale. This beautiful black cat just comes out of nowhere. He was so friendly. I petted him; he wanted to get in the stroller with the Bubs and I can tell you, she was willing. You never heard such purring and carrying on in all your life. He was so handsome."

"How do you know it was a he?" I inquired.

"Women just know, what can I say," she told me.

"It was so strange, she said. I've never seen him around here before; maybe we should ask around, he could belong to a neighbor. He had a collar on, the cutest little red one you have ever seen. It was a kind of plushy little velvet rope. It looked like a little noose tied around his neck. I hope he's not lost."

"What color were his eyes?" I inquired.

"That's so funny that you should ask me that!" she exclaimed.

"Were they blue?"

"Now how did you know that?"

"Just a guess," I tell her, finally building the rollup, and taking a bite. It needed bread!

"At first I thought he might have jumped out of the Corvette," she said.

"Corvette?" I asked.

"The red one parked in front of the house for sale. You would have loved it. I think it was new; all decked out with shiny wheels and tinted windows. I thought maybe the owner was looking at the house and might have brought his cat along and he jumped out of the car. Like I said, I've never seen him before."

"Bubs and I rang the doorbell, but didn't get an answer, so we strolled around to the back to the pool deck, but we didn't see anyone."

"Where was Blackie all this time?" I asked.

"I don't' know, he seemed to just disappear all of a sudden. When we got back to the front of the house the Corvette was gone. We never heard it start up. It was so strange."

"He was probably driving the Corvette, so don't worry about it," I told her, chuckling as another memory from the past invaded my mind…weird things were happening!

"You are so silly," she said, "and, oh, by the way, your sister called. Someone you know has died; you're supposed to call her."

You could have knocked me over with a feather.

Since I only have one sister, it wasn't hard for me to figure out who to call.

Tammie and I had been up to Birmingham, Alabama, in November to spend Thanksgiving with our two sons, their wives and the grand-children. We had spent the last night there with my sister, Fanny, who lives just north of the city; in a place they still call Black Creek, even though the town has long since vanished. It was a small mining town where we had lived when we were growing up.

Tammie, tired from the ordeal, had turned in early, but Fanny and

I had sat up late, snacking and discussing old friends and the good old days in Black Creek, something we love to do whenever we get together. She hadn't mentioned anyone being sick then, but now has called saying someone has died. Strange, I thought. I knew it must be one of my old friends, maybe it was unexpected? They're dropping off at a rate of two or three a year now, so you never know when it's going to happen. So I made the call, but very truthfully I knew what she was going to tell me before she answered. Chills, to be truthful, formed along my spine as the phone rang.

Even though you sometimes sense bad news, it's still a shock when you hear it. A sort of déjà vu, like you've been there and heard it before, but even then, you can't believe it.

It was an old friend—in fact, one whom I had asked Fanny about when I was up there in November—our conversation had begun to wane, until Fanny had mentioned seeing his sister, Jean. Then I immediately perked up. She had happened upon her in the checkout line at Walmart about two weeks before, she said. Jean's husband, Moonie, had died of a heart attack about a year ago and Jean was now living with her grandson in east Birmingham, having sold her home in Huntsville, Alabama, after Moonie died. She said Jean had told her that she might be moving out to Pinson, a small town about six miles south of Black Creek, in the near future.

God! I remember thinking. *Jean has to be seventy-nine years old by now. I couldn't fathom it.*

"How does she look?" I remember asking Fanny.

"Just as beautiful as she always was," she told me. "No one would ever guess her age. She's still spry as a fox."

I remember smiling.

I asked Fanny if she had mentioned Trapper.

She told me that Jean had told her he was still living in Shreveport, Louisiana, and said Jean had asked her about me.

Now my old friend was dead. Charles Edward Trapp—"Trapper", as everyone had called him when we were kids.

Jean had called Fanny and asked her to notify me right away. She said he had died of cancer. Had been ill for some time, but had forbidden Marlene, his wife, to discuss it with family.

Services were to be held in Shreveport. She was flying down to be with Marlene and his children. And, at his request, they were bringing his body back to Black Creek for burial.

"Trapper always thought of Black Creek as home and most all of our family is buried there," she had told Fanny. She said he had requested family only at the burial service, but she gave Fanny the funeral home in Shreveport that was handling the local services. She also asked Fanny for my address.

Saturday – May 17, 2008

It came in the mail, just as I knew it would. A letter addressed to me in Jean's handwriting, which I still recognized after all these years.

I didn't open it for a while; just let it lay on the counter in the kitchen, where I could look at it from time to time as I meandered around the house. Finally I couldn't stand it any longer.

I carried the letter out to the pool deck, where I now spend lots of time since Tammie has banned smoking in the house. I fired up a smoke and opened the envelope.

It contained the letter from Jean with another sealed envelope folded inside it. The envelope was yellowed and old, my name written on the front. "To Boogie," it said. I laid it aside. I wanted to read Jean's letter first. It went as follows:

Dear Boogie, (or maybe now I should call you Kerry) HA,

Enclosed is an envelope that Trapper insisted right up until the time he died that he wanted sent to you.

I have no idea what's in it. He told Marlene, his wife, that it was to be opened by no one but you and made her swear to follow his instructions, so we didn't dare look inside. He told her that you would know what it was and would be expecting it when you heard that he had died.

He wanted you to be notified right away, so that's the

reason I called Fanny. I would have called you, but had no idea how to get a hold of you and I was in a state of shock and in a hurry to catch a plane, so I could get down to Shreveport to help Marlene make the funeral arrangements.

We had a beautiful service for him. He had lots of friends, so there were loads of flowers, none though, as pretty as the ones you sent. I know how close the two of you were as kids, but don't know if you've kept up with each other over the years or not. I guess you have, since he was so insistent we get whatever that is in the envelope to you right away.

I'm living with my grandson in Huffman right now, but am moving out next week to a small apartment I've rented out at Pinson. Can you believe it? Almost back home, after all these years.

Do you think of Black Creek as home like I do? Trapper did, that's why he wanted to be buried there. He will probably be there by the time you get this letter.

You can't believe how many times I have thought of you over the years. You were so cute and so naughty. Do you remember?

I heard you have been real successful, but I always knew you would be. You were always so bright, just like Trapper.

The letter went on to tell me about Moonie's death and several things about the rest of her family. She gave me a phone number where she could be reached and promised to send me her new one, once she moved. She said she expected a call from me and a visit the next time I was in Alabama… "I would just love to see you," she said.

By the time I finished the letter, tears the size of horse turds were rolling down my cheeks, so I had to stop for a shot of vodka and another cigarette before I opened Trapper's envelope. I had no doubt about what was in it, but knew I would have to fortify myself to look at it, so I had a second shot and then another cigarette.

I opened Trapper's envelope very carefully, being sure not to tear it. I unfolded the single sheet of paper that was inside and when I did, a small, very old and yellowed 3x5 piece of notebook paper, with a "post it" sticker attached to it fluttered to the floor. I picked it up and laid it down on the table next to my cigarettes. I knew what it was because I have one just like it. On the Post-it sticker Trapper had scrawled, "Don't Forget."

It was time for another vodka, so I had two.

The letter looked more recent than the envelope it was in, so I surmised that it had been more recently written. It was handwritten in typical Trapper fashion—just as I remembered him…I could hear his voice in my mind as I read:

Dear Boogie,

I am dead! So get off your ass and start writing, so I can get off the "Waiting for Confession" list as soon as possible.

You might want to think of it as the last and most important mission of your life.

Just a suggestion.

See you at the Pearly Gates,

Trapper

P.S. I am currently haunting you and will until you get the fucking book done. In fact I'm looking over your left shoulder at the present moment and I must say you look like shit. And, I can't believe you're still smoking! Don't you know those things will give you cancer?

Laughing and crying at the same time is difficult, but it makes you feel so good! So good you want to feel even better and I knew just the way to do it. But, first I had to do something else.

I left the letter on the deck table and went back into the house, then into my "art room," a place I sometimes paint, but mostly is filled with all my junk and other shit I have accumulated over the years. I moved a ton of the shit aside, clearing a trail to the closet, finally reached it and opened the door.

Top shelf, far right corner, I reached up and pulled it down. An old, hard plastic briefcase, one I've had for years. I can't remember the last time I looked inside it, but I know everything that's there.

I snapped it open. Bottom-front, left-hand corner, an old tarnished gold-leaf picture frame, faded black and white photograph inside. Two boys, about twelve years old, waist-up shot bare-chested because it was summer. Arms draped over each other's shoulders, grinning like possums at the camera. I looked at it for a moment, then wiping away the tears with my shirt sleeve; I slipped the picture from the frame. I peeled the photograph from its backing and then peeled off a small piece of notebook paper that was stucked to the back of the photograph. I reassembled the picture, put everything back in place and headed to our bedroom.

My closet, underwear drawer, back right-hand corner, sandwiched under my briefs was a "joint," given to me by my brother-in-law, probably a year ago, saved for hard times. Feeling they were here, I snatched it up and headed back to the deck, on my way grabbing the vodka bottle and the shot glass.

I laid the two pieces of notebook paper side by side on the table, poured a shot, scuffed it down and lit the joint. I sucked in a big hit, coughed and wheezed and looked at the two yellowed pieces of notebook paper, thinking how many years it had been since the two of them were together.

I sat for a long time, looking, smoking, drinking and just thinking. I remember gathering up the letter and the two small pieces of notebook paper and putting them where I had hidden the joint, so I could later retrieve them easily.

I remember going back out to the deck, to the vodka and smokes, and thinking some more.

I thought of Trapper and of Jean and of Black Creek and of a promise I had made.

I remember Tammie coming home—me high as a kite and drunk beyond belief. I remember her putting me to bed and remember the last thing I said to her before I passed out, "Guess what?" I remember smiling and saying to her.

"What?" she asked.

"I think I'm going to write a book."

That's how it all started!

— CHAPTER 2 —
BLACK CREEK

IF YOU LOOK FOR BLACK CREEK TODAY, YOU WON'T find it. Like most of the coal mining towns or "camps" as they were called when I was a kid, it's no longer there. It has long since vanished, disappeared forever into the winds of time and change, leaving nothing behind but hills and hollows of kudzu vine and forgotten pine-covered mounds of tailings as monuments to its existence.

It was located on top of an insignificant east/west ridge, nestled on the Cumberland Plateau, about twenty miles north of Birmingham, Alabama, an area rich in coal, iron ore, dolomite and limestone. It was just one of the many Coal Camps that surrounded the "Magic City" of Birmingham to feed the process of "Pig Iron" to steel.

Underneath the town and reaching throughout most of northeast Jefferson County was, and still is today, a field of high quality bituminous coal. It's of a quality that can be converted to "Coke"—not the kind you "sniff" or drink as we think of coke today, but coke to be used as fuel that burns evenly and hot, creating the heat needed to produce steel and highly desired for the blast furnaces in Birmingham.

Coal had been mined in Jefferson County since the early 1800s and in and around the Black Creek area since the 1880s.

Earlier mining operations had cooked the coke on site in brick coke ovens that lined a hillside adjacent to the town. The coal was cooked under pressure for up to 36 hours and then hand-loaded into railroad cars to be shipped. No effort was made in those days to salvage by-products from the chemically loaded gasses that were released into the atmosphere. But after World War I, the process changed. Realizing the value of the chemicals in these gases, Alabama By-Products Company opened a plant in Birmingham to process them. Consequently, the Black Creek Mine, which had opened in 1917, began to ship all its coal to this facility for processing. By the time I was born in 1936, the old coke ovens lay neglected and forgotten.

Black Creek was a "company" town, owned and controlled when I was a kid by Alabama By-Products Corporation. Other than the people who lived there and their personal possessions, the Company owned everything else.

Black Creek was strictly independent of any other town or city. It had its own power plant, water system, store and monetary system. The Company money was called "clacker" for the coins and "script" for the paper money and could only be spent at the Company store. The miners bought it at a discount.

Black Creek derived its name from the small stream that flowed along the southern edge of the Camp. Various coal operations had used it over the years as a catchall for the coal washing runoff. It was filled with years of silt and sludge and its water was black as the ace of spades.

It was a typical mining town if compared to others in those days. About a mile in length and a mile in breadth, it had no streets or avenues—just one paved road that ran east to west through the center of town.

The miners and their families lived in plain, wood-frame, uninsulated houses, usually of the four- to six-room varieties. The plumbing normally consisted of one hydrant and a kitchen sink. Bathroom facilities were an outdoor privy somewhere out behind the house. My dad called them "slab houses" and said "the only good thing about them was that the rent was cheap." The houses were built along the main road and along squiggly little dirt roads that spun off the main road at various intervals throughout the town. There were no individual addresses, so everyone picked up their mail at the post office. But to further define where you lived, each of these spinoff communities had names. You could live in the "Upper End" of the Camp, or the "Lower End," and, to even narrow it down further, you could live in "The Hollow," "Up by the Pond," "Out by the Shop," "Down by the Ball Field," or just simply, "Along the Main Road."

The superintendent of the mine and most of his general management lived along the main road in the Lower End of the Camp. Since
rank had its privileges, his home had ten rooms, plus two bathrooms.
It had a large fenced-in yard with a beautiful lawn and lots of flowers, trees and shrubs, which as I remember was mowed and trimmed
daily by a crew of "day labor" blacks. The other management houses
were of the six-room variety, but better built and painted, and even
contained indoor baths.

The mining operation itself was at the center of town. The mine
entrance or portal was located down in a hollow to the north of the
main road, with the Tipple and Breaker/Washer (normally called
"The Top House") on the opposite side, on a down-sloping hill to
the south. The mining cars ran between the two on rail tracks. They
carried the miners into the mine to work and returned with the coal
they harvested. The road bridge over the "trip" track was the accepted
center of the town, the boundary line for the separation of the Upper
End to the east and the Lower End to the west.

Adjacent to the mine, just west of the trip track bridge was the
commissary, the mining office, post office and barbershop. Just
across the road about another thirty yards to the west was the school.
Kindergarten to ninth grade and, most certainly, the least liked place
in town for the kids who lived there.

Just south of the Top House, further down in the hollow, was where
the "Black folks" lived—another town of its own. It was referred to by
several different names in those days, depending on to whom you
were talking. It could be the "Colored Camp" or just the "Quarters,"
but most folks, I have to admit, called it the "Nigger Quarters."

They had their own school, their own community house and their
own churches. Basically, the only thing we shared in common was the
commissary, the post office, the mining office and the doctor's office,
where they had one side of the building and we ("the Whites") had
the other.

As a kid, I had several blacks whom I thought of as friends. In most
cases, they were the ones who did day labor work for the whites, most
usually for the bosses. Other than that, to be truthful, I personally

had very little interaction with the blacks during those years. I remember a few rock battles or air rifle "shootouts" from time to time over the "rights of possession" of the "tailing piles" or "rock dumps," as we called them, which sort of sat in no man's land separating the two Camps, but these confrontations were more battles between kids than a clash between the races. It wasn't uncommon that a few hours later, all of us (both gangs) would be congregated at the commissary buying soft drinks and candy, as if nothing had ever happened. We didn't really mingle, but there was never any carryover of the battle. In fact, we fought between ourselves far worse than we ever did with the black kids and much more violently, I might add.

You grow up fast in a coal mining camp—fast and self-sufficient or else you had better stay indoors. I knew the facts of life by the time I was four and learned to defend myself by getting my ass beat almost every day until about the third grade. By this time, I had not only learned how to fight, but was also extremely proficient in the ways and means of talking my way out of one. These achievements gave me the ability to roam the Camp at will and to feel confident that I had the courage and skills to handle any situation.

Trapper and I hung around together periodically from about the age of five, but after we were about twelve years old, you rarely saw one of us without the other.

Both he and I had plenty of other friends, but Trapper's and my friendship went deeper. I think it was because we were so much alike, not only in looks, but in interests, also. We were both avid readers, both radio addicts, both movie buffs, and we both felt superior to everyone else, including each other. We were egotistical, annoying and overbearing. We argued and fought with each other constantly, but we were friends, and in those days there was almost nothing we wouldn't try...or do.

There was no limit to our imagination. We read *The Sword in the Stone* by T.H. White and became fascinated with the young boy who later became King Arthur. We began to compare the Camp to a medieval fiefdom. The Company was the king, with the superintendent of the mine as lord of the realm. We called his under-bosses the barons, and imagined the ministers of the three churches as bishops and their churches as monasteries. We decreed the school, the commissary and the doctor's office, individual castles within the realm and considered the school principal, the commissary manager and the doctor as sort of "sub-barons" over their control. The town sheriff we dubbed the "Evil Sheriff of Sherwood Forest" and we did our best to stay out of his way. Everyone else, with the exception of us naturally, were basically serfs, who were subject to the whims and desires of the elite. We even sub-classed the serfs with "Good Serfs," "Bad Serfs" and our personal favorite, "Low Down, No Good, Rotten to the Core Serfs," and we hung out with them all. When we did, we became whomever we were with, even mimicking their manner of speech and action, sometimes consciously, other times unconsciously. We could be a corn-pone Redneck hillbilly, as well as we could quote Shakespeare, Kipling or Poe from memory to the delight of our English teacher, Mrs. Burns. It was our way of fitting in, because as we saw it, we were "special knights," two "chosen" ones with the powers of the queen on a chessboard—the power to move in any direction we saw fit in the quest to enrich our lives.

In the spring and summer it was baseball...and swimming in Turkey Creek, about three miles west of town. Fall and winter was for basketball and football, where even though we only had one basketball half-court, and no football field in town, we managed to play. And, oh yes! We had one "dirt" tennis court in town, but only the kids of the elite had rackets and they were all stingy, stuck-up little bastards who wouldn't let you use their rackets unless you kissed their asses, so Trapper and I rarely played. And then also in the fall and winter, there was school. We hated it with a passion. We prayed daily for June.

But no matter the season, we always found time for what we called, "just messing around." We would hang out at the filling station, the commissary, the barbershop, up around the mine, anywhere we could find to irritate people. And, if not doing that, you could usually find us roaming the woods, exploring or bird hunting with either slingshots or air rifles. But, most often, you'd find us in the seedier parts of town, where we learned to cuss, smoke, drink and gamble and to lie and steal with the best of them.

But through it all, two things remained consistent no matter the season—the Friday night movie at the community house and church services on Sunday.

It was also about this time that we discovered the opposite sex— when we began to bathe a little more and pay a little extra attention to our looks; when thoughts of girls and sex dominated our days and wet dreams owned our nights.

It was a wonderful life! What more can I say? And, if given the opportunity to live it over again, I'm not sure I would change a thing… except possibly one day, the day I'm compelled to tell you about. But, as I sit here, pen in hand reliving it, I'm not really sure I would even do that. It was a day when time almost stopped for Trapper and me—a day that now sixty years later is as fresh in my mind as though it were yesterday. I can still see it, hear it and smell it, as though I am actually there and as always, I start my journey back in time by remembering…my grandmother cooked my breakfast.

— CHAPTER 3 —
THE DAY BEGINS

It's a Saturday morning in early April—April 9th to be exact and the year is 1949. I'm 13 years old, finally a teenager! I wake up feeling cocky and confident. I'm ready to roll! I jump from my bed and look at the clock on the mantle. It's 6:40 A.M. I've slept late again; I wanted to be up by six. I feel cold even though a fire is burning in the fireplace. I bend down close to the flames and warm my hands, then turn around and warm my butt. Today is going to be great and I can't wait to get going!

I head to the window to observe the day. I see nothing but dark skies and rain. For the past two weeks, it has been sunny and warm, spring for sure. It has been a real drudgery sitting in school. But then yesterday in the afternoon the weather began to change. It turned cold and rainy. Granny built a fire in the fireplace, said this cold, rainy streak was going to be with us for a while, but I was more optimistic. I really thought it would clear up by today; I was wrong, as usual.

I hurry to get dressed, but not too fast, because today it has to be especially right. I want to look really good! We're going to have a party tonight at 6:30, a wiener roast at Sarah Humphries' house. The Humphries are new to the area; moved here about a year ago. They bought an old house just outside of town.

An old guy we called "Radar" used to live there. He had mirrors and tin lids, anything that reflected light, hanging from the house and all the trees. He claimed the government was trying to kill him with radar and he was reflecting it back towards them. We used to give him a hard time. We would hide and shoot at his reflectors with our slingshots or BB guns. He usually would run around his yard with his shotgun. Sometimes he would shoot it, always aiming towards the sky. I guess that's where he thought the missiles were coming from. He was always good for a laugh when there was nothing else to do.

When he finally died, the rumor was that he had a big hole burned right through his heart, but my dad says that's all bullshit. Dad said the man just died of old age. I really like the "big hole burned right through his heart" version better—maybe from a radar-shooting ray gun, mounted on a B29, high up in the sky. It's a much neater story.

Anyway, after he died, the old house was empty for about a year until the Humphries bought it. Now, you would never know it was the same place. They've taken down all the reflectors, painted and repaired the place, planted grass and flowers and even built a pretty white fence around it. I wonder why I still think of it as Radar's?

Mr. and Mrs. Humphries both teach Sunday school classes at Hughes Memorial Baptist, where I go to church. They have two kids, Sarah who is 12 and fat and ugly and Timmy who is 8, a skinny little prick who likes to sneak up on you when you're not looking and hit you as hard as he can in your stomach. He did this to me about two weeks ago at church. I saw him just as he swung at me and I flinched. He hit me right in the balls. I'm going to cuff the little fucker a good one tonight someway, somehow, for reparation, and then swear I didn't do it. My balls still hurt every time I think about it.

Even though Sarah's ugly and fat, she's really popular, so there'll be lots of kids at the party. Mainly among them will be the new love of my life, Darlene. She's my current girlfriend as of last Sunday. We've known each other our whole lives, but she's a year younger and I've always just thought of her as a skinny little kid with a big head full of blond, stringy hair. That is, until about six months ago when, as the story goes, the ugly duckling turned into a beautiful swan. Now, she's the most beautiful thing I've ever seen. All the guys are after her, even some of the eighth and ninth graders. It's disgusting. Of course, I may be being presumptuous in saying she's my girlfriend, but I don't think so. She told Sarah, who told me, that she liked me and that she really thought I was cute. Naturally after hearing this, I made my move.

It was last Sunday in Sunday school class. She was sitting on the back row with several of her friends. There was an empty seat next to her, so I sat down and said with all my charm, "I assume you're saving this seat for me?" The other girls giggled and Darlene's face turned red. I knew I had hit pay dirt by the way she blushed. Even better was the way she let me hold her hand for longer than normal when I pretended to admire a tiny birthstone ring she wears on the ring finger of her left hand. Her hands are small and soft and perfectly shaped. Her nails were painted with pink polish. I knew immediately I was in love!

After class was over and everyone else had left, we sat and talked for a few minutes. I planned it just right, for as we ascended the stairway from the basement classroom up to the main auditorium, we were all alone. About a quarter of the way up, I stopped and moved to kiss her. She didn't resist; in fact, she was the aggressor! I was only going in for a quick peck, but as my lips touched hers she literally stuck her tongue inside my mouth. I was dumbfounded!

The kiss only lasted a split second, but in that span of time my entire body was besieged with what seemed like hundreds of electrical currents that pulsated from the top of my head to the tips of my toes. She knew she had "got my goat" and it struck her as funny. She placed her hands over her mouth and began to giggle. I was in a trance, a "very first French kiss" trance. I heard her ask me a question, but it seemed to come from very far away.

"Are you going to Sarah's party next Saturday night?" she wanted to know.

"Yeah, sure," I heard myself whisper from somewhere back deep in my throat.

She giggled again, then reached up and placed her hand on my cheek and smiled. She looked deep in my eyes and said, "Maybe we can kiss some more there. You'll probably be cooled off by then." And, with that she did the hands-to-mouth giggle again then turned and ran up the stairs.

I get back to getting dressed.

I dig through the dresser drawer where my mother keeps my socks, looking for a pair without holes. I finally find a pair, but they're my new argyles that my mother said were only for Sundays. Maybe she won't notice. I sit on one of the wooden, straight-back chairs in front of the fireplace to put them on. I check the time again. It's 6:50. I've been up 10 minutes already, doing nothing but daydreaming. I need to get moving.

I head for the closet that Granny and I share, flip through the hangers and pull down my favorite pants. A pair of faded, lightweight corduroys; washed so many times they're as soft as a kitten. When my mother gave them to me for Christmas, I wouldn't wear them at all. I loved the khaki color, but the waist and seat were way too big and the legs too full and flaring. This pissed my mother off to say the least, so one day she grabbed me and made me put on the pants and commenced to put pins everywhere. Later that evening she made me try them on again. They fit great, except for the legs. They were still way too full. So I whined and bitched and my mother finally pegged them down for me; exactly to my specifications.

"Leave them kind of blousy down to the knees," I told her, "Then take out a lot the rest of the way down." I explained that the legs were way too big and that I wanted them tapered and slim at the bottom. She said I was going to look like I was wearing "jodhpurs", but she knew if she didn't get them just right, I would never wear them. So, she did it. They looked really sharp when she was done. Now I want to wear them all the time, it's a fight to get them off me. I had her wash them for me on Monday and haven't worn them at all this week.

I push down my underpants, an old pair of boxers, "army issue," that my brother gave me. I've only worn them one day and then slept in them last night. I check them for stains, but none are evident. They look okay to me. I pull them back up and check my undershirt, it looks clean. I smell my armpits and think, *Remember to use some talcum.* I look out the window again and see it's still raining. Then a jolt runs through my body as I suddenly realize that if it continues to rain, it might fuck up the party. *Oh, shit,* I think, as I pull on my pants, *Surely God can't be that cruel.*

I look for my belt, but can't find it. Then I remember that I loaned it to Trapper who, as usual when you lend him something, hasn't given it back yet. My pants are getting too tight in the waist anyway, so I don't really need a belt. I notice they are getting a little short in length too, so I pull them down low on my hips.

Trapper, I guess you could say, is my best friend. He would probably say the same thing about me. We hang out together constantly, but I'm not really sure we like each other. We're extremely competitive, challenging each other continually. I hate to say it, but he's been the most disgusting one in the group of guys who have suddenly begun to flock around Darlene.

He tried to shove me away to get the seat next to her last Sunday, but I tripped him and beat him to it. He got stuck sitting right up front. It was the only other empty seat and it was right where Mrs. Reese, who was teaching the class, could keep an eye on him. She asked him lots of questions about the Sunday school lesson that we all were supposed to have read, which Trapper and I never do. She also made him read some verses from the Bible out loud to the class.

I laughed my ass off, so did Darlene. Every time he looked back at us, I would make sure to point in his direction so he would know we were talking about him. Then I'd say something funny, so she would laugh. He was pissed and I loved it.

After class was over, he kept hanging around, trying to butt in on my conversation with Darlene. He knew I was trying to detain her for myself and he was being vindictive. He finally took the hint and left once he decided neither of us were the least bit interested in whatever he was talking about. He was pissed off that we were ignoring him and gave me a look that could kill as he stalked out of the room.

He's forever relating to me how she flirts with him, but I saw no evidence of it last Sunday. There was no doubt in my mind that she preferred my company over his, which doesn't surprise me since I'm so much better looking.

But what really capped off the day was when I told him about the kiss, especially when I informed him that it had been a "Frenchy." Every time I think about it, I laugh. I had finally gotten myself together and moved on up the stairs for the preacher's sermon. I saw Trapper sitting back in the rear of the church, in the area that's unofficially deemed the "teenage" section, a place where the two of us have now rightfully staked our claim. There was an empty seat beside him, which I knew he was holding for me.

Trapper was talking with Martha Foster, who is sixteen and has great big titties. She was nodding her head up and down, apparently agreeing with whatever he had to say. As I moved to take my seat, I noticed everything had gotten really quiet. I looked up at the pulpit and saw that Brother Kelley, the minister, was ready to begin and as I scanned the congregation, I saw that everyone had turned to stare at me. All the old women had even stopped fanning. The stare from my mother caused my bowels to gurgle. I was the last of the stragglers.

My empty seat was between Trapper and Cecil Foster, Martha's brother. Cecil is a pimply-faced prick who's a senior in high school. As I slid down the aisle, he blocked my way with his knees and wouldn't let me through to sit down. This further delayed the beginning of the sermon. Martha had to tell him to knock it off before he finally let me slide by. As I did I made sure to jam him really hard on his right thigh with my left knee. I knew I had brought forth a Charlie Horse by the feel of the kick and the way the fucker grunted. This was later confirmed when he whispered to me that in the near future, he was going to kick my ass. I told him he needed to schedule an appointment, since there's already at least a half dozen ahead of him in line.

Trapper thought my being the center of attention was funny and started giving me jabs about it as soon as I sat down, saying things like, "You must love how all the old ladies were looking at you." And, "You do realize you're holding up the reading of God's Word." I ignored him because I was too busy looking for Darlene. Since she isn't quite yet a teenager, Darlene was sitting next to her mom and dad about two rows up on the right-hand side of the church. Beside her was Larue Kelly, the preacher's daughter and Darlene's best friend.

Larue, who we all call "Lashie," after the cowboy with the whip, is another girl whom Trapper and I have had words over. In fact, it had actually ended in a fight. There had been no winner, but we had knocked each other around pretty good that day.

Larue had been my girlfriend or at least, I thought she was. I had gone up to see her only to discover that Trapper was already there, sitting with her on the front porch swing holding her hand. She was home alone and Trapper had just "happened to drop by." I could tell by the looks on their faces that they had been kissing. In fact, during the argument Trapper had admitted it. That's when I hit him in the nose.

Anyway, to make a long story short, Lashie dumped me for Trapper, who about a month ago dumped her for Bobbie Turner, who is supposedly his current true love. She's a Methodist! The rumor now is that Lashie wants me back, but that will never happen, because now I only have eyes for Darlene.

As I looked at her and winked, I saw her whisper something to Lashie. Then they both looked directly at me and did the "girly giggle." I saw her shift her gaze toward her parents for a moment and then, making sure they were fully absorbed in the sermon, she turned and poked her tongue out at me. I felt another jolt, as the electrical currents ripped through my body again.

"Looks like you struck out, partner," Trapper whispered to me and laughed.

"Looks can be deceiving," I whispered back to him.

"And what's that supposed to mean?" he asked. And that's when I hit him with it!

"It means, I Frenched her on the stairs when we were coming up. She's just letting me know she liked it," I whispered to him.

"You're such a liar," he said. But I could hear the seeds of doubt in his voice.

"You wish," I replied, as we both looked towards where she was sitting.

"And it was wonderful," I added, as we watched her poke her tongue out at me again.

Trapper hardly said anything else through the rest of the service. He didn't even sing when Brother Kelley gave his pleading invitation to come to Christ as the congregation sang the closing song. It was the old spiritual, *Just as I Am*, and everyone was standing as they sang. You could hear it echo through the rafters of the church. It felt as though God was sitting up there watching, beckoning you into the fold.

Just as I am
Without one plea
But that Thy blood was shed for me

I don't think I have ever been any happier. I sang to the top of my voice and watched Darlene as her pretty little lips moved to form the words.

And that Thou bidst me come to Thee
Oh, Lamb of God
I come, I come

And as I listened to the ending words, I couldn't resist it. So just for meanness, I nudged Trapper and said, "That's what I'm going to be doing pretty soon." Score one for me!

After church was over, we both told our parents that we were going to walk home, which isn't unusual since most of the kids like to hang out for a while after church and talk. As soon as they were out of sight, we headed down to the woods behind the church. Trapper had a Phillip Morris cigarette and two matches hidden in his shoe. The cigarette was all flattened and kind of damp from the sweat on his socks. He broke it in half and we both lit up. As we smoked, I gave him all the details.

"We started up the stairs and all of a sudden she stopped," I told him. "She put her head against my chest, she was breathing really hard. I knew she wanted me to kiss her, so I put my hand under her chin and lifted her face right up to mine. I crushed my lips down on hers and pried her mouth open with my tongue."

At this point, I took a big draw on my cigarette and blew the smoke out my nose, letting what I've told him so far sink in. After another big draw, I continued.

"She didn't resist at all. In fact she opened her mouth really wide and put her tongue so far back in my mouth, I swear I felt it hit my tonsils! We kissed three times on the way up the stairs. Every time we did it, it got better. She said that she had been dying to kiss me for a long time, that she knew I would be a good kisser and that today had really confirmed it. She wanted to do it some more, but I told her we didn't have time, that the service was about to start. After she left, I waited a few minutes so as to cut down on any talk. That's why I came in late."

All the time I was telling the story, Trapper just kept shaking his head. He didn't know whether to believe me or not. He asked me if I was lying to him. I took another draw off my cigarette and told him it was the honest to God truth. He didn't notice that I held my other hand behind my back with my fingers crossed. After that all he could say was, "You lucky bastard." He said it three or four times while we smoked and then again as we parted for home, both of us chewing pine needles, so our mothers wouldn't smell the cigarette smoke on our breath.

We were both shitty to each other the first part of this week at school. Mrs. McKenzie, our seventh grade homeroom teacher, made us sit on opposite sides of the room because we kept harassing and hitting one another. She threatened several times to take us to the principal's office for a paddling. But as the days passed, Trapper was the least of my worries. I spent most of my time daydreaming about Darlene or else looking for her during lunch period and recess.

I waited for her after school on Tuesday and walked her home. She let me hold her hand, but no kissing. I even went to prayer meeting at the church on Wednesday night, because I knew she would be there. My mother almost fainted when I got dressed to go.

By Thursday it was all over school that Darlene and I were an item. By Friday (yesterday), Trapper was back to normal; so we spent lots of time together and not one argument the entire day. We spent most of the time talking about tonight's party and planning everything we want to do today.

We were supposed to have baseball practice this morning at 8:00, but we found out last night at the picture show that it was cancelled because of the rain. Last night's show was great! The Adventures of

Robin Hood, starring Errol Flynn and Olivia de Haviland. I imagined myself as Robin and Darlene as Maid Marian all through the movie.

Darlene wasn't there, she had a cold and her mother wouldn't let her come out. That's what Sarah told me. She said Darlene said to make sure to tell me that she was going to get well and she would see me at the party Saturday night. I was completely bummed out. "Hey, don't worry about it," Trapper told me, "you can always sit with Sarah." He was happy that I was miserable. As soon as the lights were out, Trapper zipped down two rows to sit with Bobbie Turner, who had saved him a seat. They smooched through the whole movie. Trapper kept looking back at me and waving. He wanted to make sure I was watching. What a show off!

Afterwards when I tried to discuss the movie with him, he pretended not to know what I was talking about. Said he thought the movie was Abbott and Costello. Said as I could see he had more pressing matters to attend to.

I ignored him.

We did come up with the idea of getting dressed for the party early and just hanging out around town today. Just goofing off, but not doing anything that would get us dirty. This way we wouldn't have to go back home and risk something coming up that would get us grounded for the night. That would be a disaster.

We planned to meet at his sister Jean's house at 9:30 this morning. That's a little less than two and a half hours from now and I've got to stop by and see my friend, James, before I go up to Jean's.

I look at my best sweater, make a decision and pull it on. It's a light-weight wool, in sort of a burgundy color; another thing I have to hope my mother doesn't notice. The sweater is a Christmas present from my sister, Fanny. She's twenty-two and works for an insurance company down in Birmingham. She said it was really expensive, so I had better save it for Sundays and special occasions. What could ever be more special than today? I flip through the hangers. Just as I pull down my gray windbreaker I hear a shuffling sound. I turn and see Granny at the bedroom door. She's in her usual nasty mood.

"You better git in here and eat yore breakfast! You told me you wanted to git out of here early and you ain't done nothin' but dilly dally around 'til the day's half over!" She scowls at me, then looks me up and down and says, "And ain't that yore best socks you got on?"

I cringe as the words come out of her mouth, praying my mother didn't hear her. "I'll be right there, Granny," I tell her, "just as soon as I put on my shoes."

"Well, I'm fixin' to close down the kitchen so hurry up and git in here if you want some breakfast!"

I watch as she leaves, muttering something else to herself as she goes. I reach up high, to the top shelf of the closet and pull down the box that holds my almost brand-new tennis shoes. High-top blacks, the rubber soles and trim still almost shiny white, with only a few scuffs here and there from the few times they've been worn. They have multi-colored laces that I bought last week at the store. I put them in last night before I left for the show. Packaged inside the laces was a small, shiny jingle bell, *"Probably for a girl,"* I remembered thinking. But nevertheless, I attached it to the laces on my left shoe.

I sit back on the chair and tie them snug on my feet, stand up and admire how great they look, and then jump up and down to hear the bell. I walk over to the dresser and open my sock drawer again, reach way to the back and pull out my old cigar box. I also root around until I find a handkerchief, which I stick in my right-hand back pocket. I open the cigar box and extract from it the sum of my fortune: two nickels, a dime and a "clacker" half-dollar, along with four neatly folded dollar bills stolen from my brother when he was drunk and saved for a special day. At first I put it all in my pants pocket, but then I change my mind. I sit back down, remove my right shoe and push the folded dollar bills down to the toe, then put the shoe back on.

I walk back to the mirror and put my cigar box back in the drawer. I have a slight limp from the money in my shoe, but I'll get used to it. Anyway, it seems to make my bell jingle more. I check myself out in the mirror. Except for my hair, I'm "dynamite," "a *current-day Robin Hood,"* I think, smiling to myself. I check the clock; it's 7:07 A.M.

We live in a six-room, wood-frame house. By we, I refer to my mom, Mary, who is 46, my dad, Burl, age 50, my sister, Evelyn, who everyone calls Fanny, my brother, Cratham, who is 26 and a career Army man, sometimes home, sometimes not, and my Granny, my mother's mother, who has lived with us since I was four years old; since 1940, when my grandfather died. My oldest brother, J.B., who is 28, and his wife, Helen, live in a small trailer parked in our front yard, just to the left side of our porch.

Our house is typical of the other six-room Company houses in the Camp; living room, dining room, kitchen on one side and three bedrooms on the other. The front bedroom belongs solely to my brother, Cratham, when he's home. My sister is allowed to sleep there when he's away; otherwise, it's off limits, except to my mother who has to clean it. The middle bedroom is the largest and the only one with a fireplace. It's sort of my Granny's room, but I have a small daybed pushed tight into the corner. When my brother's home, my sister has to sleep with Granny—she hates it. My mom and dad sleep in the small bedroom at the back of the house. Our kitchen serves as the bathing area, since it has the only source of water in the house. Our toilet facility sits about 40 feet down the hill, a wooden outhouse (with no "moon" in the door).

As I head toward the kitchen, I hear the sound of my mother's sewing machine, an old foot-peddled Singer. She's got it set up behind the heater in the living room, right next to the radio. She's listening to music; it's too early for the soap operas. She's in deep concentration and doesn't look up. I dip into the kitchen and head directly toward the sink.

Granny's doddering around wiping off the table. "'Bout time you got in here." She says, as I stop to hang my windbreaker on the back of a chair.

"I know, I'm running late," I tell her. "I overslept."

"That ain't nothin' new," she mumbles to me.

Ignoring her comment, I push up the sleeves of my sweater and turn the handle on the hydrant. The water feels icy cold.

"There's hot water in the reservoir of the stove," I hear Granny say, as I cup my hands under the water and throw a double handful on my face. I blow really hard as I rub the water in, a practice I picked up from my dad. After checking to make sure no water has dripped on my sweater, I repeat the process again, but this time put the water on my hair. I grab the towel hanging on a nail on the wall behind the stove. Water drips on the floor.

"Why don't you git the towel over by you before you go through all that ritual?" Granny asks, doddering up behind me. "Then you wouldn't make such a mess! Lord have mercy, you're just like your daddy! Now hurry up and git your hair combed and git back in here to eat; I ain't got all day to fool with you!" she says.

"Okay, Granny," I tell her, as I head for the dining room mirror.

"What was that?" she asks.

"Yes, ma'am, Granny. Sorry!" I reply.

"That's what I thought you said; my Lord what's happening to your manners?" She asks, muttering to herself more than anyone else.

The dining room mirror is the official hair combing place for the family. It's about two-feet wide and three-feet tall in a wooden, scalloped frame that's painted gold. It looks like any other old mirror to me, but my mom says it's an heirloom, because it's been in the family for a long time. It has passed down from one generation to the next. Granny says her mother and daddy never ever hung it on the wall. They kept it wrapped in a blanket and stored up in the loft of the house. She said her daddy thought the mirror was haunted. I must have heard the tale a hundred times. The story goes that when he returned home from the War Between the States, he looked at himself in the mirror and saw the face of his dead brother. The two of them were members of the 12th Alabamians, assigned to the Army of Northern Virginia. They had fought with Robert E. Lee from 1st Manassas to Appomattox Courthouse. My great-grandpa's brother was hit in the head by a sniper's bullet as they sat drinking campfire coffee an hour before the surrender. He died instantly. Of course, this is another story that my dad says is bullshit, so who knows? Anyway,

Granny brought it with her when she moved in and gave it to my mom. My sister says it will be hers when my mother dies; that and everything else according to her. It hangs on the wall in the corner of the dining room, very close to where my mother now sits doing her sewing. Being as quiet as I can, I take my dad's rose hair oil from the shelf next to the mirror, uncap it and apply a liberal portion to my head. Then, securing the rattail comb laying beside it, I go to work on my hair. I've let it grow long over the winter months and it's getting darker too. I used to be a cotton-top, but now my mother says it's dishwater blonde. I put peroxide on it last summer and still have some lighter places on the tips.

My dad gets really upset over my hair for some reason. He almost crapped when I put peroxide on it, said he was concerned that I might be turning into a girl. He hates it when it's long. In fact, he has already said that he wants it "buzzed off" now that summer is coming. He told me to be sure I wash my hair and ears before I get it cut, because Forest Hughes, our town's busybody barber, told him last time I was in that my ears were filthy.

As I quickly part my hair and attempt to slick it down, I think to myself I need to enjoy it while I can. Dad won't wait long to drag me down to the barbershop. The back of my hair always wants to stick up, so I apply another splash of hair oil there to plaster it down. I finish with my highly developed widow's peak on the front and step back to study the results. *Sharp, sharp, sharp,* I think to myself. I take a deep breath and smell the sweet scent of the rose hair oil. *Look sharp, smell sharp, be sharp. I'm a winner.*

That's when I remember that I was going to put some talcum powder under my arms. I smell my armpits again. Nothing but rose hair oil penetrates my nostrils. I'm just naturally clean I think to myself. I nix the talcum.

Very quietly I head back towards the kitchen, but don't get two steps before the sewing machine stops. "Boogie, come in here," I hear my mother say. I quickly do a reverse and head into the living room. "Yes, ma'am", I say, knowing I'm going to get the "third degree". My mother looks me up and down as she bites off a thread that's still attached to whatever she's working on. It looks like a dress, probably for Fanny. "Where do you think you're off to so early this morning all duded up?" she asks, still looking me up and down.

"I'm just going up to Trapper's. We're probably just gonna play some Rook or Monopoly or something. Ball practice got rained out," I explain. "Maybe, if it clears up, we might walk down to the store or something."

My policy is to always be as evasive as possible when answering my mother's questions. The fewer the details the better and I always throw in "or something" for wiggle room, in case of problems later on.

"You're supposed to be cutting the grass out there in the front yard if it clears up. I hope that's a part of the *or something*," she says to me.

I had forgotten all about that, an order my dad had given me several days ago after my mom pointed out to him that even though the grass isn't growing yet, the weeds are taking over. Now I'm hoping it doesn't clear up. I walk over and open the front door and look outside. A chilly wind hits me in the face. I see water dripping off the porch roof and off the big chinaberry tree in the front yard. I see my bike, which I had meant to put up on the porch last night, still propped up against the front porch steps where I had left it when I came home from the show. It looks soaked and my front fender light probably won't work now that the batteries are all wet.

I hope my mother hasn't seen it parked there. I was told I had better not park it there again after the insurance man almost killed himself, an incident that happened about a month ago. I had come home, wheeled in and parked my bike against the steps the way I always do. The insurance guy was collecting for our burial policies and having a conversation with my mother on the front porch. Neither of them paid me any mind, as I scooted around them into the house. How was I to know that while talking to my mother he would back down the steps, trip over my bike and bust his head open? Anyway it hardly bled at all. Granny washed it off and dabbed some kerosene on it. She said it was just a scratch on the back of his head. My mother said the whole thing was my fault and that I had better not park my bike there again. Later on I heard her and my dad laughing about it when my mom told him how funny the guy looked when he realized he was falling. She reenacted the way he waved his arms around trying to maintain his balance. My dad said he would've liked to have seen it, that the guy was an asshole anyway, but he later told me that he would kick my butt if he saw my bike parked there again.

I quickly close the door and think to myself that I need to be smart and have an answer for my mother. "That's the reason I'm leaving early," I say as I walk back toward where my mother is sitting. "If it clears up, I can zip back home and cut the grass."

"Then why do you have your best clothes on?" she asks, as she stands up and stretches and before I can answer, she follows up with, "and what's that jingling sound every time you move, for God's sake?"

My brilliant brain goes into action. Avoiding the first question I go immediately to the second, for which I have an answer. "When I bought these new shoe laces, they had a little jingle bell packed inside," I show her by lifting my foot and jingling the bell. My mom laughs, which is a good sign and then says, "That's probably packed in there for girls who buy them, your dad's gonna love it."

I laugh and jingle the bell again.

"Well, get in there and eat your breakfast and don't you leave this house without brushing your teeth. I noticed them yesterday. They're yellow as a summer squash and I'll bet your breath smells terrible! I want to check them before you leave, so don't try sneaking out the back door."

I tell myself to remember to buy some Juicy Fruit gum for tonight as I say, "Yes, ma'am," and head back into the kitchen.

"What time is it, Granny? " I ask as I sit and try to swat a couple of flies that are camped out on the oilcloth covering the table. As usual, I miss them both. Granny keeps my granddaddy's old biscuit watch on a chain in her apron pocket. She keeps the official time for the whole family. She digs in her pocket, extracts the watch and adjusts her bifocals.

"Seven twenty-three, and that's the correct time. I just checked it with the radio this morning."

Granny dips snuff and when she has her bottom lip chucked full, it tends to drip out the corners of her mouth. She keeps an empty pork 'n beans tin can within easy reach at all times, because she has to spit a lot, especially when she talks. She has a habit of misplacing it and I watch as she searches for it now.

"Your spit can's next to the wood box behind the stove, if that's what you're looking for. I saw it when I got the towel," I tell her. She shuffles in that direction. The two flies are back. I make a swipe at them again, attempting to catch them in my hand. I'm foiled for the second time. "I left it there when I had to get the kindlin' for the stove this morning," Granny tells me, as she dotters back my way wiping her mouth on the dish towel, a habit that drives my dad crazy.

"A certain person went to bed last night and didn't set the stove to light for breakfast, so I had to do it."

"Sorry, Granny," I tell her, "I was thinking about that Robin Hood movie they showed last night and forgot to do it."

"Yeah, more likely that little ol' gal you been in a trance 'bout for the last week, if the truth be known. How many eggs you want?" she asks, as she gets the leftover biscuits and bacon out of the warmer of the stove and dotters over to place them on the table.

"I think I'll just have a couple of bacon biscuits, Granny. I gotta run, Trapper's gonna be waiting for me."

"Well, he can just wait! And, you can just think again, 'cause you're eatin' eggs before you leave this house. Now you want one or two?"

My stomach overrides my haste. "Cook two and break the yellows so I can put them in my biscuits," I tell her, as I jump up and head to the back door.

"Don't you bring that infernal cat back in here," she warns me. "I've throwed it out at least three times already. All it's done all morning is thread itself around my legs and whine for food. Dadburn thing ain't nothing but a pest!"

Just as I open the door, I hear the sizzle of eggs as they hit the hot grease. My cat, Kid, knows I'm up. He's climbing up the screen on the door trying to get in. I open the screen door and he jumps down and runs into the kitchen.

"Now you've done gone and did just exactly what I told you not to do," Granny mumbles, more to herself than to me. But right now I'm more concerned with grabbing Kid before he jumps up on the table. I catch him just before he jumps, hug him up to me, scratch his stomach, and sit back down at the table. I put him in my lap and scratch his head while I tell him, "Stay right there and don't move," as Granny flips the fried eggs onto my bacon biscuits.

"He's got so fat he can hardly move. All he wants to do all day is eat, sleep in there by the fireplace or on my bed, and if he ain't doing that, he's following me around aggravating me to death. Why your momma lets him hang around in this house is a mystery to me!" Granny complains, but she wouldn't take a million dollars for the cat. She loves him just as much as I do. She's the first one to start looking for him when he strays off and doesn't come back home within a reasonable amount of time. But she likes to pretend just the opposite. She does the same with me. Both Kid and I love her right back, but I do confess we both love to aggravate her.

I slurp about half of my first biscuit into my mouth, break another piece off and pass it down to Kid. He eats it out of my fingers. "Don't get grease on my pants," I tell him. Granny sets a glass down on the table and shuffles over to the Frigidaire and pulls out the milk pitcher. "Ugh, I don't want milk," I tell her, "ain't there no coffee?"

"You can forget about the coffee ,'cause while you were layed up in bed for half the morning, your daddy, your brother and your cousin, Norman, lapped it up, and I ain't perking no more 'til supper."

"Cratham and Norman got up for breakfast?" I asked her, thinking to myself, *that's got to be a first!* My cousin, Norman, is another career Army guy. He's the same age as Fanny. He lets me smoke and drink beer, if no one's around; I really like him. I didn't know he was home.

"They didn't get up, they blowed in. Both of 'em still half-drunk from prowlin' beer joints all night," Granny confides. "They almost crapped when they saw that your daddy was up, which I might say is a miracle in itself, since he's another one who likes to lay up in bed half the day. Norman told your daddy that he had come to spend the night with Cratham. Your daddy told him he needed to go back outside and look up again, because that was the damn sun comin' up, not the moon. 'Course, your Momma acted like she always does; treated them like they were a pair of little angels. Fried up their eggs and buttered their biscuits. I'm surprised she didn't spoon-feed 'em! Now they're in the bed, sleepin' it off and she's been shushin' everybody to keep quiet, so we don't wake them up, which ticked your daddy off. He left right before you got up, said he was going up to the filling station."

Interesting information, I think to myself, as I pinch another piece off my biscuit, feed it to Kid, and cram the rest into my mouth. My brother is a great source for extra cash, if I could somehow get into his room, knowing all the while that it's impossible, because my mother has it guarded.

"Stop putting so much food in your mouth at one time; you're gonna get choked!" Granny scolds, "and drink some of the milk I just poured you. It's fresh from the cow; Tulie Belle Davis sent it to us right after she milked yesterday evening. Been in the Frigidaire all night, so it's good and cold. She's sending us some buttermilk today after she churns."

Yuck! I think to myself. I take a big gulp of milk and wash down the dough stuck to the back of my throat, then hold the glass down to my lap. I laugh as Kid tries to get a taste; his tongue can't quite reach the milk, so I have to tip the glass.

Kid is a big Tom, bright yellow with an almost white belly. My dad says he thinks he has some Persian in him, but I'm not sure. His fur is real thick, but not long like a Persian. I got him about three years ago when I was just ten. I was going to the store to buy thread for my mom. As I walked past the back of my Aunt Annie's house, I saw her in her housecoat out at the edge of her yard. She was bent over, looking at something intently in a pile of weed-infested lumber that the Company carpenters had left when they were doing some patching on her house. They never came back to get it. She waved me over.

Right under a piece of 1x6 plank, at the edge of the pile, was a wallowed-out nest and in it were three little kittens. Little, fluffy balls, two gray and one yellow. She said that they had to be at least six-weeks-old, because their eyes were open.

"Are they boys or girls?" I asked her.

"My Lord, honey! How would I know that? Turn 'em over and look at 'em if you wanna know."

I examined the undersides of all three, but couldn't see anything that looked like a dick. The little yellow one was the cutest and the most aggressive; it acted like a boy. Maybe its dick was just so little I couldn't see it. I checked it again, this time looking for balls. "I think the little yellow one's a boy and the other two are girls." I told her.

She told me that their mother had got killed out on the main road, hit by a car. My Uncle Bill had seen it when he was walking home for lunch. He had picked the cat up, brought her home and buried her. She showed me the grave; it was under a big black walnut tree that grows at the edge of the fence around their yard. She told me that Uncle Bill said it would be good fertilizer. I ask her if they're going to keep them.

"The kittens? Lord, no, honey. There's no way I want one cat, certainly not three! I sneeze every time I get around one of the things. I can't hardly stand visiting with your Aunt Polly anymore because she has so many of them running through her house. Anyway, I saw your little friend, Charlie Brasher, just a few minutes ago. He was headed somewhere on his bicycle; said he'd stop on his way back and knock them in the head. I told him if he would do that for me and bury them next to their mother, I'd give him a quarter. They're just gonna starve to death anyway."

I left her standing there, said I had to get on to the store, but as I walked away all I could think about was the kittens, so I started to run as fast as I could. I ran all the way to the store. "Put the thread in one of those big paper bags," I told Mrs. Mars, when she rang up the sale. She was puzzled.

"Why in the world do you want such a big bag for a couple of spools of thread and why are you so out of breath?" she wanted to know.

I told her my mom needed the big bag for a dress she was making and that she told me to hurry to the store for the thread and to hurry back, so I ran all the way. She smiled and told me that I was a sweet little boy, as she handed me the large paper sack. I left the store in a run again; all I could think was that I had to beat Charlie back to my Aunt Annie's house. When I got there, she was nowhere in sight; probably back in the house. I hoped I was in time. I flipped the hasp on the gate, walked under the black walnut tree, looked down at the grave again, and then zipped over to the lumber pile. I heard them mewing before I got there. *They're probably hungry*, I thought. I wondered if they still had to drink milk. I tore four holes the size of a fifty-cent piece about half-way up the bag, then scooped up the kittens one by one and placed them inside, right on top of my mother's thread. I folded down the top half of the bag, making sure not to block the breathing holes, then picked it up and skedaddled away.

I could tell they were wrestling and playing with each other by the way the bag jumped up and down. I was just down the road a short way when I heard someone call my name. I turned and looked back. It was Charlie on his bike.

"Hey, Boogie! Come here!" he hollered to me.

"Can't!" I hollered back, "I got to get home."

"I'm gonna kill some kittens, want to watch me?" he hollered again.

The thought of it made me mad and sick; I didn't even bother to answer him, just turned and kept walking. After about ten steps, I turned and looked back. He was peddling his bike toward my Aunt Annie's back gate. *Fuck you and your quarter*, I thought. I felt the kittens bumping around in the bag again. I laughed out loud. I was very happy. I headed toward my Aunt Polly's house.

"I can't believe one of my cats had kittens and I didn't even know it!" Aunt Polly said to me, as she looked at the three little balls of fur I'm holding. I could hardly contain them. They kept wiggling out of my hands and crawling up my shirt. I had taken them out of the bag before knocking on her door, then folded the bag and stuffed it under a bush in her front yard. My mom's thread was in my pocket.

"Where did you say they were when you found them?" she wanted to know.

"Right out there in your front yard, under that big crepe myrtle that grows out by the road. I saw them when I was walking past your house."

"Lordy me, they are so cute! And, you want to keep the little yellow one?" she asked.

"Yes, ma'am, I thought you might let me keep it for finding them. I don't have a cat and I'll really take good care of it," I promised.

When I got home, I told my mother exactly what had happened. She laughed when I told her about Aunt Polly, but said I shouldn't have lied. She said that she was really proud of me other than that part. She let me keep the kitten.

I gulp down the last of my second biscuit and wash it down with the milk. I watch Granny washing the iron skillet in the sink and mumbling to herself.

"Where's Fanny this morning?" I ask her.

Before she answers she picks up her spit can and deposits a load of brownish gook into it, then wipes her mouth with the dish towel.

"Well, it's for sure she ain't here helpin' me wash any of these dishes, which as everybody in this house knows is par for the course. Same as always when there's work to be done."

I pick up my milk glass and drain the smidgen left in the bottom onto the tablecloth. Kid hops up on the table and begins to lick it up, just as Granny waddles towards the cabinet to put the skillet away.

"You better get that cat off the table! Fanny just went out to the trailer to take some earrings to Helen that she bought for her at Woolworths; she'll be back just as soon as she thinks the kitchen's cleaned up. She'll have a fit if she sees that cat on the table!"

The words are barely out of Granny's mouth when I hear the front door open.

"Be quiet and don't wake your brother up," I hear my mother say.

I pick up my plate and glass, take them to the sink and put them on the counter. I grab my toothbrush out of the family toothbrush jar and load it up with a squirt from the tube of Ipana. After about four strokes across the front and a couple on each side of my mouth, my teeth feel really clean. I cup my mouth around the nozzle of the hydrant, rinse out and spit in the sink. I look for the towel to wipe my mouth, but Granny has hung it back up behind the stove, so I settle for the back of my hand. Just as I turn back towards the table, my sister enters the kitchen and spots Kid.

"Get off the table, you stupid cat!" she screams, waving her hands in an effort to shoo him away. But instead of moving he crouches, blows his tail up about double its normal size and hisses at her.

"Granny, make him get that cat out of here!" she screams again.

"What did I just tell you?" Granny says to me, shaking her head.

"Okay, Granny," I say, trying hard not to laugh. "C'mon, boy, get off the table." I tell Kid, as I pick him up, give him a big hug and drop him on the floor; then watch him dive right through Fanny's legs and head into the dining room and out of sight.

"I hate that damn cat!" Fanny screams again. "Mr. Gray said he was going to shoot him if he catches him in his chicken yard again and I hope he does!" she informs me.

"Watch your language, Missy," Granny tells her.

"What time is it, Granny?" I ask, not even bothering to acknowledge Fanny's comment, but thinking to myself, "*That old fucker better hope he never shoots my cat!*"

"It's 7:38, time you got out of here," she says.

"And throw that fleabag cat out when you go," Fanny chimes in, "I don't want him back in here while Granny and I are cleaning up the kitchen."

I pull on my jacket and watch Granny shake her head and roll her eyes. I zip up and head out the back door. Nature has called!

"If you're going to the toilet, take the slop jar and empty it," Granny tells me, "It's sittin' right out there on the porch." Fanny, Granny and my mom use the thing at night when the urge hits them. They keep it tucked under Granny's bed.

The rain has stopped, but there's a heavy mist in the air as I head down the path to the toilet, slop jar in hand. It's cold and windy. The big trees along Black Creek, which runs at the foot of the big hill, about 50 yards down behind our house are in a flutter. They look stark and bare since most of them are still budding or only have tiny leaves. I shiver and listen to the sounds of the frogs as they sing in unison up and down the creek. *Perfect day for them*, I think, but I thought they only croaked when it was warm…strange?

You want to breathe as little as possible when you're in the toilet, so I take in a big breath of cold air before I open the door. I take the lid off the slop jar and pour its contents down the hole. *"Here's your breakfast,"* I think to myself, as I look down to where it's landed and watch the zillions of maggots going wild.

I pull my pants and underwear down to my knees, reach for the Sears and Roebuck catalog and hunker over the hole. The catalog's torn, ratty and wet from the rain that blows through the cracks of the toilet. I flip to the Sporting Goods section looking for the page I had turned down. It's still there; no one's used it yet. It has a picture of a neat bow and arrow set that I told my mom I would like to get as a present next Christmas. I'm hoping that she will remember. I flip through the wet book and suddenly remember that Fanny had shown her a dress that she liked, one that she thought was really cute. I turn to the dress section and sure enough, she's turned down the page! I rip it out and use it to wipe. As I head back up the hill to the house our big, red rooster is topping a chicken in the chicken yard. I think about Darlene.

"Are you sure you brushed them teeth?" my mother asks me, as she inspects my mouth.

"Yes, ma'am, I brushed them really good," I say.

"I want you to use some baking soda and salt on them tonight before you go to bed and every night for the next week. I don't want your teeth rotting out and have to spend money taking you over to Pinson to the dentist. You hear me?"

"Yes, ma'am."

"Okay, get your raincoat and put it on before you leave here and don't you get all wet and dirty and ruin that good sweater and your best socks that I did notice you have on. And I want you back here before you leave for that party, so I can see how you look. I don't want you out in the night air all wet. I don't want you catching a bad cold and then me have to baby you and listen to you beg to stay home from school. Do you hear me?"

"Yes, ma'am, but I can't wear my raincoat, I left it at school."

"You what?"

"I think I left it at school. I looked for it when I got dressed and couldn't find it anywhere."

"You better not have lost that raincoat," she warned.

"I haven't, it's in the cloakroom at school."

"Then why did you say "I think"?" she asked.

"I meant to say that I know it is. Anyway, it's not raining now, Mom. I'll jump on my bike and I'll be up to Trapper's in no time. I won't get wet at all."

"Just remember what I said about wanting you back here. You hear me?"

"Yes, ma'am." I say, as I zip out the front door, but I only get as far as the porch before I remember something I forgot. I run back inside and head back to the bedroom, open the closet door and grab my slingshot, which is hanging on a nail inside my closet. I hang it around my neck. I see Kid. He's curled up in front of the fireplace, fast asleep. I leave the room and zoom back past my mom, who is back to her sewing. I keep real quiet and head back out the door. Just before the door closes, I hear the NBC chime and the announcer say, "It's 8:00 o'clock."

— CHAPTER 4 —
LEAVING HOME

EVEN THOUGH THE RAIN HAS STOPPED FOR NOW, the sky is darkly overcast, the color of a coal miner's bath water. There's definitely more rain on the way. As I lift my bike upright from where it's laying across the front porch steps, a gust of wind racks my body and does a whirlwind through my hair. I shiver and wipe at the hair oil running down my face.

My bike is soaked, but my front fender light still works. That's good! I need to dry the bike seat off or it'll look like I pissed my pants. I don't want to go back inside for obvious reasons, so I push it over towards the garage. Maybe there's a rag or something in there that I can wipe it down with.

Our garage is sort of a lean-to affair that was hurriedly thrown up by my dad when we moved into this house. We used to live in the Upper End of the Camp, but moved down here, to the Lower End, when I was five. He had a '37 Ford at the time, but after my brother wrecked it, he sold it for scrap. My brother wasn't scratched, but the car was killed.

We don't currently have a car and my dad says we don't really need one, because my brother always leaves his here when he's away and even when he's here, he's usually sleeping off a drunk, so my dad can use his if the need arises.

Cratham's current car is a new, bright-red, '49 Ford. He's had it for about a month. He bought it when he came home from Japan. Now he's somehow wrangled his way into doing duty at the Birmingham Recruitment Office. He's going to probably be around for at least a couple of years now, which elates my mom. She said she couldn't believe Cratham was so lucky. My dad said he couldn't believe he, my dad, was so unlucky—of course, not loud enough so as my mother could hear it.

Cratham told my dad that there was no way he would park his car in "that garage." I believe he used the term, "piece of shit" garage, which I agree is appropriate, due to the fact that it really is a piece of shit. My dad built it out of "slab" lumber and roofed it with some rusted pieces of corrugated tin that he scrounged up from a scrap pile up at the mine. It's a three-sided, more falling-down than standing-up contraption that he attached to the garage of Mr. Williams, our next-door neighbor. Dad has all kinds of shit piled up in it, so hopefully I'll find a rag.

I see Mr. Williams, who by the way is a big, tall, no-nonsense kind of gentleman, looking at the red '49er and shaking his head as I approach the garage. It's obvious why. Cratham, drunker than shit when he wheeled in this morning, parked at an angle right in the middle of our two driveways, which prevents Mr. Williams, who is obviously ready to go somewhere, from being able to get his car out of his garage.

"Is he in the bed?" he asks me, as I walk up. He's definitely not in a happy mood.

"Passed out drunk." I tell him, "Him and my cousin, Norman, both. Out drinking all night, Granny says."

"Is Burl home?" he wants to know.

"No, sir, Granny said he went up to the filling station. He must've walked."

Mr. Williams shakes his head again. "Dadburn it, I could kick his ass."

"My dad?" I ask him, trying for some levity.

"No! Your brother, for the way he's blocked me in with his car. And I see he finally wrecked it last night, which ain't no surprise to me the way he drives. Come look at this right front fender," he says with a chuckle.

I lean my bike against the garage and walk around to where he's standing. Sure enough, the whole right-hand front fender is demolished, all the way from the crushed and dangling headlight, clear back to the passenger door.

"Wonder what he hit?" I ask him.

"Who the heck knows? Whatever it was, it was black," he says, indicating the streaks of black paint laminated to the red paint of the crushed front fender.

"Hope it wasn't a cop," I say, as I open the front passenger door and look inside.

"It's not locked up and the keys are in the switch," I tell him. I slide into the front seat and quickly begin a search for bounty. Hopefully some money! I see a pack of Lucky Strikes wedged under the driver's side visor. I pull it down; bingo; almost half a pack. I look to make sure Mr. Williams isn't looking and slide them into my jacket pocket. I open the glove compartment, nothing there but a mishmash of papers and a couple of old road maps. I turn and look at the back seat; nothing there, but some obviously not too old pecker tracks polka dotting the fuzzy, gray upholstery. They're going to be hard to get off, but I guess there's always seat covers. I look down at the back floor-board and see a pile of flimsy material lying in a heap, pushed almost up under the front seat. I scale over the seat to the back, reach down and pick it up—panties; and from the looks of them they belong to a really fat girl. I wad them back up and stick them under my jacket. Looks like somebody got lucky; probably Norman, he loves fat girls.

Mr. Williams opens the driver's door and slides into the seat. "I'm gonna move it so I can get my car out," he tells me. He starts the car, backs it up, then backs it back into our driveway, front end facing out, so that the obliterated fender will be the first thing my dad sees when he comes home. He didn't say this, but I know that's why he did it. As he gets out of the car, he drops the keys in his pocket.

"I'll give these to Burl later when I see him up at the filling station. I'm going up there to get some gas," he says. What he means is, "I hope the fucker wakes up and wants to go somewhere and panics when he can't find his keys."

As he leaves I unfurl the panties and use them to dry my bike seat. When I'm through, I stretch them over the dangling headlight of the demolished fender. *Hit her in her fat ass and snagged her panties. At least that's my verdict*, I think to myself.

I hop on my bike and head up the road toward the top of the hill. The road's level for about 50 feet, then inclines upward at about a 30-degree angle for about a football field and a half to the top. The road is rough and rutted in the best of conditions, but today it is also squishy with mud and pools of water. I hit a big mudhole, no way to miss it. I lift my legs high off the pedals in an effort to keep my pants dry. It slows me down, but I recuperate and pump as hard as I can on up the hill.

James lives in the last house on the right at the top of the hill. There are six houses between his house and mine. Twelve if you count the other side of the road. I make it to the second house on the right before I hear someone call my name. "Hey, Boogie, where you headed?" I look to my right and see Margie Skinner. She's sitting on her front porch steps smoking a cigarette. "Come here," she hollers to me. I slam on my brakes, drop the bike on the edge of the road and head up the steps to where she's sitting. Her house sits up really high. There are about ten steps up to her porch. She's about five steps up; she has her hair in rollers. In actual years, Margie is the same age as me, but in body, action and mind, she's at least twenty-one. By the time she was eleven years old, men from six to sixty found themselves tongue-tied when she was around. We've known each other since we were babies. When we lived in the Upper End of the Camp, her family lived right across the street. When we moved down here to the Lower End, they followed us about a month or so later.

She's the first girl I ever kissed and the first to ever show me the difference between boys and girls. We were probably about three or four years old at the time. She has a sister named Annette who's two years older than us. The three of us used to play doctor and nurse, which required a lot of examination of each other's bodies. I'd still be game for it now, but Margie has no interest in me whatsoever. She says I'm just a kid. She goes for the older guys. Her current boyfriend is about seventeen. He just quit school to join the army. It was a surprise to everyone because he's been a high school sport star in both football and baseball. In fact, she's wrapped up in his blue football sweater now and has on a pair of short shorts. She's got great legs and loves to show them off. She shivers as she sucks on the cigarette.

"Where you headed all duded up so early in the morning?" she asks me as I move up the steps to where she's sitting.

"Why are you sitting out here on wet steps?" I ask her back, ignoring her question to me and at the same time trying to make a decision as to whether I want to sit down with her and get my pants wet or continue standing up. I decide to stand.

Margie is one of those happy-go-lucky types who can always find something to laugh about, but today there isn't even a smile.

"I broke up with Ken last night and I'm sad," she tells me as she wipes away a tear that has just run down her cheek. Her eyelashes are long and black, like the color of her hair and I can see more tears starting to pool in the corners of her blue eyes.

"He's way too old for you anyway," I tell her, "and he's telling everyone that he's joined the Army, so he won't even be around. You'll get over him in no time," I assure her. "You must have at least a hundred guys chasing after you now anyway."

She stands up beside me yawning and stretching. She takes another draw off the cigarette, starts to flip it away, then changes her mind and hands it to me.

"Cup it in your hand when you smoke it or else your daddy might catch you smoking," she says and finally laughs as she watches me inhale a big drag.

"Why do you say that?" I ask.

"Because he's sitting in there in the kitchen drinking coffee with my mother right now and he's liable to walk out here on the porch, you dummy. Catch his little baby smoking," she explains.

"My dad's here?" I ask.

"First thing this morning, right after my dad left. It's funny, he always seems to show up when my dad's not home," she says with a smirk.

I ignore her comment, take a final drag on the cigarette and flip it out in the yard. No use stretching my luck. She stretches and laughs again, then rubs her hand through my hair.

"What'd you do? Use a whole bottle of hair oil this morning?" she inquires, as she wipes her hand on my jacket and then pulls at my slingshot. "You're so juvenile! Still like a little baby. Even got a little bell on its shoe!"

"Now I wish I was sitting down. I can see why she still thinks of me as a kid. She's at least three inches taller than my five foot three, and she's built like a brick shithouse. Even with her hair in rollers and no makeup, she's sexy as hell.

"You never did tell me where you're going," she chides at me again.

"Just up to Trapper's, but I've got to stop up at James' first. Anyway, I gotta get going," I say. I see her eyes light up and a sly smile form on her lips when I mention James' name.

"Ugh! I hate James! He's so gross. But he is cute," she says. "Every time I see him, he asks me when I'm gonna let him fuck me. He asked me up at the store the other day, right in front of Ken! Walked right up to where we were standing. Stood there smirking and licking a Popsicle. Propositioned me right there. I shook up the Coca Cola I was drinking and sprayed him with it. He just stood there laughing; I couldn't believe it. And Ken didn't do a thing, 'cause he's afraid of James. Ken's two years older and at least twenty pounds heavier; can you believe it? James is so gross!"

"Are you?" I ask her.

"Am I what?"

"Since you've broken up with Ken, are you gonna let James fuck you?" I ask.

"Get out of here!" she says, but she laughs anyway and she doesn't say no.

"See you later." I tell her, and start down the steps, then decide to say something else. I stop and turn back, "Hey, don't be sad about losing Ken. He's not worth crying over, you know."

She laughs again. "It's not Ken, you ninny. I'm already over him! I'm sad because he told me he wants all the stuff he's given to me back, the fuckin' 'Indian giver!' This sweater and that pretty necklace and bracelet set he gave me for Christmas, all that kind of shit and my mother says I have to do it. It's not fair, 'cause I've given him things that he can't ever give back to me, if you know what I mean."

No shit, I'm thinking to myself. *Old Ken and several other guys, if you can believe the stories the "big boys" are telling.* "Call me next time you're in a giving mood," I tell her, as I skip on down the steps.

"And after I stop laughing, we can ride your bike and shoot your slingshot," she yells to me as I head up the hill, pumping as hard as I can. I know she's watching, hoping that I have to get off and push ,so she can laugh at me again. What a bitch! But, she's my friend and I know she always will be 'til the day we die. I nearly kill myself, but finally I make it to the top. On the way up I see very little activity. Louis Whitworth's out wiping his car down with a towel. *Don't the dumb shit know it's just gonna get wet again? Look at the sky, Louis!* I'm thinking to myself.

I see old man Dorman sitting on his front porch swing. He's got on a starched white shirt and his overalls. No coat, but he's got his hat on and holding his cane. Probably waiting for his son to pick him up to take him somewhere. "Hey, Mr. Dorman!" I yell to him. "You need a coat out here today!" I get no response, but it does start the old fart to swinging. He's a crazy old man. My dad says he's "touched in the head."

I swing my bike into James' yard. The air has become heavier with mist. When I stop, the tail wind that made it possible to conquer the hill flattens my clothes and turns my exerted sweat into icy water that rolls down my back. I prop my bike against an overgrown hedge next to the porch and hear a banging sound coming from their garage, another dilapidated structure that looks even worse than ours.

I walk over and look inside. I see James sitting on an old barrel in the back. He's holding a kerosene lantern for Charlie Brasher, who's banging on something and grunting like a hog. "Hey, it's daylight outside if you two haven't noticed," I inform them as I walk back to where they are. Charlie's banging away with a hammer on a wrench he has tightened around a rusty bolt on the side of an old, worn-out, push mower.

"The fucker can't see what he's doing, so I'm holding a light for him," James tells me.

"We got a new blade and now can't get this old fucker off," Charlie pipes in. "Hold the light down closer, James, I'm gonna put some more oil on it."

"Why don't you use some vaseline, Charlie," I say to him, "You're used to getting things off with that!" James laughs! "Fuck you, asshole," Charlie tells me, as he clicks the oil can 'til it floods the rusted bolt. "Let it soak in for a while and we'll try again," he says to James.

"Hey, James, did you cut my slingshot rubbers?" I ask him. I get no reply. He's too busy concentrating on holding the light for Charlie.

"Goddamn it, Charlie, hurry up! It's soaked long enough!" he tells him.

"Whose mower is it?" I ask.

"Why you wanna know?" James asks me. James is a weird duck to say the least. He's one of those guys that you somehow know immediately can beat the shit out of you. In my case, there's lots of guys who fall into that category, but I'd put James up in the top five. He's one of those "loner" types; keeps to himself for the most part. If he's your friend, you're okay. If not, watch out. And, to be James' friend takes years. I've known him for as long as I've known anybody. He's fifteen now, he'll be sixteen in August. In appearance he's not much different from other guys his age; maybe slightly taller and certainly a lot stronger, although you don't perceive this at first glance. It's when you look into his eyes or attempt to have a conversation with him that you realize he's different. His eyes are the lightest of blue, like the morning skies of October. They are uncommonly round and staring, giving the impression that he's constantly surprised. But, they have a look that's vacant and expressionless and they rarely blink. He's secretive as hell and sometimes goes for hours without saying a word. When he does talk, he can be blatantly direct.

"Why do you wanna know?" He has just asked me.

"No reason," I tell him, "just making conversation." He makes no comment. I stand and watch as Charlie attempts to dislodge the rusted bolt. I remain silent.

"It ain't gonna move, James, I'm gonna have to cut it off, Charlie says, standing up and heading toward the door. "I'll be right back, I'm gonna go get my dad's hacksaw." Charlie lives right next door. I know he won't be gone for long, so I seize the moment and ask again. "Did you remember to cut my rubbers?"

"Charlie!" James hollers, just as Charlie's exiting the garage. "Do you know what size bolts you need for this thing?"

"Yeah, I think so," Charlie responds.

"Then scour up two, 'cause you're gonna have the same problem on the other side. And, hurry the fuck back!" he tells him.

Charlie's smart as hell when it come to fixing stuff, but he's fat and slow as molasses. "I'm gonna kick his ass if he cuts off those bolts and ain't got none to fit," James mumbles more to himself than to me. I watch Charlie as he walks away. His big fat ass is about to bust out of the overalls he's wearing.

"Well, you got a big enough target," I say to James, who hasn't moved. He's still sitting on the barrel holding the light, deep in concentration. What the deal is with the rusted-out mower is apparently important to him. Who knows? I certainly am not asking again.

I stand and wait, watching him hold the light. Finally, after what seems like about five minutes, he moves. He jumps off the barrel, sits the lantern on the floor, walks over to a shelf, and pulls down a large fruit jar. There are several more just like it sitting on the shelf. Inside them is where he stores that precious commodity that has become so hard to find—real, red rubber, inner tube, a "must have" product for the construction of a slingshot. James is about the last person in town to have any, since after the war all the tubes have gone synthetic. James has an unknown source of supply. I think it's his uncle, who owns an auto shop over in Pinson, a small town about six miles away, but he would never tell you.

He cuts up the tubes in exactly 6-inch widths and 12-inch lengths, puts wax paper between each piece, then rolls them up and stuffs them down in fruit jars. He has exactly 13 strips in every jar. Don't ask me why; it's a crazy numbers game he plays with himself. The number 13 is a lucky number according to him. Each jar is the equivalent of 78 sets of ½" x 12" slingshot rubbers, which is the perfect size according to James and the only size that he will cut them. As I watch him open the jar, I go for some fun.

"You cut them 7/16" for me, didn't you? I asked him.

"I ort' to have cut 'em ¼", for those weasely little arms of yours," he tells me, as he rolls back the wax paper and pulls out the set he has cut for me.

"Fifty cents and they're yours," he says, making sure not to give me the rubbers before he gets his money. I reach into my pocket, pull out the "clacker" ½ dollar and hold it out to him.

"I ain't takin' no clacker," he says to me. "I want real money, the silver stuff."

"Clacker's real money," I attempt to persuade him.

"Yeah, if you're shopping at the commissary, but unfortunately you're not, you're dealing with me," he replies.

I know there's no use arguing. I reach back into my pocket and pull out the two nickels and the dime. "Twenty cents is all I got," I tell him as I hold out my hand. "Can I owe you the other 30 cents?"

"I'll take the clacker half and the twenty cents since it's you," he says, "I'll even tie them on for you."

We make the transaction. I take my slingshot from around my neck and hand it to him, then watch as he pulls on each of the rubbers and inspects them.

"'Bout time you changed 'em," he tells me. "These are dry-rotted; ready to break any minute. Where'd you get them anyway?"

"I cut 'em off a piece of tube that J.C. Logins had. Most of it was rotten when I cut 'em," I tell him.

"You done a shitty job," he informs me.

Everyone's not as precise as you, I think to myself as I watch him take a small pen knife out of his pocket, cut the strings that hold the rotted rubbers to the stock and then slowly unwrap each one and discard the strings to the floor. I would have just yanked them off. He checks the pocket strings and unloops them from the old rubbers. "These are still in good shape," he declares as he reloops them back onto the new ones, about a ½ inch up from the ends. "Never try to attach the rubbers directly to the pocket," he says. "It's dumb and you lose accuracy, but some folks never learn. Of course that's debatable," he goes on to add.

"Hand me that mayonnaise jar on the shelf next to the fruit jars," he tells me. I retrieve it and hand it his way. He opens the jar. It contains a roll of black fishing line, still on the original spool. "25 lb test," he says, "that's what you should always use." He pulls the end of one of the rubber opposite of the pocket over one of the notched out stock forks and begins to wrap. "Always keep the line tight and don't do more than four wraps," he tells me after tying it off and trimming the line with his pen knife. He performs the same ritual on the other side, then closely examines both rubbers to be sure they're even. "Perfect!" he says. "Let's try it out! There's some steel balls in that Bull Durham sack over there on that same shelf. Grab 'em," he tells me as we walk out of the garage.

We're shooting at his mother's clothespins on a line about 25 feet away, pretending they're birds. The wind is moving them around, making them hard to hit. James demolishes the first two he shoots at, then passes the slingshot to me. I shoot at one and miss. "That fucker would've had to be the size of a buzzard for you to hit it," he tells me. "You jerk too much when you shoot." I shoot again, this time with a smoother release and the clothespin explodes. James is unimpressed. He takes the slingshot from me and looks it over again. "Next to mine, this is probably the best slingshot stock I've ever seen," he comments. "How long you had it now?"

"Since 1945, when J.B. came home from the war, he made it for me then; whittled it out of cedar. So, I've had it about four years, I guess," I tell him.

James lifts the stock to his nose. "You can still smell it," he says. "This is the original pocket, too, ain't it?" he asks, as he inserts another steel ball into the worn leather pocket. "Last one," he says.

"Yeah, it's a good one. My granny's still bitchin' 'cause I cut the tongue out of one of her shoes." But he doesn't even hear me; he's looking around searching for something else to shoot. We hear Charlie behinds us. He's opening the gate to the fence around his yard. He has a hacksaw, another big wrench and an RC Cola that he's robbed out of his mother's Frigidaire in his hands. He takes a slug of the RC and sits it on top of the gate post while he opens the gate. Two seconds later, it disintegrates. "Three for three," James tells me and laughs.

Charlie's pissed about his RC, but even more pissed that a piece of the glass cut his ear. "It's just a fuckin' scratch," James tells him. "Quit whinin' like a baby. Hurry in there and cut them bolts."

"I gotta go before it starts pouring," I tell the two of them as I walk over to where they're standing. "Give me my slingshot," I tell James, who has already hung it around his neck. I know he likes it and I'm expecting some resistance, but he hands it to me.

"You orta' let me keep it here, so it don't get wet," he says.

"Can't, I'm heading up to Trapper's," I tell him. "We're probably gonna go bird hunting later."

"Better take that stupid bell off your shoe or you'll scare 'em all away," Charlie tells me, still wiping at his bloody ear.

"Hey, you guys going to the weenie roast over at Sarah Humphries' house tonight?" knowing before I ask what the answer will be.

"I don't go to those pussy little parties and Charlie didn't get invited," James informs me, as I jump on my bike and begin to pedal away.

"Wait a minute," he tells me. I stop. He has a grin on his face.

"That mower belongs to Margie's daddy. I was talking to him up at the store the other day and he was complaining that he had ordered a new blade for it and couldn't get the old one off. Asked me if I thought I could fix it. He dropped it off this morning. As soon as Charlie gets it fixed, we're gonna take it down there and Charlie's gonna cut their grass," he tells me.

"What if it keeps raining?" I ask him.

"Who gives a shit? He's gonna cut it rain or shine," he says.

"What are you gonna be doing while Charlie's cuttin' the grass?" I ask him with a grin. I get a bigger grin back.

"You boys better stop shooting the clothespins off my line!" I hear someone yell. It's Mrs. Love, James' mother; she's sweeping off the porch.

"Do you know what time it is, Mrs. Love?" I ask her.

"It's about twenty minutes 'til nine; I just glanced at the clock on my way out here," she says.

"See you," I say to James as I peddle away, thinking to myself that James is gonna get fucked and old Charlie's gonna get wet. No justice in the world, but in his case, Charlie deserves none.

Old Boogie's gonna get wet, too if I don't hurry up. I've got plenty of time to make it to Jean's by 9:30, but a sprinkle of rain has begun to fall. Pretty soon I'll be soaked. It's about another 200 yards from James' house up to the main road, a big S curve that's fairly level and a smoother grade than the hill. I pump the pedals as hard as I can. I see no one or anything of interest on the way and feel only the rain as I hunker down and pump.

The dirt road meets the main road pavement right in front of the school. I take a right and coast on the asphalt for about 25 yards, then angle off to the right and coast down the dirt road to the commissary. I've just remembered the Juicy Fruit and stopping by the store will give me a break from the drizzling rain. The commissary is the Company store where they "rob you without a mask or gun," according to my dad.

My older brother, J.B., works here and so does my Uncle Bill. J.B. runs the cold drinks and candy section and my Uncle Bill works in the meat market. "Sweets and Meats" is how my dad refers to the two of them. I laugh every time he says it. There's a long, wide, rutted, dirt parking area in the front. It serves the commissary and the Company mining office that sits about 20 yards to its right. The people going to the post office and barbershop also park here. The building they're in sits about 20 yards to its left. There're lots of cars here today.

As I coast by the mining office, I see a lot of activity, more than usual. Bingo! Payday Saturday, dummy! That's where my dad's headed, not the filling station. He could be right behind me, so I'll have to get in and out of the store fast or he might have several "cups of coffee" and be detained for a while. It seems as if I remember his "coffee time" with Mrs. Skinner has been the subject of several loud conversations between my mother and him when they thought no one else was around. In that case, I'll only have to deal with my brother when I buy the gum, for which I have no money to pay, unless I take off my shoe.

I slam on my brakes, hop off my bike and lean it against the cement steps along the front of the store. As I walk up the steps, I survey the area. Even though it's windy, rainy and cold, the big thermometer right outside the door says it's almost 60 degrees. It feels much colder. As I look toward the parking lot, I see the usual gathering of Payday Saturday miners. They're bunched up together in small groups with their hats pulled down and their shoulders hunched against the drizzling rain talking. The largest group is standing under the only tree in the parking area that has survived; a medium-sized elm. There are probably 8 to 10 of them gathered in a circle. In the center is a big, gray-headed man holding an umbrella. He's got a .45 caliber pistol strapped to his waist with the butt out on the left side, set up for a cross draw. And even though you can't see it, I know he carries a black jack in the right-hand back pocket of his pants. He's the town sheriff, Dorcey Britt; known to most folks as just, "Britt." He's holding court, telling some of his tall tales to all who will listen. His crowd's smaller today due to the weather. On a good day, it's sometimes triple this size and he can keep them in awe and stitches for hours. If you're under 18, or even look like you are, he'll run you off, but sometimes when everyone's really caught up in a good story, you can sneak up without being noticed. I've heard some great tales this way.

Britt's tough; he's not somebody you want to fuck around with. Man, woman or child, black or white, he'll black jack your ass in a second, if he thinks you're breaking the law—especially if you give him any shit. The niggers are scared shitless of him. Just to the right from where Britt is holding court, I see only one peddler in the lot; old man McCombs, with his horse and wagon. He's rigged a big umbrella over the wagon and the wind is wreaking havoc on it as he weighs out his produce for several women who are holding umbrellas and shopping. It's gotta be pissing off Mr. Barns, the commissary manager, because he hates the peddlers due to the competition. Usually there's three or four of 'em; I guess the weather has the others grounded.

I head through the door; there's more people shopping outside than inside. I look to my right and see my Uncle Bill propped up on the counter, smoking a cigarette and bullshitting with a woman

I know, but can't recall her name, while she looks over the meat displayed in the case. I make a left-hand turn and head toward the candy section. Three nigger men are in a group in front of the counter. Two of them are drinking Coca Colas and bullshitting and one is taking a Stanback headache powder and chasing it with a Buffalo Rock. My brother, J.B., is taking the money for a couple of RC Colas he has just sold to two little nigger kids with snotty noses. They look at me and roll their eyes, then move in the direction of the men, whom I presume are their daddies.

"What are you doing up here?" my brother wants to know.

"I need some chewing gum and want to see if you'll loan me the money for it," I tell him. "I'm heading up to Trapper's to play Monopoly."

"Where's your raincoat? Does Momma know you're out without it?" he asks.

"I left it at school. It wasn't raining when I left and she said it was okay," I reply.

"We don't sell on credit here, unless you got a job," he tells me. I hear the niggers laugh; I turn and give them a dirty look. That just makes them laugh again, even the little kids that are swirling back and forth between their legs join in.

"Why stop if you don't have any money?" he continues.

"Well, like you said, it started raining and like I said, I thought maybe you'd give me a loan. It's only a nickel, J.B. C'mon…please?" I beg.

"Damn kids nowadays don't know the value of a nickel," I hear a voice behind me saying. I turn and look and see Britt. He's shaking the rain out of his umbrella onto the floor. "When I was his age, my daddy had me out in the field chopping and hoeing. Made me earn my money," he goes on to say. I hear a shuffling of feet and see the niggers head out the door. "Give me one of the coldest Coca Colas you got back there, J.B., and charge it to my account, would you? And give this young fellow whatever he wants for that nickel. What was it, boy?" he asks.

"Juicy Fruit gum, Mr. Britt."

"That's it! Juicy Fruit gum! Charge that to my account, too, J.B., would ya? Old Boogie here's a pretty good little ol' boy. I catch him in a little mischief around town every now and then; have to kick his ass a little, but he ain't near the problem you was when you were his age. Else I'm just gettin' old and slow—is that the case, boy?" he asks, as he turns and looks at me.

"No, sir, Mr. Britt; you're sharper than ever!" I tell him.

"Throw that boy a couple pieces of that bubble gum, too, J.B. He might hanker for a different flavor later on."

"Whatever you say, Britt," my brother answers as he hands him his Coca Cola. He hands me a pack of Juicy Fruit and two pieces of Double Bubble and if looks could kill, I'd be dead. There's no way he's gonna charge it to Britt. He'll pay for it himself. But, that's not why he gives me the look. It's because he knows that I 'Uncle Tom'ed' Britt for the gum. That's why he's pissed.

"Could I bother you for the time, Mr. Britt?" I ask, smiling at my brother. I know I'm gonna pay for this later.

"It's almost nine," J.B. says, looking at his watch. "Time for you to get going."

"Thanks for the gum, Mr. Britt!"

"No problem, boy, now skedaddle your little ass out of here, I wanna talk with J.B." They didn't have to tell me twice.

I hit the main road again; this time blowing bubbles. The rain has let up and I'll swear the sky looks lighter. I looked at the thermometer again on the way out of the commissary and the temperature was the same, but now the wind seems to be coming from the north; no wonder it's so cold.

Just as I cross over the trip track bridge, a big bubble pops and sticks to my face. As I'm pulling it off, I hear shouting voices from over by the Top House. It sounds like kids. I look over that way, but don't see anyone. I look to the left. My friend, Wayne, lives in the first house on the left after you cross the trip tracks. I see him and another friend, Albert, on Wayne's front porch. They're shooting air rifles and now I know what's happening. I take a left, head into Wayne's yard and lean my bike against the big oak tree that grows next to his house.

Albert's bike has a kickstand. It's parked over next to the steps; it's a lot newer than mine.

"Hey! What're you guys doing; shooting at the niggers again?" I ask as I walk up on the porch.

"Those little jungle bunnies are over there stealing the coal that falls out of the washer again," Wayne tells me as he shoots in their direction. "We're pelting them with BBs."

"It don't hurt 'em from here," Albert says. "I know, but it pisses 'em off," Wayne tells him.

"They been calling us all kinds of names, hollering for us to go fuck ourselves; all kinds of shit," they tell me in unison; we all laugh. They're both shooting Daisy Pumps and have now stopped to reload. Both taking a mouth full of BBs and spitting them in the magazine. It eventually rusts out the spring when you load it this way, but it's the quickest way to do it. "That's what I don't like about a pump, I tell them. "It only holds 50 BBs. You have to load it too often."

"They shoot a lot harder than that piece of shit Red Ryder you got," Wayne informs me. "You ready?" he asks Albert. I don't argue with him because he's right. My old Red Ryder has seen its best days. Anyway, I'd rather have my slingshot. Cocking and firing as fast as they can, each of them rain seven to eight BBs down toward the washer, about a 100 yards away, then take a couple of deep breaths and do it again. I know they're probably not hitting anybody, but it must sound like a hail storm when the BBs hit the tin roof of the Top House. "I think I hit one," Wayne tells us, "I heard him squeal!"

Wayne and Albert are both fourteen, a year older than me. Wayne's dad works in the coal mine and Albert's dad is the principal of our school. There was a time when the three of us were the best of friends, but even then we had a tendency to get along better if we were in twos rather than if the three of us were together. But, then Wayne hit thirteen and started acting like a big shot, I guess because he was a teenager. We still call him that to his back…"Big Shot." He knows we do and he hates it. When Albert made the transition, he started acting the same way. Then the two of them started hanging out more together and calling me a "kid" and all that kinda shit, which really pissed me off. That's when I started hanging out with Trapper who, by the way, neither of them like.

Now that I'm thirteen, they have sort of welcomed me back in the fold, but at this point, I'm sticking with Trapper. Even though I'm not sure I like him either; we have more things in common. I watch them do their cock and fire routine again. "I think I hit one this time," Albert tells Wayne. "I hope the wind's not blowing them off target," Wayne says, as they fire away again.

I hear the door open and the screen door slam. I turn and see Mrs. Watson, Wayne's mother. She's got her hair all twisted up with bobby pins with wave clamps across the front. She has on an old faded-out checkered robe. She's short and slightly heavy, but has a very pretty face. "Ya'll leave them lil' colored kids alone, they're just getting' a lil' coal so their mothers can build a fire. It's cold out today and this wind cuts right through you. Anyway, you could hit one of them in the eye and they'll be hell to pay when your daddy finds out," she says looking directly at Wayne. "And, speaking of your daddy", she says, still talking to Wayne, "he left here this morning with the last pack of cigarettes and I only got about two or three left in my pack." She pulls out a crumpled pack of Chesterfields and lights one up with a Zippo lighter, then blows the smoke out her nose and pinches tobacco off her tongue. "You're gonna have to go down to the store and get me some. Get three packs and tell Mrs. Mars to charge them to our bill. Tell her your daddy's gonna pay some on it today." "Yes, ma'am!" Wayne salutes her, then reaches for her crumpled pack of Chesterfields. "Give me one and I'll go right now," he tells her.

Wayne's parents let him smoke, contrary to my parents, who would probably kill me if I got caught. She hands him a cigarette and the lighter. "And you get right back here; don't you let me run out," she tells him. "Dibs on the butt!" Albert says real fast as Wayne lights up, then gives me that "I just snookered you" look. Instead of bumming a cigarette off her as I usually do, I reach in my jacket pocket and pull out the Lucky Strikes. "Surprise, surprise," I hold them up and say.

"My God! Miracles will never cease," Mrs. Watson says, as she takes another draw off her Chesterfield and pinches more tobacco off her tongue. Everyone laughs. "What did you do, rob Burl's cigarette carton?" she wants to know. "He smokes Camels," I tell her. She shakes her head. "Well, I'm sure you came by them by some devious act, if I know you." We all laugh again.

I take six cigarettes out of the pack and hand one to Albert, who looks surprised. I pass one to Wayne, which he pokes in his shirt pocket for later and hand three to Mrs. Watson. "Stick these in your pack, in case you have nicotine fit before Wayne gets back," I tell her. I put the other one in my mouth. "Who's got the Zippo?" I ask.

"Boogie, you know something?" she asks.

"What's that Mrs. Watson?"

"Even though you're a little shit most of the time, we all love you and I think your little bell's cute."

"Oh, his little bell is so cute!" Wayne and Albert chime in together in unison.

"Thanks, Mrs. Watson," I tell her.

"And Wayne, if you see your daddy, tell him to get on home. We're supposed to be going down to north Birmingham to see your sister, Ruth. Tell him I'm ready to go. And don't shoot at those colored kids anymore," she says, as she closes the door.

"Come on and go down there with me," Wayne tells us, as he walks down the steps and heads towards Albert's bike. "I'll ride double with you and hold the air rifles," he says to Albert.

"I'm heading up to Trapper's," I tell them. "You and Carol going to the party tonight?" I ask Wayne. Carol is Wayne's current "love interest," the lucky prick. She's a real knockout.

"Wouldn't miss it for the world, but if we play kissing games don't start trying to slobber all over Carol. She's out of bounds, buddy," he replies.

"So is Darlene, buddy," I tell him.

"You going, Albert?" I ask.

"He's going," Wayne answers for him. "He can't wait to put the tongue to Sarah."

"Fuck you!" Albert says to Wayne. Wayne and I laugh.

"Fuck you later!" I tell them, as I flip my cigarette away and hop on my bike.

"Fuck you later, too," echoes back to me as we head in opposite directions.

Damn! I meant to ask Mrs. Watson what time it was and forgot, I think to myself, as I head on up the road toward Jean's house. I must've been screwing around with Wayne and Albert for about fifteen minutes, plus the time it took to ride up there, which was about five minutes, so it's probably around 9:20. I've still got plenty of time; in fact I'll probably be early, which will be even better.

It's starting to mist rain again and the sky that had looked lighter a short time ago has reverted back to a gloomy gray. Passing cars throw up water from the road and the wind whips it across my body. I pass the Baptist church and think of Darlene's tongue; but then, even though I try not to, I find myself scanning around the parsonage next door to the church for any sign of Lashie. Everyone says she wants me back. What's the harm in giving her a little encouragement; as long as Darlene don't find out? That shouldn't be too hard for a "woman's man" like me to handle. I look all around, but see no signs of life; the house is dark and deserted. The preacher's car is gone; they're probably visiting some family or friends or maybe shopping down in Birmingham. *Get Lashie out of your mind,* I tell myself. *You're asking for trouble.*

Just past the church I take a right onto a dirt road that runs down a hill. It's very similar to the one in front of our house and in very much the same condition. At the foot of the hill, just before the road begins an upward slant, is a giant mud puddle. I slam on my brakes, jump off and push my bike around it, making sure to get as little mud on my shoes as possible. Jean lives three houses up on the left. I continue to push my bike the rest of the way.

— CHAPTER 5 —

JEAN

LIKE THE MAJORITY OF HOMES IN BLACK CREEK, THE houses along this road have that worn, weather-beaten, gray look—the look lumber takes on when exposed to the elements over a long period of time, but Jean's house is easy to spot. It's the only one with a white picket fence and grass growing in the yard. Jean loves her lawn and "Moonie," her husband, has to maintain it to perfection to keep her happy. Keeping that Bermuda growing is one of the things she's adamant about.

I lean my bike against the fence, open the gate and head up the gravel walkway towards the porch, stopping to wipe the mud away from the soles and sides of my tennis shoes on the grass. I notice the grass is turning a nice shade of green due to the recent warm weather and the rain, and then I jingle up the steps. There's a balustrade that runs along the edge of the porch; it's about four feet high. Randomly spaced along the top rail is a variety of plants, mostly ferns and geraniums, planted in an assortment of buckets and pots. Jean loves her plants and flowers. An old-fashioned three-man swing hangs on chains from the porch ceiling. It's accompanied by two high-back rocking chairs. All are painted green.

I finger comb my hair to the best of my ability and wipe the water off my face. My hands come away oily, so I dry them off on the back of my pants before wiping the water off my jacket. I don't feel wet, just slightly damp all over. I unzip my jacket, check my sweater and find it basically dry. I'm not as cold, since I got up on the porch where much of the wind is blocked. In fact, as I hitch up my pants and knock on the door, a familiar warmth begins to radiate right in the center of my groin.

Her real name is Imogene, but when she was about five years old, her mother saw Jean Harlow in a movie called, *Dinner at Eight*, and came to the conclusion that her young daughter was a miniature version of the actress. She immediately started calling her Jean; I've heard the tale a hundred times. And, her mother wasn't wrong, for over the years as she has become older, the resemblance has remained; everyone says so. She even has the same slight cleft at the base of her chin. As for me, I've seen a picture of the actress who is dead now, and I think my Jean is much more beautiful. In fact, she's the most beautiful woman in the world, at least to me she is. I know, I know, I'm in love with Darlene. And I said Darlene is the most beautiful thing I've ever seen. And I really meant it, but there's a difference, believe me; Darlene is a girl! Jean's a woman! And without feeling any sense of betrayal to Darlene, I must confess that Jean is number one on my jack-off list. I literally lust after her, as do a large majority of the other males in town and the surrounding territories.

As I wait at the door, I can hear it begin to rain harder. It feels misty on my face as a big gust of wind blows water up on the porch. I open the screen and put my ear to the door. I hear music, a soft melody, and someone singing. I knock again and just as I do, Jean opens the door. It's Bing Crosby crooning, *As Long As I'm Dreaming*, very apropos as I look up and see "my" dream. She's holding Mikie, her little boy who is eight months old. He's wiggling and kicking and pulling at her hair. He smiles real big when he looks and sees it's me. "Hey, Buddy", I say and cluck him under the chin, then shake my foot and jingle the bell. He's not interested in the least; all I get is a yawn. Jean laughs. "I heard the knock and figured it was you", she tells me, "but Mikie was just waking up so I had to get him before I answered the door. He's fretful and hungry as usual when he wakes up, so I'm gonna have to feed him. Come on in out of this rain before you catch your death of a cold."

Bingo! Bingo! Bingo! She hasn't fed him yet, I've timed it perfectly! I congratulate myself as I walk in and she closes the door.

"I've got a fire in the fireplace, stand over there in front of it and dry yourself out," she instructs.

"It's cold out, too," I tell her. "It must be the wind; it's blowing real hard. The thermometer at the commissary says it's almost 60 degrees, but it feels a lot colder than that."

"Something wrong with that thing," she says. "Mine on the back porch showed 50 degrees when I was out there just a little while ago, but of course, as you know, everything's always higher at the commissary!" We both laugh.

"Is Trapper here yet?" I ask her, knowing he won't be when I ask, because (and now I must confess) I had told him I would be up here around 10:00 A.M. Nine-thirty is Mikie's feeding time, a fact I have deduced over the months since Mikie was born, by dropping in at various times on Saturday mornings just to "play with him." Sometimes I come by with Trapper to make things look less obvious, but most of the times without. There doesn't seem to be any particular set time for afternoon or evening feedings, but in the mornings Mikie always alarms for breakfast at 9:30 A.M. He must do the same during the week; I can't wait until schools out, I hope she doesn't wean him before then!

I position myself in front of the fireplace. It feels warm and toasty on my legs and back as I stand looking at Jean. "Your little bell's real cute," she says to me. I tell her its story. She pulls a small wooden chair from in front of her sewing machine that is set up in the corner next to the radio and drags it over to the hearth next to me. Old Bing's still crooning, *Accentuate the Positive*, a real catchy tune. *Jean must have a record on or else the disc jockey is hung up on Bing*, I think to myself. All the while I'm wondering why all women like to sew and why do they all have the machine set up the same, next to the radio?

"Take off that wet jacket and hang it over this chair so it can dry," she tells me. "Lord! I can't believe you boys go out in this kind of weather without a raincoat. And you watch, Trapper will blow in the same way, soaking wet. You did say he's supposed to meet you here, right?"

"Yeah, at 10:00", I tell her, "but I think I got here a little early; I rode real fast because it was raining."

I think that's the end of it, but she doesn't let it go. I see a smirk begin to form on her lips; as she takes on that "you lying little shit" look my mother always gets.

I know exactly what's coming so I answer her before she asks, "I forgot and left it at school." Damn! My mother, my brother and now, Jean! "Anyway, it makes you look like a little kid," I tell her.

"What makes you look like a little kid?" she asks as she makes herself comfortable in the big stuffed chair she uses for nursing. It sits just in front of the fireplace, maybe three feet from where I'm standing.

"Wearing a raincoat," I say, "Everybody says it."

She has on her old, white, chenille robe over one of Moonie's old, white t-shirts and she's wearing a pair of shorts. It's the common attire for Jean every day, unless it's really, really cold. If she goes out, like to the store or the post office, she puts on a brassiere, but when she's home she rarely ever wears one. Of course she usually has on the robe, so you can't see anything. In real cold weather she usually wears blue jeans or slacks. I'm glad it's shorts today; I love looking at her legs.

She adjusts Mikie around and pulls his head up close to her breast. He starts making all kind of crazy gooing sounds and pulling at her robe. His little lips are smacking and spit's running out the corners of his mouth. He knows what's coming and he can hardly wait. I feel the same way! I reach up and wipe at my mouth.

"It makes you look stupid when you don't," she says to me.

"Don't what?" I ask, as she unbuttons the top of her robe and pulls it to the side, exposing her right breast. It's still under the t-shirt but little is left to the imagination as it bulges underneath the thin, cotton fabric.

"Wear a raincoat when it's raining," she says, then looks at me and laughs. Mikie's going crazy, he's pulling at the t-shirt, trying to get at her breast.

"He can't wait," I say to her. *Neither can I!* I think to myself.

"Just a second, little man," she tells him, as she hikes up her shirt. And then, there it is, in all its glory. I only get to see it for a moment before she plunges it into his mouth. I stand transfixed, watching Mikie as he slobbers and sucks and then, as he always does, he releases the breast and goes for the one on the other side.

That's when I get my first good look. It's hanging just to the right of his head, jiggling up and down as she struggles to get it back in his mouth. It's big and white and full of milk, with just a trace of blue veining under the skin. The big circle around the nipple that I can spell, but can never pronounce, the one I looked up in a health book in the library, the "areola" is a deep, reddish-pink. It looks puffy and soft and has some tiny bumps on it. But it's the nipple itself that fascinates me. It's ruby red, as big around as my thumb, and at least an inch long. It's still oozing milk. I stand mesmerized as I watch a drop of the cloudy looking honey drip off the end of Jean's nipple and spot the arm of Mikie's blue pajama top.

My mouth fills with saliva so I swallow real fast. I'm turning into stone, starting with my groin. Jean pulls Mikie back and he lunges towards the nipple and sucks it back into his mouth. His little feet are just a kicking. I swallow real fast again. Suddenly she looks up at me and smiles. I immediately turn towards the fireplace to warm my front, even though certain parts of me are burning up.

She laughs and says, "I'll swear, he's just like Moonie. He can't get enough tittie! Well, I've got news for this little glutton; he's gonna start getting weaned next week. Momma says I should have already done it."

"Trapper says you have a new girlfriend, is that right?" she asks me.

Certain things have quieted down, so I turn back around. I look at Jean. Her eyes are closed and she's scrunched down all soft and cozy in her big, overstuffed chair. She has a beautiful, tranquil smile on her face. Her feet and legs are resting on the footstool that matches the chair. She has kicked off the fuzzy house slippers she was wearing and is now barefoot. Her feet are highly arched, long and thin and graceful; very pretty feet. Her toenails are painted red to match her fingernails. I look at her hands as she holds Mikie and just like her feet, they're perfect.

Her legs are to die for; long and muscular but extremely curvy. When she was a cheerleader at Mortimer Jordan High School, even though the football team sucked, Jean packed the stands—record attendance for the three years she was there, just to look at her legs. Needless to say, she drives the guys crazy every summer when she goes to the commissary or the post office in her shorts.

She's a very strange and uncommon person. For example, she would never even consider letting any man other than Moonie see her breasts, but she doesn't relate the nursing of Mikie to showing her breasts at all. It has never entered her mind. And, don't think I'm the only one to ever have seen this performance. No matter where she is, if Mikie's hungry, he gets fed. She did it one Sunday when the new preacher at the Methodist church was preaching his sermon. She and Moonie were sitting on the front row. The preacher almost swallowed his false teeth; lost his whole train of thought. For the next two weeks, he visited her every day for what he termed "prayer sessions." Moonie finally had to have a few words with him, then he and Jean switched, to the Baptist church; that is, when they go.

She's done it all over town. When she takes Mikie with her to the store, all the men who work there will tell her how hungry he looks. The best story, and I think the funniest one, is when she and Mikie went with Moonie to get a haircut and Forest Hughes, the big-mouth barber, got so enthused with Jean's titties that he gapped the shit out of Moonies hair. Ended up he had to give him a buzz cut. It was all over town within hours; everyone was talking and laughing about it. Moonie was pissed, threatened to sue Mr. Hughes, but backed off when he heard that Mr. Hughes said he would subpoena Jean. He said there wasn't a judge alive that would convict him of not being able to cut hair when he saw that set of tits.

But none of this has ever had any effect on Jean or produced any reaction from her. She lives in her own world; a never-never land, where everyone is always happy and everything is always good. To do anything intentionally wrong would never cross her mind. She's just a beautiful, unassuming, 20-year-old who is content with her life. She has her romance novels, her fashion magazines, her radio and a love of preening herself. She has her home, her baby and her man, who, by the way, is the "love of her life" and as Jean says, "her love for life."

Why she picked Moonie out of the multitudes chasing her is a mystery to everyone. He's the exact opposite of Jean. He's self-centered, possessive, vindictive, and extremely jealous, even of me and Trapper, who's her brother. Jean just laughs at the way he acts. Says that's the way he's always been.

"Know why I call him Moonie?" she asked me one day. I had no idea; I guess it never crossed my mind. Since he wasn't a Black Creeker, I had just assumed it was a childhood nickname like mine.

"Well," she goes on to tell me, "the first time I met him I was at a party. After we were introduced, I couldn't get rid of him. He hung around me the whole night, showing his ass. Every time I looked up he was there. When I got home, I told my mother about this strange, sweet guy I had met, but when she asked me his name I couldn't remember it. The very next morning, he was knocking on our door just as we were getting ready for breakfast. It was a Sunday and when my mother answered the door, he told her he was there to take me to church. I was still in my room, in my pajamas, when she came back to get me. She told me the guy I met at the party the night before was at the door. She said, 'It's the guy who hung around you like a moon.' 'Ole Moonie's here?' I said to her, so surprised that I couldn't believe it and she said that, 'Yes, old Moonie was waiting to take me to church and I better hurry and get dressed.'"

We both laughed at the story. "Are you okay?" Jean asks me. Mikie's asleep, but still giving a little suck every now and then. I watch as she slides the nipple out of his mouth and pulls the t-shirt back down. The fabric puckers and forms to the oozing nipple. "Yeah, I'm fine. Why?" I ask her.

"I asked you about your girlfriend and you never answered me." She says, as she stands very slowly so as not to wake Mikie. "I'll be right back as soon as I put him back in his bed. Do you want something to drink? I got Coca Cola and some Grapicos if you want one," she says in almost a whisper.

"I could go for a Grapico," I tell her, knowing they're Moonie's favorite and that he gets pissed when Trapper and I are here and drink them. As Jean leaves the room, I walk to the window, pull open the curtains and look out. The weather hasn't improved, but doesn't seem to have worsened either. I walk back over to the fireplace and look around the room. Everything seems so quiet. No music! I hadn't even noticed when it stopped. It must have been a record; Jean's got a big collection and she loves Bing.

Her house is small, only four rooms—five if you count the small, unfinished bathroom that Moonie built by closing in half of the back porch. So far it only has a commode and a big, oval galvanized tub. It's the typical Black Creek house, which with a few exceptions, are either four- or six-roomers. My dad calls them slab houses, but the rent is cheap to match the houses. It has a living room and kitchen on one side and two bedrooms on the other. Mikie's at the front of the house and Jean and Moonie's room on the back. They have it fixed up real nice. Moonie has a real good job and he buys the best for Jean. He works at the post office over at Pinson and has to work a half-day on Saturdays, so he'll be blowing in here before long.

Funny thing about the bathroom is that you can see right in it from their bedroom, through the window that faces the porch. Instead of converting the window into a door so you enter the bathroom from the bedroom, dumb-ass Moonie cut the bathroom door to face the porch. Consequently, to enter the bathroom, you still have to go out the kitchen door to the porch. My next goal is to drop by one day when Jean is taking a bath. She always forgets to lock her door. Just as the thought goes through my mind, she comes out of Mikie's room and heads toward the kitchen.

"What time is it?" I ask her as she walks by, "Trapper oughta be here soon."

"I'll look at the clock in the kitchen," she tells me. Trapper's just like me; he's prone to be late. I hope it holds true for today. I love spending time alone with Jean.

"It's almost ten." She tells me as she walks back in and hands me a Grapico, then sits back down in her chair to drink her Coca Cola.

"We oughta be drinking hot coco on a day like this!" she says and shivers. "Now, tell me about this girlfriend of yours, she's Mr. and Mrs. Wilson's little girl, Darlene, right? She's so pretty." She sits her drink on the lamp table by the chair.

"She's not so little anymore," I tell her.

"I know! All you kids are growing up so fast I just can't believe it," she says, as she props her right foot on the ottoman and inspects her toenails. God, her legs are fantastic!

"I French kissed her at church last Sunday." I volunteer.

"You what?" she exclaimed.

"French kissed her, you know, when you stick your tongues in each other's mouth when you're kissing." Jean's still inspecting her toenails, but now she's got the other foot.

"How in the world do you know about things like that?" she asks me, never looking up.

I don't answer her question, but continue to go on. "It makes you feel real funny when you do it," I tell her.

Jean's rummaging around in the lamp table drawer looking for something. She pulls out a file and returns to her toes. I continue, "You start breathing real hard," I say.

"Boogie!" she says, turning and looking at me, "you are so bad! I just can't believe that you kids are doing things like that!"

I love playing this game with Jean. It's almost as much fun as looking at her. I do it frequently when I'm up here. I invent wild tales and confess them to her, just to watch her reaction. She acts so gullible, seeming to believe everything you tell her, yet never getting too overly excited about it. She never really questions the validity of the story. She's always preoccupied, usually with herself; listening, but not really listening to anything that I'm saying.

I continue my game. "I'm not a kid, I'm thirteen," I say.

"Well, to me you're still a kid. I guess it's because I've known you since you were a baby. I forget sometimes that you and Trapper are now big, grown up, he-men." Sarcastically said, but she laughs. "Anyway, that little girl's way too young for you to be kissing."

"The older girls won't let me kiss them," I tell her.

"Well, you shouldn't be kissing any girls, especially the way you said."

"Why's that?" I ask her, continuing to work the bait.

"Because it makes you have thoughts about things you're too young to be thinking about, that's why," she replies.

I smile and observe her, trying to think of a good reply. She's inspecting her hands now, apparently satisfied with her toes. The hands pass muster and she puts the file on the table next to her cola, then rises and stretches.

"Shoot! No wonder it's so quiet in here," she says, as she heads toward the radio, "the music's off. I hadn't even noticed it 'til now."

She has a radio/phonograph combo, a big mahogany colored thing with the record player and a place to store the albums in the top. I continue to watch as she lifts the lid and slides Bing off the turntable.

"How about some Como?" she asks, as she slips another record out of its cover.

"Fine by me." I tell her.

"I just love him, he always makes me feel so romantic," she says, as she sits back down and sips her cola. I finish off the Grapico and look for a place to put the bottle. "Just sit it on the mantle," she tells me, "I'll put it with the other empties later."

Listening to the music and the warmth of the fire gives me a comfy feeling. I feel my pants and sweater and then check my jacket hanging on the chair—everything's dry. Jean's back in her nursing position, eyes closed, listening to Perry's "Prisoner of Love" and how he "needs no shackles to remind him." *Neither do I*, I think to myself. I begin the game again.

"How old were you when you first started French kissing boys?" I throw at her.

"A lot older than you; anyway, who says I ever did?" she throws back at me, still absorbed in the music.

"I bet you and Moonie do it."

"Moonie and I are grownups."

"What's the difference?" I ask.

"The difference is that grownups can do things that kids aren't allowed to and shouldn't do. And, as you and Trapper always say, 'everyone knows that!'"

"How did you know how to do it with Moonie if you hadn't done it before?" I ask, trying to work her into a corner.

She gives a big sigh, finishes her drink and hands the bottle towards me. "Put that on the mantle with yours, please."

I take the bottle and place it next to mine, but I don't give up.

"How did you?" I ask again.

Now she's checking her legs, ankle to calf then up to the knees.

"I'm gonna have to shave these hairy things before we go to the drive-in tonight," she comments.

"How did you?" I ask for the third time.

"I guess there's just some things that you don't have to practice; things that just come natural to you. You'll find that out as you get older," she finally answers. "Anyway, stop asking me all these silly questions. Let's talk about something else."

I'm undaunted. "You know Martha Foster?" I ask, watching as she opens the drawer again and fishes out a small mirror and some tweezers.

"You know that I know Martha Foster, silly," she says.

"I kinda didn't tell you the truth when I said that thing about the older girls," I say.

"What are you talking about?" she wants to know. All the while looking in the mirror and tweezing her right eyebrow.

"I kissed her once. She stuck her tongue way down in my throat." And before she even has time to answer, I go on to add, "She let me touch her titties, too." And before she can catch her breath, "James Love says he's done it to her."

That did it. That got her attention! The mirror and the tweezers go on the table and ever so calmly she turns towards me. "Boogie, honey", she says to me, "you're just saying all kinds of silly things that I'm not going to listen to anymore. And if you don't shush, I'm going to get up from this chair and wash your mouth out with soap. You wanna hear another record?"

But before I can answer I hear a banging on the door. "That's probably Trapper, let him in," Jean tells me as she heads toward the record player. "He's probably soaked."

Thinking, "*I hope so,*" I walk to the door and open it. It's Trapper, he's waving at some people in a car. It's Brother Kelley and Lashie's hanging out the back window. "See you at the party tonight," she yells at him as they drive away. He's dry as a bone! "Man! I can hardly wait for that party tonight," he tells me as he walks in the door.

"Wasn't that the Kelleys?" I ask him.

He gives me a shit-eating grin. "They picked me up just as I started walking down here. They'd been over to Pinson to buy groceries; picked me up on the way back. Mrs. Kelley wanted to get the meat in the Frigidaire, so we stopped off at the parsonage. Me and Lashie waited in the car while they unloaded everything and then her and Brother Kelley brought me on down here. I don't have lipstick on my mouth, do I?" he asks, poking out his lips for inspection. It would've been a great zinger, if I didn't know that the only time Lashie wears lipstick is when she's out of her parents' sight. I pretend to look. "Don't see any" I say. "You're lucky; she got that shit all over my dick last time I was with her." We both laugh as we head toward the fireplace.

"That song's as old as the hills," Trapper tells Jean as she walks over singing along with the Andrews Sisters, *"Don't sit under the apple tree, with anyone else but me...."*

"I know it is, but I like it. And, anyway, I need something to cheer me up on this 'okie' cold day," she says. She does a little dance step, laughs and continues on. *"Don't go walking down lover's lane, with anyone else but me...."*

"Don't you have no Eddie Arnold or Hank Williams?" Trapper asks her. She ignores him.

"I can't believe you aren't soaking wet like Boogie was when he got here," she says.

"I'm smarter than he is; he's a dummy," he replies.

"Birds of a feather..." I say to him.

"Well, I hope you got a cleaner mouth," she says, pulling back on the stock of my slingshot and stretching the rubbers, as though she's gonna shoot it at my face. "I can't believe some of the things he's been saying."

"They're all lies. You can't believe anything he says," Trapper tells her.

"I get it from hanging around with you," I retaliate, not bothering to deny the accusation.

"Hey! We gotta get going," I tell him.

"Is Mikie asleep?" he asks her, ignoring what I said, as usual.

"I just fed him and put him to bed and hopefully, he'll sleep 'til Moonie gets home," she tells him.

"Shoot! I wanted to talk to him," he says, as though Mikie can talk.

Trapper is trying to teach him. He wants his first words to be, "Fuck you, Moonie." He says it to him constantly, hoping he'll parrot it back. "That's the way you teach the little fucker to talk," he told me once when he was doing it. He's a nut! But, I guess I am, too.

In fact, there are a lot of people around town that can't tell us apart, which we both take advantage of at every opportunity. I don't think it's that we really look alike so much. It's more that we have the same kind of look. Trapper's hair is a lighter blonde than mine and he's fairer in complexion. Since we're constantly measuring and weighing ourselves, I know for a fact that he's half an inch taller and I'm three pounds heavier. He says it's because I'm fatter, whereas I brag to him that it's penis size. We never let up on each other. We even argue about the color of our eyes. His are blue and, according to him, women find blue eyes more attractive in a guy. I contend it's green, the color of mine. Last Wednesday night at church, Darlene confessed that what first attracted her to me were my beautiful green eyes. I haven't hit him with it yet; maybe at the party tonight!

I might also give him hell about the way he's dressed. He's got on a sweater that he got for Christmas. It's got all kinds of stars and snowflakes and stripes; it's a fuckin' Winter Wonderland. I wouldn't be caught dead in it, but he loves it. He's got on his favorite jeans, which don't look too bad since his mother cut 'em down to fit him. And, of course, his tennis shoes; identical to mine. His real weak spot is that stupid coat he wears. The one he calls an "Ike Coat." I keep reminding him that it's an "Ike Jacket," but he don't listen. It's a whitish-gray color and all fuzzy looking. Nothing that I think the "General" would have been particularly interested in. All in all, as I size him up, it's obvious as always that I'm much better looking!

Since the possibility of playing with Mikie is out, he and Jean are now discussing something about his older brother, Eddie, and some girl he's fooling around with.

"Mother's really upset," she tells him, "but, he keeps seeing her."

I make no comment, so as to stay on Jean's good side, all the while knowing I'd do the same as Eddie if I had the opportunity. The rumor is that his girlfriend "fucks like a mink." At least that's what the "big boys" say.

While they're talking, I walk back to the window to check the weather. The rain has stopped again and, as before, it looks brighter in the sky. Maybe it will clear up before the party. "Now's a good time to get going," I suggest to him again, as I walk back to where they're talking.

Jean's back in her chair, mirror and tweezers in hand, attacking her eyebrows.

"What's the deal with that stupid bell?" he asks me. "I thought you were gonna take it off after everybody at the show last night said you were turning queer."

"Trapper! You can just watch your language too!" Jean informs him, as she continues to pluck.

"And why'd you bring your slingshot?" he wants to know.

I completely ignore him. What he's really pissed about is the multi-colored laces in my tennies. I could tell by his reaction last night when he first saw them. The music's stopped again. Jean's the first of us to notice it. She rises and heads back toward the record player.

"I can't believe how the two of you argue and fuss all the time," she says as she walks away. That's what everybody says, but that's the way it's always been. It started in kindergarten when we first met. But I guess that's not really when we first met because we've known each other since we were babies. Kindergarten is where the conflicts began.

Mrs. Terry, our teacher, was befuddled that among the little monkeys that showed up in her kindergarten class in 1941, three of them could already read and write; Trapper, Nell Lang and me. Her first thought was to move us up to first grade, but she found that our parents weren't in favor of that. Anyway, before she could convince them, Mrs. Stevens, the first grade teacher nixed it. She said we were too advanced for her class also and suggested a double promotion. "Stick 'em in the second grade," she told Mrs. Terry; which, by the way, was quickly vetoed by Mr. Jergins, the school principal seconds after the second grade teacher stormed out of his office.

So she was stuck with us and she wasn't happy about it, but we were elated. We drew and colored and ratted out all the other little monkeys when we felt it was necessary—sort of appointed ourselves "top sergeants." Short of that, we did little else other than fight among ourselves—a quest for domination that remains with us even now.

"Nell's so stuck up and high falootin' that I can hardly stand her anymore," Trapper said to me recently, then went on to add, "but I'd sure love to suck them big ol' titties of hers." There is one thing, however, that we're completely unanimous on. We're convinced that if old man Jergin hadn't intervened that day, Mrs. Terry would have eventually got us a cap and gown. "Our IQs are superior," Trapper contends. I guess that's another thing we agree on.

"You ready to go?" he asks, handing me my jacket.

"Couldn't be more ready," I reply.

"Where ya'll headed?" Jean wants to know.

"Just messin' around," we say at the same time, which makes us laugh.

"Ya'll be careful now. And, stay dry!" she says.

"Don't worry about us, we'll be fine," Trapper tells her, as he opens the door.

We leave to the sound of the great Eddie Arnold's baritone voice, "I'll hold you in my heart, 'til I can hold you in my arms."

I turn; look at Jean, sigh, then close the door.

BOGGED DOWN

I continue to struggle with my self-inflicted task. My inability as a writer clearly evident, I sit for hours, pen in hand, staring at blank pages in my composition book. The words won't come. When they do, I sometimes write for hours, only to later judge them inferior and toss them aside.

Tammie chides me for not using my computer. "So much easier than all that scratching out and rewriting you do," she said. "And then, when you try to read it back, you can't decipher it."

She's right! There's only one problem. I don't type. I'm disgusted with myself. "There is no way I can try to remember a story and 'hunt and peck' at letters on a keyboard at the same time," I told her. So, she installed *Speech Dragon*, hoping it would understand Southern. It didn't. I wasn't surprised.

"But what good are all the modern, fancy gadgets anyway, if you can't write?" I asked her. "Other than business letters and a few love poems here and there, I've never written anything," I continued pleading my case.

She wanted to know who besides her that I have written love poems to and then didn't believe me when I told her, "my mother."

"You shouldn't start something, if you don't have confidence in your talent to do it," she said. "Anyway, you've read a zillion books; you should know how to write one. Just get yourself refocused!"

These encouraging comments really perked me up.

I've always been an avid reader—always avid, but not thorough. Thorough is when you read all the boring parts and look up the meanings of the words you don't know. Realizing this makes me more disgusted with myself. I vow to read more thoroughly in the future.

I've concluded that one of my problems is trying to relive the past, when living in the present is so frightening. I need to knock off TV, which for the record, I'm also disgusted with, especially the news.

Watching TV to me is like a cold keg of beer after a baseball game, on a hot summer's day. You know when you continue to slug it down, well past your limit, you're going to be sick, but for some unexplainable reason you continue to drink. And, as I said before, the news is the worst.

I've dialed the "networks" out altogether and have now locked in on a channel on cable news. Although I seem to get a more balanced coverage there, the narcissism of some of their commentators makes me sick. I don't think there's one of them that hasn't written a book telling us how great they are.

But I've got to tell you. If for nothing else, watching TV news has convinced me of one thing. We've become way too civilized—a bunch of secular dominated fat cats who comfortably sit back convinced nothing could ever happen to us.

Bad things happen when you least expect them, which gets me back to my story. Trapper and I were feeling fat and cocky that day as we left Jean's. Little did we know what lurked just around the corner!

—CHAPTER 6 —
MESSING AROUND

IN MOST CASES, IF YOU'RE HEALTHY AND FEEL SE-
cure, life is wonderful; especially when you're thirteen years old.
Your body is in a stage of change and in that situation, the highs
normally far overshadow the lows. Then, there's that extra, extra,
high, when some event or events that happen push you to the up-
most, where every cell in your body is pulsating to its maximum
output and you just know that it can't get any better, that this is as
good as life can get. It's a marvelous feeling and, in my short life, I
have identified two things that take me there. One is when the final
school bell rings signaling summer vacation and the second is being
in love. I'm at this plateau, as I follow Trapper down the steps from
Jean's front porch.

The day is crazy. First it rains and then it stops, then it rains again,
on and off, off and on, as though God can't make up His mind. The
sky is in shambles, going from almost black to light gray, then back
to dark again. There's no thunder or lighting, so it's not really stormy,
just cold, windy and dark. The rain has stopped for now, but you can
feel that it won't be for very long.

Trapper grabs my bike.

"Jump on the seat," he tells me, as he straddles the cross bar, "I'm
driving."

Not even out of Jean's house for five minutes and he's already trying to take command. *Fuck you*, I think to myself.

"Duh! I don't think so," I tell him. "Anyway, we're heading up the
hill and then out to the main road. There's no way you can pull me, so
if you want to push it up, be my guest."

He looks perplexed and questions my decision.

"Why do you want to go that way? That's stupid, dumbo!"

"Because I'm not going through that big mudhole at the bottom of the hill again and get my shoes muddy, dummy—that's why," I tell him.

"Screw you, I'm not pushing it unless I can drive when we get to the top," he tells me, as he gets off the bike.

"Tuff shit" I tell him.

I push him out of the way, grab the handlebars and begin to push the bike up the hill. He follows along, peppering me with sarcastic remarks. He's still pissed about me "shooting him out of the saddle" with Darlene. I think it's funny and chuckle. He continues to jab.

"If you weren't so puny, you could ride it up," he says to me in a shitty tone of voice.

"Hey! Good idea!" I tell him, as I offer him the bike. "You can ride it to the top and I'll take over from there."

"I would, but your fuckin' chain slips," he tells me, making no move to take the bike.

I begin to push the bike again, happy that it's bugging him that Darlene's got the hots for me.

"I'm gonna get my pants all wet from the seat," he complains and I ain't riding side-saddle on the crossbar." "No big deal, you can wipe it off," I tell him, "or else not ride at all and just trot along beside me."

"With what?" he wants to know, ignoring the suggestion about trotting.

I laugh!

"Either your hands or your skinny ass, take your pick," I tell him and continue to laugh!

"Funny, funny," he says, and then giving me a questionable look he extends his arm and touches my jacket right below my neck with his forefinger. Like a "sucker," I look down and when I do, he curls his finger, flips up his hand and catches me right on the underside of my nose.

I've just fallen for the oldest fuckin' trick in the book.

"Laugh at that, asshole," he says, and then laughs himself.

He really didn't get me good, so it only stings and hurts for a few seconds, but it does serve to finally piss me off.

I stop and immediately cup my hand over my nose, like I'm really hurt.

"Hold the bike for a minute while I get my handkerchief. I think you bloodied my fuckin' nose," I tell him.

"God, Boogie, I'm sorry. I was only kidding around," he says, looking at me all sorrowful like.

"Just hold the fuckin' bike," I tell him.

"I'm sorry," he says again, as he takes hold of the bike. "I didn't mean to hurt you. Fuck!"

Continuing to hold my nose, I tip my head back and reach towards my back pocket for my handkerchief, but instead of pulling it out I fold my fingers into a wedge and before he even sees it coming, I snap my arm forward and drive my wedged fingers right into his left bicep—right into "Frog" city.

He yelps and lets go of the bike and grabs at his arm. I catch the bike before it hits the ground.

"Sucker," I yell at him.

"God damn it, Boogie, that hurt," he tells me rubbing his arm.

"Good! I meant for it to! You're being a whining asshole!"

"No shit!" he says, "I hadn't noticed!"

We both laugh!

"Hey, if you got a match, I got something to soothe your pain," I tell him, as I reach in my jacket pocket and pull out the crumpled cigarette pack and open it up.

"There's two left," I tell him, as I watch him dig into his pants pocket searching for a match.

"And one match," he says, holding it up. "What would you do without me?" he asks.

"Just don't let the wind blow it out. Hang on for a minute," I tell him as I hand him a cigarette. I roll the bike to the edge of the road and prop it against the ditch bank along the shoulder, then unzip my jacket and pull it out wide to block the wind.

"Stand up close to me when you light it," I tell him. He knows the routine. He moves in very close, strikes the match with a flick of his thumbnail, cups it in his hands and lights up. He takes a deep drag and hands his cigarette to me. I light mine off his and hand it back.

"Pain's gone already," he says and laughs smoke out his nose.

I inspect the cigarette pack again just to make sure it's empty, then crumple it up and toss it aside.

"Where'd you get 'em?" he asks.

"Stole 'em out of my brother's car this morning while he was asleep."

He shivers, then jerks his head back, then takes a puff and exhales.

"Shit, I wish there'd been more than two. We got the rest of the day and then tonight. I was gonna steal a pack from my dad, but he only had two packs left in his carton and I knew I'd get caught. Maybe we can buy some? Whatta you think?" he wants to know.

"You got any money?" I ask him.

"I got about a quarter, how about you?"

I know he's probably lying, so I do, too.

"About the same," I tell him."

"The commissary's out, unless we can get somebody to buy 'em. Nobody there'll sell 'em to us. Think we could get Wayne to do it? He buys 'em there all the time for his mom," he says.

"Yeah, he'll probably do it, but then he'll want at least half of them for what we owe him," I reply.

We stand silent for a while and smoke. Gusts of wind rip at our clothes and hair. Trapper's hair is baby fine and he keeps jerking his head back in an attempt to keep it out of his eyes. He looks spastic.

I laugh!

"What?" he asks.

"Nothing," I answer, just as he does it again.

I fish my chewing gum from my pocket.

"Want a Juicy Fruit?" I ask him.

"Sure," he answers back.

I've smoked a little more than half the cigarette, so I snub it out and put the butt in my jacket pocket for later, then I unwrap the gum and stick it in my mouth.

Trapper does the same, then amazes me by picking up the bike and commencing to walk it up the hill. I guess the "frog," the cigarettes and the gum have humbled him. "Yeah! Sure!"

"Let's go down to Harley's and see if we can find somebody there to buy 'em," he says.

Harley's is a small general store that sits at the western edge of town, down close to the baseball field—a mom-and-pop operation and the only competition to the commissary in Black Creek. Neither Mr. nor Mrs. Harley can ever tell Trapper and me apart, so I usually charge stuff to his dad's account and he does the same to mine just to confuse them.

"We'll have to find somebody, cause there's no way the Harleys will sell 'em to us," I say. "They got strict orders from both our dads."

"I know," he says.

We move on up the hill.

"Man, I can't wait until tonight!" He tells me all excited. "Mr. Humphries is gonna have to leave just after the party starts to go down to Birmingham to see his sister in the hospital and Mrs. Humphries has promised Sarah that if everybody behaves, she'll stay in her room and listen to the radio. She always falls asleep when she does."

"How do you know all that?" I ask him.

"Lashie told me. She said as soon as Mrs. Humphries's asleep, that Sarah said she wanted to play kissing games. How about that?"

"Who the hell would wanna kiss Sarah?" I ask.

"Nobody I know of, but anyway, Lashie said we're gonna play Spin the Bottle, Walking and Dark Room Gamble, but we'll have to do it real quiet so Mrs. Humphries don't wake up."

Trapper stays excited as he relays all this information to me. I suspect that most of it's bullshit, which he's prone to emit, so I begin to separate the fact from the fiction.

"Lashie told you all this?" I ask him.

"Yeah! I told you she did."

"It don't add up," I say, giving him a questionable look.

"What don't add up?"

"Well, in the first place, if the weather stays bad, the party might get cancelled. You can't roast wieners if it's raining, dummy," I tell him.

Trapper's ready with the answer.

"You can if you cook 'em at the bar-b-que pit that Mr. Humphries built that's attached to their back porch, dummy. That's where the fire's gonna be. Never even know it's raining. All that shit's handled. The party's on, rain or shine, believe me."

I throw another one at him.

"There's probably gonna be at least twenty of us there, even some eighth and ninth graders. Sarah told me she was inviting lots of people, so you're telling me that there's only gonna be Mrs. Humphries there to supervise us. You're full of it."

Trapper babbles on, he's done his homework.

"Only about fifteen and eighth grade is the cutoff, except for two people," he tells me. "Sarah reconsidered after Bobbie and them talked to her. God! You don't know anything," he says. "There'll be a few grownups there 'til the thing's over. It's from six-thirty to nine-thirty and then they all leave. It's the afterhours when things really get started. That's when the fun begins."

"Whatta you mean?" I ask, now confused more than ever and feeling somewhat out of the loop.

He rolls his eyes and shakes his head in exasperation.

"Sarah's having a pajama party, dimwit. A lot of the girls are sleeping over and a few choice 'male specimens,' including me and you, have been invited to hang around, if you know what I mean?"

Now I really feel left out. I hadn't heard any of this.

"Are you making all this shit up?" I ask him.

"No, I told you, Lashie told me, plus Bobbie had already filled me in about how they conned Sarah into not inviting so many people and convinced her to have the pajama party. That's why they invited Martha Foster and Bert Anderson, dumbo!"

This statement blows my mind. Bert Anderson is the mine superintendent's son. He's sixteen, fat and I've heard, queer. He goes to school in Birmingham and never associates with the locals, the Camp people.

"Bert Anderson's coming to the party?" I ask.

"Yeah! Can you believe it? Bobbie, Darlene, Lashie and Carol marched right up to the Super's door and knocked. Mrs. Anderson came to the door herself. They told her they wanted to give Bert a personal invite to Sarah's party. They told her that they had heard how great Bert plays the violin and since they would like to have music at the party, they felt that a talented violinist would be a welcome relief from the current trashy music the Black Creek youth is hearing over the radio. The old lady ate it up; said Bert would be there with bells on. Pardon the pun!"

I hate a wise ass! I think to myself.

"Why did they really invite him?" I ask.

"Sarah's got a crush on him. Can you believe it?"

"My God! He's ugly, he's fat and he's got a million zits. What's more, he's queer as a three-dollar bill."

Trapper shrugs his shoulders. "Love's blind! What can I say?"

"And Martha Foster?" I ask.

"She's Mrs. Humphries' supervisor for the pajama party. The girls convinced her to pick Martha. They said she had a good Christian outlook on life and was mature enough at sixteen to supervise young girls. They said it would also set an example to everyone as to how a sixteen-year-old should act, since all of them are approaching that age. They said they felt their model should be a mature, Christian teen."

"What bullshit!" I say. "What's the real reason?"

"She knows how to play all the kissin' games and she don't give a shit what we do. She'll want to join in. Man! she's got some great big ol' titties and she don't get mad if you 'cop a feel.'"

Where the hell have I been all week, I wonder? Everyone seems to know everything that's going on except me. You'd think Darlene would have filled me in.

"You been knowing this all along and haven't told me?" I ask.

"All except what Lashie told me today and I was gonna tell you this past week, but you were being such a weird asshole 'til Friday and then I forgot all about it 'til today."

"I hope you get Sarah every time in Dark Room Gamble," I tell him.

"Sarah's gonna get Bert. The girls will see to that."

We both laugh at the thought of it.

"They fix all the games so their boyfriends don't get mad," I say.

"Yeah, but Dark Room Gamble's the hardest to fix," he says. "Who knows, I might get Darlene."

"And you might get your other arm crunched, if you don't wipe that smirk off your face, asshole."

Trapper starts running the bike, me behind him with my fist drawn back. We laugh and run all the way to the top of the hill.

We've seen no signs of life on the way up. No people, no animals, no cars. But, just as we get to top, where the road makes a tee, I hear a coarse barking sound to my left. It's coming from the house the Skinners used to live in. Our old house is right across the road. A big black and tan hound runs off the porch, raises itself up on its hind legs and props its front paws on the fence gate. It's barking like crazy and wagging its tail.

His name is Simon. He belongs to Margie and Annette Skinner's older sister, Faye, who still lives in the house. I've known him since he was a puppy. We walk his way. Tapper leans the bike against the fence and we both give Simon a pet through the gate. He whimpers and slobbers on our hands, wants us to let him out, wants to play! "Sorry Simon, no time to play today, we're in a hurry," I tell him. He seems to understand what I've said. He gives one final whimper, then turns and runs back up on the porch.

I get the bike and push it back to the road.

If you go to the right, the road runs down to the rock dump, about seventy yards away. There's only one house on this section of the road. It's where James used to live. The rock dump itself is a big round mountain of a thing, which covers about three and a half acres of earth and is about two hundred and fifty feet high. It serves a dual purpose: for the mine, it's a place to dump the tailings or residue from the breaker/washer where the coal is readied for shipment. But more importantly, especially for the kids of Black Creek, it serves as a dam for the big pond that runs up the hollow behind the house where I used to live, all the way to the main road, about sixty yards to my left. The pond is a great place for fishing and also for frog gigging, but no one swims in it and very few will eat anything caught from it, except the niggers. As I look I see two of them fishing now. They're bundled up and have umbrellas and have at least ten cane poles staked out between them. I point them out to Trapper.

"Bet they're fishing for catfish," I tell him.

"Hell, they don't care what it is as long as they can fry it," he says. We laugh!

I straddle the crossbar of the bike.

"Hop on," I tell Trapper. "We can ride from here." He hops on the seat.

We head to the left, towards the main road. The road is muddy and full of potholes of water and the wind is in our face. I'm standing on the pedals pumping as hard as I can, but with Trapper's extra weight on the seat behind me, the going is difficult. I'm seriously considering letting him drive.

"Quit hittin' so many fuckin' mudholes. You're splashing water all over my pants and shoes," he tells me.

I see a big one just ahead and hit it dead center on purpose. Just as I do my chain slips and we nearly crash, but my skill and dexterity and the chain taking hold keeps us upright.

"Damn it! You did that on purpose," he yells.

I ignore him and continue to pump the pedals as hard as I can, laughing like hell to myself. We hit the main road just in front of Darlene's house. I stop the bike. Trapper slips off the seat and begins to wipe at his pants legs and shoes. I hold the bike and do the same.

"I knew this was why you wanted to come this way," he says to me.

"And that's supposed to mean?" I ask.

"So you might see your little baby, that's why."

I raise my left foot and jingle my bell and laugh. "God! You're so brilliant," I tell him.

But he's right; I do want to see her. Maybe get a chance to ask her about the party tonight. Is she over her "bad cold?" Is she going? How much of this bullshit Trapper has been telling me is true? I look all around her house. The only sign of life I see is smoke coming out a small chimney on the roof. Disappointment floods my body. Then, a misty rain begins to fall.

"You think she's home?" I ask him.

"Oh sure she is," he says. "Just waiting' for her lover to come court-ing.' So why don't you just go over there and knock on the door and tell her momma that 'lover boy's' here. I'll just stand out here and wait in the fuckin' rain. I'll even hold your fuckin' bike."

Disregarding his sarcastic remarks, I change the subject and ask him a question about something that has been nagging at me.

"How are we gonna explain being out so late tonight?" I want to know.

He throws his arm out, palms up, and gives me that "how the hell should I know" look.

"Other than not gettin' soaked, that's the next biggest problem we got. Let's go! We'll figure something out," he says, as he jumps on the seat.

We're off again, heading west—the wind ripping at our clothing and a misty rain painting our skin. Riding double is a breeze now that we're on pavement.

"Come on! Peddle faster," Trapper yells, as he sits on the seat with his legs thrown out to keep the water and the mud from the tires, off his clothes.

Just as I speed up, my chain slips again.

"This bike's a piece of shit, I told you the chain was slippin'" he hollers to me.

"It just needs oiling," I yell back.

I hit the pedals hard for about four more turns, then stand on them and coast.

"When we get down to Harley's, use some of that 'rose' that's drip-ping off your head," he tells me and laughs. "Asshole!!"

We hit the curve at the Baptist church. I dip to the right and take it on the inside to stay away from an oncoming car that we meet in the turn. Whoever's driving the car begins to honk their horn.

Trapper turns to look.

"Fuck you!" he yells at 'em.

I pump hard again and coast. It's downhill all the way and once more the rain has stopped. We sail past Wayne's house, no sign of him or Albert or the niggers. We hit the bump on the trip track bridge and fly past the commissary.

"Who drives a maroon 41 Ford?" Trapper yells to me.

"Was that the car that Mr. Horn Happy was driving?" I ask.

"Yeah, a two-door Super Deluxe.

"No idea," I tell him.

We pass the school and the Methodist church and then head down the steepest hill in town, the one everybody calls Drugstore Hill, even though there hasn't been a drugstore here for years. The filling station is now where it used to be, and as we whiz by, I see my Uncle Sam, who runs the station, talking to some old men sitting on stacked-up drink crates whittling. The filling station is the gathering place for whittling and gossiping for the old men around town. Trapper shoots them a bird. I hope one of them isn't my dad. I turn my head, scrunch down and pump the pedals. We're zooming.

Halfway down the hill, we see John Lester, a mental retard about five years older than us. We call him, "Ha Ya," because he can't speak plain. He has a *Grit* paper route. He's wrecked his bike and *Grit* newspapers are blowing out of the front basket and scattering everywhere. The bike's in the ditch along the shoulder of the road with Ha Ya under it holding his knees and crying. We don't bother to stop because he wrecks about ten times every day, but Trapper does take the time to shoot him a bird and yell, "Moron."

At the foot of the hill, the road makes a checkmark right in front of the community house, a long, narrow wooden building used mostly for the picture shows on Friday nights.

"Take a right and let's check out the ball field while it's not raining," Trapper hollers, but he waits too late and I'm going too fast to make the curve, so I continue going straight.

"We'll check it when we come back. Let's go on down to the store and dry out for a while," I yell back to him.

As I whip pass the turn, the road levels out for about thirty yards and then it's downhill again, all the way to Harley's, about a football field away on the right.

I pump it hard and coast. As I glide across the Black Creek Bridge, I notice the water. It's still as black as china ink. It takes a lot more rain than this to muddy that fucker! I take a deep breath. I feel wonderful!

"WHEEEE!" Trapper yells as loud as he can, "Ain't it great to be alive!"

"You bet!" I yell back, as I make the turn into Harley's parking lot and listen to my shoe play *Jingle Bells* as my bike tires hit the bumpy rocks.

We're both laughing as we get off the bike. I lean it next to the steps.

"Why you want to check the ball field?" I ask; "You know it's gotta be full of water."

"I hope it don't rain out the men's practice game tomorrow, I want to get us a couple of new baseballs," he tells me.

"Answer me truthfully," I say to him. "Do you honestly believe that your checking the field will have any influence on the weather?"

"I know! I know! But, we need some new baseballs," he says and shoots me a bird.

What he really means is that baseballs are hard to come by, especially for young boys in coal mining camps, so we steal them from the "big boys," the "men's" team every home game! We chase their fouls and you can be assured that there are always two or three balls that can never be found. If they complain, we just steal more, like last year.

Just before one of the home games started, Enoc Sandler, who is the appointed "king" of the men's team, tells us that he's going to personally kick all our asses if one baseball gets "rat holed" during the game. That pissed our whole team off, so we all went to work. By the sixth inning, they were down to two baseballs. They stopped the game, both teams screaming threats at us. Some of them even tried to chase us down, but none of them could catch us. People who were at the game started leaving and one of them must have told Britt, 'cause the next thing I know, he was there, wheeling up in his big black Buick and jumping out.

"I hope somebody didn't get me out of my Sunday easy chair for nothing," he tells Enoc Sandler, who met him three steps from the car.

They all gathered around him, Ol' Enoc waving his arms and talking a mile a minute. That's when we all started moving in. With Britt there, we knew we were safe.

We heard Britt say, "You're telling me that you had to stop your ballgame 'cause you ain't got no balls?" Then he started to laugh. "Hell, Enoc," he said, "I've known near all of you fuckers your whole doggone lives and I've always know'd you didn't have no balls." He turned and looked towards us and laughed again.

"Move in here closer, you little 'burr heads.' I wanna talk to you," he yelled over to us, waving us in towards him.

"Who's the chief burr head here?" he asked us. Naturally, before any of the rest of us could move, Wayne, Mr. Big Shot, grabbed the spotlight. He moved right up into the circle of complainees, stood all stiff and erect and cocky like he always does and told Britt, "I'll do the talking."

"You're Frank Watson's boy, ain't you?" Britt asked him.

"Yes, sir, Mr. Britt."

"OK, now, I've heard these ol' boys' side of the story, let me hear yours."

Wayne was prepared and it was a hell of a story! About how we had always worked really hard during the ballgames to chase down the fouls and how hard it is searching for lost balls in the weeds, and in the woods and along the snaky little creek down behind the backstop and how diligent we've always been in doing it. About how we've never asked for any compensation and continued doing it, even though we were always accused of stealing the balls that were just impossible to find. Hell, tears were starting to pool in my eyes before Britt finally shut him up.

"OK, OK," he told Wayne, "Enough, enough!"

Britt took off his hat and ran his hand through his hair, then put it back on and snapped the brim down to shade his eyes. He hitched up his pants and adjusted the .45 that hung butt out on his left side, then looked Wayne right in the eye and asked, "Then why was today any different, boy?"

Wayne was ready with the answer.

"'Cause Mr. Sandler told us if one ball couldn't be found, he was going to personally beat our asses and it scared us. So I guess everybody figured that the more balls that got lost, the less likely we would be to get our asses beat, so I guess we all didn't look for them as good as we should have.

Britt stood there for a few moments. Shaking his head, then pulled out a big cigar from his breast pocket, unwrapped it, bit off the end and stuck it in his mouth.

"Anybody got a light?" he asked.

There was a flurry of pocket patting, but before anyone else could find a match, Wayne whipped out his Zippo, flicked it once and lit Britt's cigar. He took a couple of big puffs to get it going good, then blew the ashes off the tip, squinted up his eyes and looked at Enoc.

"Did you tell them boys that?"

Enoc's all flustered and red in the face. He stretched up his neck and told Britt, "Well, I guess I might a said something to that effect, but I never meant no harm. Them baseballs are expensive. I just wanted to caution them about stealing 'em."

"You got any proof of that?" Britt asked him.

"No sir, other than the fact that they's always got new balls to play their games with and they shore don't have the money to buy 'em."

"They got new balls?"

"Yes, sir, brand new balls, "Enoc told him.

"Then them can't be yours," Britt said.

"Why's that?" Enoc wanted to know.

"'Cause your balls that you've lost are 'used balls.' They've been throwed and hit Enoc, that's used, not 'brand new.'"

Enoc had trapped himself. He didn't know what to say.

"How many balls you normally lose in a ball game?" Britt asked him.

"Two or three, four at the most," Enoc told him.

"How many got lost today?"

Enoc had to think for a minute.

"We had fifteen new ones when the game started. We're down to two now, that's why we stopped playing."

"Thirteen missing" Britt said.

"Yes, sir."

"An unlucky number, wouldn't you say?" Britt asked him.

"Yes, sir."

"How much is a used ball worth?"

Enoc had to think again. He didn't know where Britt was headed; He pulled off his cap and scratched his head before he answered.

"I'd say about a quarter if it's used. That'd be about the average."

"A quarter, huh," Britt stated.

"Yes, sir, a quarter."

"So if I looked in the trunk of my ol' Buick and I just happened to have some used baseballs in there and I said to you, Enoc, you can finish your game if you'll pay me a quarter a piece for them balls what you reckon-on you'd say?"

"Enoc's really confused now.

"I guess I'd say OK."

"You guess or you know you would?" Britt asked him.

"I know I would," Enoc answered.

Britt shook his head up and down and then turned back towards Wayne.

"Here's what I want you boys to do," he said. "I'm gonna open the trunk of that big ol' black Buick over there and I want you boys to go back out there and hunt really hard for them lost balls. I'll bet if you do, you gonna find at least ten of 'em. Then, when you find 'em just bring 'em back here and put 'em in that Buick's trunk. That's what I want you boys to do. Understand?"

"Yes, sir," Wayne said.

"OK, get moving and if I was you, I'd work extra, extra hard."

It didn't take long. Not more than 15 minutes could have passed before 10 formerly lost baseballs were now lined up in the Buick's trunk. Britt had leaned against the front fender and finished his cigar while the process happened. When the last ball was in the truck, he strolled over, looked in and smiled.

"Hey, Enoc," he said. "The damndest thing just happened. I just looked in this ol' Buick's trunk and found ten 'used' baseballs.

Now as I remember, you said you'd pay a quarter a piece for 'em, is that right?"

"Yes, sir, that's what I said."

"Well, let me see now, that'd be about two dollars and fifty cents. Soon as it's in my hand, I don't see no more reason for this game to be delayed, do you?"

"No, sir."

"And by the way, Enoc, no fuckin' clacker!"

They had to take up a collection. When they were through, Enoc handed Britt the money. He made a big production out of folding the bills and putting them and the coins in his pocket.

"By the way, Enoc, I forgot to ask what the score was when you had to stop."

"They had us six to three, Mr. Britt," Enoc told him.

"Damn," Britt said, "it's gonna be a shame if you lose your balls and then the game on the same day. A real shame! And by the way," he said, looking directly at Wayne, "I think about three is the most balls that should ever get lost in a Black Creek ballgame, ever again. Whatta you think?"

"I think you're right, Mr. Britt," Wayne told him.

"Good! Nice doing business with you fellows," and with that he gets in his Buick, guns it a couple of times and pulls away.

Black Creek lost nine to three!

Enoc was pissed!

As we move inside the store, we're still laughing. It's a great day, even with the bad weather and it seems like everything we say is funny. It looks like we're the only customers. Mr. and Mrs. Harley are standing at the checkout counter in the center of the store, apparently discussing the handful of papers he's holding. They spot us as we come in. I turn and look at the clock that hangs over the door. It's 10:55.

We head in separate directions, Trapper to the right, me to the left. It's a game we play every time we come in. The Harleys are paranoid about the kids around town swiping from them, so we like to tease them a little. We always wander all around the store touching and feeling everything in sight before we finally convene back at the checkout counter, where they sell all the good stuff, like the candy, the dopes and the ice cream and—the cigarettes. Mr. Harley takes Trapper and Mrs. Harley drifts toward me.

"Now, are you the Trapp boy or the Smith boy?" she asks me. "I can never tell you boys apart."

Then, before I even have time to answer, she continues to go on.

"Ya'll look so much alike, you'd think you were twin brothers."

I'm in the can goods section, rubbing my fingers along the corn and the peas and the beans as I walk down the aisle.

"My mom cans all this stuff," I tell her, "Except she puts it in jars where you can see it."

"That's nice," she tells me.

"She says people spit in the stuff they can in the factories," I tell her, as I pull a big can of tomatoes off the shelf and hold it out towards her.

"They probably harked a big oyster right in this can!" I say.

I want to laugh as I watch her lips turn downward and her face begin to pale, but I contain myself."

"An oyster?" she inquires.

"Yeah, you know, the gooie snot that drips out of the back of your nose into your throat that looks like a oyster when you hark it up," I tell her, as I slide the can back into place and move on to the mayonnaise and ketchup.

She blanches a little whiter and holds her hand up to her mouth.

"We are brothers," I tell her. "Blood brothers—the ketchup reminded me, 'cause it looks like blood."

"Oh, my!" she says and kinda fans at her face with her hand then moves it down to her chest and takes a deep breath.

"Like the Lone Ranger and Tonto or Tom Sawyer and Huck Finn." You know, loyal companions," I go on to tell her.

"We did it when we were nine," I continue, as I move onwards towards the back of the store and stop at the meat case.

It's a big, white, boxy looking thing, with a glass front. Not as big as the one at the commissary, but it looks newer and a lot cleaner.

It's full of pigs' feet and knuckles and fat back, all the kind of things that people like, especially the niggers who trade here regularly. She's right behind me, following my every move.

I look to my right and see Trapper over by the mops and brooms. He's running his mouth a mile a minute to a confused-looking Mr. Harley, who's standing beside him scratching his head. I can't hear what he's saying, but I would venture to say that it's some far-out, bullshit story that he's telling.

I give Mrs. Harley a big smile and then tell her, "You have to fuse your blood and take an oath, then cross your heart and swear to God."

She furrows her brow and gives me a bewildered look.

"I'm not really sure what you're saying," she tells me. "My goodness! You're a talker."

"To be blood brothers—that's what you gotta do," I tell her. "Wanna hear something funny and weird?" I ask.

"I guess," she says, "but I can't imagine what could be weirder than some of the things you've already told me."

"It's about when we were nine and got to be blood brothers," I tell her, as I walk the length of the meat case putting handprints on the glass.

"Remember," I said, "you have to fuse your blood."

"Did your mother send you down here to buy meat?" she wants to know.

"This is the funny part" I say, ignoring her question. "We didn't want to cut ourselves, so to get blood, we peeled some impetigo scabs off our legs and pressed the bloody sores together, while we swore our oaths, crossed our hearts and swore to God. It's funny, 'cause we wasn't sure it would work."

She's taken off her apron and is using it to clean my prints off the glass, all the while shaking her head and looking towards Mr. Harley.

"Please be careful and not touch the glass," she tells me.

"Now here's the weird part," I go on.

"The day we done it, we were shootin' birds with our air rifles. I'm talking about real birds, not the kind you shoot with your finger and we was pretending they was Japs. Part of our oath was that we would protect each other from our enemies. That's how we know it worked."

She stops wiping the glass and gives me that same perplexed look again.

"I think you lost me," she says, looking over towards Mr. Harley again.

"We knew it worked, 'cause a few days later, God ordered the U.S. Army to drop some super bombs and they killed about a zillion of 'em."

"Birds?" she asks, as she looks at me and sorta screws up her face.

"No! Japs, and then they surrendered. Ain't that weird? And then the War was over!"

I'm tiring of playing the game, so now that I have her totally confused, I do an about face and head up the main aisle towards where you pay and where all the goodies are. Trapper sees me and does the same. The Harleys follow suit.

There's a small glass case on top of the checkout counter that holds a variety of pocket knives. Both of us stop to admire the contents and manage to smudge it up pretty well with our fingerprints as we point out the knives we'd like to have. Mr. Harley checks the back of the case to make sure it's locked, while the misses searches under the counter for a rag to clean it off.

We head for the cold drink box that sits adjacent to the counter. It's a two-sided contraption, hinged in the middle. I raise one lid, Trapper takes the other. The water in the box feels icy cold as we search for our choice.

"Them dopes are in there by brand, so it ain't necessary to handle every one of them" Mr. Harley tells us. "The big ones are all on your left side, so try not to mix 'em up."

We already know this before we go through our ritual. He tells us the same thing every time we come in. We just do it to irritate him. Trapper drops his side of the lid and it slams shut with a bang. It startles the Harleys and both of them jump.

"Oops! Sorry," he says.

We dip in again on my side. Trapper comes out with a Pepsi and

I choose an RC Cola. Mr. Harley is giving us the eye, so I softly close the lid, then raise my foot and jingle my bell. We both laugh! We open the drinks on the side of the box, take a big swig and put them on the checkout counter.

"I'm gonna need a Zero bar, too," Trapper tells Mr. Harley.

"And a pack of peanuts for me," I chime in.

"And a pack of Wings cigarettes for my dad," Trapper goes on; saying it in a confident voice in hopes of conning Mr. Harley.

I suddenly get a gurgle in my bowels, knowing if by some chance he gets them, he'll charge them to my dad's account and I'll be in a fix when my dad looks over the charge slips. But then the thought of having a whole pack of Wings, which is equivalent to having two packs of cigarettes since they're so long we usually cut them in half, diminishes my concerns.

"Are you the Trapp or the Smith kid?" Mr. Harley asks Trapper.

All of a sudden, I see an out. Just as he answers "Smith," I volunteer "Trapp" at the same time.

"Can you believe these boys?" Mr. Harley asks, looking at the wife, "or anything they say?"

She shakes her head in agreement.

"Boys who don't tell the truth, that smoke and kill things usually wind up in the penitentiary," she tells him, looking at us.

"Well, whichever one you are, you can forget about the cigarettes," he tells Trapper. "Them's orders from both your dads. Now do you want anything else before I make up these tickets, 'cause I'm sure you wanna charge these dopes and candy to your daddies' accounts."

"Peanuts ain't candy," I inform him, but before he has a chance to reply the chiming sound of the store door opening distracts him.

We all look towards the entrance and see two niggers coming in. I recognize them immediately and although they both have the appearance of being young boys, I know one of them's not. They head directly down the aisle towards us.

"I think you two boys need to be gettin' on along," Mr. Harley tells us. "Finish drinking them dopes outside and don't run off with them bottles, 'cause I didn't charge you no deposit. Put the empties in one of them crates out there at the side of the store when you're through, you hear?"

I hear what he says and I'm sure Trapper does too, but neither of us answers; our full attention is on the approaching niggers.

The biggest of the two, we call "Square." He's about 15 years old and the leader of a gang of niggers about our own age. We've had several "run-ins" with them in the past.

He's not real tall, only about three inches taller than me, but he's large-boned and powerfully built. His identifying feature and I might add, the reason for his name, is his head. It has the appearance of a square box with a face—very interesting and very odd looking, to say the least.

He's wearing a heavy gray button-up sweater that looks too small, over a tattered-looking checkered shirt that's stuffed into a pair of faded bibbed overalls that look like they might be his daddy's, 'cause they're way too long. On his feet he's wearing a pair of old sneakers that his toes have worn through and he has a red-and-blue striped sock hat on his head, pulled all the way down to his eyes.

The smaller one is a "sight for sore eyes." Everyone calls him, "Snooks." He hangs around the commissary a lot and the white boys like to devil him until he pulls out his knife, a switchblade he carries in his coat pocket. When he pulls it and waves it around everyone has a laugh. He's less than five feet tall, probably in his 30s, though none of us know for sure, and, to make matters worse, he's also retarded, a "pinhead" and a "harelip." His attempt at talk comes out as guttural grunts and he's always dressed the same, no matter the season of the year: an old gray wool "newsboy" cap, with the earflaps pulled down over his ears, a heavy brown overcoat about three sizes too big that hangs almost to his feet, a pair of what looks to be old khaki army pants and old worn-out brogans on his feet. I've never been able to determine whether he wears a shirt or not, since he always has the coat buttoned right up to his neck.

As they approach, Trapper starts in on Snooks. "Nooks! Nooks! Nooks!" he says real loud, getting right up in his face. Snooks backs off, rolls his eyes and slides his hand inside his coat pocket.

"OK, you boys, outside! We ain't gonna have no devilment in here. This is a place of business," Mr. Harley tells us.

Trapper and I both laugh and surprisingly so does Square.

"How's Missa' Gene's haid?" he asks me and laughs again.

"Sore as hell, with a great big red welt that looks like another mouth right over his eyes," I tell him.

"He really looks much better," Trapper adds. "Two mouths become him, he's such a FREAK."

This statement breaks us up! Even Snooks starts to laugh, even though he has no idea why.

What we're laughing about happened about a month ago.

It was a windy day, early in March, warm for the season of the year. Several of us guys were up on the old rock dump. Another big, round mountain of a thing that takes up the hollow between the commissary and where James currently lives. It hasn't been used for years and is now almost covered with pine trees, seemingly the only thing that will grow there.

Charlie had rigged up a sled to slide on the pine straw and James wanted to try it out. Trapper was along and so were the Tanner brothers, two younger kids who live next door to Charlie. Also in the group was Gene Tiddle, a fat, loudmouth 14-year-old, who lives in the Upper End of the Camp. He had hooked up with Trapper on his way down and Trapper couldn't shake him. None of us really wanted him around, because to be truthful, Gene isn't an easy person to like. In addition to being a loudmouth, he's also a spoiled, domineering, bully prick.

We had been up there less than an hour, when bored with sledding, he began shooting his air rifle (which he had brought along) at kites some nigger kids were flying about 25 yards up the dump above us. They were just little kids, with a small amount of string, so the kites weren't flying very high, but still Gene's BBs were having little effect on them. This pissed him off, so he began moving up the dump closer to the kids, hoping to "knock 'em out of the sky," as he had bragged to us he was going to do. As he moved up closer to them, the kids spotted him and realizing his intent, they began to quickly wind in their kites and run away. That's when he began to shoot at them.

"Gene! Get your ass back down here and leave them lil' nigger kids alone," James hollered at him, but Gene paid him no mind, just kept heading up the dump, cocking and shooting the air rifle.

"I'm gonna beat the fuckin' shit out of him," I heard James say, and the next thing I knew he was heading up the dump after Gene and so as not to miss any of the action, the rest of us followed right behind him.

Gene had reached the top of the knoll where the kids had been standing to fly the kites and we were about thirty feet down the dump behind him, when I saw James suddenly stopped his ascent and point towards the top, about another fifty yards above us.

Square was standing right on the peak with about ten of his gang lined up beside him, about five on his left and five on his right. It reminded me of Indians up on the ridge in a western movie. Gene must have seen them at about the same time we did, because as James was pointing them out, I saw Gene do an about face and barrel back down the dump in our direction.

We all knew what was coming next, so we all dove for cover. I wedged myself in a cleft behind a small pine and watched as shards of the shale that covers the dump left their hands and like a covey of flushed quail came flying in our direction. While the first barrage was still in the air, they released a second one and just as the first barrage hit the ground, they released a third before I saw them stop and stoop to gather more ammunition. Most of the sailing missiles seemed to be directed towards Gene, who had almost made it back down to our position, then veered off about forty feet to our right to take cover in a fissure of layered shale, but plenty of them came our way, several too close for comfort. After the third barrage hit the ground, all of us, with the exception of Gene, made a mad dash back down to the cover of the pine thicket where we had been sledding. He elected to stay in the safety of his ditch, where although heavily bombarded, he had remained unscathed. In fact, during the ammo gathering time on the peak, he rose to his knees and began to blast BBs towards them as fast as he could cock and shoot before he had to fall flat again for the second round of the attack.

It came almost like the first. One barrage, then two, then three, this time with only a few of the shards sailing down towards us. The others were all directed towards Gene.

And, as I said, it came almost as the first, but not quite. For this time, as the third barrage was released, Square held up and didn't throw with the rest of his gang. He waited until all the other rocks had all landed before he threw. Square is a southpaw and the piece of flat shale that he released was the size of a saucer. I watched it as it left his hand seemingly going far out to the right of where Gene was taking cover, then while it was in the air, it began to break up. Two small pieces crumpled off and fell away, which seemed to create a boomerang effect on the larger portion, which remained intact. Somehow, someway, as the flat piece of shale arched through the air, I realized exactly what was going to take place, but I was unable to do anything other than watch in awe as it happened.

Gene, thinking that everything was clear again had decided now was the time to head for the safety of the trees and had jumped to his feet to lay down a round of retreating shots before he ran. As he pumped off the final one, he shot a bird and took the time to scream. "You fuckin' niggers can't hit shit," a statement which proved to be vastly untrue since it had scarcely escaped his lips before Square's arcing projectile exploded on his forehead. Blood squirted one way and Gene went the other, about twenty feet down the dump, sliding on his back.

"Holy shit, what a throw!" James said, making a general statement to the group.

"I knew that fuckin' rock was going to get him as soon as it left Square's hand," he went on the say.

We all agreed.

I looked toward the top of the dump. Everyone but Square had disappeared. He was waving his arms in front of his face signaling a timeout and was strolling down towards us.

"We'd better check Gene out," James told us and we began to move up towards him.

He seemed to be out cold, but just before we got to him, he began to move and wipe at his forehead. His hand came away all bloody. He turned and looked toward us and tried to sit up, but immediately lay back down. His face was covered with blood, but I noticed he was still holding on to his air rifle as we formed a circle around him.

"Hell, Gene! You'd been better off if you'd stayed up there in that ditch where you was hidden," James informed him, as he and Charlie squatted down beside him.

Charlie took a greasy looking red bandana handkerchief out of his back pocket and began to poke at the bleeding cut on Gene's forehead.

"They's some of that rock still stuck in there," he said to James, as he dabbed at the cut. "Something white-looking, too."

"That's his fuckin' skull, you moron," James told him.

"It looks like a fuckin' tooth," Charlie said and laughed.

"Does it hurt?" he asked Gene.

"Them niggers shot me in the head," he said, as he attempted to sit up again.

"Grab his arms and let's pull him up, Charlie," James said. "We'll take him down to the doctor's office and get him all sewed up."

"Is he daid?" I heard a voice from up above us ask.

We all looked up. Square was standing on a knoll about twenty feet away.

"Naw, he'll be OK. He's just knocked silly," James answered.

"He hadn't orta' gone an' shot at them lil' chilrun," Square told us.

"You did the right thing, Square," James told him. "Except for throwing at us. I was on my way up there to kick his ass before I had to stop and start duckin' rocks."

Square grinned.

"We'se got 'fused a mite bout who wuz doin' the shootin, 'cause ya'll all looks alike," he said.

We all laughed, as Square walked back up the dump.

Anyway, we took Gene by James' garage and he poured some kerosene on the cut, which by that time was also a big lump and then up to the doctor's office, where Doc Hooker doused it with alcohol

(Gene screamed like shit), sewed it up (only 14 stitches) and wrapped a bandage around his head.

"Is he gonna be all right?" I asked Doc Hooker.

"Long as he stays away from niggers with rocks," he answered.

We all laughed!

Gene still claims he was shot in the head by a nigger with a shotgun.

"Let's get out of here," Trapper says to me. "See ya, Square," he says.

"Yeah, see ya, Square," I say, as we head towards the door.

"Hey, Missa Boogieman," I hear him say.

"Yeah" I answer, turning back to look at him.

"Nex' time you up on da dump, wears that lil' bell, so I knows which one is youse," he whispers to me, "knows where to 'di-rect' my rocks."

Then he laughs. So do I, but I leave wondering whether he means direct them toward me or away from me?

As we head out the door, the clock says 11:15. The day seems to be dragging by.

Once again the rain has stopped, but from the looks of the sky it could start again any minute.

"Let's go check out the ball field," Trapper says.

"Will you get off the ball field thing!" I tell him. "We need to get somewhere to hang out where we won't get wet."

Trapper grabs my bike.

"Get on the seat; we'll go get under the creek bridge while we finish drinking these dopes. Hold em' and don't drink out of mine."

Just as he says this, we hear the honking of a horn. We look toward the road. It's the same car that honked at us up by the Baptist Church, the maroon '41 Ford. It's parked right at the edge of Harley's parking lot, under the big sweet gum tree that grows just off the edge of the road.

The horn honks twice again and then the driver's door opens and a man steps out of the car.

Harley's store sits about seventy-five feet off the road, so I don't recognize who it is. All I know is that he looks big and heavy.

"Who the hell is that?" I ask Trapper.

"Beats the shit out of me," he replies.

"He's waving for us to come over, let's go see," I tell him, as I start walking towards the car.

Trapper leans the bike back up against the steps and follows me. I hand him back his dope.

"Hang on just a minute," Trapper says, as he stops to open up his Zero bar and take a bite. I open my peanuts and began to pour them in my RC Cola. It won't hold them all. "Trade you what's left of these peanuts for a piece of that Zero," I tell him. We make the exchange and move on. Trapper screws me on the deal.

The guy's waiting for us by the car. He's big and fat. Not fat-fat, but big like muscle that's turning to fat. He's about six feet tall, give or take an inch, probably around 250 lbs., and as we approach him, I give him the once-over. He's dressed in a pair of old, faded, bibbed overalls and a washed-out, blue chambray shirt. Instead of a jacket, he's wearing what looks to be, the coat of an old, black, sharkskin suit. It probably fit him 25 lbs. ago. It's frayed at the collar and cuffs and worn at the elbows. On his head is a stained and tattered-looking gray, felt fedora, with the brim pulled down low, like he's trying to hide his eyes. I look down at his shoes. They're the kind the farmers wear—big, brown brogans, the ones with the heavy thick soles, except his are worn thin. They're all scratched and scuffed. His little toes are breaking out of the sides.

He sort of reminds me of a farmer. A farmer coming to town and he could have been except for his long, shaggy looking hair and the at least three-days growth of whiskers on his face. He's too dirty looking! Farmers clean up when they come to town.

His hair is a dark, dark brown, almost black, probably attributable to its greasy, unwashed condition; tinges of gray are invading both it and his beard. His complexion is ruddy, with penny-color blotching on his face and his hands. His nails are long, unkempt and dirty. No, definitely not a farmer! I try to judge his age—forty, maybe? I give a questionable look to Trapper and get the same back from him. I look at the guy again. I'm almost close enough to touch him. I finally recognize him, the minute he opens his mouth.

"God Damn!" I thought ya lil' fuckers had decided to camp out in there all day," he says to us. And then he laughs. It's a laugh that's unmistakable—a braying-like he-haw sound that ends with a snort, usually three to be exact, a laugh that matches his looks to a tee. He has a head that is uncommonly long, with a wide, almost lipless mouth that sets low on his face, which gives the appearance of having very little or no chin at all. A bona fide "Andy Gump," a name I've heard people use when referring to him in the past. His eyes, though large, are heavy lidded, so he appears to be looking through slits. His long wide nose sits almost flat on his face and bows downward, almost to his mouth, then tips with extremely flared and open nostrils. His teeth are yellowed and they're big and bucked, and protrude outward over his lower lip. Great for eating corn off the cob, Trapper and I used to joke. Yeah! He could be called "Andy" and that's probably what we would have called him were it not for his large, pointed, almost lobeless ears that are right out of the tales of Pinocchio. When you put the ears together with the face, you have the perfect donkey. His name is Bill Brady. We always called him, "Donkey" Bill.

He used to drive the Birmingham bus when I was younger, probably about ten. Then he got fired, or so everybody said, but he continued to hang around town, mostly around the school where he entertained the junior high boys with tales of his "so called" wrestling days and gave them demonstrations of various "holts," which was his word for holds. Then about a year ago, he just disappeared. There was a lot of talk and speculations as to why, and a lot of tales were told, and I guess that the general consensus that was finally reached was that he was a pervert, and that most of the "holts" were actually "hugs."

Trapper and I could have told them he was queer from the start. All the kids knew it, especially the boys. They all kidded and laughed about it. There was even rumors that he had actually had some success with a few; one in particular, which was one of the best stories of all, but there was nothing known for certain, 'cause there ain't no way anybody's gonna admit to anything like that. Actually, the only run-ins we ever had with him was when we used to hang around when he was showing off for the older boys and mock his laugh and call him Donkey Bill. He used to tell us he was going to kick our asses and even tried to chase us down a few times (without success), but nothing other than that.

One day he picked me and Wayne up, when we were going up to the peach orchard to swipe some peaches and he waited in the car while we made the raid (we gave him six big clear seeds), then he brought us back to town. He picked Trapper and me up once and gave us a ride to the creek. That was right before he vanished. He was OK on that day. I guess, to sum it up, he always seemed queer to us, but was never queer for us.

If he hadn't opened his mouth, I'm not sure I would have recognized him. He's really changed. He's gone from fairly clean-cut and in good shape, to fat and shabby, and in the past year, has aged to the point that he looks much older than I think he probably is.

I look at Trapper and can tell he's recognized him, too. "Remember what they say about a bad penny?" Trapper mumbles to me.

I laugh! He's right. Seeing Bill fits the old saying to a tee.

"How's it going, Bill?" Trapper asks as he finishes off his Zero bar and throws the wrapper to the wind, then pours the remainder of my peanuts in his Pepsi Cola.

"Yeah, Bill! Long time no see, where you been?" I say.

"Thet's fer me to know and ya ta find out," he tells me, then gives us another one of his donkey laughs.

"I gots more important thangs to do thin hang 'round this piece of shit town, thet's fer sure. I've places to go and thangs to do, man! But I'm here today and ol' Bill needs a lil' help and I knowed I was in luck when I saw two of m'good buddies whupping down the road on thet there bike. I honked atcha up there by the church, but I knowed ya din't know who I wuz."

"What kind of help?" Trapper asks.

"Matter of fact, I couldn't be eny luckier," he continues to go on, ignoring Trapper's question completely.

As I listen to Bill talk, I notice other changes in him from the way he used to be before. He's more nervous and fidgety and he seems to be ill at ease about something. His eyes keep darting around and he keeps turning his head, scanning the road in both directions. He reaches in his bib pocket and pulls out a pack of Camels, it looks almost full. I notice his hand shakes when he pulls out a cigarette and puts it between his lips. Then he starts to pat for a light. Coat pockets, pants pockets (both front and back), then coat pockets again before he finally finds it in his bib pocket; the same one his cigarettes were in. It's a shiny, silver Zippo.

"Fuck," I hear him mumble.

He strokes the wheel about three times before he finally gets a flame, then lights up and takes a big lung-busting drag and expels it in my direction. Riding just behind the flavor of the smoke that fills my nostrils is the aroma of pot whiskey.

He takes another puff and shivers.

"God damn this fucked-up weather!" he says.

I take the last drink of my RC and throw the bottle to the opposite side of the parking lot entrance, about 30 feet from where we're standing. It hits in some weeds and rolls to a stop right on the edge of the road. Not to be outdone, Trapper follows suit. His bottle hits in the same bunch of weed and rolls almost next to mine.

"How's thet fer a fuckin' shot?" he says.

"Whatta you mean you need some help and why's bumping into us so lucky for you?" Trapper says again, as he turns back towards Bill.

"'Cause I knowed thet ya know where the 'Big Rock' is, 'cause I took ya there once. Remember?" Bill says as he takes another drag off the Camel.

The Big Rock is a well-known and favored swimming hole over on Turkey Creek. If you stay on this same road, it's about three miles west of where we're now standing. It derives its name from a huge outcropping of limestone rocks that forms the bank along the creek for about 25 yards on its eastern side.

"Why you gotta problem with the Big Rock?" I jump in and ask.

"'Taint with it, it's at it. I got a truck stuck plumb up to the axle over there."

"Whose truck is it?" I ask.

"Now who the hell do you think it would be's, if I'm the one's wastin' m'time trying to git it out? It's my fuckin' truck—'47 Chevy pickup, clean as a fuckin' pen," he tells me, getting a little testy.

"Whatta ya want us to do?" Trapper asks him.

"Damn, I guess I'm gonna hafta draw you a fuckin' picture. I need ya to help me git the fucker out," Bill tells him, waving his cigarette hand in front of Trapper's eyes, like he's testing him for a trance.

"How you drive two cars at a time?" I ask.

"Whatta ya mean?" he asks, flipping his Camel away.

"I mean you say you gotta truck stuck and you got a car to drive to hunt up somebody to help you get it out. Two vehicles, one driver," I say. "Git it?"

Bill shakes his head and reaches back to scratch his ass before he answers, then shakes his head again.

"Got the truck stuck over there yesterday evening if'n ya gotta know, and if it really matters," he informs me, then proceeds to hark a wad out of his throat and spit it into the wind. I smell the whiskey again.

"Damndest thang I've ever seen," he says. "Ask two good buddies fer a lil' favor and they wind up givin' you the fuckin' third degree." He shakes his head again then takes a deep breath and releases it in exasperation. He fumbles in his pocket and pulls out his cigarettes and lights another one up.

"Don't know what this world's comin' to when friends won't help friends," he goes on to say.

"Uh! Hang on a minute Bill," Trapper tells him. "I don't remember us saying we wouldn't help you yet, but if you want it official, they ain't no fuckin' way I'm gonna mess up my clothes and shoes pushin' a truck out of mud. I don't know about Boogie."

"Me neither," I tell him.

"Anyway if we's such good friends, how come you ain't even offered us a smoke?" Trapper asks him.

I can tell the conversation's not setting well with Bill. He takes another big drag of smoke and blows it right towards Trapper's face, then mimics a reply.

"Well! You jist hang on a fuckin' minute yoreself 'cause here's the whole damn story, so as I don't hafta keep on answerin' fuckin' questions.

"We wuz a fishin' over at the Big Rock yesterday in the evenin'. By we's, I mean me un' a good buddy of mine who lives over there at Newcastle. We'd had a few brewskis and he said he had a hankerin' for some fried catfish and I said, 'Hell! Let's go ketch us some.' He wanted to know whir' and I said, 'Shit, I know a place that's close whir' there's tons of fish,' 'cause I remembered what you two told me thet time I gives ya a ride over there. Remember? I asked you if they's wuz any fish in thet there creek and ya'll said, 'Shit, yeah, it's full of 'em.'

"'Grab your fishin' pole,' I told him, 'and let's git goin'. He said, 'But Bill, it's a rainin',' un' I said, 'You dumb shit, thet's whin the fuckin' catfish bite.'

"So anyways, we jumped in m' '47 pickup and lit out over there. I remembered right whir' it wuz. The onliest thing I didn't remember wuz how bad that lil' ol' dirt road thet goes down to the creek wuz. But we made it down there all right and shore nuff, jist like ya said, they's wuz plenty of hungry fish. Hell! By the time we finished off a few more brews, we already caught enough of 'em to feed him and all his kin, so I said, 'Hell, let's git out of here and go fry 'em up.' Thet's whin thangs turned to shit. By thet, I mean thet's whin I got the fucker stuck. Backed her up in a fuckin' ditch and marred her up, clean up to the axle. We pushed and pulled and tried to gun her out but that fuckin' '47 was stuck tight."

"What'd ya'll do?" I jump in and ask.

"Hell! We had to walk out. Kerried our fish though, got wetter then shit. Fuckin' rain wuz spatterin' down like a tall cow pissin' on a flat rock."

"Ya'll walk all the way to Newcastle?" Trapper asks him.

"Naw, jist walked to that lil' ol' store there at the crossroads, there at Crosston. They wuz a feller there a gittin' gas. He wuz a headin' off down toward Birmingham so he give us a lift back to m'buddy's house. We give him two big 'cats' for his trouble, tickled the shit outta him, said he loved fried catfish.

"Enyway, this piece of shit Ford I'm drivin's m'buddy's. Drove it over here whir' I knowed I could find some friends to help me out; un' by the way, we ain't gonna get muddy a pushin' nothin'—brought a chain to pull 'er out. All I need ya fellers fer is one to steer the fuckin' truck and the other to relay instructions back to him while I'm doin' the pullin.'"

"Why ain't your buddy helpin' you?" Trapper asks.

Bill shakes his head again and gives us another deep exasperated sigh.

"'Cause the fucker had to work today. That's the fuckin' reason why! Now, I bet the next thang ya'll gonna wanna know is what color his ol' lady's pussy hairs are?"

And, with this statement we get another short rendition of the donkey laugh.

"Oh! And another thang I fergot to mention is there's a 'fiver' in it for you if you wuz to decide to help," he goes on to tell us.

"Five dollars, you're saying," Trapper asks, with his eyes lighting up.

"Yeah, you knows, thet little slip of green paper, the one with thet piece of shit Lincoln's picture on it? That'd be, let's see, two fifty a piece? And if you want some smokes, I gotta whole fuckin' carton in the truck. How's a pack a piece sound for a bonus?"

What the hell, I think to myself. *Two whole packs of cigarettes and man, all the stuff I can buy with two dollars and fifty cents, plus, we got plenty of time to kill—why not do it, making money. If Bill's dumb enough to pay us that kind of dough for just steering out his truck, why not take advantage of it?*

I look at Trapper. Somehow I know he's thinking the same thing.

"Whatta you think?" he asks me.

"And you'll bring us right back here as soon as we get the truck unstuck?" I look at Bill and ask.

He rolls his eyes.

"Wudn't thet what I already said?"

I really don't remember him saying that, but anyway I go on.

"What if for some reason, we can't get it unstuck—do we still get paid?"

"God damn, don't you ever run outta questions?" Bill asks me, flinging up his arms, like he can't believe he's still being quizzed.

"Yeah Bill, that's a good question," Trapper tells him.

"Look!" Bill explains. "It's gonna be a simple thang. We hook up the chain and pull out the truck, end of story. But no matter what, I pay ya and brang you back here, so I can go git m'buddy and then come back to git my truck. Now, you want the deal or not?"

Something tells me to say no, but my greed overrides my good sense. I look at Trapper and shrug.

"Heck, let's do it," he says.

"Give us a pack of cigarettes up front and I'm ready to go," I tell Bill.

"I jist told you, all the cigarettes are in the truck, all 'cept the ones I'm smokin'. Come on, let's git the hell outta here before it starts fuckin' raining again," he says, opening the car door to get in.

"You can buy us a pack right inside the store there," I tell him.

"Yeah, a pack of Wings," Trapper says.

"Fuck thet shit. I ain't about to do no business with this little 'piss ant' store or thet asshole, Jew bastard, what runs it, so ya kin fergit thet."

"Mr. Harley's not a Jew or an asshole," I tell Bill. "He's a real nice guy," I go on to say, which is the truth, even though it is fun to harass him a little every now and then.

"Well, ya ain't the one thet the fucker turned down fer a lil' credit. Said he din't know me, kin you believe it! I was driving the bus here ever' day and he don't know me! Bullshit!

"He's a fuckin' nigger lover, too! Look! There's a pair of 'em coming out now. They's all loaded up and you know it's on credit; 'cause ain't none of 'em got no money. See what I mean! He'll give a fuckin' nigger credit, but not a white man. Fuckin' nigger lover! He's fuckin' lucky I didn't burn him out like I started ta do."

While Bill rambles on, I watch Square and Snooks as they walk across the parking lot towards the road. They skirt far to our left and avoid even looking our way. Both are carrying a big sack of groceries. Just as they reach the road, Snooks spots the cold drink bottles.

He bends down and picks them up and places them in his overcoat pockets, then turns towards us and "walls" his eyes and smiles. He'll sell them to the commissary. He knows they're a gift from us.

"Bingo!" Trapper says.

"Yeah, Bingo," I reply.

"Are we gonna go or stand here all day and look at niggers?" Bill inquires.

"Let's go for it," Trapper urges.

"OK," I tell him, "but I'm riding 'shotgun.'"

— CHAPTER 7 —
BAD JUDGMENT

ONE OF MY DAD'S FAVORITE SAYINGS IS: "WHATEVER feels good to you is bound to be good for you!" Does that mean that things that feel bad are bound to be bad? I hope not, because I don't really feel good about the decision Trapper and I have just made. As Bill starts the car, the happy, carefree mood that I was in only minutes ago is suddenly replaced with a feeling of doubt and apprehension. I hope we haven't used bad judgment. I try to shove it to the back of my mind.

The maroon '41 that we're in isn't a bad-looking car, definitely not a piece of shit. Someone, be it Bill's "friend" or whomever, has taken good care of it. The paint job is still good and I only noticed a few "dings and scratches" as I walked around to get inside. It has a sort of round, curved body style that makes it look like a four-door, although it has only two. The tires are white walls and look to be fairly new.

The inside is just as clean. The gray cloth interior is almost spotless and hardly worn at all. It has a grain-looking dash trim and a glove box mounted clock that says it's 11:35. The owner, however, must not be a music lover, since there's no radio, but there is a monotonous beat from the rapid fanning of the windshield wipers, as they labor in vain to clean the road-scummed windshield.

Bill cuts the wipers off, shifts into low, guns up the motor and pops the clutch. We're off! A cloud of gravel rains out behind us.

Up ahead, almost to the Black Creek Bridge, I spot Square and Snooks. They turn as they hear the sound of the car. Bill taps the clutch and without letting up on the accelerator stuffs it up to second gear and steers directly towards them. They head for the shoulder and dip off the road on the trail next to the bridge, we're about five feet behind them, more off the road than on. Bill has to quickly jerk the car to the left to miss the bridge abutment. He's braying to the top of his lungs as he rights the car, then slows down and drops it into third.

"God damn! Almost had me a pair of niggers for hood ornaments," he says, between snorts.

"You get ten points for a nigger," he goes on to tell us. *What an asshole*, I think.

I look at Trapper. He's got that, "my ass is eating seat covers" look on his face. Mine probably looks the same. *"My ass will be grass"* with *Square now*, I think to myself. *Maybe I'll give Trapper the bell. Yeah, good idea!*

"Uh, excuse me, Bill," Trapper asks, "where the hell are you going?"

"Whatta ya mean?" Bill wants to know.

"I mean the Creek and the big rock's in the opposite direction from where you're headed. You're going in the wrong fuckin' direction. That's what I mean!"

Trapper's right! Where Bill's truck is stuck is about three miles west of us, we're headed east, back into town, or so I thought, until we take a left at the community house and head north on the Trafford Road. Now I'm confused.

"Jist a lil' change of plans, 'cause Bill's thirsty," he tells us. "Don't git all fuckin' excited and start askin' a bunch of questions agin."

Trapper ignores him.

"If you're thirsty, why didn't you get something to drink at Harley's?" he asks Bill.

"'Cause that fuckin' Jew don't sell what I'm thirsty fer, if ya gotta know," he answers sarcastically.

I look to my left as we pass the cutoff to the ball field. It looks like a lake. I'm surprised Trapper doesn't ask him to turn in and check it out, but he doesn't pay it any mind, he's too busy bantering with Bill.

"They ain't a store this way for another six miles, 'til you get to Trafford," he tells Bill.

Bill just laughs, "Did I fuckin' mention a store?" he says.

That's when I realize where we're headed.

Bill laughs again! Gives us a wiseass riddle, "What Ol' Bill's thirsty fer is in a can. It starts with a 'S' and ends with a 'Z' and if'n I ain't mistaken, a fucker whose name starts with a 'B,' usually has a good supply, and he lives jist up the hill a ways from here," he tells Trapper.

Trapper finally catches on.

"So, you're going up to Boodle's to buy some beer. Schlitz to be specific," he says to Bill.

"Brilliant deduction," I say to him.

"Thet's my brand," Bill says and laughs. "Ya know, ya ain't as dumb as ya look."

Thank God! I think to myself and chuckle as we continue to whiz along.

"Better slow down, Bill, you gotta take a right just up ahead. The road's right before the old Redman Hall. You'll run past it, 'cause it's hard to see," Trapper tells him.

But Bill pays him no attention, it's started misting rain again and he's fiddling with the wiper switch.

I can feel the swaying of the car as the gusting wind engulfs us.

Bill's pissed, says he can't see, because the windows are streaked and, sure enough, we miss the turn!

"God damn it!" he swears when he overshoots the road.

"I told you," Trapper reminds him.

"Shut the fuck up!" Bill tells him. I laugh.

Mr. Jim Faucet's house sets just up the road on the left. We flip into his driveway and turn around. Bill guns it back to Redman Hall and takes a left. We're headed to the Top of the Hill, up to Boodle's.

The road up the hill is bad even in good weather. Today, with all the rain, it's very probable we won't make it to the top without getting stuck. As we move upwards, Trapper is rattling instructions and directions to Bill: "Watch out," "big mudhole," "slow down." Bill is swearing and telling him to "shut the fuck up."

The car is bumping and bouncing and sliding. I can hear the sounds of the mud and gravel as it flies out behind the spinning back wheels. I sink down into the seat, close my eyes and tune it all out.

Clyde Davis, code name Boodle, is our local bootlegger. That's the reason he lives out here away from everyone else on the outskirts of town. That, plus the illegal chicken fights he holds up here almost every Sunday at the Top of the Hill, as everyone calls it. Sometimes during baseball season, they have to be delayed or postponed, but normally they get worked in, you can bet on that! Saturdays are usually reserved for the dog fights over in the Nigger Quarters, but they're usually held at night. Since a substantial element of the miners and the farmers in the surrounding areas love to drink and gamble, Boodle does a good business. You'd think the road would be paved.

He lives in an old rundown farmhouse, just over the other side of the hill. I guess it's his, because I've heard that his daddy used to live there before him. "Sorry piece of shit was borned there," I remember hearing Britt say one day down at the commissary.

Boodle's a sight for sore eyes. He's Mr. 5x5—five feet high and five feet wide, from whence he gets his name. Everyone, including Boodle, has lost count of how many kids he has. There's at least one and sometimes two in every grade at school. They come and leave in a pack. One of them's, Leonard, who everyone calls Snakeman, because he looks just like a fuckin' snake, is in my class. He's real smart, a neat guy, I like him, but he's stranger than shit.

Boodle's a good businessman; he buys his beer from Jabo, who runs the Rock House, a beer joint over in Pinson, which is the next closest place to buy liquor; either there or Hersh Lindsey's place over in Trafford, about the same distance away. Boodle marks it up and sells it to the folks who don't wanna make the drive and also, which I think is a very good business decision, he takes clacker. The moonshine, which everyone around here calls "pot whiskey," and the home brew he sells, he makes himself, in cahoots with several of his friends. Boodle makes no bones about what he does and everyone in town accepts it. He's just one of the good ol' boys, plays second base on the men's baseball team.

Britt pretends to hate him, always saying he's "gonna arrest him" or "gonna run him out of the county," but it's all just talk. I know! I've been to the chicken fights, lots of times. Everybody's so drunk and so focused on which game cock is going to slit the other one's throat that they normally pay you no mind. I see a lot of the same men that I just saw in the morning at church holding a Bible and praying to God for their souls, but now they're holding a beer or a fruit jar of pot whiskey and praying to God that their rooster will win. I'm fully convinced that the town prefers Boodle to Britt and I'm sure he knows it, too. That's just the way it is in Black Creek.

I suddenly feel the car stop and I quickly come out of my trance. Bill's braggin' about the skillful way he maneuvered up the hill. Trapper's giving him some shit.

"Hell! 'Old Lucky Teter' himself couldn't done a better job then thet coming up thet there hill," Bill crows, hoping someone will agree.

"That's the reason he's dead, doing crazy shit like that," Trapper tells him.

He looks over at me for confirmation.

"Ain't that right, Boogie?"

"Why are we stopping?" I ask, seeing we're not yet to Boodle's.

"So's you kin ketch yore breath and wipe yore ass. Scared the shit outta ya, din't I?" Bill says to me and donkey laughs.

"Did you see him, Trapper? He was all snookered down, pale as a ghost and holdin' his breath. I thought he wuz a man, not a little chicken shit."

"Fuck you, asshole," I tell him.

"Why'd you stop?" I ask him again.

He ignores my question for the second time.

"Ain't none of them sons a bitches gonna git up here tomorrow for no chicken fight. Only cocks they's gonna be playin' with are their own, or maybe one of their queer buddies," Bill informs us, then gives us an extended donkey laugh in appreciation of his wit.

"Now, which 'un of ya lil' fuckers gonna go down there and buy me some beer?" he wants to know.

It's gotta be at least a couple hundred yards on down to Boodle's. "I ain't walking it," I tell him.

"Me either, Bill," Trapper says. "Drive on down there. What's the deal stopping way back here?"

"Yeah! And why does one of us have to buy it?" I ask him, and then go on to say, "Seems to me that Boodle would rather do business with a grownup rather than one of us." I don't say a "kid," because at this point in my life I have definitely moved beyond that.

Bill doesn't answer my question. He opens the car door and gets out. I do the same. I see him fish in his pocket for a cigarette and light it up, then look all around as though he might be looking for something or someone again. "What a fuckin' miserable day," I hear him say. "I agree!"

I look around. We're parked just to the side of the road, right at the top of the hill. I can see the pit where they fight the chickens. It's in a cleared-out area about 35 feet away. It's half-filled with water. The wind is playing havoc through the trees and loosens the water in their branches. It splatters across the car and on my head. I duck back inside and close the door, so does Bill, but not in time to miss another barrage of the wind-driven liquid that centers on his cigarette and turns it to sog. He cusses and throws it on the floorboard. Trapper and I look at each other and laugh.

"If we're going to just sit here and screw around the rest of the day, I wish you guys would keep the car doors closed," Trapper says.

Bill takes off his hat and bangs it on the steering wheel, the water bounces on Trapper.

"Fuck ya," he tells Trapper, as he fits it back on his head.

"Boodle don't give a shit who he sells beer ta," he looks at me and says, continuing the conversation we were having previously. "He'd sell it to a fuckin' baby were it to crawl up here with some money, so don't give me thet shit! He's probably got some bottles already nippled up just in case the 'sit-ze-ation' arises," he goes on to say, then follows up our chuckle with a three-snorter.

"And, don't tell me ya lil' fuckers ain't slipped up here and bought beer before, 'cause I know better," he says, as he starts up the car.

"I'm gonna pull on down there closer, so ya'll better be deciding which 'un's gonna go down there and git it, 'cause I ain't drivin' down ta the house, ya can fergit 'bout that. Thet fat fucker won't be alive tomorrow if I do."

He shifts into low and as we try to pull out, the back wheels just sit there and spin. He throws it into reverse and rocks it back, then into low again and pours on the gas. We fishtail out, blowing an airborne trail of mud and muck about 30 feet behind us.

"Good fuckin' thing I know how ta handle a damn car," he tells us.

"Too bad you don't have the same talent with trucks," Trapper says, then looks at me and we both laugh.

"Very fuckin' funny," Bill says, but he isn't laughing.

Bill parks the car along the edge of the road just past the driveway that goes down to Boodle's. The house sits about 50 yards off to the right on the downslope of the hill. The driveway goes down to the house and then circles back up to the road about 60 feet in front of where Bill has parked the car.

It's a big, old, "dog trot" house that used to be the family home of one of the original families that settled this neck of the woods, but that was probably about a hundred years ago. I think it was one of my mother's family, but I'm not really sure. I know that I've heard my Granny describe how pretty it used to be up here when she was a girl.

"We used to visit them sometimes on a Sunday after church," she's told me. "We'd ride up there in your Grandpa's buggy, we wuz jist a courtin' back then," she'd go on to say with a chuckle.

"It wuz such a perty drive, especially in the spring and fall. The house was so perty and the yards were all bermed and terraced, and full of the most beautiful trees and flowers you can imagine. They had a big grape arbor and a great big vegetable garden out back. Raised their own cows, pigs and chickens, so they always had plenty to eat.

"We used to stay for supper sometimes! Lord! I can still taste those meals. They had a big ol', fat nigger cook, and boy did she know how to lay out a meal. Fried chicken, and I mean golden brown fried and creamed potatoes with gravy and every kind of fresh vegetable there is. They always had ice for the tea when the weather was hot and I have never tasted better buttermilk anywhere.

"But! That was way back then. Lordy, how time does fly!"

From where we're parked you can't see down to the house. There's a big berm about four feet high just off the edge of the road between the two driveways. I don't think this is one that my Granny talks about, more likely one that Boodle has constructed for privacy—either that or to hide what the house and yards look like now. Thank God, Granny can't see 'em!

Trapper and I flip a nickel that he has in his pocket to see who goes down for the beer. I lose! Bill is asking questions and giving instructions.

"How much is Boodle robbin' people fer beer nowadays?" He asks us, as he extracts his wallet from his inside coat pocket. It's old and worn, one of those long flat foldout kind made from leather, usually with a belt chain attached to it. Bill's has the chain ripped off. I can see a tear in the leather where it was attached. As he unfolds it I catch a glimpse of gold-leaf initials branded on the front. They're worn almost off, but appear to read S.R., certainly not initials that coincide with his name.

"I think he's getting 35 cents a can," Trapper tells him, but I ain't really sure."

"Ain't it 35 cents, Boogie?" he asks me.

"Somebody told me it was 45 cents," I say, knowing its 35, but say it anyway, just to piss Bill off.

"That's fuckin' highway robbery!" Bill spouts, "No fuckin' way I'm paying thet Fat Fucker more'n 35 cents and I ain't happy 'bout thet."

"You can always take your business elsewhere," I say to him.

"Yeah! Well, I ain't 'un of 'em dumb-ass coal miners, I knows what a beer's worth," he retaliates.

His comment pisses me off.

"I'd watch out what I say about coal miners, if I was you," I tell him.

"Whatcha gonna do? Shoot me with thet lil' 'pea shooter' ya got hangin' 'round yore neck or tickle me ta death with thet sissy little bell ya got tied to yore shoe? I'm just fuckin' tremblin' all over," he says.

"Are we gonna buy beer today or not?" Trapper asks.

I look at the dash clock.

"Not before noon," I tell him, 'cause it's past that now.

"We gotta get going, Bill, otherwise, I ain't going. We got a party to go to tonight," I say to him.

"OK! OK! Don't let your 'ass fly up'! I just hate to be ripped off!

Thet's all!" he replies, as he slips two ones out of his wallet and a dime from his pocket, then hands them to me.

"Get six fuckin' Schlitzs," he says, "and you ain't buying 'em for me, if anyone asks."

"What if they're 45 cents?" I ask him, just to antagonize him some more.

"Boogie! Please just go get the damn beer," Trapper says, "so we can get going. OK?"

"At your service, Master," I say to him, as I exit the car.

"Remember! Ya ain't with me," Bill yells, as I walk away.

As I head down the hill towards the house I zip my jacket up as high as it will go and stuff my hands in the pockets. It's not raining at the present moment, but the wind is still whistling through the trees. They look stark and forlorn against the dark gray sky.

It feels colder up here and I begin to feel "spooked." A chill runs down my back. Something's different, I think to myself. It's too quiet. I don't hear the sounds of the dogs! That's it! The dogs! Boodles got a passel of them and normally they raise a ruckus when I've come up here before. Wonder where they are today? Most of them are hounds, but intermingled amongst them is a few little "off breeds" and a big black chow that likes to bite.

The driveway's wet and muddy; I stay to the edge in the weeds so as not to screw up my shoes. I continue to listen and watch for the dogs.

As I get closer I hear the crowing of a rooster. Boodle keeps them in pens out at the back of his house. *If this is the "noon crower," his clock's off,* I think to myself.

To my right is nothing but weeds and woods, to my left is weeds and trash, a proverbial dump that stretches all the way from the berm almost to Boodle's front door—old junked cars, junked appliances and furniture and garbage. Tons of it, you name it, it's there. Everything Boodle and his Pappy before him didn't want anymore, they've dumped in the front yard. So much for my Granny's "beautiful flowers and trees." Now it looks more like a cemetery—a cemetery of "dead stuff." No wonder I'm spooked!

I shiver again and keep walking down the hill. I see a couple of cats slinking around the base of an old wood stove. Tough looking scared up old Tom's. One of them has one of his ears chewed off. They probably live off rats and lizards. I wonder what else lives in here, and also begin to wonder if anyone's at home.

Just before I get down to the house, I hear a bleating sound and a loud rattle, like something or someone walking on lumber. My eyes follow the sound and I see three goats looking at me from atop a pile of slabs stacked up just at the end of the dump. Probably Boodle's firewood, I surmise.

They appear to be a daddy, a mommy and a baby. They must be a new addition to Boodle's family. I don't ever remember ever seeing them before.

The daddy goat don't seem pleased to see me and as I move forward, he proceeds to jump off the lumber pile and position himself between me and the house, stopping about 35 feet in front of me, daring me to come any closer.

I immediately stop and watch him. I think of "Billy Goat Gruff." *Stand real still,* I tell myself.

He's a mean looking son of a gun, dirty white in color and about three feet high to the top of his back. His neck is skinny and long and is topped off with about the scariest looking head I've ever seen on a goat.

He only has one eye that's working and it appears to be seeing red. The other eye and his entire forehead is nothing but raw and bloody scar tissue.

He's a "butter," there's no doubt about it.

Both his horns are broken, one at the tip and the other in half. He cocks his head to the side and begins to size up his prey with his one good eye. I very slowly remove my slingshot from around my neck. *Damn! Why didn't I think to get a couple of steel balls while I was with James?* I think to myself. *How fucking dumb can you get?*

I sense I'm in trouble, so without moving I glance down at my feet. I'm in luck. I see a couple of roundish pieces of sandstone peeking out of the muddy ruts in the road. They're about ½ inch in diameter;

I crouch down and pick them up. My movement seems to indicate something to the goat. Possibly that I have gone into a battle position, because all at once he begins to charge straight at me, head down, ready to butt!

I stand firm and hurry to get a rock into the pocket of my slingshot. But, then he suddenly stops, about 20 feet away, when he hears a voice behind him.

"That fucker'll butt you!" I hear someone yelling. I look towards the house and see its Leonard. He's standing on the front porch steps. I've been so busy watching the goat, I failed to see him.

"That fucker'll butt the shit outta ya if ya don't stay still," he yells to me again and then laughs. "He don't like your jingle bell."

"He must have good hearing," I yell back to him, still keeping my eyes on the goat, my slingshot set on ready!

"Hell! I heard you, too!" he says, as he moves down the steps and walks towards the goats, stopping about 15 feet from its rear end.

The goat keeps its same distance from me, but circles to the right, closer to the trash dump. His head is still down and he's pawing at the ground with his right foot.

"I can't believe you heard my bell," I say to Leonard.

"Snakes have keen hearing," he says and laughs.

I laugh, too.

"That fucker bites, too," he says, "bit me last week. I knocked him in the head with a two-by-four. See where he's bleeding?"

"It's over there by the wood pile, if you want me to go get it?"

"Naw, that's all right," I tell him. "I got something here that he's gonna like a lot worse than a two-by-four" and with that I draw my rubbers back and let fly.

I don't try to hit the sucker 'cause I don't want to hurt him. He probably suffers enough just having to live in this crap every day. I just want to scare him off to get him to leave.

My shot flies true and hits just where I intended. Just to the left of his front feet, so that the ricochet of the rock wouldn't hit him, but close enough to create a splatter of mud and gravel on his feet and legs.

He doesn't even flinch! He's ready to charge, I can see it.

"Hell, Boogie! You missed him," Leonard cries out.

"I can't believe you can't hit as big of a thing as a goat, at that distance."

He laughs.

"He must really have you spooked! I thought you was supposed to be a good shot with that thing."

I take the jab and don't bother to explain. I had tried to do a good deed, but it was unsuccessful and also unnoticed, so now is the time for a different approach.

I pocket the second rock and let it fly.

Once again the shot flies true. The rock nicks him on the left side of his long skinny neck, just in the middle. A shot, not to hurt, but to sting like a "bee."

It works! He jumps sideways to the right, lets out a whining bleat and scurries away from me up the hill. I breathe a sigh of relief.

The momma and baby who have been watching the action from atop the woodpile, jump down and forge up through the dump after him.

I walk on down to the house. Leonard is all smiles.

"Ain't that the meanest fuckin' goat you ever seen?" he wants to know. "I still can't believe you missed him the first time. You barely hit him the second shot!"

Snakeman just don't get it, I don't even bother to reply.

"Momma wants to shoot him, but Boodle won't do it 'til July," he informs me. "He's gonna kill 'em all then. We're gonna bar-b-que 'em for the Fourth. Boodle says we'll eat the momma and the baby and he'll sell the old billy to the niggers, 'cause it won't be fit for anyone else to eat."

I feel nauseated!

"Where did you get 'em?" I ask.

"Boodle traded some old farmer up in Blount County some pot whiskey for 'em. His wife made him get rid of 'em cause the old billy was buttin' and bitin' their kids. Boodle don't give a shit whether he butts and bites us or not, all he's thinkin' about is his belly." He laughs!

I look back up the hill. The goats are standing almost to the top, in the middle of the dump. The billy is looking directly at me, while the momma attempts to console him and fight the baby off her teats at the same time. I feel really depressed.

A big gust of wind roars down the hill. I can hear the screeks and the howls as it threads its way through the rusted out graveyard of the dump. A slight drizzle of rain begins to fall again. I'm not only nauseous and depressed, I'm also spooked again.

Leonard runs up on the front porch. I follow close behind him. "I'm tired of this rain," I say. "It's gonna clear up later in the day," he informs me.

"They say it on the radio?" I ask him.

"Naw , I just know," he says, "I kin feel it."

"Don't tell me!" I say," Snakes can predict weather, too!"

We both laugh.

"Where is everybody, where's the dogs?" I ask. "It's so quiet, I didn't think anybody was here."

"Boodle took 'em to get 'em dipped. They's all eat up with the mange. Half the kids loaded up in the back of the truck and went with him. Ever' body else is either asleep or listenin' to the radio.

"Who's dippin' 'em?" I ask.

"I think its ol' man Harrison Smith. That's your grandpa, ain't it?"

"Yeah, that's my grandpa," I tell him.

"Boodle better watch out, or he'll dip the kids, too" I say.

We both laugh!

"He dipped me once when I had dandruff," I tell him. "My mom's still pissed about it. Cleared the shit up though. My head was all broke out and itching, I'd scratched it until it was bleeding. Grandpa was dipping Nigger, his black cocker spaniel, so he just grabs me by the nape of the neck and ducked my head in the mix. Ain't never had a problem since. My head peeled for 'about a month though."

Leonard thinks this is funny.

"They say he's a crazy old bird, is that right?" he wants to know.

"He's strange," I say.

"Some folks say he's a warlock," Leonard goes on, "that he can cast spells?"

"I think that was started by my mother," I say.

We both laugh!

"What you doin' up here in this kind of weather?" he asks me.

"I came up to do some business with Boodle, but since he ain't here I don't know."

"How much business you wanna do?"

"Six cans of Schlitz, can you sell 'em to me?" I ask, hoping he's gonna say yes.

"Can't do it, Boodle keeps 'em locked up," he says. "My momma's got a key, but she won't sell 'em to nobody under sixteen and you won't pass for that, anyway, she knows you and how old you are."

Fuck, I think to myself.

There's two rocking chairs on the porch. The sound of the rain hitting the tin roof is making me sleepy. I sit down in one and yawn. Leonard sits in the other.

I pull my jacket tight to my body, I'm cold, but Leonard seems impervious to the weather. His only clothes are a pair of jeans. He's wearing no shoes nor shirt and I don't see even a goose bump on his body. He seems to read my mind.

"Snakes don't git cold either," he says.

"Who was you gonna buy it for?" he asks me.

I lean back and rock the chair, trying to appear casual. He looks exactly like a snake I think to myself. Tall and extremely skinny, dark shiny skin, with those slanty eyes and hardly any forehead at all, exactly like a snake.

"Me and Trapper" I reply.

I continue to rock and yawn, hoping the rain will stop.

"Now it don't look like for anybody," I go on to say.

"Where's he at?" he asks.

"Who?"

"Trapper."

"Oh! He's up in the car."

Leonard grins. "Figured he was around close somewhere, since you two are 'joined at the hip,'" he says.

I laugh and keep rocking, really undecided what to do. Bill's gonna be pissed, he's gonna have to come down here and buy it himself if he wants it bad enough. *Fuck him,* I think to myself.

I stand up to leave.

"Who's drivin' the car?" the Snakeman asks.

"Just someone who drove us up here," I tell him. "I gotta go," I say.

"Secrets, secrets, secrets," Snakeman says.

I raise my hand and give the Scout sign.

"Hey! I promised, OK?"

"I understand, no sweat!" the Snake says.

"How much money you got?"

"Two and a dime, why?"

"I can sell you six Sterlings," he says, "for two and a dime. If you'll settle for Sterlings."

I look at him, confused.

"They're mine. I stash a few back ever' now and then," he says to me.

"For hard times?" I ask him.

"Yeah, fer hard times," he says and laughs.

"They're hot though and they're flat tops, so you gonna need a 'church key.' I get a dime extra fer that."

"I thought the church key came free," I tell him.

"Not at the Snake's store," he informs me.

"So two, twenty gets six Sterlings and a key?" I verify.

"You got it! No wonder all the teachers say you're so smart," he says and laughs.

"Sold!" I say, "but I'm gonna have to owe you for the key. I'll pay you Monday at school, OK?"

"It's a good thing I like you," he says.

Bill's gonna be pissed that I bought him Sterling beer. As Leonard jumps off the side of the porch, and heads towards the back of the house, I sit back down in the rocking chair and wait.

I look for the goats and see them back down on the far side of the lumber pile. They're standing in the road, just where it circles to go back up the hill. They're watching two of Boodle's game cocks who have apparently escaped their pens circling each other in a sparing match. Both have their neck feathers ruffled out and their wings shifted to low. Neither seems prone to attack. It's like one's afraid and the other one's glad of it. I'm trying to think of a way to save the goats when Leonard comes back. He's been gone only a few minutes.

"Must have a close hiding place," I tell him.

"Figured I could sell it while Boodle was gone," he says. "Had it already sacked. Be careful—the sack's damp," he says, as he hands it to me.

I hold it under my arm while I fish out the money and pay him. He stuffs it in his pocket and comes back out with the church key.

"Don't ferget, you owe me a dime for this on Monday," he says.

"Right," I tell him, as I drop it in my jacket pocket.

"Pleasure doin' business with you," he says.

"Pleasure's all mine," I tell him as I walk down the steps and head back up the hill.

I walk fast. The sooner I'm out of here, the better. I'm not anxious to see Bill because I know he's gonna be pissed about the beer, but anything's better than this spooky place. I shiver and start to trot.

Once again the rain has stopped. As I approach the car, Trapper and Bill are standing on the outside smoking. Bill is lighting a fresh Camel and it appears Trapper is smoking the remainder of his "butt" from earlier this morning. I remember I have one, too, and finger it out of my jacket pocket. Just what I need when I'm all out of breath.

"Give me a light," I say to Trapper.

Bill grabs at the sack and yanks it from under my arm. The bottom gives way and the six silver Sterlings hit the ground and begin to roll. Bill drops his lighter into his left overall pants pocket and scurries after them. The lighter falls out the leg of his pants and flips open on the road.

"God damn it!" he yells as he picks it up and wipes it off, then puts it in his bib pocket where he had kept it previously.

"Must have a hole in his pocket, so he has something to play with." I say to Trapper and we both laugh. I inhale a big draw off my cigarette and the laughing makes me cough.

"I told you to get fuckin' Schlitzs," Bill yells at me. "These are 'green ass' Sterlings," he says as he picks them up and sits them on top of the car. "I wanted 'cone top' Schlitzs, and I wanted 'em cold, not fuckin' hot Sterlings thet I kin't open. These're gonna taste like piss," he moans.

"That's all I could get. Sorry 'bout that," I tell him. I want to laugh but I'm afraid to.

"Whatta ya mean?" he asks, all bent out of shape.

"Boodle's not home. I had to buy these from Leonard, that's all he had. I thought you'd be happy."

"Is thet thet fucker thet looks like a fuckin' snake?" he wants to know.

"That's the one," I say.

Bill shudders and screws up his face.

"Thet son of a bitch used to make m'skin crawl ever' time I saw him," he says.

He picks up the last beer, but continues to look around on the ground, kicking at the mud and gravel where the beer had fallen.

"I hope ta hell ya got a church key," he says, when he fails to find one on the ground.

I decide to have some fun! "You didn't give me enough money. He wanted another 15 cents for one," I tell him as I take a final drag off my cigarette and flip it away.

"Church keys are supposed to be free!" both Trapper and Bill say to me at the same time. Seems like everyone but Leonard knows it.

"Says it right on the fuckin' can!" Bill goes on to say.

"Yeah, I know, I told him that," I inform them, "but he told me 'tough shit.' What was I to do?"

"Well, ya kin jist march your ass right back down there un' git one," Bill tells me.

I hold out my hand.

"Give me 15 cents and I'll go," I say.

"The fuck ya say. I ain't payin' fer somethin' that 'sposed ta be free."

"Then how do you reckon I'm gonna get it," I ask.

"I don't give a shit! Kick his ass. Thet'd be a start," he says, "fuckin' snakie lil' bastard."

"Yeah, right!" I say.

Bill shakes his head, he's pissed. He reaches in his pocket, the one without the hole and pulls out some change. He hands me a dime and a nickel. "I alluz knows you wuz a lil' chicken shit," he tells me. "So's now ya better run both fuckin' ways and don't fuck 'round like ya did afore or else'n we'll leave yore ass," he tells me.

I drop the coins in the pocket of my pants.

"I can do better than that," I tell him. I reach into my coat pocket, pull out the church key and hold it up. "Ta-da!" I say, as I hand it his way.

"Ya lyin' lil' fucker," he says, as he snatches it out of my hand.

I hear Trapper laughing.

Bill grabs a beer and slits a small hole in the top of the can. Knowing it's hot; he holds it close up to his mouth and catches the foam as it gushes out the top. He then turns the can and slits the other side. He consumes the contents in three big swallows and throws the empty in the ditch along the edge of the road. He lets out a belch.

"Ya might as well dig thet 15 cents outta yore pocket, 'cause I wants it back," he tells me as he opens the driver's door and bends down to retrieve something in a brown paper sack from under his front seat.

"No way," I say to him.

He opens the bag and takes out a quart fruit jar. It's filled almost to the top with a clear white liquid that I recognize immediately as "pot whiskey." I quickly surmise that the missing inch or so is the reason for his whiskey breath at Harley's.

He flattens the bag and lays it on the top of the car, then sits a couple of the beers on top of it to anchor it from the wind.

Trapper and I stand and watch as he uncaps the jar and takes two huge slugs, then opens another beer and swallows it down as a chaser.

He screws the top back on the jar of whiskey, puts it and the four remaining beers in the sack and puts it all back on the floorboard of the driver's seat, then lights up a Camel, belches really loud again and farts.

"Ya'll pay fer rookin' me outta thet 15 cents," he looks at me and says, acting real mean.

"I already did, with my own money," I tell him. I told you he charged me for it.

He doesn't answer.

"Let's go," he says and gets in the car.

I don't feel guilty at all about lying to Bill about the 15 cents for the beer opener. I have to pay Leonard for it Monday, so big deal, I made a nickel. It was worth more than that to walk down to get the beer.

I do however have a concern about his statement that I would "pay for it." Hopefully all he means is that he'll take it out of my share of payment for helping him with the truck. *That's probably what he means,* I tell myself, as I close the door of the car.

I thought the subject was closed, but he no sooner starts the car before he brings it up again.

"If I din't think ya wuz lyin' 'bout the money fer thet church key, I'd go down there and slit thet slitherin' lil' fucker's throat," he looks over at me and says.

When I don't reply Trapper gives me a questionable look, which I shrug off, then goes to my defense. He's been real quiet up to this point.

"Boogie and I ain't liars," he tells Bill. "Anyway, you'd better be turnin' around so we can get out of here and on over to the Big Rock if you wanna get your truck out today."

Bill ignores him as usual and keeps driving straight ahead, being a real prick.

Boodle's place is usually the end of the line for anyone driving on this road. After that, it becomes very narrow and overgrown, reverting back to the logging road it was in the first place. It winds down the hill from Boodle's, then up another smaller hill and then follows its ridge for about two miles through the woods and through some pastures where the Holland family keep their cows. It intersects with another dirt road right by their barn, at the front of their house.

The Holland's son Robbie is the same age as me and Trapper. I've never been through here in a car before, but Trapper and I have biked through here several times to visit Robbie and to swim in some strip pits over behind his house.

"Do you have any idea where you're going?" Trapper asks Bill.

"Jist where the fuck I said I wuz going, ta Turkey Crick," Bill replies.

"Well, I hate to tell you, but you're headed in the wrong direction again," I chime in to say.

Bill grunts, "What seems wrong ta ya might seem right ta me." He looks over to me and says, "Enyway, I've drove through here lots of time. So don't sweat it."

"Then I guess you know you gotta ford Dorman-Chandler Creek at the bottom of this hill," Trapper interjects, irritating Bill some more.

"Ya know what ya'lls problem is? Ya'll worry too much and ask too many fuckin' questions," Bill informs us. "Enyway, what's at the foot of this hill ain't what I'd call a crick, 'tain't nothin' but a lil' ol' branch that's dry most the time. I told ya, I've drove through here afore, so quit fuckin' worryin' 'bout it."

Trapper looks at me and circles his index finger around his head and then points to Bill—an indication of what an idiot he thinks Bill is.

"Yeah, well I guess none of the rainwater that's been fallin' since yesterday is gonna be flowin' through it, huh?" Trapper goads, then repeats the finger routine again.

"And if you're lucky enough to get cross the creek, you gonna have to drive through barbed wire if you make it over to where the Hollands live. They fenced off this old road about a year ago to keep their cows from wandering off," I add.

"Damn! You lil' fuckers are jist full of information," Bill says and stops the car.

We're at the foot of the hill. The creek's dead ahead. It runs down the narrow valley between the two hills about 40 feet to the front of where we've stopped.

Bill fishes out another Camel, belches again repulsively, and lights it up. As usual, he doesn't offer one to us. Manners aren't high on his list of priorities.

It's not raining, so I roll down my window to let some of the smoke out. I can hear the sound of the creek but can't see it. It's hidden by the heavy growth of trees and bushes.

"Sounds like it's up to me," I say. "I can hear it from here."

"One of ya'll walk down there and see. If'n it's up, I'll make a run at it from here." Bill tells us. "I'll need some speed to git up the bank on the other side, 'cause it'll be slick."

"It'd be better just to pull on down there and drive across it slow and steady, then gun it up the bank when you're across," Trapper tells him.

Bill's paying no attention. He's busy digging in the paper sack on the floorboard. He comes up with the jar again, unscrews the top and takes a big slug, then wipes his mouth with the back of his hand.

"Damn! Thet shit's good!" he exclaims as he takes another deep drag on his Camel.

"Just go on down there and do what I said, one of you, I don't give a shit which. You'll know if I can drive across it, Hell! You know everythin' else! Come back and let me know."

He screws the lid back on the jar and puts it back in the bag, rolls down his window, takes a final draw off his cigarette and flips it out.

"Go on now!" he demands, starting to get mean.

Apparently Trapper hasn't noticed. "I still think my way would be better," he says.

This really gets to Bill. I see his jaws clench. "I don't give 'diddly shit' what ya thank," he tells Trapper. "I wuz driving a car when you wuz still 'shittin yellow,' and if you mention enythin' 'bout a truck agin, I'll slap the shit out of you. Yore really startin' to piss me off."

"You can go," I say to Trapper in an effort to settle Bill down, "I went and got the beer."

I open the car door and step out. My shoes sink down in the mud and leaves along the edge of the road. I expect some resistance from Trapper, but get none. He slides out of the car.

"This is bullshit," he says and bumps my shoulder.

"Walk along the edge of the woods, so you don't fuck up your shoes," I tell him and laugh.

I scrape mine off on the running board and climb back in the car.

Bill lights up another Camel and leans back against the door looking all satisfied. He has a shit-eating grin on his face.

"It really pains me that I gotta get a lil' rough with ya boys to git ya ta do what I wants," he says in a fatherly tone, like he expects me to fall for that kind of shit.

Yeah, right! I think to myself.

I lean back on the seat and watch Trapper as he picks his way along the edge of the road up close to the trees, trying hard to stay out of the mud.

A gust of wind rips through the trees and shakes the car. Water off the branches splatter across the roof and hood. Trapper shoots us a bird over his shoulder. He undoubtedly got drenched.

"This shit makes me sleepy," Bill says.

The rain or the booze I wonder? But, I don't ask.

"Makes me get up a hard, too," he goes on to say.

I look over. He's rubbing at his dick.

"Ever had enybody suck you off?" he asks me.

I don't like the glint in his eyes, so I pretend to look for Trapper and ignore his question, hoping he'll drop the subject. He don't take the cue.

"That's what I need now," he says. "A good blow job. Wouldn't thet feel good?"

I glance over towards him again, he still pulling at his "pud" through his overall pants. What a weirdo!

"You really want thet five dollars I'm gonna pay ya'll, don't ya?" he asks.

"Sure," I say, answering his question in hopes of changing the subject. "That's why I agreed to help you. For the money. Why else would I be here?"

"Ya only gonna git half of it," he says.

"No, shit!" I reply, surprised he can divide by two.

"There could be some extra money, jist fer you, if'n ya'd be interested," he says.

I get his drift and I want to puke.

I look through the windshield and see Trapper headed back our way. He's almost to the car.

"There ain't printed that much money," I tell Bill.

He doesn't have time to reply.

"It's up, but not as high as I thought it would be," Trapper says as he opens the door of the car. "We oughta be able to make it across."

I slide out and let him in.

"I still think you could cross it better the way I said," he tells Bill as he scoots into the car.

Bill looks over at me and smirks.

"Close the fuckin' door," he says.

— CHAPTER 8 —
MISGIVINGS

MOST OF THE GUYS I KNOW HAVE NO RESERVATIONS at all when it comes to killing a mockingbird. They consider them fair game for their air rifles, or slingshots. Nor would they ever understand you trying to convince them otherwise. It would give you a reputation of being weak, of being a sissy, so I never do, but it's a bird that I will never kill.

I'm not really certain why I spare them. Maybe it's for their beauty or maybe for their song, which they usually sing far better than most of the birds they're imitating, or maybe it's for their bravery, because they are by far the bravest birds I know. Whatever the reason, they're safe when it comes to me.

There's always a good excuse for missing a shot or always a good reason for not taking one and I've used them all when it comes down to killing a "mocker" and I've done it so well, nobody has ever noticed.

I watch now as two of them break from the cover of the clouds and begin a "peck and flutter" aerial attack on a red-tailed hawk that has only minutes ago glided along the floor of Holland's pasture to seek refuge on the lower limb of a tall oak tree that grows along the edge of the pasture fence.

I watch as the hawk takes flight again, staying low to the ground at first, then with a few flaps of his wings, he catches the wind and swirls upwards. The mockingbirds are with him all the way, like a "chicken on a June bug." Peck and flutter, peck and flutter. I lose sight of them as they enter the trees.

The birds seem to have no misgivings at all about attacking their prey. When provoked, they protect eggs, their young, their territory and also themselves, no matter the cost. I wonder if I could ever be so brave, as I stand and ponder my ever-increasing misgivings about agreeing to help Bill, especially after the recent incident in the car.

He tried to make light of it after Trapper returned to the car.

After advising Bill again on how to ford the creek, Trapper turned and asked for my opinion in hopes that I would agree with him. Not that he really wanted my opinion, he never does—just the verification that he was right. When I didn't answer, he proved me correct. "Ain't I right, Boogie?" he asked. I knew it was coming, because he does it constantly. And, it annoys the hell out of me—today, under these circumstances, more than ever.

"I don't give a shit what you do," I told him... and was going to add, "I'm out of here," but before I could say it, another gust of wind rocked the car and splattered it with water, so I quickly changed my mind.

I'm stuck out here in the woods, in the middle of nowhere. It's cold and rainy. Walking out of here would be dumb, so instead I said, "I want to go back the way we came."

Bill laughed and started the car. "No fuckin' way" he said and started to pull out, but stopped when Trapper grabbed the steering wheel.

"Hold up a minute, Bill" Trapper told him.

"What's the problem?" Trapper turned and asked me.

"He's all pissed off, 'cause he kin't take a joke," Bill volunteered before I could open my mouth. "I wuz funnin' with him and he took 'tall serious," he told Trapper. "I wuz just a kiddin' ya know," he looked at me and said.

"Yeah?" Well, that ain't my idea of funny," I told him.

"What happened?" Trapper asked.

I looked over at Bill, his donkey mouth was set in a smirk and he was staring at me hard through his slitted donkey eyes.

"It wuz jist a misunderstandin', so let's jist drop it from here," Bill said, as he continued to stare at me. "Enyways, I said I wuz kiddin'. So come on," he said and grinned, softening his donkey face. "Let's go git the truck, OK?"

"Then tell us why you're going this way," I said. "At least you can tell us that."

"Yeah, Bill, I'd like to know that, too," Trapper told him. "If you'd gone back the way we come, you coulda already been half-way there."

"Uh, huh! Yeah! Yore right!" Bill replied, the smile now gone from his face. "And I could be arrested and halfway to fuckin' jail, too! Know what I mean?"

After saying this, he rolled his window down and harked a big concoction of beer and whiskey from his throat, then spit it to the wind. He fished out a Camel, lit it up, then looked back at us.

"Ol' Bill ain't no fool!" he went on to say. "He knows full well thet there's a ol', fat piece of shit sheriff out here at Black Creek thet'll arrest him in a minute he sees him drankin' with two young boys in his car. That son's a bitch thinks he's the King of the fuckin' Cops. I know! I've had run-ins with thet fucker afore and let me tell you somethin'..."

But it didn't come immediately. He took the time to repeat the spitting process again and to inhale a lung-blasting suck off his Camel before he went on.

"Thet bastard fucks with me today, he'd be the sorriest fucker ever lived. Bank on thet! Yeah! He'd stop me all right if he saw us together, no fuckin' doubt 'bout it."

He stopped again, took a final drag off his cigarette, rolled the window down and flipped it out.

"But it wouldn't be fer ya two fuckers they'd arrest me fer, ya kin bet on thet. It'd be for guttin' that fucker like a hog and stickin' that .45 of his and that blackjack up his ass. That's what it'd be fer. Yeah! That's what it'd be fer! Sorry fucker!"

Bill took a deep breath, smirked his lips up a little tighter and dropped his lids almost closed, then nodded in approval, both to and of himself, a smug, "don't fuck with me" look on his face that at first struck me as funny, until he opened his eyes and looked directly at me. That's when the funny turned to fright, 'cause when I looked in those eyes they told me a story. They told me that he would really do it. No doubt about it!

Bill broke his stare and let out a sigh, then leaned back against the seat. He took his hat off, ran his fingers through his hair and put it back on, then sat in meditation.

I looked at Trapper, he looked at me. We both raised our brows. Trapper rolled his eyes; I gave him a silly grin. We both turned and looked at Bill. He was looking at us. Trapper broke the ice.

"Uh, for some reason I get the impression that you and the sheriff ain't gonna go campin' together anytime soon," he said to Bill. "Ain't quite skippin' rope together—right?"

I chuckled and looked at Bill. He sat there for a moment looking at Trapper and then he chuckled, too.

"Ya might say thet," he told Trapper, "but 'tain't worth gettin' electrocuted over, so if ya'll're through runnin' yore mouths, we'll jist move on outta here and go git thet truck. And, jist to be safe, we'll circle 'round the back way.

Bill's reason for skirting town was logical and made sense, but I didn't believe it for a minute, not all of it anyway, and the way that we finally crossed the creek gave me a further reason for doubt.

Instead of crossing at a high speed the way he had informed us he intended to do, he did right the opposite. He eased cautiously down the bank and drove easily across at a slow, steady speed. Trapper's instructions almost to a tee. As we gunned up the hill towards the ridge, he looked at me and smirked.

Of course, Trapper was elated that Bill had followed his plan and kept telling him how smart he had been to listen to him. Hell, Bill never had a plan in the first place. All he wanted to do was get one of us alone. Blind-ass Trapper!

We made it up the hill and across the ridge with hardly a problem. A few slips and slides and some tire-spinning in low places, but nothing serious.

It wasn't until we arrived at the Holland's pasture, where we're currently parked, that we encountered a problem…

The pasture is fenced, just as I had warned Bill it would be and the road is blocked by a gate. The gate is in two sections that are hinged to gate posts on opposite sides of the road and swing together in the middle. I think it's called a "swing gate."

It's made out of "hog wire," framed and braced with "two x sixes" and it's locked tighter than a drum, a fact I discovered after crawling through the barbed wire to check it out, per Bill's instructions.

Too bad! I think, then chuckle to myself. *Bill's gonna be pissed when I tell him, but screw him! He deserves it.*

I take a deep breath—the air smells damp and musty, tinged with an odor of cowshit and the only sound I hear is the sound of the wind as it forces its way through the branches of the trees.

I look for the mockingbirds again, but don't see them. I look across the pasture for any signs of life. I see nothing, not even a cow. Everything looks dark and dank, a look that fits my mood.

"Well! Is it locked or not?" Bill yells to me.

He and Trapper are standing outside the car where he has stopped, about ten feet in front of the fence.

I crawl back through the fence and walk back towards the car. Trapper meets me halfway.

"Cheer the fuck up," he says to me.

"Fuck you," I tell him, taking it out on him because I'm pissed at Bill.

We both walk towards the car.

"Well, is the fucker locked or not?" Bill asks me again.

"Locked up tight," I tell him. "I guess the gate's for their convenience, not anyone else's."

"Well, I got news for 'em! It's agin' the fuckin' law to block off a fuckin' road," he grumbles, as he reaches back into the car for his paper sack of refreshments.

"It's their land, they can do anything they want," I tell him, as I watch him take out a beer and set the sack on top of the car.

Once again he has to pat his pockets for the opener, then finds it in his right-hand coat pocket. It's tangled with something else bulky that's stuffed in there and he grumbles as he works it free.

"Why don't you keep it in the sack?" I ask him.

He gives me a shitty look.

"This is not a sanctioned road anyway," Trapper informs us.

"What the hell does thet mean?" Bill wants to know as he slits the

Sterling and sucks out the foam. About half of it misses his mouth and lands on the front of his coat, which he doesn't bother to wipe off.

"It means it's just a 'pig trail' that runs through the woods. You own the land, you own the pig trail, if that's clearer to you," Trapper replies.

"Why didn't you jist say that 'stead of using all them fancy words?" Bill chides back. "Both you lil' fuckers are jist full of 'em."

"We get 'em out of books, Bill," Trapper tells him. "You know! Those sort of rectangular things, that's made out of paper, that's got pages that flip." "They got words in 'em and you can learn 'em, if you don't just look at the pictures."

"They're what's inside those balloons that you see coming out of people's mouths when you read your comic books," I interject.

Trapper and I both laugh!

Bill gives us the evil eye and shoots us a bird. He lets out a big belch and sits the beer on the car, then digs in the sack for the jar. He unscrews the top and takes a slug, then chases it with the beer and the Camel.

"Is they just a hasp lock on thet gate?" he asks me, letting out another belch.

"There's a hasp with a lock in it, so I guess it could be called a hasp lock," I tell him.

"A locked hasp would be more appropriate however," Trapper adds.

"Sorry, locks aren't my forte," I tell him.

We both laugh. Bill glares at us and shakes his head.

"Real smart asses," he mumbles.

"Guess this is the end of the line, huh," Trapper inquires, as Bill stuffs his booze back in the car.

"Guess agin," he says, as he flips away his smoke, then bends the empty beer can and throws it over the fence.

"Pile yore asses in if'n yore ridin' with me," he informs us, as he slides back under the wheel.

"I hope you ain't gonna try to knock that gate down," Trapper says to Bill, as we settle back inside the car.

"What fuckin' gate?" he asks as he starts the engine and pulls slowly forward. "Watch and ya might larn somethin'," he says.

He continues to move forward and butts the sharp nose of the Ford up against the gate, right in the center where the two sections meet.

"Perfect fuckin' fit" he says, as he continues to gingerly apply the gas.

The car moves forward and the gate begins to bow. I can hear the cracks and snaps of the framing as it begins to give way to the momentum of the car and I can hear the spinning of the back wheels as they grope for traction in the soft mud of the road.

Bill suddenly stomps down on the gas, the tires gain traction and with a final ripping sound the gate gives way, flying out to our front on both sides of the car as we lunge into the pasture throwing a trail of grass and mud behind us.

"You probably just skint' the shit out of your buddy's car," Trapper says to Bill.

Bill just chuckles.

"And the Hollands are gonna be pissed that you tore up their gate," he goes on to say.

Bill laughs, a short one snorter and looks over at me.

"I didn't see no gate! Did you, Mr. Boogieman?"

"You better stop and let me go back and try to close it," Trapper tells him.

"Fuck 'em!" Bill says and drives on.

The pasture is soft and squishy, what used to be the road now overgrown with grass. Bill drives slow and cautious in an effort to stay on the original road bed. Just before we reach the Holland's barn, I see two cows who have left shelter and braved the weather to graze.

"Ever fuck a cow?" Bill asks, right out of the clear blue.

Neither of us answers.

Trapper looks at me and circles his finger around his head again and points at Bill.

"How 'bout a sheep?" Bill goes on.

I look at Trapper and nod my head in approval of his diagnosis.

"Whir' I come from, they's some folks do it all the time," he goes on.

"And where would that be?" Trapper asks.

Bill belches, then reaches down and adjusts his balls.

"Great State of Texas, son," he brags.

"I didn't know there was a Pervert, Texas. You ever hear of it, Boogie?" Trapper looks over at me and inquires.

"I think it's out in the western part of the state. Out close to Queer City," I tell him. "You know! Where the "deer and the antelope play.""

"They fuck them, too, Bill?" Trapper asks.

"What?"

"The deer and the antelopes. Ya'll fuck them, too?"

"Fuck you," Bill tells him.

We can't help but laugh.

We pass the barn and pull up to the gate at the fence. It's another "swing gate," except this time it's a one-piece job, a corrugated metal one that looks almost brand new.

"Get out and see if'n the fucker's locked" Bill tells me.

"Un' make it fast," he adds, as I exit the car.

We're in luck. The gate's not locked, only held secure with a wraparound chain. I swing the gate outwards and signal Bill to drive on through.

We've come to what most everyone calls Dean Road, a country dirt road that wiggles through the hills and hollows for three or four miles between the Trafford Road and the Blount County highway. Just across, on the other side is the Holland's house. I look all around, but see no signs of life. I feel relieved. I wouldn't want them to know that I was party to the destruction of their gate. This is short-lived, however, for just as Bill drives through, I get a mental image of someone looking at us from a window, so I hurriedly close the gate and run for the car, "jingling all the way."

Bill takes a right on Dean Road. It's slippery and wet, dotted with potholes of water.

"Better be careful through here or you'll really get stuck" Trapper tells him.

Bill grunts and cuts his eyes towards him and sneers.

"If I kin drive through the fuckin' woods, I kin drive on a road," he informs Trapper.

And to prove it, he accelerates the car. We're right in a curve as he does it. We fishtail to the left, it's more than Bill expects. He lets off the gas and fights the wheel to right the car. "God damn! That was a close one! That fucker is slick!" he exclaims, then gives us a two-snorter.

"You otta' quit playing 'Lucky Teter' when you're full of liquor," Trapper advises him. "I'd be a lil' more careful if I's you."

Bill ignores him, "Ain't we nearly down ta the paved road?" he asks.

"About another mile," Trapper tells him, "so take it slow."

After fighting the wind and rain all morning, the drone and movement of the car begins to make me sleepy again. I yawn and look at the clock; it shows its 1:05.

"Is this clock right?" I ask Bill.

"How the hell would I know?" he questions me back.

"You'd think you'd know if your clock's right."

"Well, I knows it's right two times a day, jist ain't shore this is 'un of 'em," he quips.

Trapper laughs, which entices Bill to honor us with another two-snorter.

"Real funny, be sure you don't piss your pants," I tell them.

"Damn! He's a mind reader, too, 'cause thet's jist what I'm 'bout to do," Bill says to Trapper, inducing more laughter.

I settle back in the seat and tune them out. We're coming to the end of Dean Road. We're going have to make another turn. There's only one logical way to go and that's to the right. If we head in that direction, there's two ways to get to our destination. One would be to take the Black Creek Road about a mile or so away and go the way we should have gone in the first place. This, however, would take us right through the center of town, a place Bill says he wants to avoid. The other, would be to bypass the Black Creek Road, continue south for about three more miles and circle back to the Big Rock on the Narrows Road, a rutted-out dirt road that snakes along beside Turkey

Creek for about five miles, as it flows through a narrow gorge on the western side of Pinson Mountain. It's an illogical choice and way out of our way, but knowing Bill, I'm almost sure it's where he's headed.

Trapper brings me out of my thoughts. He's deduced the same thing.

"I hope you ain't thinking about going all the way over to the Narrows Road and circling around to Big Rock that way," I hear him say to Bill.

"Damn! Ya tryin' ta read minds, too?" Bill grumbles back to him.

"If you are, it's a bad move, 'cause you ain't gonna get through there today with all this rain," Trapper goes on to tell him.

"Is thet the road thet passes by thet big ol' rock thet looks like a oyster settin' on the bank of the crick, at thet place all the Rednecks 'round here call the falls?" Bill asks.

"That's the one and it's gonna be washed out big time. Hell! You can hardly get through there in dry weather. That's why there ain't no-body lives out there. You get stuck in there; they ain't gonna be a soul in miles to help get us out on a day like this. Ain't I right, Boogie?" He looks at me and asks.

"I sure as hell wouldn't try to go that way, that place gives me the spooks," I reply, just as Bill slows for the stop sign.

"Ya fuckers worry too much," he tells us, as he runs it and takes a right.

Just as we turn on the pavement, a slow misty rain begins to fall again. Bill flips on the wipers and the windows begin to streak. This irritates him. He begins to mumble obscenities and complains that he can't see, but at the same time accelerating the speed of the car. We're weaving all over the road and narrowly miss hitting an old ratty pickup truck coming from the opposite direction.

"I hope to hell you ain't drunk," Trapper tells him.

"Don't fuckin' worry 'bout it, I usually drink more then I have today afore breakfast," Bill replies, "but it's a good fuckin' idea."

If he's not drunk, he's well on the way, I think to myself. *He's had three beers and four big slugs of whiskey. Hardly noticeably, when we were slipping and sliding on the narrow country roads, but now that we're out on the highway, it's obvious and to make matters worse, he's still got lots more left to drink.*

"They's ain't nothing but redneck farmers and black-neck miners live out here in this fuckin' neck of the woods," Bill suddenly volunteers, "but their women shore do have some sweet pussy," he goes on to add.

"What color are their necks?" Trapper asks him, which is ignored by Bill.

Bill slows the car as we approach Hopewell Baptist Church. Seeing it reminds me of Bobby Ford.

Trapper and I were just here two weeks ago for his funeral. Bobby was two grades ahead of us, just had turned sixteen, just had got his driver's license. His dad let him use their new Buick to take Suzy Creel to the movie over in Pinson. They never made it. They said he was driving way too fast, showing off for Suzy. He flipped the car and was killed. Suzy is still in the hospital. They say she might die...

Bill swings off the road. We drive around to the back of the church and head into the cemetery on the hearse road and stop.

"Why are we stopping here?" I ask him.

"Yeah! We gotta get going. We told you, we gotta go to a party this evening," Trapper chimes in.

"Just hold yore fuckin' horses. I gotta take me a piss and then I'm gonna drink me 'nother beer, afore we move on.

"Find somethin' to clean thet windshield off and maybe I'll let ya'll split one," he tells us, as he gets out of the car.

I open the glove box and look inside. I see nothing there but some yellowed folded-up papers.

Trapper is leaning over the seat, peering into the back of the car.

"Nothing to clean with in the glove box," I tell him.

"There's a 'tow-sack' full of something back here on the floorboard," Trapper says.

"Hey! What's in this tow-sack?" he hollers out to Bill. "Any rags in it?"

Bill's standing just outside the car, he's left the door open. His dick is hanging out the fly of his overalls. He's holding it taking a piss. I can hear it as it splatters on the muddy ground. The smell of it wafts in the air and through the car.

"Don't fuck with thet bag, ain't nothing in there concerns ya," he tells Trapper, then farts and sighs and continues to piss.

"Screw him, let him clean his own windows," Trapper tells me as he sits back down in the seat and begins playing with the knob on the steering wheel. It's a big ruby-red one, with a shiny chrome mounting bracket.

"I'm gonna put one of these on my steering wheel when I get a car," he says.

"Yeah, me, too," I agree.

This place gives me the creeps, he says. "It makes me think of Bobby. I hope Suzy don't die or we'll have to go to another funeral."

"Yeah, but it'll be at Bethel Church," I tell him.

"Who says," he wants to know.

"My dad, he's gonna help dig the grave."

"Well I guess ya don't wanna beer," Bill says, breaking into our conversation, "since ya ain't cleaned the winders off!"

He's turned towards us, his dick still in his hand. He's milking it back and forth as he talks.

"Don't forget, Bill, if you shake it more than two times, you're playin' with it," Trapper tells him in a laughing manner!

Bill slides back into the seat, his horse still out of its stall. Water drips off his hat and coat. Trapper slides closer to me.

"God damn! I need some pussy!" he says, as he yawns and stretches. Shame to waste this boner. Look at thet thing!"

"Ever see a prick this big?" he asks, shifting in his seat to afford us a better view.

Trapper looks over at me. I look out the window of my door, neither of us interested in Bill's tallywacker.

Yeah, you! I think to myself, but neither of us reply.

"Nine fuckin' inches soft," he continues as though either of us gives a shit, "and you don't wanna know how big 'Ole Bob' is whin he's hard—or maybe you do," he says and gives us a one-snorter.

I suddenly think of the dead kid again. Probably because Bill called his dick, Bob.

"Hey! Why don't we all beat off?" he says. "Whatta you think?"

"I think you need a new ruler," Trapper tells him, then looks over at me and we both laugh.

"Or maybe he's looking at it upside down," I say, which makes us laugh even harder.

I look at Bill. He's giving us a cold icy stare. He's a pervert and he's starting to really scare me. I feel a stirring in my bowels, a prelude to the squirts. Suddenly nothing about this is funny.

"You gonna sit here and pull at your pud, or go get your truck?" Trapper asks him.

I don't wait for an answer. I open my door; the rain has almost stopped again. "Come on Trapper," I say, "let's get the hell out of here."

I'm halfway out of the car, Trapper right behind me when Bill begins his personality change again.

"Hey! Wait a minute. Whir ya'll goin'?" he asks, in an almost pleading manner as we begin our exit.

"Look, Bill!" Trapper tells him. "We agreed to help you get your truck out of a mudhole. That didn't include sittin' in a cemetery watching you play with your dick and it sure the hell didn't include joinin' in with you for no circle jerk. So either we start doing what we agreed to do or we're outta here."

"Aw, come on! Git back in the car." Bill begs in the same pleady tone, as he stuffs his "Johnson" back in his pants and begins to fasten his fly.

"I wuz jist fuckin' 'round, you know, jokin' with you guys. Kin't ya' take a joke?"

The transformation is complete. He's now Bill, the good ol' boy, just one of the gang.

"Come on, let's have a smoke," he tells us as he digs in his pocket for his Camels and Zippo.

Trapper eases back inside the car, enticed by the lure of a cigarette. I stand firm.

Bill puts the fire to the smoke, takes a deep drag, then leans back and exhales the smoke out his nose and mouth with a sigh. "God damn! I'd walk ten miles for a fuckin' Camel," he says, then in appreciation of his wit again, gives us a double-snorter.

"Here, ya'll want one?" he asks, extending the pack towards Trapper who snatches it from his hand with the speed of a cobra strike.

"Don't mind if I do," he says, as he fingers one from the pack.

"You want one, Boogie?" he asks, looking around at me.

I hesitate for a moment before I answer.

"Do you or don't you?" Trapper inquires again.

"Sure," I say, "get one out for me," all the while hating myself, because I'm as weak as he is.

"Slide over," I tell Trapper, "I'm getting' cold out here."

He moves over about a foot. Just enough space for me to sit down. He's staying as far away from Bill as he can and as an added safety measure, I leave the door open.

We're gonna need some fire, Bill. Let me have your "Zippo," Trapper says to him as he hands him his cigarettes back.

But Bill has other priorities, stuffing his cigs back in his pocket, he immediately hand dives for the sack on the floor, then comes out with two beers and his jar, which he deposits on the seat before commencing a pocket pat in search of the church key.

"We need a light," Trapper says to him again.

"Hold yore horses, I don't know what I done with the fuckin' opener," Bill tells him, as he continues patting himself down, then having no luck, starts searching in the gap between the seat and the back rest.

Trapper shifts closer to me.

I give him an ass bump and jar him back towards Bill. "Keep your ass over some, you're pushing me out the door," I tell him.

"Look good on the floorboard, see if that opener mita' fell down there," Bill issues an order, as he wiggles out of the car.

Neither of us breaks our necks.

"He's killing time for some reason," I whisper to Trapper. "What you say we cut this show short?"

"Yeah? And get soaked walking back! Are you nuts?"

"Nuts for being here and so are you," I advise him.

We both look towards Bill. He completes another pat down of his overall pockets, then bends down and looks towards us.

"Ya'll find enythin' on the floorboard?"

"'Tain't in here," Trapper tells him.

"I told you that you otta keep it in the sack," I remind him.

He gives me a fuck you look and shoots me a bird.

"Did you look on the ground? Maybe it fell out that hole in your pocket," Trapper tells him.

Bill gives him a questionable look, then turns and begins to search at his feet.

Trapper looks back at me and lowers his voice.

"He's an idiot and a drunk, but if we can keep him sober, I don't think we're gonna have a problem."

"You left out pervert," I remind him, but before he can reply, Bill finds the church key.

"Shit!" I hear him exclaim as he reaches down and picks it up from the ground.

"God damn it, pissed all over it!" he complains as he slides back in the car wiping it off on his pants leg.

We can't help but laugh.

"Look at it as a positive," I tell him.

What the hell's thet 'sposed to mean? he grumbles as he uncaps his whiskey jar.

"It'll improve the taste of that Sterling," I tell him.

We continue to laugh!

He ignores my levity and follows his usual ritual: slug of pot, double slug of beer, disgusting belch and then the Camel.

"While you got the lighter out, give us a light," Trapper says again, still holding on to the two cigarettes he plucked out of the pack for us.

But Bill's in no hurry to accommodate.

"Jist a second," he says.

He drains the last of the beer, tosses out the can and closes the door of the car; then with a shit-eating grin on his face, he belches and strains out a thunderous fart at the same time.

"Can't light ya up now or I'll blow up the fuckin' car," he tells Trapper, which is good for a one-snorter.

I almost gag as the smell of the fart hits my nostrils. I hold my breath and step back out of the car. I fill my lungs with cold misty air, then lean back in for the continuation of the Trapper and Bill show.

"Put 'em in yore mouth if you wants 'em lit," Bill tells Trapper. "Both at the same time, 'cause I gotta save fuel," he jibes.

"Hold on now, I gotta do a safety check," he says, as he strokes up a flame and waves the lighter around in the car then up close to Trapper's face and over his head; all the time in a fit of snort, thinking he's funny.

"Come on, Bill," Trapper mumbles around the cigarettes, fanning his nose at the same time.

Bill smirks, then finally relents and holds the flame up to one of the smokes allowing Trapper to light it up. As he moves to fire up the second one Bill flips the lighter closed in an attempt to snare the cigarette, but Trapper is way ahead of him, it's an old game he and I have played lots of times.

Anticipating Bill's intention, he quickly jerks his head to the right, which not only foils Bill's plan, but also serves to brand his fingers that are holding the lighter with the lighted end of the other cigarette.

Sparks and burning tobacco fly everywhere. Bill yelps and drops the lighter.

"God damit, ya burnt me!" he cries as he inspects, then looks and sucks at the burn.

Trapper picks up the Zippo, which has fallen on the seat and brushes away the ash and stray bits of tobacco from his coat, but before he can light our cigarettes Bill snatches the lighter from his hand. He takes a final drag on the cigarette he's smoking and flips it straight at Trapper's head. It misses and comes out the passenger door where I'm standing. It misses my face by about an inch.

"I hope ya burnt a hole in yore fuckin' coat," he tells Trapper.

"It ain't my coat you better be worried about. Look at your buddy's car seat," he tells Bill, as he points down at the seat between them.

I peer in for a closer look and sure enough there's a burn hole about the size of a dime, right in the center of the seat.

"I'd go for seat covers if I was you, 'cause there ain't no way you gonna repair this old gray upholstery so it don't show," Trapper informs him.

Bill gives Trapper a sneer, then leans back into his own space and inspects his wound again. Apparently deciding he's going to live, he lifts his arms above his head and stretches, then fishes out another cigarette and lights it up. He picks up the jar and the second beer still sitting on the seat at his hip, puts the jar back in the bag and then deciding to keep the beer out, puts it back on the seat beside him. He takes another deep drag on his cig and exhales the smoke out his nose. He turns and looks at us, first at Trapper, then at me, then back at Trapper.

His eyes are hooded, almost closed. He looks all relaxed, a half-sneer, half-smirk on his face.

"Now what wuz we talking 'bout? Oh, yeah, the car," he says, answering his own question.

"Let's see now. First I skint it on the fuckin' fence, now I got me a hole burnt in the seat and now Mister Trapperman," he nods his head towards Trapper here, "thanks, I otta be worried. Well, I got somethin' to tell ya."

Before continuing he takes another lung blaster off the Camel, looks at us again and then sort of lowers his head.

"Sorta a confession," he goes on to say.

"Kin ya'll keep a secret?" he asks.

Neither of us answers right away, because (and I'll speak for the both of us) neither of us can figure out what the hell's going on!

"Kin ya?" he asks again, looking first up to me, then down at Trapper.

Trapper doesn't hesitate.

"Once you divulge something only you know to someone else, it's no longer a secret," Trapper tells him. "If you're asking me if I can keep something you tell me to myself, the answer is, 'yes I can.'"

Bill looks up at me.

"Ditto" I tell him, flowing on the draft of Trapper's wind.

"Well, here goes," he says.

"Fact is, that it don't make no difference what happens to this ol' car—none at all, 'cause, fact is, I jist stole this fucker last night," he tells us.

I feel my jaw drop. It possibly hits Trapper's head, because he immediately looks up at me with the same expression.

The two of us look back at Bill. He's looking at us all sorrowful-like and shaking his head.

I feel the gurgle return to my bowels.

I look at Trapper again; he looks back up at me.

That's when it happens!

A record-breaking laugh that rocks the car. A four-snorter, followed up by a two and then a whee!

"God damn! Got yore goat on that 'un, din't I?" Bill manages to get out through breaks in his laughter.

"Had you lil' fuckers believin' it, didn't I? Thankin' you was ridin' 'round in a stole car!"

"Man! Was that a good un' or a good 'un?" he asks, as he rolls down his window, flips his cigarette butt to the wind and immediately lights up another.

Trapper looks at me again, then back at Bill. I want to tell him to add bullshitter to Bill's list of credits, but hold my tongue.

"So you was lyin' to us about the car?" he asks Bill.

"Funnin' with ya', and, boy, did ya swaller it," he tells Trapper with a chuckle.

"You sure?" Trapper asks again.

"Hey! Whatta I gotta do? I was funnin'."

"Give me the lighter," Trapper tells him.

Bill looks puzzled.

"Whatta ya mean?" he asks.

"You asked what you could do. You can give me the lighter, so I can finally light these two damn cigarettes," Trapper tells him and laughs.

I don't follow suit.

Bill chimes in with Trapper and tosses him the Zippo. The good ol' boy's back.

Trapper lights the two cigarettes and hands one over to me, then slides over to make room for me to sit, but I'm not sitting.

"I'll be back in a minute," I tell him and attempt to close the car door, but Trapper twists on the seat and catches it with his foot.

"Where you goin'?" he asks.

"I said I'd be right back," I tell him again, then I turn and walk away, heading deeper into the cemetery. I need to think.

I take a draw off the cigarette, inhale too much smoke and begin to cough. It makes me dizzy. I hear Bill holler something derogatory concerning my manhood, but can't quite make it out. He and Trapper both laugh. I turn and look back at the car. Trapper hasn't closed the door, so I shoot them a bird, then take another draw and look up at the sky, then turn and continue to walk.

The rain has stopped again, but its presence since yesterday has turned the cemetery into a sea of mud that sticks to my shoes. Everything looks forlorn. The sky is a dark smoky gray and the trees in the cemetery stand black and stark against it like stick figure drawings. The sheen on the tombstones from the cold misty air makes them appear luminous and ghostly white. Goosebumps racks my body. I stop and look around.

A sudden gust of wind howls through the trees. Its force and sound cuts through my body like a knife, causing icicles to form on my spine and my hair to stand on end.

"What the hell am I doing here?" I think to myself.

I shiver and pull my jacket up tight to my body, then walk towards a heart-shaped tombstone I spot just off to my right.

It has three heart-shaped picture frames hanging on it. Hung with red ribbon, probably on Valentine's Day, I surmise. The pictures are of a twelve-year-old boy who drowned in a strip pit—the one over behind the Holland's, as a matter of fact. His name is Jimmy. He was a year ahead of me at school. I squat down, take a big draw off my cigarette, blow the smoke on Jimmy's grave, and then watch as the wind inhales it.

"Just in case you're having a nicotine fit, Jimbo," I say out loud, remembering how he used to hang out with the rest of us guys down behind the school where the bigger boys smoked, hoping to catch dibs on their butts.

"Too bad he had to die, he'd be one of the big boys now," I think to myself.

I rise back up and move on a few more steps, then decide I've seen enough graves, so I turn and head back towards the car. As I pass the Valentine tombstone, I take a final pull off the Camel and drop the butt on Jimmy's grave.

Trapper doesn't seem to think we're going to have a serious problem with Bill, I can tell by the way he's acting. Either that or he wants the money Bill has promised to pay us so bad, he's willing to take the chance. As for me, I'm uncertain. Maybe he has been just kidding around with all his sexual overtures. Everybody knows he's a queer, maybe that's just how they act. What concerns me most is his dilly-dallying. He originally said he was in a hurry to get his truck, yet all the while, he's been in no hurry at all. I'm undecided about going on. I want the money, too, but not bad enough to risk getting molested by a queer. I need to come up with something.

On my way back, I devise a plan for a possible ploy.

As I approach the car, Trapper is still sitting with the door open, holding a beer in his hand, which by the way is unopened. Bill is bending his ear with stories about his sexual escapades. I arrive just in time to hear one of the more lurid ones.

"Move your ass over so I can sit down, it's cold out here," I tell Trapper.

Trapper moves over without even looking at me, he's all enthralled with Bill's tale. Bill doesn't miss a beat. Ignoring me altogether he continues to expound.

"You wouldn't believe all the pussy ya git whin yore an athelete," he's telling Trapper. "Un' here's one fer yore fuckin' books!" he continues.

"Here while back, I wuz fuckin' this little ol' blond. She'd been married before, had a kid 'bout eleven or twelve years old, but he wuz a runty looking lil' thang so he looked a lot younger. He wuz a retard, crazy as shit, no more then a fuckin' monkey. She kept the lil' fucker locked up in the house, wouldn't let him go out, said the other kids picked on him, made fun of him. I liked the lil' fucker, used to bring him candy and shit. He loved fuckin' candy. He used to lay on the bed and eat it while I fucked his mammy. Her and me used to laugh 'bout it.

"Then, this one night, I woke up getting' the best damn blow job I ever had in my life and let me tell ya' now, ol' Bill's had a lot of 'em. I thought, you damn bitch, how much more dick you need? Hell! I'd already fucked her twice afore we went to sleep, but enyway, I weren't complainin' 'cause it wuz feeling really good. Then, and this is the crazy part, I hap's to look over and I sees she's a layin' next ta me. I thought, Hell! What's a going on, so I threw back the covers and by damn if it weren't thet lil' ol' moron down there just a suckin' the hell outta ol' Bob. Hell! I din't know what to do, but by this time it wuz too late to do a thang anyhow, 'cause ol' Bob was just about to puke, so I jist layed back and let him have at it. Little fucker ate that load I shot in his mouth like it wuz candy, then jist curled right up and went to sleep. Craziest thang I ever seen."

Bill stops to light up another Camel.

"I'd give you'ens another 'un, but I'm runnin' low," he tells Trapper, which is fine by me, since I'm about to puke myself from listening to his story. He takes a big drag and continues.

"Next morning I told his mammy 'bout it while she wuz a cookin' my breakfast. She jist giggled, said he had probably a seen her a doin' it. Said he really looked up to me, 'cause she had explained to him that I wuz a famous athelete."

"But here's the kicker," he goes on to say after another big drag on the smoke.

"I know this feller, richer than shit, do some work ever now and then for him. Well, not long after this happened him and me wuz a talking and for some reason, this lil' ol' boy come up and I broke down and told him what happened, not that I'm proud of it you know, and anyway, he felt real bad about it and ya won't believe what thet feller done.

Bill pauses for another drag. I guess this is where the both of us are supposed to be on the edge of our seats saying, "What? What?" But since I could give a shit less, only Trapper takes the bait.

"What'd he do?" Trapper asks him.

"Fucker moved thet kid and his mammy into a big fine house he owns down in Birmingham, jist give it to 'em, rent fuckin' free. Become like a daddy to thet lil' ol' boy. Bought him a new bicycle, all kinda new baseball shit, takes him out ta see the Barons play all the time.

"Hell! He's bought him footballs and skates, jist ever kinda thang you can thank of that a boy would want, he's bought him, and to top it off, he gives the lil' fucker ten dollars ever' week for spendin' money!

"Hell! That lil' bastard's got more friends now then you kin "shake a stick" at. Hardly ever goes in the house now, last time I heard."

"Just long enough to suck your rich buddy's dick, sounds to me like," I say to Bill.

"Yeah, nobody buys a kid all that stuff for nothing," Trapper adds.

"Naw, naw! 'Tain't like that a 'toll. They's some folk's jist do thangs out of the goodness of their hearts. This feller's one of 'em," Bill protests.

"You'd know it if'n ya met him. He'd really like ya'll, I know he would. Anyway, that lil' ol' blond's probably "hauling his ashes" ever' night, so he's well took care of."

"Yeah, I bet!" Trapper says.

I'm tired of listening to Bill's bullshit stories, so before he can get started on another, I change the subject of the conversation.

"What's the plan, Bill?" I ask him. "Are we gonna go get your truck or not?"

Bill looks at Trapper, who he now considers an ally and shakes his head.

"Funny ya asked," he says. "Me and the Trapperman wuz jist talking 'bout thet while ya wuz off visitin' with the dead folks. Conclusion was thet soon as ya got back, we wuz gonna drank this beer that we've been a holding since afore ya left, 'cause we thought ya might want some of it, and then zip on over the road to git the truck." "Ain't that 'about it, Trapperman?"

"Yeah, and let's hurry," Trapper says, handing him the beer. "I need a swallow to get the whisky taste outta my mouth."

I look at Trapper surprised!

"Bill give me a drink while you was gone," he tells me. "Said you could have one if you wanted it when you come back. Want one?" he asks.

"No way! That shit tastes like rottin' eggs," I tell him.

"You've drunk it before, I've seen you," Trapper says back to me.

"Well, I ain't drinking it today, so let's get on with the beer, so we can get the hell outta here."

Bill has the opener ready and slits the top of the can. He gulps about half of it down, let's out a big belch and hands it off to Trapper who takes two big swallows then passes it on to me. I don't really want any, but I take a slug to speed up the drinking process then hand the can back to Trapper. It tastes like hot piss smells. Probably Bill's from the opener, I think to myself.

Another big swallow from Trapper and another from Bill completes the task.

"Well, 'nother 'dead soldier,'" Bill says, as he rolls down his window and drops the can in the cemetery. "Close the fuckin' door, if ya wanna git outta here," he says to me, as he lights up another Camel.

"There's one other thing we need to talk about," I spring on him.

"God damn! I thought ya'd talked out. What's the fuckin' problem now?" he wants to know as he starts up the motor.

I step back outside the car and lean back in to talk.

"I ain't going if you're going over there on the Narrows Road," I tell him. "Either you take the Black Creek Road or count me out."

Trapper looks at me, surprised at my decision.

"Come on, Boogie," he says, "get in and let's go."

"No way," I tell him. "Either Bill goes through Black Creek or see ya."

"You'll get soaked and freeze your ass off if you walk back home from here," he goes on to say.

"Don't worry about it, I'll get a ride and if I don't and freeze to death, I'm in a good place to get buried," I reply.

"So much for 'one for all,' I guess," Trapper jibes at me.

"Sorry, left my sword home today," I tell him and chuckle.

"Hold the fuck on," Bill interjects.

I was wondering when he was going to jump in. He's just been sitting there with his eyes hooded down; watching us banter, but what he says throws me for a loop.

"Just hold on fer a minute," he says, looking at Trapper. "The Boogieman's probably right, thank 'bout it a second," he says.

Somebody help me out of the cemetery mud, I can't believe what I just heard him say, I think to myself as Bill continues.

"Now I ain't one who 'preciates somebody making a promise to me then backin' out on it, I don't want you thankin' thet, but on the other hand, we's been kinda fooling 'round, so's the time is gittin' away and like ya said, that ol' Narrows Road is probably fuckin' mudded over. Probably couldn't git through on the fucker anyway. So, maybe ol' Boogie's right. Maybe we otta go through Black Crick."

Trapper looks at me, then grins and shakes his head.

"Hell, you don't have to convince me," he looks over at Bill and says, "that's what I told you to do in the first place."

"Are you serious?" I ask Bill.

"Serious as a hard dick," he says and snorts.

"Come on! Git in. I gots another beer and half a jar of whiskey left in this ol' sack. We'll have us a celebration when we git thet truck unstuck."

"Come on, Boogie, let's get the hell out of here," Trapper says and pulls on my arm.

I look at Bill; he's gunning the motor, ready to go.

"And we're going through Black Creek?" I verify with him again.

"Fuckin' Boy Scouts honor," he tells me, giving me the pledge with his hand. "Now git in!"

I slide into the car, hoping and praying I've made the right decision. Bill backs out, throws the Ford in low and with a shower of mud, we leave the dead behind. A glance at the clock says it's ten 'til two.

— CHAPTER 9 —

FEAR

I FEEL COLD AND DAMP AND WHAT'S MORE, I'M START-
ing to get really hungry as we take to the pavement and move away
from the church.

I fish in my pocket for my Juicy Fruit, unwrap a piece, stick it in
my mouth, then hand a piece to Trapper. There's one piece left, so I
put it back in my pocket.

"Thanks a hell of a lot fer the gum," Bill says to me in a snippy,
sarcastic tone.

"I'd give you some, but I'm running low," I assure him, being just
as sarcastic back.

I know chewing the gum is just going to make me hungrier, but
it at least gets the pissy taste of the beer out of my mouth. A peanut
butter and banana sandwich and a glass of sweet milk would be the
perfect thing, but for now the gum will have to do.

Bill has got the pedal to the metal, going way too fast for the wet-
ness of the road, plus he's weaving erratically, moving back and forth
from straddling the yellow line to our left, over to the gravel on the
shoulder of the road to our right, his intake of booze really evident.

Just as we top a rise in the road, we meet a car. Bill is hogging his
lane, so we both have to swerve. Bill heads back towards the shoulder, but not before road water from the oncoming car's wheels flood
our windshield. The wipers labor furiously, but can't keep up. The car
bumps up and down as we hit the jagged pavement along the edge of
the road and I can hear the sound from the gravel along the shoulder
as it pelts the underside of the car.

The windows clear somewhat just as we begin our downward
slope! Suddenly, there's an object in our path! Hidden from view just
over the rise, and with our windshield smeared, none of us had seen

it. But there it is now! Not more than 50 feet away, it's either stopped or moving really slow.

"Watch it, Bill!" Trapper yells, as both of us brace ourselves back against the seat and begin stomping at imaginary brakes.

Full of alcohol and partially brain-dead, Bill's first reaction is to slam the brakes on hard. We begin to skid and almost fishtail before his logic kicks in.

Unable to swing to the left and pass, due to an empty pulpwood truck barreling towards us, Bill shifts into second to gear us down, then pumps like mad on the brakes. We roll under control about three feet from the back end of a rickety cow trailer. It's being pulled by a farmer (I guess), with a tractor. Two cows are loaded inside and he's traveling about five miles an hour. Probably just changing their pasture, because less than thirty yards from where we almost annihilated him, he turns off a side road that angles down towards a pasture with a gate.

Bill is furious.

"Crazy, dumbass, piece of shit farmer," he yells, as he rolls his window down and shoots him a bird over the roof of the car. "If I weren't in a hurry I'd stop and beat the dog shit out of 'em," he says in a huff.

"I wouldn't piss him off if I was you," Trapper tells him.

"What the hell ya mean by thet?" Bill wants to know.

Trapper looks over at me and smiles, then looks back at Bill who's speeded up again and is now weaving even more, because he's trying to light up a cigarette.

"Well, I just happened to notice that them was two fine-looking cows—a possible double date for you and one of your buddies tonight, if you're in good standing with their daddy," he says, then looks at me and laughs.

"Don't you think so, Boogie?" he asks.

"I found the black and white one extremely fetching," I say.

Both of us break up laughing.

"I want fergit that 'un," Bill tells Trapper, and he ain't laughing.

I sit back and stare out the windshield at the road ahead. The rain is still at bay and Bill has cut off the wipers so as not to streak the glass any worse. Through a semi-clean place right near the top of the windshield, I survey the sky through a break in the trees. Far to the south, I see a patch of sky that looks like blue, but it's only there for about a minute before it disappears. I wonder if the Snakeman's right?

I look over at Trapper—he's sucking up to Bill, trying to appease him for his joke about the cows. Bill's telling a new version of the story about his rich friend and the moron kid that sucks dicks and Trapper is pretending to be intently listening. It's disgusting.

We're almost to the Black Creek cutoff. It's time for phase two of my ploy, so I interrupt Bill's story.

"Hey, Bill! Stop down at Herman Ronson's and I'll buy a Coca Cola and pour it on the windshield to clean it," I tell him. "Ain't nothing cleans a windshield better than a Coca Cola." *Cast the bait, then sit back and wait for a strike,* I think to myself.

Herman Ronson is a "shade tree" mechanic who lives at the northwest corner of the Black Creek intersection. He's in competition with Boodle for the "King of Junk," except unlike Boodle, all of his junk is cars and trucks. The hillside along the front of his house is filled with them. Just across the road on the southwest corner is Herman's Garage, which consists of a small cement-block structure, slightly larger than a two-seater toilet with a roofed, open-air bay along the side for working on cars, and a couple of pumps out front for kerosene and gas. Herman sells the normal things you find at a filling station, like cold drinks, candy bars and rubbers, but his specialty is car repair and used parts.

Regardless of what Bill has promised us about the route he will take to the creek, I believe he's lying. I gambled when I got back in the car—gambled that I could get him to stop here, where it'll be a cinch to get a ride back to town because a lot of the old men from there hang out here. It's another one of those designated centers for whittling and gossiping, plus, Herman is a good friend of my dad's and if all else fails, I can always con him into taking me home.

"Anyway," I go on to say, "I'm getting' hungry and we can get a candy bar or something to eat."

"Yeah, I'm starving," Trapper adds. "My belly thinks my throat's been cut."

Bill makes no comment to my suggestion. He sucks down a final drag and cracks his window just enough to flip his cigarette butt out. The wind catches it and propels a shower of sparks back at his face. We take another excursion along the shoulder of the road while he's batting them out.

Trapper and I both laugh.

"What da' you think about my idea?" I pry at Bill again.

"What fuckin' idea?" he asks me, playing an asshole as usual.

"About stopping and getting a Coca Cola to clean the windows," I remind him.

"I'll vote for it," Trapper chimes in.

"If I wuz to spend good fuckin' money on a dope, I wouldn't be dumb enough to pour it on a fuckin' car winder," Bill informs me.

He's giving me the runaround. He has no intention of stopping, just as I feared when I decided to take the gamble. He's not gonna go through Black Creek either—I can feel it in my bones, also in the pit of my stomach. But I took the gamble, so I gotta play it through. "I said I would pay for it, not you," I tell him. "Heck, I don't mind springing for a dope to clean your windows with. You'll be able to see a lot better, if they're clean." And then I think to myself, *You're a big, fat, queer fucker, and probably a liar, too.*

Bill looks over at me and smirks. He gives me sort of a semi-snorter, then taps Trapper's shoulder with the back of his hand.

"Then I guess we knows what thet makes ya," he tells me, then finishes up the rest of his snort.

"I gotta go to the toilet, so we gonna have to stop," Trapper says unexpectedly. "Ya'll can argue about the dope and the winder while I'm takin' a piss." Then he looks at me and smiles, expecting one back, showing that I appreciated his witty use of Bill's lingo.

I give him a big one, then add, "Me, too. Really bad," I say.

I really didn't have to go until Trapper mentioned it, but now I have to. If Bill stops, I'm gonna have to get money out of my shoe some way, so the toilet's perfect. I can kill two birds with one stone—*if* he stops…

The intersection is just around this next curve, then down a short grade and still no verification from Bill on his intentions. I give it one final shot.

"Tell you what!" I blurt out, "When we stop, I'll spring for a cold drink and a candy bar for all of us, my treat."

Maybe that'll do it, I think to myself, but I'm probably wrong.

I get a "that's great" from Trapper, but nothing from Bill. He just looks at me with a smirky grin.

We go through the curve and head down the grade towards the intersection, I see it ahead. I calculate how long to get there. I figure ten seconds. If he's not braking by five, he's not stopping. I start counting: 10-9-8-7-6-5. Bill applies the brakes, the speed of the car decelerates—I breathe a sigh of relief.

We roll through the intersection at the right speed and Bill's going through all the motions that indicate a turn into Herman's. He even rolls down the window and gives a right-hand turn signal. Then, all of a sudden he pops the clutch, throws it into second, stomps the gas, and continues going straight. I swallow my fucking chewing gum.

Bill celebrates his deception with a three-snorter, as he drops the gear back to high. He thinks it's funny.

Trapper, over the initial shock, bears in on him.

"What the hell's going on, Bill? I told you I had to take a piss and you said you'd stop. You can just turn around and go back. Right now!"

"Never said no such thang," Bill tells him, with the jackass smile still on his face.

"Well, you fuckin' indicated you was, didn't he Boogie?" Trapper tells him and then looks over at me for verification.

I'm furious; not only at Bill, but also at myself for the stupid chance I've taken.

"He's a liar," I say to Trapper, "a damn liar."

Bill lets up off the gas, looks over and stares at me hard and mean.

"What the hell'd ya say?" He hisses at me.

I give him the same look back.

"I said you were a damn liar," I tell him. "What the hell you gonna do about it?" I go on to say, with a challenge.

I hope he's going to say that he's going to stop the car and kick my ass. I'll be out the door and gone before his fat ass is out from under the wheel and I hope Trapper has enough brains to be right behind me. Up to this point, he doesn't seem to sense that Bill might be up to something other than what he's told us as I do. Nevertheless, he's got to make his own decisions.

But, instead Bill says, "Them's fuckin' fightin' words wher' I come from, good buddy. I thank ya better take 'em back right now."

"Yeah! What? When ya'll ain't fuckin' cows, you're beatin' up kids! Is that right?" Trapper comes to my defense and asks him.

Maybe he's starting to see the light.

"I ain't taking nothin' back," I tell him. "You lied when you told us you'd go through Black Creek and now you ain't doin' it. You turn around and go that way and then I will."

"You're right, he lied about that, too," Trapper looks at me and says, still pissed that Bill hadn't stopped at Herman's.

"I done just what I said I wuz' gonna do from the start," Bill looks at Trapper and says, "so stop with the bitchin' and fuckin' complainin' and knock that shit off 'bout me lying. Anyway, ya two lil' fuckers made me a promise and I'm holding you to it, and if'n I'd of stopped back there, both of ya'll wuz all set to abandon ship. I wudn't borned yesterday! I saw through your lil' plot, which by the way, makes both of you liars in my fuckin' book!"

"That's just another lie you're telling, to prop up the ones you already told," Trapper says to him.

I don't say anything, I'm thinking of some way to get Bill to stop the car. We're on the straight away, just before the trestle on the railroad that runs into Black Creek to get the coal. It's the halfway mark if you're going from Black Creek to Pinson. We're three miles from home, about two if you walk down the railroad tracks.

The trestle or Truss Bridge as some folk call it is a large wooden contraption constructed out of huge creosoted logs, built to take the train rails up and over the highway. Just as you go through it, the road takes a sharp turn to the left. Dead man's Curve everyone calls it, because of all the car wrecks that have happened there. My Aunt

Mertie lives in the first house on the right, just after you go through. A lot of the accidents have been in her front yard.

"Stop down at the trestle and let me out," I tell Bill, confident I can get either my aunt or uncle to take me home.

Bill gives me no reply, just accelerates the speed of the car.

"You better slow down!" Trapper tells him. "You hit that trestle curve at this speed, you gonna kill us all."

"Two lil' chicken shits," Bill glances over at us and says, then speeds up some more.

But like Bill said, he wasn't borned yesterday,' so just before we get to the trestle, he slows and takes the curve at a normal speed, then accelerates again, completely ignoring my request for him to stop and let me out. I consider opening the door and jumping, but have enough sense to know that I'd probably break my neck, so I don't do it.

Bill's foot on the gas stays heavy as we zip along up the hills and through the hollows. A misty rain begins to fall again. Bill turns on the wipers with a curse. No one's talking, which seems to magnify the humming sound of the car wheels and the clacking sound of the wipers.

Trapper's staring straight ahead. Just after Bill called us chicken shits, he looked over at me and threw his hands up in the surrender sign. I think he's just waiting now to see what happens next. I hope he's thinking about some way to get Bill to stop so we can get the hell out of this car, because I think we're in real trouble.

We pass Jimmy's Gas and Groceries and approach the turnoff to a dirt road that would take us back to the Black Creek Nigger Quarters, if Bill was so inclined. I had completely forgotten about this road. I take a final shot.

"You can still go through Black Creek, if you take a right just up ahead," I tell him.

I waste my breath. His only reaction is to look at me and smirk as we fly pass the turnoff and to curse at the wipers again and again as we continue to follow the crooks and dips of the road that weaves its way around the base of Pinson Mountain. The Narrows turnoff is a mile or so ahead. If he passes that one up, I have no idea where we're headed.

We swing down into Pinson Valley, cross Turkey Creek Bridge and hit the big *S* curve that follows immediately. Bill takes it too fast and I feel the car fishtail, but then it regains its traction and we move on through the curve.

"Ain't we almost to that turnoff?" Bill asks Trapper, finally breaking his silence.

"Next road to the right," Trapper tells him and then asks, "What you gonna do if you can't get through that way?"

"Thet's fer me to worry 'bout," Bill tells him. Then out of the blue, he volunteers some information that we haven't heard before.

"Hey, ya might get to meet m'buddy!" he says.

"I thought you said he had to work today," Trapper inquires.

"Not that 'un, the other friend I wuz tellin' you 'bout," Bill clarifies, "him what helped that 'lil ol' boy.'"

I feel a cold chill ripple up my spine.

"Where we gonna meet him?" I quickly ask Bill.

He thinks for a minute, the screws turning in his head looking for the right answer.

"He said he might be out this way today," he tells me, flipping the wipers off, then on again, trying to appear nonchalant.

"He know your truck's stuck?" Trapper asks him.

"Ya'll really like him, he's a great guy," Bill goes on to say, ignoring Trapper's question.

"If he does, why ain't he helping you get it out?" Trapper continues to question him.

"Yeah, why's he coming out here?" I add to the interrogation.

Bill fools with the wiper switch again, this time leaving them off. Once again the rain has stopped. He slows the car—the Narrows cutoff is just ahead.

"This is it, ain't it?" He looks at Trapper and asks, still not answering our questions.

"Make your own decision, you ain't answering anything we ask you," Trapper tells him.

Bill makes the turn. The dirt and gravel road is narrow and rutted. The muddy rainwater that fills the ruts flows down towards us. About the first 100 feet of the road is uphill before it dips down into the gorge of the creek. Bill gears down to second and we begin our climb.

"Ya sure this is the right road?" Bill looks over at us and asks. "Seems like I remember it bein' a bigger damn road then this."

"That's why they call it the Narrows," Trapper tells him, then looks at me and grins.

"No shit," Bill says, as we slip, slide and spin our way up, this time with no advice from Trapper.

From the looks of the road we're the first car of the day, which proves to be fortunate for us, thus not having someone else's screw-ups to try to maneuver through. We make it to the top with a minimal amount of trouble, only having to use low gear once when dumbass lets the right back wheel slide into a shoulder ditch.

I thought he would stop at the top to brag about his accomplishment, but we continue on down the hill towards the creek. I'm still considering jumping out.

"Thet was a fuckin' snap" Bill says to us as we bounce down the water-soaked hillside.

"That was the best part of the road. Wait 'til you get up the hill just past the falls before you pat yourself on the back," Trapper tells him.

Bill fumbles in his bib pocket and pulls out his lighter and cigarettes, but when he fishes in the pack it's empty. "Fuck," he says, as he crumbles the empty pack and tosses it into the back of the car. He pats at his coat, then slides his hand into the inside pocket on the right and pulls out a fresh deck. He peels the cellophane wrapper from the top and opens the pack with his big, bucked teeth, taps one out and lights up.

Thought you were running low," Trapper comments.

"I am, I smoke about four packs of these fuckers a day and this is the last pack I got with me," Bill tells him.

We reach the bottom of the hill. The road almost levels as it follows the path of the creek through the narrow gorge with just a slight decline as it heads west, the direction in which we're headed.

It will stay like this for about another mile, until right before the falls, where at this point, it will be downhill again, still following the creek as it tumbles over a bed of limestone ever deeper into the gorge. That's where Bill's problem will begin. For just at the foot of the falls, a high north-south, ridge blocks the creek and turns its flow to the north. The road still continues to follow it, except now it's cut into the hillside, about halfway up the ridge. Getting up that hill with the road in this condition will be extremely difficult, if not impossible.

I nudge Trapper and say to Bill, "So if your friend's coming out here, why ain't he helping you?"

"Yeah, Bill, if you know he's coming out here, he must know your truck's stuck," Trapper adds.

Bill belches again and shakes his head as though he's trying to stay awake. "I need 'nother drank," he says as he reaches down and pulls his sack from the floorboard.

"Hold the wheel a minute and don't steer it off the fuckin' road," he says to Trapper.

Trapper grabs the steering knob with his left hand and sits up on the edge of the seat so he can see the road while Bill unscrews the lid off his jar. He takes a big gulp just as Trapper steers us into a big bump in the road, half of it runs off his chin and splatters on his overall bib and coat.

"Keep it in the fuckin' ruts," he yells at Trapper, then takes another big slug and belches.

"They ain't nothin' like good whiskey to clear the cobwebs," he says, taking a final draw off his cigarette before cracking the window to toss it out.

He puts the whiskey back in the sack, drops it in the floorboard and then takes back the wheel.

"We was talkin' about your friend," Trapper reminds him.

"Yeah, your friend," I say.

Bill shakes his head.

"Hell! I don't know what he knows or don't knows, he's a rich man. Rich men don't get trucks unstuck; theys pays somebody else to do it.

Best remember that when you meet him and go along with whatever he asks you and you could have a rewarding day."

"And what would that be?" Trapper asks.

"Probably one or both of us to suck his dick," I say to him, answering for Bill.

"Sorry, not one of my family traits, nor will it ever be," Trapper quotes, then turns towards me and we both break out laughing.

"Hey!" he goes on to say, "maybe Bill can do it while we're getting' the truck unstuck."

"Yeah! The rich guy can steer the car while Bill takes care of him, that'll leave both you and me to give directions," I add.

"On the blow job?"

"No, on gettin' the truck out, dummy."

We both continue to laugh.

"Hey, Bill, do rich guys steer cars?" Trapper asks.

Bill's pretending to ignore us, but the sneer on his lips lets me know, he's thinking of something to say to get us back.

"Ain't we almost down to them falls whir that big oyster-looking rock is?" He looks over at Trapper and asks with a big smirky grin on his face.

"I thought you knew your way around this neck of the woods," Trapper tells him.

"Went swimmin' there once, in thet big ol' pool by the rocks," Bill goes on to say, ignoring Trapper's sarcasm. "'bout a year or so ago, best I remember. Be a long time afore I ever fergit thet day."

I don't want to hear another one of Bill's stories so I halfway tune him out. We're approaching the falls, he's correct on that, and it's about time for him to take another piss. If he stops, I'm definitely out of here after hearing about his friend. I tune back in when I hear Trapper say, "Big deal, lots of people swim there. It's a great swimming hole."

"Yeah, but this wuz special," Bill goes on: "'Twas on a week day, real hot. I wuz motoring through here, had some brewskis in the car, so I thinks to myself, why not stop and go down there and set on that big ol' rock where it's cool and have a cold 'un. I'd bought 'em over at the Rock House and had 'em all iced down, you know. Anyways, 'tweren't nobody down there but me and I gotta tell you that water looked so good, the next thang I know'ed I wuz a strippin' off and divin' in."

"What's so special about that?" Trapper asks him. "Sounds like a normal thing to do to me."

"I'm 'bout to get to thet if'n you'll jist shut up and listen," Bill tells him, then continues… "Well, I'd only been in fer a few minutes when lo and behold, I heard some talkin' and I looked up and saw this couple, a man and a woman, a walkin' down towards me. Lord Almighty, she wuz the prettiest thang I ever laid my eyes on, before or since. Blond hair, great big blue eyes, had this lil' black bathing suit on that them big luscious tits of hers was 'bout to bust out of, and legs, Lord God, I didn't even know theys made 'em like that. Long and lean, all curvy like you know. I could see the outline of her pussy betwist 'em, her bathing suit was so tight. Ol' Bob got so excited he jumped plumb out of the water and slapped me in the face afore I got 'em under control. Man, what a sight she wuz."

"The crème de la crème," Trapper says to him.

I have to laugh.

"The what?" Bill asks.

"The very best there is," Trapper answers.

"You can fuckin' say that agin, the fuckin' very, very best," Bill tells him.

I'm listening to this bullshit story and I'm marveled at the way Bill has described the woman. I have a picture of her in my mind, I wait for him to continue.

"Enyhow," he goes on, "she spotted me right off and jumped in the water and headed right out m'way. Left the guy, who I later find out wuz her hubby astandin' up on the rocks with a quilt and a fuckin' basket in his hands. He was a roly-poly, lardass fucker, looked like a fuckin' dough ball."

Bill's descriptive talent is amazing. I know where the fucker's going and I know he's lying and I know I should call him on it now, but the pervert that I am is dying to hear the rest, so even though my blood is boiling, I continue to listen.

"Well I'm astandin' out there in 'bout waist deep water," Bill goes on. "She swum right up to me and said, 'Whatcha' doing?' I said, 'Well, I wuz a'coolin' off, and doing a pretty good job of it 'til I saw you, now I'm hotter than a fuckin' chili pepper.' She just giggled. 'I thought you might be fishing,' she said to me.

"'Naw,' I tell her, 'but afore you get in here too close, I gotta warn you, I ain't got no bathing suit on, I'm as naked as Adam on the first day, honey.'

"'Thet's what I wuz atalkin' 'bout, silly,' she says to me, "you know, atrollin' your worm!'

"She wuz cuter than shit when she said it, made me laugh. I told her, 'Honey, they's more then a worm hangin' 'tween these legs— more like a fuckin' cobra snake. You might wanna jist dip down there and check it out, and maybe make up with it a little bit for the insult afore it jists pops over there and gits you.'

"She laughed and winked at me and said, 'I love big ol' snakes and I know jist how to tame 'em down.'

"And then, by damn if she didn't jist fill up both them titties with a big ol' breath of air and disappear under that water like a fucking eel."

I've finally had it. This is disgusting, I refuse to listen to any more of Bill's make 'em up as you go stories.

"You're a goddamn liar," I say to him through gritted teeth.

If looks could kill, I'd be dead.

"Thet's the second time ya called me a liar today," Bill tells me, his eyes burning a hole in my face, "and yore definitely gonna pay for it. Believe me, ya 'lil' fucker!"

"You know where he's going with this, don't you?" I say to Trapper.

"Duh! I didn't just fall off the turnip truck yesterday," he tells me.

"I've had enough, too, Bill," Trapper looks at him and says.

"Come on! Yore missin' the best part," Bill says, with a shit-eating grin on his face.

He looks over at us suddenly, like it just dawned on him.

"Hey! I bet you guys know her. She lives over there in Black Creek.

Doncha wanna hear about how it felt when she sucked my dick? Well, I'll tell ya enyway. In thet cold water, it felt like ol' Bob wuz stuck up to the hilt in a hot watermelon, ya know, one thet's been laying out in the field all day, 'cept this 'un has a big ol' tongue thet rolled all around and little nippy teeth that like to tease and bite."

"We said that was enough," I say to Bill again.

But he pays no attention to me at all. He's having too much fun goading us, paying us back. He gives us a one-snorter and continues.

"Or maybe ya'd like to hear about how I horse-fucked her right there in the water 'til she was screamin' with delight, while that fuckin' milk toast husband of hers was alayin' up there on his tummy a browning his dough. About how ever' now un' then he'd holler down, 'Are you having a good time, honey?' or 'bout her hollering back, 'The best time of my life, sweety.'"

"We're at the falls," Trapper tells Bill. "Stop the car and let us out."

"Yeah, I see thet big ol' rock down there. Thet's where I fucked her. Finished off up her ass, which by the way she loved, if you're interested."

"Stop the car," I yell at Bill.

"So, I guess it do run in yore family to suck dicks," Bill says to Trapper, with a snort.

"Stop the car," I yell again.

"Fuck ya," Bill says to me.

I've got to make a decision, we're just at the cutoff to the parking area of the falls. If we don't make it up the hill, we can probably jump out and run. If we do, who knows? I decide not to take a chance.

I push Trapper aside and swing my fist at Bill's head as hard as I can, an old-fashioned roundhouse that catches him square on the nose. Blood flies everywhere. He's caught by surprise, can't believe he's been hit. He lets go of the steering wheel and clutches at his nose with both hands and screams in pain.

My intent is to force him to stop the car, but that's not what happens. The shock of the blow makes him forget he's even driving. All at once a current of fear invades my body; time seems almost to stop. Everything's happening in slow motion. I see Bill looking at the blood on his hands. I see him wipe at it as it drips off his chin and lands on his overalls and coat. I see the shock and surprise in his eyes turn to hate. I see his mouth open and hear the bellowing scream, "Ya god-damn dirty lil' fucker! I'll fuckin' kill ya!" he cries out.

I see him lunge in my direction.

I see Trapper grab the steering wheel and frantically stomp at Bill's feet trying to find the brake pedal. I see him knocked off the seat to the floorboard as Bill propels across him to get to me and as he falls, I see his hand continue to grasp the Ruby red steering knob.

I feel the car swerve sharply to the right, hit a bump and leave the road. I feel us airborne, we seem to float.

I feel two crashes almost simultaneously, the first when the wheels of the car come roaring back to earth and the second, when a back-handed swing from Bill detonates on the left side of my face. The blow is glancing, due to the lurch of the car, but still the force of it drives the right side of my head hard against the passenger door window. My head feels like it's exploding.

Oddly, time seems to normalize, but only for a few moments. I feel my face begin to swell, my head begin to throb and the speed of the car all at once and then time slows again.

I look at Bill and see the panic on his face as he tries to get the car under control, but he has no success. Trapper is blocking both the gas pedal and the brakes, still holding tightly to the red steering knob.

I see Bill hurdle towards me again, but this time he goes face down on the seat with his hands locked over the back of his head to protect himself.

I feel and hear another loud crash as the front wheels of the car hit something large and stationary. The right side of the car lurches up and spins to the left, we're airborne again. My head hits the wind-shield. I see trees and sky and then nothing...

A while later I hear the pitter, patter of rain. I hear voices and the sounds of a struggle. I try to focus on them, but they seem far away.

I'm wedged down between the front seat and the floorboard of the car. I grab at the seat and attempt to raise myself up. My head feels like a balloon. I'm dizzy, only half-conscious and don't make it on the first attempt. I fall back. I shake my head and open and close my eyes. My vision is blurred.

I feel at my face. It hurts like hell. As I pull my hands away, they feel wet and sticky. I bring them down close to my face. They're covered with blood. I feel at my face again. My left eye feels swollen and so does my nose. The left side of my mouth is busted open and my lips have swelled. My teeth hurt when I move my mouth. I touch my right ear and on around to the side of my head, where I feel a large knot. My ear feels swollen and hot, like it's on fire.

I hear voices again. It sounds like Bill and Trapper. Trapper screams something at Bill, then I hear a thud and the car shakes and then the voices stop.

I gather all my strength and pull myself up on the seat. I attempt to sit up, but my head is spinning, so I lay back down. I know we've wrecked the car and wonder how bad I'm hurt. I know I must have been knocked out. I remember us spinning out of control and hitting the trees. It doesn't seem very long ago, so I must have not been out for long. I wonder if I'm going to die like Bobby Ford did! I begin to tremble, I'm scared and cold. I begin to cry, but stop when snot begins to gather in my nose and I can't breathe. I attempt to clear it with my finger. It comes back bloody.

I sit up again. I'm not as dizzy. I look at the windshield. It's cracked on my side of the car. I feel my head and ear again as I look at the broken glass.

Outside, I see broken tree limbs lying across the hood of the car. I try to concentrate, to visualize what has happened.

When Bill knocked Trapper off the seat, Trapper was attempting to guide the car to a stop. As he fell he hung on to the steering knob, which pulled the steering wheel to the right. He must have fallen on the gas pedal, so we must have literally jumped the incline from the road down to the parking area. That's when I felt the first crash. Right before Bill hit me.

The parking area is just a clearing at the top of the hill, about 60 yards up from the creek. It's about 15 yards wide. We must have zoomed across it and hit something else, most probably one of the boulders along the hillside or more likely, the big one at the head of the trail down to the creek. That's when we went airborne again—up and over the small trees and shrubs that grow in profusion along the edge of the parking area, then, downward to a rest, amid the trees, vines and boulders that pocket the hillside.

I look to my right out the passenger door window. The car is turned almost parallel to the creek. It's wedged against the trunks of a group of mid-size oak trees that grow along the edge of a shelf, just above the trail that leads down to the creek. That's what stopped us, else we would have flipped. I look down through the branches of the trees to the foot of the hill and see the creek about 35 yards away. I watch it for a moment as it ripples downward over its terraced limestone bed before it turns north and pools in front of the big oyster-looking rock the size of a house.

I look to my left. The driver's door is standing open, but not all the way. Just enough for someone to squeeze out. I can see why. It's blocked by a heavy undergrowth of vines and shrubs. "Good thing we hit in the bushes," I think to myself. It's a lot better than landing on the rocks.

Suddenly, I feel sick to my stomach. My bowels begin to gurgle. A cold chill of fear knifes through my body again. I feel as though I'm going to throw up. I slide towards the open door, but stop when I hear the rustling of bushes and the unmistakable sounds of Bill.

The first thing I see is his brogan, as he kicks at the door in an effort to open it wider. The next thing I hear is his message.

"You better be dead in there ya lil' son of a bitch or ya gonna be the sorriest little motherfucker that ever lived."

The next thing I feel is warm and wet. I've pissed my pants.

Bill peers into the car. His hat is off his head. His hair is wet, sticking out in all directions. His eyes are opened wide, they look wild and crazy. Drops of water run down his face streaking blood where it has dried.

I slide quickly to the passenger door and try to push it open, but the oak trees are holding it tight. Fear and panic rip through my body like bolts of lighting. I'm trapped, there's no way out.

"You better leave me alone," I scream at Bill at the top of my lungs as he leans into the car and reaches for me. I try to hit him again, but he's already on me, grabbing my hair and dragging me across the seat face down. The nappy fabric of the seat digs into my face and tears at the open wounds. I feel lost and helpless.

Just as my head is out the door, Bill pivots to his left, clutches the seat of my pants and literally throws me over his shoulder out of the car. I land on my back in the undergrowth, the bushes failing to break my fall. The breath is knocked out of me. I struggle to breathe. Bill's on me before I can move.

I feel my slingshot being ripped from around my neck. "You ain't gonna need this peashooter no more," he says as he tosses it down the hill towards the creek. I see it hit a tree and fall into the bushes adjacent to the trail.

He flips me over face down, takes hold of my legs at the ankles, pulls them up and spreads them apart. He's holding me like I'm a wheelbarrow. I'm aware of everything he's doing, but my body is numb from fright.

"Better make me a wheel outta 'em hands or I'm gonna drag ya," he tells me, as he begins to push me forward.

He guides me towards the rear of the car. The rocks on the hillside cut into my hands, the bushes snag my clothes.

"Gitta up," he yells and begins to push me faster.

My arms fold under me, I can't keep up. He drops my legs. I roll into a fetal position and begin to cry. My brain feels scattered, one thought after another races through my mind, but the one that's clearest is that I'm probably going to die!

Bill grabs my legs again and turns me back on my stomach. I raise my head and look back at him over my shoulder. I try to tell him to please stop hurting me, but before I can get the words out, he straddles my body, falls to his knees, then lays flat. He presses his full body weight down on me and pushing his crotch hard against my rear. He brings his mouth to my ear and begins to lick it with his tongue. His weight is smothering me. I begin to squirm and gasp for breath again, which only entices him to press into me harder. I stop and lie still. The smell of him is sickening, I want to throw up, but haven't the breath to do it.

He grabs my hair and begins to lick at the side of my face, then back to my ear. I can feel, smell and hear his heavy breathing as he continues to push his crotch into my rear. He's becoming excited, I recognize the sounds. He stops licking and begins to whisper to me.

"Pissed yore pants, din't ya? Know what I'm gonna do? I'm gonna pull them lil' ol' britches off ya and I'm gonna stick ol' Bob right up that little tight ass of yores. Bet ya won't have no doubt about his size then, 'cause he's gonna feel real big. I'll bet ya might even like it, bet ya probably done it before. Like whin ya and yore lil' ol' buddy Trapper's out in the woods a beatin' off, nobody around. Bet ya'll played the ol' 'cornhole' game didn't ya? Ain't that right?"

His hand is still clutching my hair. He shakes my head up and down to indicate a yes.

"See there, I knew it," he whispers.

His breath is putrid and I begin to gag as he licks at my face again. My head is on fire from his tight grip in my hair, but I'm helpless and the gagging takes almost the last of my breath.

"I'll bet ya really like it, don't ya?" he continues to whisper, "Tell ol' Bill."

And, as before, he shakes my head up and down to indicate that he's right.

"Then," he whispers, "after I've torn ya a new asshole, I'm gonna let yore lil' ol' buddy, Trapper, suck yore shit off, clean ol' Bob up real good. That sound all right to ya?"

He shakes my head again.

At this point, my breath is almost gone. My consciousness begins to ebb away. I can hear the things he's saying, but they really don't register. The only thought in my mind is, *Please let me breathe,* and so with the last ounce of my breath I force it out between my lips. "Please, please, let me breathe!" I rasp.

I feel him shift his weight and I gasp for a token of air. He tightens his grip in my hair and begins to laugh.

"Ya think I give a shit ya can't breathe, ya lil' fucker? Ya outta thought of that before ya hit me in the fuckin' nose, God damn ya, afore ya caused me to wreck the fuckin' car. But don't worry, I ain't gonna let ya die. Both ya lil' fuckers're too important to me fer thet. Business afore pleasure. Ain't theat what they say?"

And with that, I feel him roll off my back.

I gasp for breath and feel the sweet air as it hits my lungs. I can't get it in fast enough. I strangle and begin to cough.

Bill's still holding my hair. He rolls me over to my back and pulls me up to a sitting position, then pulls me to my feet and begins to push me towards the back of the car.

My legs feel cold and numb, like the rest of my body. I'm scared beyond words. I start coughing again, I stumble and almost fall, but Bill's tight grip in my hair keeps me erect. He pushes me forward again and then pulls me to a stop. I lean against the fender of the car for support.

The trunk of the car is open. Inside is an old spare tire, a rusted-looking scissors jack and the burlap tow sack Bill had in the back of the car. They are all lying loose. I see no sign of the chain he supposedly had to pull his truck out. The sack has been opened. It's filled with rope and what looks like another tow shack that has been cut up into strips of various sizes.

I hear a grunting sound and look to my right. I see Trapper lying on the ground about fifteen feet away. He's been hog-tied and gagged with the same type of burlap strips that are in the bag. He also has a rope, with a one-loop noose, cinched tight around his neck. The opposite end of the rope is tied to the trunk of one of the larger oaks that grow along the shelf. Bill has left about three feet of rope between Trapper and the tree when he tied it off. Just enough to hang him, if for some reason he rolls off the ledge, I guess. Trapper's straining and thrashing around in an effort to free himself, which is pulling the noose even tighter. I can see a blood ring where the rope has chaffed his neck already, and I can see that he's having trouble breathing due to the gag tied in his mouth. He looks towards me pleadingly.

Bill still controls me by the hair, but he has no control over my recovered lungs.

"Can't you see he's choking to death?" I scream at him as I lunge forward, trying to pull away.

"Take that fucking gag outta his mouth!" I scream again.

Bill pulls back hard against my scalp. I feel his control, but oddly I'm still feeling no pain, still numbed with fright. *I have to get to Trapper* is all I'm thinking of. *Get the gag from his mouth, get him loose. How? How? How?*

I stop trying to pull away, turn and face Bill.

"Thought you weren't gonna kill us? Thought we was real impor-tant to you?" I say to him. "Well, looks like you gonna fuck up again, if you let him die, if you don't get that gag outta his mouth."

Bill grabs me by the seat of my pants and begins to push me forward.

"Ah, ain't that jist terrible," he tells me, as he throws me face-down on the ground next to Trapper.

A jagged tree limb cuts a gash in the palm of my left hand and another digs a furrow across my right cheek. I scramble towards Trapper, try to reach the gag, but I don't make it. Bill is still in control.

He grabs me by the legs again and drags me back towards the trunk of the car, laughing, giving me a two-snorter, funny to him that he played with me by letting me almost reach Trapper before he yanked me away. It infuriates me. I gather all my remaining strength and try to twist over on my back, kicking my legs as I do in an effort to break his hold. But Bill's too strong and I'm too tired and weak, so I give it up and just lay there and watch as he pulls a long piece of burlap from the trunk and begins to tie my legs together at the ankles.

"Yore lil' buddy's so scared, he pissed his pants," he hollers over to Trapper, "and, boy, do he stink!"

My legs are already numb, so there's hardly any feeling as he cinches them tightly together.

"Why are you tying us up?" I ask him as he reaches for another piece of burlap.

"Shut the fuck up," he tells me as he pulls my arms behind my back and ties them together at the wrists.

"Don't tie them so tight!" I scream at him as the burlap digs into my skin, which only makes him pull it tighter.

"Please don't gag me" I say to him, as he grabs another strip of burlap and begins to drag me over next to Trapper who is hardly struggling any longer. It's taking all his energy to breathe, and now that I'm up close to him I can see why.

His nose has been busted, either in the wreck, or by Bill's fist. Both nostrils are swollen and caked almost shut with dried blood and snot. This, plus the gag, is cutting the air flow to his lungs to a trickle.

His skin has a bluish cast to it and as he looks at me his eyes seem to be rolling up inside his head.

His clothes like mine are soaked. I know he's cold. I watch as he shivers and gasps for breath.

Bill has yet to gag or hog-tie me like Trapper, so I can still maneuver. I go for the gag again, this time attempting to grab it with my teeth, but a hard lick on the back of my head, courtesy of Bill stops me.

He pulls me away and draws back to hit me again. I twist away to take the blow on my back, but it doesn't come. I turn back towards him to see why, just in time to see him pull a yellow-handled knife from his coat pocket. I watch as he flicks it open with his thumb and bends toward Trapper.

"Don't hurt him!" I scream as loud as I can.

Bill turns and grabs me by the hair and presses the knife to my neck.

"Ya scream like theat one more time, ya lil' fucker, I'll cut yore fuckin' throat!"

I stay perfectly still, holding my breath—couldn't move if I wanted to. I'm literally scared stiff.

I try to keep my voice calm as I tell him, "If you do, then you'll be a murderer and if you let Trapper choke to death, you'll be a double-murderer.

I feel the sharp point of the knife pressing down on the soft skin of my throat. He tightens his grip in my hair as though he intends to rip it from my head, but he hesitates on cutting me. Instead he harks up a mouthful of phlegm from the back of his throat and spits it right into my face. The smell of it and the feel of it on my skin is more than my stomach can bear. I immediately begin to retch and puke.

Bill lets go my hair and jumps back, but not before the excrement from my stomach splatters across the top of his wet brogans.

"Ah shit! Goddamit, ya got thet shit all over m'shoes," he laments, as he rubs his feet in the wet vines and bushes in an attempt to clean off the vomit.

He grabs my hair again and pulls my head up, so I'm looking him straight in the eyes.

"Didn't like thet, did ya?" he says. "Well ya know what?" he goes on, getting right down in my face. "Thet's what ya lil' fuckers mean to me. Ya don't mean spit."

Vomit is still dripping from my mouth, off my chin, landing on the front of my wet jacket.

"I wuz gonna cut the gag outta yore lil' buddy's mouth afore you started yore fuckin' screamin', but no! You had to show yore' ass and start makin' a lot of noise din't ya?"

When I fail to answer, he shakes my head up and down as he had before to simulate a yes.

"See! Ya know ya done wrong and ya ain't gonna do it agin, are ya?"

This time I shake my head from side to side to indicate a no.

"That's the onliest smart decision ya made today," he tells me as he releases his grip in my hair.

"Now ya jist lay back down there and be real good un' if ya gotta puke agin, it better be real quiet and not fuckin' on me, else I'm really gonna lose m'temper and ya don't want that, do ya?"

I shake my head no and begin to cry, not from pain but from humiliation. My nose and mouth are clogged with dried blood and vomit. *If I live, he'll pay for this,* I think to myself over and over. *I've got to stay alive; I've got to get free.*

I watch him as he hovers over Trapper. He uses the knife to cut the gag from his mouth and his fingers to pull out another piece of burlap that was rolled up and stuck inside. I hadn't realized that a piece of the shit was in his mouth. No wonder he couldn't breathe.

Trapper breathes heavily and begins to cough as fresh air finally hits his lungs. Bill reaches behind his back and cuts the piece of burlap that has him hog-tied, allowing him to stretch out his legs, which he does immediately. I look in his eyes. He looks back at me. I know he's feeling better when I see him wink.

"Can you take that noose off his neck, too?" I plead to Bill, knowing I'm pushing my luck.

He rises to his feet and looks down at us, completely ignoring my request.

"Now here's the rules," he tells us.

"Both ya lil' fucker're gonna lay there real quiet. I've showed ya jist now that I kin be a real nice guy if'n ya jist cooperate. Now, I don't wanna hear a sound, no talkin' no coughin' un' 'specially no fuckin' screaming, got it?"

We both nod our heads yes.

"And, ya don't fuckin' move," he adds, as if we could get very far with our hands and feet tied.

"Good!" he says.

"Now, ol' Bill's gonna check out the car. See if'n we might kin get it out and back on the road, and for the sake of ya lil' fuckers' health, I hope we can."

We lie quietly and watch him as he walks away. He reaches down in the undergrowth, picks up his hat, shakes the water off it, and puts it on his head, then moves on around to the front of the car. I hear him swearing as he pulls at the bushes and small trees that are wedged against the front wheels. I lose sight of him as he bends down to survey the damage.

I look over at Trapper and whisper, "Are you OK?"

"Yeah, I think so," he whispers back. "Just my nose where he hit me, I think it's broke and my left arm hurts real bad. I couldn't breathe 'cause he had that piece of tow sack stuffed in my mouth. I thought I was gonna die. My neck hurts where this rope's cuttin' it. Does it look bad?"

"You got a blood necklace," I tell him.

"How about you?" he asks.

"I'm OK."

"Your face looks really bad. He must of really beat the shit outta you for hitting him in the nose. I couldn't believe it when you did it. You fuckin' really knocked the shit outta him."

"Listen," I say to him, "We're in real bad trouble. That pervert's gonna rape us for sure and then he's gonna kills us. We gotta figure some way to get loose and get away from him.

Trapper shakes his head. "No, he ain't gonna rape and kills us, not right off, or he says he ain't. He's gonna sell us first."

"Whatta you mean, sell us?"

"That's what he told me when he was tying me up. That story about having his truck stuck over at Big Rock is a whole lot of bullshit, Boogie. He conned us really good. The only reason he came out to Black Creek today was to look for young boys. He said he's done it before, at other places. He gets them for his queer buddy. He says his buddy pays him a lot of money for them. That's what he meant when he said we was gonna meet him."

"You gotta be shittin' me," I say.

"No! He's gonna sell us to him. His rich buddy, the one what helped the little boy." (nervous chuckle) "Bill brags about knowing this guy, how rich and important he is. Says he's meeting him out here on the creek. Bill gets the money, his buddy get us. Gonna take us down to Birmingham where he lives, Bill says."

As I listen to Trapper's story, the numbness I felt before begins to disappear. My head and face begin to hurt and I'm suddenly aware of every cut and bruise on my body. What's more, I'm soaking wet and cold and, worst of all, I smell like piss. I begin to shiver.

"I'm cold as hell, too," Trapper tells me, "and I'm really scared. Bill said that this guy will get tired of us after a week or so and that he'll give us back to him. Says he can't wait. Says you're gonna really pay then for hitting him in the nose. That's when we'll get killed. He'll rape us, then kill us."

"I told him he was gonna get put in jail and electrocuted for doing this, but he just laughed at me."

"We got to get away," I say to Trapper.

"How the hell we gonna do that?" he asks. "Bill's gone to fat, but he can still run faster than we can crawl. I guess you ain't noticed that I'm tied to a tree with a fuckin' noose around my neck."

"There's got to be a way," I say to him. "Let me think about it and you better be thinking about it, too."

"Duh! No shit," he says back to me.

I hear the rustle of bushes and see Bill rise back to his feet at the front of the car. I watch as he takes off his hat and shakes the water off again, then scratch at his head and put it back on. I hear him mumbling to himself, but can't quite make out what he's saying, although a few seconds later, I have no problem hearing the "goddamn it" that comes out of his lips as he slams the palm of his hand down hard against the hood of the car.

"It must be really bad," I think to myself.

He walks back to the driver's door and kicks it hard, forcing it open wider, then bends down and reaches inside. He comes back out with his sack of goodies, which apparently survived the crash.

He turns and starts to walk back towards us, then suddenly stops. He stands and listens for a moment then does a little hop and skip, then stops and listens again. He bends down and surveys the undergrowth around him, then kicks at it, listens, then kicks at it again, then shakes his head. He picks his way cautiously back to where we're lying on the ground, keeping his eyes directed sharply at his feet.

"Goddamn snakes ever' where 'round this fuckin' place," he informs us. "Think I jist saw 'un of the fuckers over there by the car. Fucker tried to bite me."

"Yeah, they love to eat big fat queers," Trapper replies. "Crawl right up inside them, eat their nuts first."

Bill looks at us and smirks, we watch with no further words, waiting for the retaliation. But it doesn't come. He just looks at us, deciding what to do next. I feel a strong need to piss.

He takes out his whiskey jar, drops the sack at our feet and holds the jar up to checks for quantity. It looks about a quarter full. Satisfied, he unscrews the lid, clears his throat and takes a huge swallow. I watch his Adams apple bounce up and down like a basketball as he swills it down his throat. He fishes the church key from his bib pocket, sits down between us, recaps the whiskey, digs the beer from the sack and slits the top. He starts to take a drink, but hesitates and rises back to his feet. He does a detail search of the ground where he was just sitting (I presume for snakes), then gives it an all clear and sits back down. I notice that he's becoming wobbly, unsteady in his step. I watch him for a few more minutes as he sits there, alternating between smoking, drinking and belching and then my eyes drift towards the sky.

No rain is falling but the wind seems to have picked up. As it whistles through the surrounding foliage, drops of water catch a ride and pelt at my body like tiny bombs. The sky is still gray, but lighter; especially towards the south. Upper winds are driving the darker clouds through the heavens fast and to the north. Snakeman said it was going to clear up. I think he's right.

I've lost track of time, but know it's got to be somewhere around three o'clock, although I was out for a while, so it could be later. I start to feel sleepy.

I hear the water dripping off the trees and the sound of the creek as it rushes down the falls. I hear the far-off cawing of a crow and the sounds of Bill swallowing and belching as he finishes off the booze.

He's sitting with his back to us, just at our feet. I watch as he drinks the last of his whiskey, shaking the jar over his open mouth to get the very last drop, then chase it with the last of the beer. The wind is blowing his long hair that's hanging from underneath his hat back and forth across the shoulders of his wet suit coat. He tosses the beer can on the ground, picks up the jar and stands up. He staggers slightly to his right, then holds out his arms for balance. "Whee! That shit do have a kick," he says with a snort. He walks in between us, to the edge of the ledge behind us. We follow him with our eyes. He uncaps the jar and shakes it over his mouth again, hoping for another drop; then recaps it and slings it down towards the creek. I hear it break on the rocks below. He walks back over, checks the ground again and sits back down.

I look at Trapper questionably? He shrugs his shoulders.

Bill takes off his hat and runs his fingers through his hair, rubs at his eyes and then begins to talk.

"OK! Here's the way 'tis, so listen the fuck up. Thanks to Mr. Boogiemen, we gonna hafta do some walkin', thet car ain't going fuckin' nowhere; axel's broke and two tires'r busted, radiator's all fucked up. Thet fucker's junk-yard bound, so let me brang ya up-to-date on the sit-ze-ation.

"As I told Mr. Trapperman here, before we gonna meet up with m'buddy. He jist loves young boys like ya two lil' fuckers here and he's in the need to replenish his supply. What's more, he's got the money and he'll pay real good for 'em. Onliest thang is, he don't like em if they're all marked-up, wants 'em all nice and purty. I've learn't that from some of the other lil' fuckers I've brought 'em. Hardly made nothing on 'em, for my time. But, if they're nice and purty, he'll pay top dollar. Now, I can explain them few lil' scratches ya got right now. I think he'll be OK with thet, 'specially when I tell him how ya made me wreck the car. He's gonna 'preciate the fact that yore a lil' on the wild side. He likes lil' tigers in his bed, likes to tame 'em. I've seen 'em afterwards, din't hardly recognize the lil' fuckers.

"Now, if'n I was you, I wouldn't get all happy 'bout this, start acting all up again, athinkin' ol' Bill's hands are tied—a'thinkin' he can't afford to put no more marks on us so we'll jist give him a hard time and he won't do nothing about it. Yeh, if'n I's you, I wouldn't thank thet 'cause, ya know why?"

He's holding the empty beer can in his right hand and for effect makes a production out of crushing it flat. He does it effortlessly, then rises to his feet and turns to face us.

"'Cause you know why?" he asks us again, looking all wild and crazy-eyes and then throwing the crushed beer can right between our heads into the bushes.

We both flinch back, then continue to stare at him, neither saying a word.

"'Cause my buddy alluz tells me, 'Bill, if ya can't brang 'em to me nice and purty, then jist kill 'em, save both us'n some time.' Thet's what he alluz tells me, and oh, by the way," he says, reaching into his side coat pocket and extracting a small shiny object, "did I ever show you lil' fuckers my gun?"

So that's what the bulge in his pocket was, I think to myself.

It's a nickel-finished Colt, a .38 caliber Detective Special, with a two-inch barrel, a snub-nose—one of the older models, with the squared butt configuration and the wooden handles—a "belly gun," they call it in the movies. I recognize it immediately. My Uncle Coy has one just like it. He's let me shoot it lots of times on Sunday afternoons down on the creek behind our house. He's told me lots of things about it. "Good up close, but after about thirty feet, forget it for accuracy, which has proven to be true the times I've shot it. It's a small gun, hardly visible in Bill's big hand, but it packs a big wallop if someone's lucky enough to hit you, which by the way is very possible, since it holds six bullets and very probably if the person you're shooting at is tied hand and foot.

"Snub nose .38," Bills tells us, as he holds it out for us to see. "Blow a fuckin' hole in ya the size of m'fist," he goes on to say. "So if there's any trouble, know what? I'm just gonna put it right up to yore lil' fuckin' heads and pull the trigger. Blow yore fuckin' brains out, leave ya for the damn buzzards. So both a'ya better keep thet in mind, understand?"

I understand we're probably as good as dead, I think to myself.

Bill goes on, "Now, as I said we's gonna do some walkin', a lil' piece down the creek. M'buddy's gonna be there with his car. It's not far, we kin walk it easy."

"How we gonna walk if we're all tied up?" I ask, breaking Bill's rule of silence. I know I've gone too far by the way he turns and looks at me.

Instead of answering my question, he moves beside me and squats back down on the ground facing me. He reaches out and puts the barrel of the pistol right between my eyes. I try to shy away but he grabs my hair again and holds me tight.

"Thought I told ya to be fuckin' quiet?" he says to me, getting right up in my face. "Maybe I jist orta' shoot ya now, shut yore lil' smart Alec mouth up once and for all. That's what I'm fuckin' tempted to do."

I close my eyes and hold my breath, certain he's going to shoot me, certain that I'm about to die. I feel the pressure of the gun barrel as he grinds it into my forehead. *Please God, don't let me die like this,* I think to myself. I tremble and wait, but no shot comes.

It feels like forever, but I'm sure it's only moments later that I feel the pressure of the gun lifted from my head.

"Naw, you ain't gettin' off that easy," he tells me. Yore little ass is gonna suffer 'fore ya die. I'm gonna personally see to that.

I open my eyes and look at him. He's got that "I wanna hurt you bad and I got the power to do it" smirk on his face.

He pulls my hair tighter, lowers the pistol and drops it back inside his coat pocket, then replaces it with the beer opener, which he fishes from his overall bib. I watch as he twirls it in his fingers.

"Come on, Bill! Leave him alone," I hear Trapper cry out. "We can't do nothing. We're gonna do ever' thing you say. You don't need to hurt us no more."

"Shut yore fuckin' mouth or I'll be on yore ass, too," he tells Trapper, as he pulls my head closer and slides the sharp point of the opener between my lips.

"How 'bout if'n I jist pull me a tooth, smart guy?" he says to me, wedging the rim catcher of the opener under my front teeth.

The very thought of it panics me and I try hard again to pull away. Bolts of pain rip through my head from his grip in my hair. My busted mouth and nose start to throb and begin to bleed again. I'm power-less. I feel pressure on my teeth and the sharp point of the opener as it bites into my upper gum.

"Your queer buddy ain't gonna like it if you mess up his mouth any more," I hear Trapper yell at Bill.

I cringe at what Trapper has implied, but his words have an immediate effect, for as soon as he says them Bill releases my hair and pulls the opener out of my mouth. But my reprieve is short lived, for in the next instant he grabs my hair again, presses the sharp point of the opener just under my bottom lip and with a flick of his hand cuts me deep.

I scream as I see the blood run off my chin and splatter down the front of my jacket.

"Shut the fuck up or I'll cut ya agin," he tells me, holding the opener back up to my face and tightening his grip in my hair.

Trapper lunges towards us, but the rope around his neck holds him back. "Come on, Bill," he pleads. "Leave him alone, you've paid him back already. OK? Please don't cut him again. We've promised not to give you no more trouble."

"You say 'nother word, you're gonna git worse than this," he hollers back to Trapper. Enyways, it's just a lil' ol'cut. Probably leave a scar, but chances are, he ain't gonna live long enough to worry 'bout it.

He thinks this is funny and laughs a two-snorter, releases my hair and rises to his feet, then all of a sudden he ducks back down again.

We all hear it at the same time—the sound of a car. It has a bad muffler, I hear it backfire as it slows down and I hear the crunch of gravel as it turns off the road into the parking area above us. The driver has the radio up real loud. Ernest Tubb, belting out *Filipino Baby* floats on the wind. My spirits begin to rise, but only for a moment.

Bill pulls the gun back out of his coat pocket and points it at us. "Ya make one sound and ya die," he whispers.

He scoots quickly to Trapper, changes the gun for his knife and cuts the burlap binding off his legs. He unties the rope from the tree, wraps it firmly around his hand, then moves to me. He cuts my legs free, drops the knife back in his pocket and grabs me by the hair again.

"OK, both of ya, up and in the trunk, and remember, one sound and I'll kill ya. That fucker in that car kin't see us. We're too far down the side of the hill, but if he hears enythang, he might get nosey and head down this way. He does, I most likely will have ta shoot 'im. Hell! I might do it enyways and take the car. This could be a lucky break, save us from walkin'. On the other hand, theys could be more thin one in thet car and I might kin't do nothin', so git in there so I kin go check it out, and remember, ya make a lot of noise, ya might cause folks to die."

We climb into the trunk, Trapper first and then me. We lie down flat and watch Bill as he wets his hands from the rainwater accumulated on the car and wipes at his face, then dries it with his coat sleeve—trying to clean up, so as not to arouse suspicion. He adjusts his coat, straightens his hat, lights up a Camel and closes the trunk.

It's dark and cramped and everything smells wet. My head is resting on the dead spare and the rusted jack is cutting into my legs. I feel Trapper squirming behind me.

"Can you move forward some?" he whispers, "I can hardly breathe back here. This rope is choking the shit outta me."

"I'm up as far as I can go," I tell him as I try to adjust myself forward a little more.

"My hands have gone numb," he says.

"So are mine," I reply.

"At least it's warmer in here than outside," he continues to go on.

"Duh! No shit," I mutter, but loud enough for him to hear it.

"How's the cut under your lip?" he asks.

"It's still bleeding," I say.

"Does it hurt?"

"Yes, it hurts."

"Well, if you think about it, it's better than having your teeth broke out."

No shit, I think to myself, but make no comment. *I just wish Trapper would stop talking so I can think. I'm cold, wet and scared and I don't want to talk. I just want to concentrate on finding a way to get us away from Bill; to get us free, but he continues to yak.*

"Good thing I thought about that mouth thing," he says, then chuckles, "or I know what you'd be asking for, for Christmas. And did you notice that he didn't even get upset when I called his buddy a queer?"

That's because he was too busy hurting me, you dumb shit, I think to myself, but once again remain silent, hoping he'll shut up.

"Yeah, good thing I'm a fast thinker. You got what I meant, didn't you? About the mouth? I mean, you know what queers want you to do? Bill sure did! Got that beer opener right out of your mouth soon as I said it. Wish he hadn't cut you though."

I cringe at the thought of it and what's going to happen to us. I wish Trapper would knock it off. He always talks a lot, but when he's really scared, you can't shut him up.

"You sure you're OK?" he asks.

"I told you I'm OK. We just gotta get away."

"You're not talking much."

"You're talking *too* much," I tell him. "Anyway we need to be quiet, listen for gunshots. He's probably gonna shoot whoever's in that car."

"Duh! He's probably gonna shoot 'em, whether we listen or not, dumbo."

Trapper's right, but I continue to listen. I wonder if we can hear a pistol shot from inside the trunk?

"I got it all figured out," he goes on, "how we're gonna get away, I mean."

"And how's that?" I ask, amazed that he may have thought of something I haven't.

"Simple," he says. "We're gonna run! Our legs ain't tied no more if you haven't noticed, so when he opens the trunk to let us out, we make a run for it."

"Great plan!" I tell him. "We try to run and he shoots us both dead. Are you nuts?"

"Yeah! Well, we're dead anyway if we don't do something, so I say we chance it. Maybe at least one of us can get away. He probably won't shoot us 'cause he wants that money too bad and we ain't worth nothin' to him dead."

"So, we just get out of the trunk and start running," I say. "with our hands tied behind our backs, up and down the hills and the rocks, and probably through the water. What if we fall? We'll break our necks. Anyway, I'm ripped and cut all over and weak from vomiting. I'm not sure I can run. Have you thought about that?"

"Yeah, I know. I hurt real bad, too, but I don't see any other way. This may be our only chance. I say we take it."

"I don't know," I say. "Shut up and let me think."

"You better think fast. He could be back any minute. Might even be standing out there right now listening to us. You sure you're all right? I can feel you shaking and, boy, do you smell like piss."

The thought of Bill coming back is running chills up my back. Trapper's right, he could be standing by the car right now, but even if he is, I don't think he can hear us whispering. He's also right that unless we do something, we're as good as dead. Oh God! Why did I get myself in this mess? Why didn't I just tell him to fuck off when he first told us that bogus story about his truck? Why do I do these dumb things?

"If we do it, we'll have to create some kind of a diversion," I whisper to Trapper. "He'll have that pistol on us all the time we're getting out of the trunk. He's no dummy. He'll know we might try to run. He'll shoot us if he has to. He knows he's fucked if we get away."

"Plus drunks do crazy things," he adds, "and he's drunk. Did you notice how he's wobblin' and swayin'?"

"That could be an advantage to us," I tell him.

"Think he'll tie our legs again before he gets us out of the trunk?" he whispers.

"I don't think so. He'd have to put his gun up. He can't tie us with one hand. Anyway, he said we was gonna have to walk."

"Not if he kills whoever's drivin' that car," he reminds me.

"We'll still have to walk up to the car, so I'm betting he won't tie us up right away," I say, hoping I'm right.

I can feel Trapper wiggling about.

"Wish I could get my hands untied," he says, "but I can't get 'em loose."

"He's got us tied good," I say. Remember, he's had plenty of practice. Ain't that what he told you?"

"Well, he brought enough rope and stuff to do the job."

"Where is it?" I ask.

"I'm laying on it" Trapper says.

We both lay quiet for what seems like a long time, but I'm sure it's only minutes. It starts to rain again and I begin to feel sleepy as I listen to the sound of it beats down upon the car.

Suddenly I hear another sound, but before my mind can register that it's the turning of the trunk handle, the trunk is already open and

I feel the rain upon my face. I look up, I see the bulk of Bill towering over us, pistol in hand. My heart sinks. We've waited too long. We don't have a plan.

"Now ain't that a purty sight," he says, two little assholes alayin' jist like I left 'em."

"Betcha been a hatchin' up all kinda schemes, ain't ya. Figurin' how to git away from Ol' Bill. Bet ya have, ain't ya?"

He's taunting us, wearing that shit-eating grin on his face and waving his pistol around. Not only that, but somewhere along the line, he's scored another beer. A Pabst Blue Ribbon that he's sipping while he talks.

"Well, if'n ya have, ya kin forgit it, 'cause 'tain't gonna happen. Yore lil' asses belong to Ol' Bill and it's gonna stay thet way!"

"Can we get out of this trunk now?" Trapper asks him. "I'm smotherin' in here."

Bill takes a sip of his beer and leers down at us. "Ya git out when I say ya kin git out. Now, ya jist lay there nice un' quiet 'til I hear thet car crank up and drive off, then we's gonna head outta here ourselfs."

He's no more than said this when I hear the roar of a motor and the sound of crunching gravel as the car pulls out on the road. The radio is still turned up high and as the car pulls away, my dream of help flies away with Roy Acuff, on the wings of that *Great Speckled Bird*. As the sound of his voice fades into the distance, tears begin to roll from my eyes. They mix with the falling rain and they sting as they seep into the wounds on my face.

Bill is still talking, but I've tuned him out. *Please, please God help us*, I concentrate as hard as I can. *Please, please, please, just make him go away.* I bow my head and close my eyes, but when I open them and look up, he's still there.

"OK, looks like 'em fuckers 'r gone," he's telling us as he finishes off the beer and slings the can down the hill. "Now here's what we's gonna do.

"First we gonna git you lil' crybabies outta the trunk and then we's gonna take a nice lil' stroll down the creek to whir' my buddy is."

"Thought you was gonna get that car so we wouldn't have to walk," Trapper chides him.

"Naw, I said I might git it, Mr. Smartass," Bill retaliates. "Anyway, 'tain't none a yore concern, so keep yore fuckin' mouth shut and listen."

He reaches in the trunk with his free hand and grabs a handful of my hair again. My scalp is sore, I wince with pain and I wish I had listened to my dad and had my head buzzed.

"OK, Mr. Boogieman, jist roll them legs out real gentle like and stand up real still. And you," he says, pointing the gun at Trapper, "ya stay right whir ya be."

My legs feel rubbery and weak and as I attempt to stand, my head begins to spin.

"Stand the fuck up straight," Bill hollers, as he yanks me upright.

"What did you do, chicken out?" Trapper yells out to him and then adds a zinger. "Musta been growups in that car!"

"Jist keep on and you gonna git a dose of what yore lil' buddy here's already has," Bill tells him. "I been easy on ya so far, but that's gonna change real quick, ya keep runnin' yore mouth.

"Anyway, for yore information, tweren't nothing but three fuckin' hillbilly rednecks, in a ol' piece of shit '39 Buick that looked worse than this wreck here. Had a big ol' fat whore with no fuckin' teeth with 'em. She was passed out!

"Said they just stopped to take a piss and to drink another beer. Hell, they were already half-drunk.

"Crazy fuckers had a twelve-gauge shotgun propped up in the front seat between 'em and a big ol' huntin' knife alayin' on the dash.

"They wuz a heading over to Crosston 'til I told 'em the road was washed out un' they wouldn't git through.

"I told 'em me un' a buddy wuz running some 'trotlines' we set out last night for cats and soon's we wuz through, we wuz gittin' the hell out of here ourselfs.

"They asked me if I wanted to fuck that ol' fat gal, said she had some really good pussy. Told 'em if they didn't mind I jist settle for a beer. Dumb fuckers give me two. Soon as I finished off the first one, they decided to head back out the way they come in. Jist as well, 'cause ain't no ways I wuz gonna mess around with a bunch of Rednecks with a fuckin' shotgun—my momma din't raise no fool. Anyway, them fuckin' hillbillies weren't worth wastin' bullets on.

"That ol' car did have a good fuckin' radio though," he adds.

He tightens his grip in my hair and bends to look into the trunk.

"Whur's that tow sack?" he asks, then apparently sees it protruding from under Trapper's legs. "Shift back off thet sack," he tells Trapper, as he drops the pistol into his coat pocket, then reaches in and yanks the sack free. He opens it up and pulls out a long piece of rope. It's identical to the one around Trapper's neck, noose and all.

"Made these 'specially for ya, jist in case I gotta hang ya" he says to me, giving me a one-snorter.

"Remember what I told you about m'buddy, about him saying to jist kill you if somethin' goes wrong? Well, what he really said was to hang ya', not shoot ya. 'Course I may hafta do both, you keep fuckin' with me."

Bill's wobbly and beginning to slur his words. Not only is he securing me by holding my hair, he's also using his grip on me to maintain his balance. He also isn't shutting up. Those last two Blue Ribbons have given him "diarrhea of the mouth," so I have no alternative other than to listen as he continues to enlighten us with a character study of the "good ol' buddy," the one he's gonna sell us to, somewhere down the creek.

"Now, I wouldn't want him ta know I said this," Bill goes on, "but he's one mean, crazy bastard, a cold fucker!

"College educated, too! Would ya believe it? Went down there to Tulane. Made hisself a big fancy lawyer. He's richer then shit. Got a big ol' house over in Mountain Brooke where all 'em fancy folks live and a great big farm up in Walker County, which I'm shore ya'll gonna git to see."

This last statement strikes him funny, he pauses for a one-snorter and then continues.

"Yeah, he's bout the craziest fucker I ever seen, but hell! What else kin ya expect, him bein' from Mississippi un' all!"

He stops for another one-snorter, tosses the rope over his shoulder then reaches back and grabs the seat of my pants and pushes me firmly against the car. He tilts me inside the open trunk, right over Trapper.

"He jist loves to fuck lil' white boys," he says in a whispery tone as he massages my ass.

"You fuckin' queer!" Trapper says to him.

He gives us a snorter and goes on.

"Won't fuck no nigger kid 'tall! Hates fucking niggers. Said his daddy wuz a 'Klucker,' wouldn't be surprised if he ain't one hisself. Never knowed no white man from Mississippi thet wudn't."

Another pause for another snorter and, he finally lets go my ass as he continues to talk.

"Said his daddy use ta hang lots of niggers. Said he alluz used a fifteen-foot rope, rigged up like these here."

He takes the rope off his shoulder and waves it between us, then chuckles.

"Yep! Rigged up jist like his daddy's."

"Told him I wouldn't need 'em, but he insisted I brang 'em. Now's looks like they's gonna come in handy gittin' you lil' fuckers down the creek.

"Yeah, he's a crazy fucker. A lot like his daddy, 'cept 'tain't niggers he likes ta hang, it's lil' white boys.

At this point and with this statement, I begin to shiver, which produces another loud donkey laugh from him and encourages him to further expound on our fate.

"That's what he does when he gits tired of 'em," he says. "Hangs 'em and gits one last fuck up their asses while they're chokin' ta death. Says thet's the best fuck of all. Usually does it in thet big ol' barn up on his farm.

"Course, sometimes he gives 'em to me, when they're special to me, like you two are. Glad I got these ropes now, 'cause I'm really gonna enjoy using 'em.

Bill's really enjoying telling his gory story. Loving the fact that he has us totally dominated, that there's nothing we can do.

He releases my hair and slides the noose around my neck.

"Hey, how 'bout that!" He says. "It's a perfect fit!"

He pulls the rope tight. I choke and gag.

That's what it's gonna feel like when I hang ya, 'cept a lot worse," he says, with a smirk and then a chuckle.

I know if I beg him to loosen it, he'll only pull it tighter, so I don't say a thing and when I don't, just like I'd hoped he'd do, he pulls the noose a tad looser.

"But thet's a pleasure I'm gonna enjoy later," he says. "Right now I gotta rigs you boys up for thet stroll down the creek."

Holding my rope tight, he reaches inside the open trunk and grabs the rope attached to Trapper. "OK, Mr. Trapperman, roll out real slow, and ya make one false move, yore dead," he tells him.

The rope has been on my neck less than two minutes, but I can already feel it cutting into my skin. I wonder how Trapper has been able to endure it? Plus there's not a place on my body that doesn't itch—it started the minute he tied my hands. The only time I forget it is when he's actually hurting me. I'm cut, banged and bruised, but the itch is the worst of the lot.

He leads us back to the same spot where he tied Trapper before, pulls the two ropes together and ties them to the same tree.

"Sit the fuck down and don't make a sound," he tells us. "It's time for a piss, a Camel and some serious thankin' and I wants it real quiet while I do it."

We sprawl on the ground and watch as Bill opens his fly, pulls out his dick and lets go a torrential yellow stream right at our feet, all the while pulling a bent-up Camel from his pack, then flipping his Zippo to light it up. He closes his eyes and sucks his lungs full of smoke then exhales it through an oval mouth, tapping gently at the side of his cheek in an effort to produce smoke rings. He has no care whatsoever that his putrid piss is splattering over our shoes and pants, nor the fact that his effort to produce a ring is foiled immediately by the gusting wind. Eyes still closed, he sways to and fro on unsteady feet as he drains his bladder down to the last dribble, then shaking his dick, more than once, and, with some regret, clearly obvious by the contented smile on his face, folds it back into his fly and closes it up. He takes another big drag off the Camel, hikes his leg and farts, then belches and sighs. It's totally disgusting.

Upon our knees now to escape the pooling piss, we watch as he strolls back to the car and fetches the burlap bag, then returns and drops it square in the middle of the foaming froth.

He looks at us indignantly, then after taking a final drag off his cigarette, he flips it directly towards us. We duck away as the amber sparks rain down on our bodies.

"OK, on yore feet," he tells us, breaking the silence, "we gotta get the fuck goin."

We rise to our feet, apprehensive of what's to happen. Trapper begins to babble.

"We can't walk down that creek with our hands tied," he says to Bill. "We'll fall and break our necks. There's hardly any trail at all down that way. Lots of big rocks to climb over and some places we'll have to wade, 'cause they ain't no bank to walk on. There's high cliffs and the creek comes right up to them. There's vines and bushes and…"

"Shut the fuck up!" Bill screams at him, but he babbles on.

"I just thought you outta know, and it's real snaky too. Cottonmouths! And they'll be all stirred up because of the rain!"

Trapper's really getting to him and I can see he's gonna pay for it. Bill's glaring at him, clinching and unclinching his jaws, breathing really hard, and then, so fast I don't even see it coming, he grabs Trapper by the hair and crotch, lifts him up as high as he can, until the rope around his neck goes taunt, then brings him crashing back down on his feet. Trapper screams as his legs fold under him. He falls to the ground and begins to cry.

"Get your ass back up," Bill screams at him again.

Trapper's in pain, he makes no effort to rise. "I hope you're happy, you fucking pervert," he screams at Bill, taunting him once more. "You've really hurt my legs, I probably can't walk at all now."

Bill grabs his hair and begins to pull him to his feet. Trapper winches in pain. "You can't walk, you gonna die right here," Bill tells him. "Now shut the fuck up."

All through the affray, I remain quiet, wishing I could help but knowing there's nothing I can do. Bill lets go of Trapper's hair, digs out another Camel and lights it up, then blows the smoke right into Trapper's face. He's had way too much to drink and he's starting to realize it. He takes several deep breaths and looks all around, then turns back towards us.

"Hell! I was walkin' down cricks when ya was still 'shitten yellow,'" he tells Trapper. "Ya think a few lil' ol'snakes scare me?"

My ears perk up! So Bill has a weakness, I think to myself. I look over at Trapper. I can tell that he's thinking the same thing. He gives me a wink and then, despite the situation, I have to smile.

Bill "hot boxes" his cigarette and flips it away, then reaches down into the sack and pulls out a handful of the burlap strips. He sorts out four of the longest ones and drops the rest on the ground. He lays the four strips he has selected across his left shoulder and pulls out his yellow-handled knife.

"Turn the fuck 'round," he tells Trapper, positioning him as he turns so he can keep an eye on me.

"Sit!" he tells me, "and no fuckin' advice or I'll cut his fuckin' throat."

"Sure," I say to him and proceed to kneel on the ground, but just as I do, I suddenly jump up again, so fast I almost lose my balance. I look down at my feet, then sort of dance around, kick at the under-growth and pretend to listen.

"What the hell ya doin'?" Bill wants to know, looking around on the ground himself.

"Nothing, just thought I heard something crawling around in the bushes," I tell him. "Hold it! There it is again," I tell him, looking down towards where he's standing.

He jumps and hops back a step, surveying the ground at his feet, a look of apprehension on his face.

"What did it sound like, Boogie?" Trapper asks me in a panicky tone.

"Shut yore fuckin' mouth," Bill screams at him, poking his finger right up in his face.

"I don't know," I say, pretending Bill's not even there. "Just something slithered in the bushes and sorta hissed. Probably wasn't nothing but the wind. Can't never tell over here, 'cause this place is haunted."

Bill's recovered enough to be curious. "What the hell's that supposed ta mean?" he looks over at me and asks, still pointing his finger at Trapper's face, daring him to say a word.

"That's the reason I didn't wanna come this way," I tell him.

"Who gives a shit about thet? Whatta ya mean 'bout bein' haunted?" he barks back at me.

"Everybody knows it, that's lived around here any time—all kinds of weird shit happening to people over here. They say it all caused by him. I guess you ain't noticed nobody lives over here. Wonder why?"

"Set your ass back down," he tells me, pointing the knife blade towards my face.

I check the ground at my feet again, kick around a few times, then slowly sit back down. *You asshole,* I think to myself, *I may not be able to hurt you, but I can sure torment the shit out of you.* It's all I can do to keep a straight face. I feel my balls begin to grow.

"Now, jist who the hell is 'him' supposed ta be?" he looks down at me and asks.

I hesitate a few moments before I answer, trying to remember some of the scary tales my Granny has told me about this place, along with some scary stories that I have read. *Sleepy Hollow* jumps to my mind.

"Most folks say it's a 'headless horseman,' I tell Bill, but others say it's a bloody skeleton that flies through the air. It changes forms. Sometimes it's a black panther that cries like a baby and other times, it's a gigantic man-eating snake. You just never know."

Bill has stopped pointing at Trapper and has drifted closer, looking at me, a sly grin on his blood-streaked face. He senses what I'm up to and he's enjoying it.

"Ya think I believe eny a thet Redneck superstitious crap, yore outta yore fuckin' mind," Bill says to me, as he grabs Trapper and jerks him back towards him. "Keep yore ass turned 'round like I told ya," he says to Trapper. "Now, raise yore arms up."

I'm kind of bumfuzzled, I really don't know what Bill's up to. I stay quiet and watch.

He wedges the knife blade against the bindings and cuts them from Trapper's wrists. Trapper immediately bends down and begins to rub at the calf of his right leg, only to be roughly pulled up again. "Stay still and turn 'round facin' me and hold yore arms straight out," Bill tells him, while all the time grabbing his shoulders and forcing him around himself.

I watch Bill very closely. I want to see everything he does and, also, the order in which he does it.

He takes one of the burlap strips from his shoulder and wraps it several times around Trapper's right wrist, then ties it off tight, leaving a tail of about ten inches dangling. Using a second strip of burlap, he duplicates the process on the left wrist, then takes the dangling ends and ties them together, leaving a gap of about six inches between Trapper's hands.

Trapper's sermon to Bill about walking down the creek may not have penetrated his pickled brain, but it seems to have sparked a tinge of common sense.

"Now, you lil' crybaby, if ya fall ya kin catch yore lil' ass 'fore ya break yore fuckin' neck," he tells Trapper, "and ya' better damn well not make me sorry I done this. Now set yore ass the fuck down."

Trapper doesn't reply, just kneels and then sits.

Bill moves over to me. Without waiting to be told, I stand, turn my back to him and raise my arms. I feel the pressure of the knife blade as it slices through my bindings and then the wonderful feeling of relief as my hands are finally free. I want to rub them and shake them to stimulate the feeling back, but Bill pulls me toughly around, giving me the same orders he gave Trapper. "Hold yore arms straight out."

This is the moment I've been waiting for. My hands and legs are now free. The only thing restraining me is the noose around my neck. My balls are now the size of baseballs. This is probably my last chance. It's now or never!

I scream as loud as I can and point to the ground. "Watch it, Bill, there's a fucking snake!"

He literally does a pirouette, actually turns in the air and when he hits the ground, the snake strikes—a snake called Trapper. It's coiled tightly around Bill's leg, sinking its fangs deeply into his calf, right through his 401 denim overalls.

Bill screams in panic, he thinks it's really a snake and then screams again when he realizes what's happening, this time in sheer anger.

He grabs Trapper's hair and tries to pull him from his leg, grabs at the rope around his neck and tries to choke him, but Trapper is locked tight both in teeth and body, intertwined in the rope, so all Bill's pulling is for nil. Bill does a curtsy to his left, grasps Trapper's jacket and pulls him up off the ground, but it's a bad move. The weight of the aggressive snake and the angle of his body, along with Bill's intake of alcohol throws him off balance, and he falls to the ground.

My intention had been to distract Bill long enough to get the noose from around my neck and run. Trapper's action was completely unanticipated. Watching it has put me in a daze, but Bill's fall to the ground has sparked my brain. I come back to reality.

I reach to my neck, loosen the noose and pull it over my head. I look for a rock or a limb or anything to crush Bill's skull with, but they're never there when you need them. I hear Trapper screaming. It doesn't register so I look towards the sound. Some way Bill has finally pried Trapper from his leg and is now on his knees, holding him under his arm like a sack of potatoes. Trapper screams again and now I hear it clear. "God damit, Boogie, run! Run! Run! And with only one thought in mind, I run. I run like I've never run before. *I'm free! I'm free! I'm free!*

LIVING IN THE PAST

Trying to write this book is driving me *nuts*.

I need to live more in the past than the present, staying away from the future altogether, but find my concentration corrupted by things that are yet to be.

My son, Mike, tells me I'm going to be dead before I ever finish the thing. Now, during the day, thoughts of dying periodically flash through my mind. In and out, off and on, like fireflies at twilight.

At night I hear sounds, a train whistle in the far distance, or the squawk of a night bird as it patrols the small lake behind my house or maybe just the sudden silence of croaking frogs, all relaying the dreaded signal that the end is near.

I have good days and bad days, but I always hate the nights. They serve to remind me that another day in my life has passed.

I prompt myself to the fact that everything exists only from moment to moment. That time erases everything as it goes, that there would be no past or any future if time traveled alone. But both to the good and to the bad fortunes of mankind, this is not the case. Because somewhere, loosely embedded in the vast cloak of time are three traveling companions; awareness, memory and imagination and unlike time, they leave a trail. Like metal shavings to a magnet, they cling to the human psyche to become its spirit, its soul, the very source of its existence.

Why only mankind was chosen for this honor has always been debatable. Some say it's the hand of God, while others swear it's only by chance, just an accident. Then there are those who never think of it at all. "Who gives a shit," they say when asked.

I remind myself that the price we must pay for knowing we have lived is to know we must die. *Life is a death sentence* for us all.

So, I go on, staying as far away from the future as possible, living from moment to moment in the present and dwelling reluctantly in the past as time moves on, advancing towards my final chapter.

And if another person asks me if I've finished my fuckin' book, I'm going to scream!!!

Why did I ever open my big mouth? "Once a dummy, always a dummy," the words of Trapper come to me bright and clear.

So, with a shrug and a chuckle, I continue...

Oh, how wonderful it felt to be free on that day! I remember thoughts of "Jack, the Giant Killer" and "Seven League Boots" flashing through my head and I remember running like the wind.

— CHAPTER 10 —
DOWN THE CREEK

I HEAR WHAT SOUNDS LIKE THE BUZZING OF BEES over my head and right behind it, the sound of gunshots—two of them.

The sound of the gun reverberates off the surrounding hills and echoes down through the creek valley below.

I'm running down the trail towards the creek. No planned reason, that's just the way my legs carried me. The trail is steep, a ribbon of rocks and dirt that wiggles through the boulders and bushes like a drunken snake crawling its way down the side of the hill.

I jump to my right off the trail. I stumble and almost fall. I take this opportunity to look behind me. I expect to see Bill right on my tail, but he hasn't moved. He's still standing at the edge of the ledge the car is resting on, about 25 yards away, pointing his pistol down towards me. He's holding Trapper in a chokehold under his left arm. I fall flat on my stomach and crawl behind the biggest rock I see. My heart is beating about a thousand miles a minute. I feel weak and dizzy, no idea what to do.

Bill grabs the rope right at Trapper's neck, pulls him around facing down towards me and puts the gun to his head.

"Ya got ten seconds to git yore ass back up here or the next 'un goes in yore lil' buddy's head," he screams down at me.

"Don't do it, Boogie!" Trapper screams right behind him.

He tries to pull away, but Bill raps him on the side of the head with the barrel of the pistol, one, two, three times and he falls to his knees.

"I'm gonna kill him!" Bill screams again, pointing the gun back at Trapper's head.

I'm scared beyond belief. I don't know what to do next and my mind refuses to work. Think! Think! Think, I keep telling myself.

"Go get help!" Trapper screams at me again, then pays for it with another rap of the gun barrel on the side of his head.

"You kill him, they gonna electrocute you!" I scream back up at Bill. "I'm a witness! I'll tell them everything you've done!"

"Ya ain't gonna tell shit, 'cause after I blow this lil' fucker's brains out, I'm gonna track yore lil' ass down and put a bullet in yore head," Bill hollers back at me.

More than ten seconds have passed and Trapper's still alive. *Keep him talking,* I think to myself.

"Ain't no way you'll ever catch me, you fat pervert," I scream. "I'll be there when they fry your ass down at Kilby Prison. I hear you shit your pants when they pour the juice to you," I add for good measure.

I can tell that Bill is thinking about what I've said, because he doesn't answer back right away.

I yell back up to him again. "Let Trapper go now and we'll walk away, let bygones be bygones," I yell to him. "We'll keep our mouths shut about today. You ain't done nothing so far you gotta die for."

Bill pulls Trapper towards the tree where the rope is tied, shifts the pistol to his left hand, unties the rope and pushes Trapper back towards the car. He apparently says something Bill doesn't like and gets a swift kick in the ass. I lose sight of them and then hear the trunk lid slam. Trapper's back in the trunk.

He's gonna come after me now, I think to myself.

I look around to get my bearings. I'm about halfway down to the big oyster rock—it's about twenty-five yards away. The creek is about thirty or forty feet behind me. I have no cover here unless I'm flat to the ground behind this rock. If he heads this way, I'll have to run again. I can't let him get close enough for an accurate shot.

Bill walks back to the edge of the ledge, drops the pistol into his coat pocket, fishes out his cigarettes and lights up.

"Come on up and let's talk it over," he yells down to me. He must think I just fell off the turnip truck yesterday.

"I can talk just fine from here," I yell back up to him.

He's quiet for a minute, just standing there looking down towards me smoking his cigarette. He's trying to decide what to do. I decide to help him along.

"Trapper and I'll walk out one way and you go the other. You won't ever hear from us again. This never happened," I yell up to him.

I watch him closely as he continues to smoke his Camel. Something in the back of my mind tells me that he's going to come at me again before he ever consents to any deal. He's not going to give up easy. If he comes at me, it will have to be down the trail and he will have to move about twenty feet to his right to pick it up; otherwise, he's going to have to jump down off the ledge, about a four-foot drop, and pick the trail up as it angles down the hillside about twenty-five feet below and in front of where he now standing. That twenty-five feet is covered with small trees, bushes and rocks and will be slow going to come at me that way.

Just when I start to dismiss that possibility, he flips away his cigarette and flips himself down off the ledge at the same time. Even though I'm watching every move he makes, this move surprises me. He's off the ledge in a wink and comes charging down the hillside like an enraged bull. "I ain't gonna make no deals with ya, ya lil' bastard, I'm gonna kill ya," he screams at me at the top of his lungs.

I seem to be frozen to the very spot where I'm laying for just a moment as I watch him, gun back in his hand again, charging down through the bushes and rocks.

Run you fool! I think to myself, jarring my mind out of its reverie and then, quick as a cat, my legs go into action. I'm up and running again, not daring to look back until I hear the sound of the gun again and then when I do I see that Bill has tripped and fallen and has involuntary pulled the trigger of the pistol as he attempted to break his fall. *Thank God for pot whiskey and beer* runs through my mind.

I reach the big oyster rock and skirt around it to the left, the side opposite from the creek. Halfway around, I climb to the top, fall to my stomach and look back towards the trail. Bill is standing where I had been just a few minutes ago. He has his left leg propped on the rock I was hiding behind. He has pulled his pants leg up and is rubbing at his shin. It's the same leg Trapper bit.

I can't resist the taunt. "I hope you shot yourself!" I scream to the top of my lungs, pressing my head flat to the top of the rock, hoping he won't see me.

He pulls his pant leg down and walks a few more steps down the trail in my direction, then stops. His eyes scan the big rock from side to side and then across the top, but he has yet to see me.

I lie as still as I can, but I'm ready to move in case he comes down any further.

"You thank yore real damn smart, don't ya," he hollers down towards me, looking all around, trying to get me talking again so he can pinpoint my location. It's hard not to banter with him. I'm tempted, but I bite my tongue and keep quiet.

"If ya'll come on back up here now, I'll let both of ya'll go," he yells. "Come on back up and we'll work it out. Hell, I was just funnin' with ya, guys, so come on back!"

Yeah, and the devil don't live in a hot place, I think to myself, but I still hold my tongue.

"Ya don't, ya jist signed yore death warrant and after I've killed ya, I'm gonna kill the rest of yore whole damn family. Yore mommy and yore daddy and that smartass brother of yores that works down at the store. Hell, I'll even kill yore goddamned granny, if you got 'un," he screams down at me.

A chill goes through my body at the thought of what he has just said, but instead of frightening me to the point of giving up, it strengthens my resolve to stay free, to be able to tell the whole world if necessary what's happened here today, especially if he harms Trapper. There's no way I'm going to let that pervert get his hands on me again, so I continue to lie silent and watch him.

He continues to stand where he's stopped, looking down towards me. I expect any minute for him to move on down the hill, but then it dawns on me that he doesn't want to get too far from the car, where I'm sure he has Trapper locked back in the trunk. Someone else might decide to brave the muddy road over to the creek. I'm sure Trapper's making enough noise that if someone else drives up and happens to see the wrecked car, they'll have no problem hearing him. Bill realizes the same thing.

He stands there for what seems like forever, but I'm sure that only a few minutes pass, then he yells down to me again. "OK, don't say I din't warn ya," then he turns and starts walking back up the hill. He only walks for a few steps before he turns back towards me. "I'm gonna start by killin' your lil' buddy," he screams. "Listen for the shot. It's gonna be right between his fuckin' eyes," then he turns and continues walking up the hill towards the car.

Waves of guilt flood my body. I feel guilty that I'm the one free and not Trapper, but then again, he's the one who bit Bill's leg and he's the one who yelled for me to run. I would have done the same for him under the same circumstances, I think. Maybe I should have done something while Bill was retying Trapper's hands. Was I chicken or did I just not think to do it? It's all too confusing to try to think about it now, but it does break my code of silence. I wait 'til Bill's back up to where he fell and then I stand up on top of the rock in full view and yell up to him, "I'm gonna laugh when they fry your ass for murder and don't expect any help from your queer lawyer buddy, 'cause they gonna fry him, too!"

He turns back in my direction and sees me standing on top of the rock. He lifts the pistol and points it down towards me. He stands there for a few more minutes, but he doesn't fire. It would be impossible to hit me from this distance, I think, but to be sure I fall flat on the rock again. When I look back up, he's moving on up the hill.

I watch him until he reaches the top of the ledge, then lose sight of him as he moves back towards the car. I'm trembling all over, my whole body aching. My throat seems to close up and I gasp so hard for breath, I begin to hiccup. Tears begin to roll from my eyes stinging the open cuts on my face. *Stop it! Stop it,* I tell myself. *Stop laying here crying like a baby. You've got to decide what to do, so get yourself under control,* but my body doesn't cooperate. *Get up!* I tell myself, so I rise back to my feet and begin to take deep breaths as I peer for a sight of Bill and listen for the gunshot that will end Trapper's life.

The deep breathing helps. I get my sobbing under control and my hiccups go away. I remember the hanky in my pocket, pull it out and wipe at my face. It comes away bloody. I wet it in the water trapped in the crevices of the rock and hold it as a compress over my busted nose and mouth. Some of the hurt seems to go away. I wet it again and hold it against my swollen ear, all the time watching the ledge and listening for the shot.

Minutes seem like hours. All I hear is the roar of the creek as it throws itself downward over the boulders and terraced lime-stone on its way through the gorge. Suddenly over the roar, I hear Trapper's voice and then I hear Bill, but don't understand what either of them is saying. Then, I see them; they're up on the road to my right, just before the bend, where the road cuts up the hill to the north to follow the creek. The road is cut into the side of the ridge just above eye-level to where I'm standing on top of the rock and it's only about 50 feet behind me as a crow would fly. If Trapper hadn't yelled, they might have walked right up behind me while I stood fat and dumb looking the other way. Trapper's paying for it, too, for as I watch, I see Bill slap him about three times on the back of his head and push him forward. Trapper's walking to the front, his hands still tied in front of him. Bill's walking about four feet behind him holding the rope that's still noosed around Trapper's neck, pointing the gun at his back.

I stay where I am and watch them climb up the hill. Trapper moves to the edge of the road to stay out of the mud. Even with a gun at his back and a noose around his neck, he's still worried about screwing up his shoes.

I move down off the front of the rock and head back up the trail towards the car. I move slowly, walking backwards, so I can watch their movements.

They're both watching me at the same time. Just as they reach the top of the hill, Trapper yells out to me again, "Go get help!" only to be kicked in the ass again by Bill, who screams out, "Ain't nobody can help you two little fuckers, 'cause yore dead. Ya hear me? Yore dead!"

"Hang in there, Trapper," I scream, "I'm going to get help!"

I move on up the trail and watch them as they pass behind the big oyster rook and on down the road along the side of the ridge. I watch them until they move out of sight behind the trees that grow along the edge of the road.

I'm surprised that Bill is taking the road. When he told us we were going down the creek I had imagined walking along the bank and I think Trapper did, also, but why not take the road? It's certainly the fastest way down to wherever he's going to meet his queer buddy and with the road in the condition that it's in, nobody will probably be traveling it today. If by chance they do, he'll just move down into the woods where they can't see him or else shoot them and take their car. Whatever the case, I know that the only way I have a chance to save Trapper is to follow them. I have to stay close enough to get a tag number if he takes a car or meets up with his buddy, but not so close that he might shoot me or catch me again. Going for help is out of the question, if I ever expect to see Trapper again. I've made a decision.

I move off the trail just to the left of where Bill jumped off the ledge and then beat at the bushes in search of my slingshot. I know this is the general area that it landed when Bill threw it down the hill. I find it nestled in the needles of a small pine tree, fish it down and hang it back around my neck. I veer off the trail and move quickly down to the creek. Lying prone at the edge, I submerge my face in the icy cold water, then scoop it up in my hands and drink. I pat my face down with my handkerchief, then move back as fast as I can up to the top of the big oyster rock so I have a view of both the road and the trail down along the creek, in case Bill might decide to tie Trapper to a tree and double-back in an effort to get me.

I sit down and take off my wet shoes. My socks are soaked. I take them off, wring them out and put them back on. Before I put my shoes back on, I dig the soggy rolled-up dollar bills from the toe of my right shoe—they've been killing my toes. I fold them gently together and slide them into my back pocket. I also remove the jingle bell from the laces of my left shoe and wrap it in my wet handkerchief, which I keep in my other back pocket.

I stand and stamp my feet up and down, they feel much better, ready to go. My clothes feel heavy. They're soaked and stick to my body. The inside of my thighs are chafed from the wet corduroy. But suddenly I feel warmer. I look around me and then up to the sky. I hadn't even been aware of it until now. The heavy winds have stopped and the sky has turned from a murky asphalt-gray to a bright cobalt-blue. The sun in the sky sits to my west at which I reckon to be about a four o'clock high, but the brilliance and warmth of its rays feel more like high noon. Tiny tendrils of steam rise from my jacket like miniature campfires, as the warm sun beckons stored-up rainwater back into the welkin.

I push my wet hair up out of my eyes, take a deep breath and move down off the back side of the rock. I move slowly and with caution, keeping my eyes on the road above me and the trail down along the side of the creek to the north. It would be just like Bill to double-back, hoping to catch me unaware and either capture me or put a bullet in my head. Until I can get up to the road so I can see them again, I've got to be extremely careful—I can't screw up.

I walk down the creek trail for about forty feet to where the trail forks. The path to the right continues on down the creek, the one to the left leads up the hill to the road. I take the left. Every sound I hear fills me with anticipation. I hear the shrill twirling rattle of a kingfisher as it plunges to feed on a minnow and my heart almost stops. I startle and fall into a crouch at a sudden "machine gun" rat-a-tat-tat from the hillside above me, as an Indian hen drums loud and resonant into the bark of a tree in search of grubs. Its loud ringing cry down through the valley of the creek gives me chills when it finally gives up and flies away. Every snap of a branch or rustle of a bush brings an image of Bill as I move slowly up the hill.

The high ridge the road is cut into begins to fall away about thirty yards past where the trail I'm on joins the road. At this point the heights of the hills above the valley of the creek are pretty consistent all the way to the Newcastle Road, which is about four miles away. The road pretty much follows the path of the creek in a roller-coaster fashion. When the creek turns down in the valley, the road in most cases turns with it at the top of the hill. If Bill is headed to Big Rock to meet his friend, he's got about a four-mile walk to the bridge over the creek on the Newcastle Road and then about another 300-yard walk down the creek to the Big Rock swimming hole. He'll have to cross the creek at the bridge because the big rocks are on the eastern side of the creek.

I reach the road and gaze to the north following the path of the road with my eyes. It runs pretty much straight for about a quarter mile before it makes its first turn. I see them about 250 yards down the road, about halfway to the curve. I breathe a sigh of relief when I see Bill that far away. They haven't been moving very fast. Bill probably dilly-dallied around trying to decide what to do about me, but it looks like at this point he's made a decision and has speeded up. As I watch them, he pushes Trapper forward and kicks him in the ass—within a few minutes, they're out of sight around the bend. Bill knows the same thing I do. Dark is only a few hours away and I'm betting his friend won't wait long after that.

Feeling safe from Bill for the moment I break into a trot and as strength comes back in to my legs, I begin to run.

The first bend in the road is to the right towards the northeast, then after about 100 yards, the road snakes back to the general direction that it's now heading. The slope of the creek valley off to the right is extremely steep and heavily covered with trees and large boulders. The opposite side of the road is thinly covered with a growth of small pines and baby oaks along with a heavy growth of bushes. At some time in the past, it has been cleared and farmed. Just before I reach the bend in the road, I take this direction.

I move about twenty-five feet off the road amongst the small trees and bushes. I bend low and move as fast as I can without giving myself away, in case someone's just around the curve waiting. I reach the bend, squat down to gather my breath and listen. I hear the caw-caw of a jay and the clicking sound of a red bird, but nothing that sounds human. I try to look down the road, but I'm too far back to get a good view. I spot a group of taller bushes about ten feet from the edge of the road, move forward to them and lie flat.

Peering around the bushes, I have a clear view of the road ahead. No sign of Bill or Trapper, but for some reason I get the "willies" again. I freeze, lay flat to the ground and hardly breathe. I may have just played right into Bill's hands. If he's laying in wait for me, this would be the side of the road he would hide on—*definitely* not the valley side. He might have been watching me all the time, just waiting for me to get close enough for a bullet in the head. I'm unsure now of what to do, so I continue to flatten myself tight to the ground and listen. I'm suddenly overcome with urges—to clear my throat, to scratch and especially to pee, but I fight them off and lie still.

In the distance, I hear someone scream and immediately recognize it as Trapper, then another voice shouting something back, that can only be Bill. I stand and look to my left towards where the road turns back. I hear Trapper yell something again and then I see them. They're well past the second bend in the road, probably about 200 yards from where I'm standing and they're moving fast. As I watch, they go over a knoll in the road and out of view.

I clear my throat about three times, scratch myself all over, whip my "weenie" out and pee as fast as I can, then I'm off again.

I'm sore and stiff, hurting all over. My left eye is almost swollen shut, which severely hampers my vision. My face feels like a balloon where it has swollen and breathing is a struggle through my busted nose and mouth. I seem to have stopped bleeding everywhere except where Bill cut me under my bottom lip with the beer opener. It hurts like a bastard and when I touch it, my hand still comes away bloody. The running probably isn't helping, but it can't be avoided. I've got to stay up with them, stay undetected and last, but not least, get ahead of them. That's the only way to stop the anticipation of an ambush at every turn in the road and it will also help me to determine exactly where Bill is headed and ultimately get there ahead of him. Fortunately I know just where I can do it. It's about a mile ahead, the one place where the road doesn't follow the flow of the creek—that's where I can get ahead. It will probably be my only opportunity. I forget about my pain and will my scraped and scratched legs forward.

Until I can get in front of them, I follow my same established pattern as I continue my pursuit, staying off the road and sneaking around the curves, then identifying their location by sound or sight before I move ahead. Trapper's tendency to yap long and loud helps. I am now less than 100 yards behind them and Bill has yet to give any indication that he suspects I'm following.

Trapper and Bill have come to the point where the road veers away from the path of the creek, where hopefully I have a chance to get ahead. A blip in the earth at some time in history has created a high hill just in front of them and were the road to go straight, it would have to go up and over it. Apparently the road builder was lazy; he decided it was easier to go around. Or maybe it was originally the animals or even the Indians, because they say most roads are built following the paths of old trails. Whatever the case, the road veers around the hill to the west away from the creek and makes about a mile half-circle before it reaches the other side of the hill and then re-establishes its course along the path of the creek.

I watch them as they turn to the west and continue along the road. My plan is to go straight, up and over the hill. I plan to do it fast, to beat them to the other side with room to spare, so I can watch them come towards me, not the other way around, as it is now.

As I exit the road and start up the hill, I can see that this is not an original idea. The hillside slopes at about a 30-degree angle and though heavily wooded, there is a definite and clearly a worn path that leads to the top, about 75 yards above me. Lots of some bodies or some things have cut this gap before.

Just before I reach the crest of the hill, I stop and squat to my knees. Everything sounds natural, just the calling of birds and the sounds of the creek in the valley below me. I hear a rustling sound above me and see a pair of fox squirrels playing tag through the trees.

I force my mind back to the job at hand and still remaining low, I slowly crest the hill, making sure to stay behind the largest trees and bushes so as not to be seen. I move behind a big oak tree that grows at the very top of the hill and peer down the hill towards the west. I want to see if I can see any part of the road from here. I see nothing but bushes and trees, which is good. If I can't see them, then it's pretty certain they can't see me.

Even under the cover of the trees, I can feel the warmth of the late day sun now that the rain clouds have moved away. Many of the trees are covered with small new leaves or just starting to bud, while others are still stark and bare. The bushes and undergrowth that I've been wallowing in and wading through is in the same stage of growth, some with buds or small leaves and others bare as bones.

I shed my jacket, tie the sleeves around my waist and let it hang down over my butt. My sweater is damp from rainwater and sweat. I take it off and wring it out—it smells like a wet dog. I pull it back on, tuck my slingshot safety under it, take three deep breaths and look around me. The warming sun seems to signal that spring is here. In a few weeks these hills and valleys will be a wonderland. They will be filled with the colors of dogwood and redbud, scented with the fragrance of honeysuckle, laurel and sweet shrub and serenaded by the mating music of the mockingbirds and thrashers, but will I be around to see it? Will Trapper? I take another deep breath and with that question in mind, I begin to run.

Other than an occasional turn to snake around limestone formations or cavities in the earth, the trail across the hill runs almost straight. Along its path numerous trails jut off to the east and worm their way down the hill to the creek. A lot of people camp and fish here, because all along the foot of this hill the creek runs wide and deep. It's also not dominated by the weekend swimmers who are too lazy to walk. They haunt places like the falls or the Big Rock where there are plenty of places to park their cars. That's how I know about this trail. I've camped out here several times, adult-supervised, of course. Quickly bored with fishing, we kids spent most of the time exploring the surrounding hills and hollows.

I've also tube-fished the creek, all the way from the falls to the bridge on Newcastle Road, the same four miles I'm traveling today. I've done it twice with my Uncle Coy, the one with the gun like Bill's. It was on this section of the creek last summer that I had my first "up front" view of sex—that is, I mean, between a grown man and woman:

Late August, last summer, on a Tuesday I think, Uncle Coy picked me up early. Aunt Norma was with him. She dropped us off at the falls and kept the car to pick us up at the bridge later in the day. The tubes belonged to Uncle Coy—big red truck tubes with black rubber waders attached "Rube Goldberg," style by Uncle Coy.

Hot as hell that day. Coy (which he says is OK to call him) said even if we didn't catch fish, at least we would be cool, which was fine with me. I didn't give a shit about the fishing anyway, I just like tubing down the creek.

Coy was right, nothing was biting. Too darn hot! By the time we arrived at the deep wide section in the valley below, I had stopped fishing altogether and was kinda dozing in the tube. I only started back when he bumped my tube and signaled to me that we might catch something through this part of the creek.

Coy likes to tube very quietly. No talking, hand signals only, which is also fine with me.

I was fishing the west bank, the bank below the hill, while Coy was fishing the opposite side. My line caught and hung on a tree limb over the creek. I gently reeled myself in towards the bank so I could snap off the twig I was hung on and save my fly. I had just completed the task when I heard the sound, a sound like someone tuning a guitar.

I looked over at Coy who was floating the opposite bank, up about 15 feet in front of me. He was giving me the finger across the lips sign and also a signal to move towards him to the opposite side of the creek, however, a signal I ignored. I kept floating straight forward about 15 feet out from the bank. I floated no more than another 10 feet before I saw the guitar plucker.

It was a he, mid forties, early fifties? Small and wiry, wearing baggy red swim trunks, he had a "farmer's tan," was rawboned and lined, and looked like he had been ridden really hard. He was sitting on a limestone boulder that jutted out over the creek. He had his feet in the water, his guitar in his hands and a cigarette hanging from his lips. A bottle of what looked like blended whiskey was balanced on the rock beside him. He was doing a twist and twang on the guitar strings. Cigarette smoke curled up into one eye and long, stringy, dishwater hair hung over the other.

I floated right in front of him. He looked up and gave me the Indian "How" sign with his hand. Neither of us said a word.

About 20 feet past him, on the other side of a bush that grew beside the rock he was sitting on was where I hit the jackpot. The show of my lifetime, with a ringside seat—a she, pleasantly plump, carrot-colored "Holy-roller" hair, and skin the color of Frigidaired dough. She was naked as a plucked chicken and shaped quite similar. She was lying on a quilt, on her stomach, her face turned towards me. She had a can of beer in her right hand, her knees tucked up under, and her ass pointed to the sky.

Behind her, up on his knees, up tight and snug between her open thighs was a carbon copy of the guitar man. They could have been twins, who knows? The only significant difference was that he had on blue swim trunks that were pulled down to his ankles. He was polishing his pole so hard and fast he never saw me, but just before I floated past them, she opened her eyes, looked at me and grinned.

I looked over at Coy and pumped my right fist up and down. He just shook his head and smiled. Neither of us has ever mentioned it again, which is certainly all right with me.

I don't think I'm any worse for the experience, except now, even the fat girls are giving me woodies.

I'm over the hill and down the other side. I can see the road out in front of me as it curves back from the west and then turns back towards the north to follow the creek.

I take cover along its edge, looking and listening for Bill and Trapper. I see or hear nothing. I know without a doubt I've beaten them here, but I have no idea by how much.

My heart is pounding in my chest, partly from the run over the hill, but mainly due to fright. I take some more deep breaths to try to settle myself down. I need to think about what I should do. Right now the only plan I have is to stay in front of them and watch and to hopefully get a tag number if and when Bill meets up with his friend. If I do, I can give it to Britt and he can give it to the police. The only problem is, by the time they find Bill and his friend, Trapper will probably be dead. As I think about this I start feeling guilty again, so I try to put it out of my mind.

From where I am now, it's probably a couple more miles to the

Newcastle Road, maybe a little less. I have never actually walked through here before, but I have ridden through here many times. I need to settle down, unscramble my brain and concentrate on what I know about the road ahead of me.

Before I even get started, I hear a yell. It's got to be Trapper. I look in the direction from which they will be walking. The way the road curves, I'll be able to see them when they're about 75 yards away. I'm not sure that's far enough. I look back down the road again. Still no sign of them. In front of me the road slopes upward and then over a small hill, probably 25 yards to the top. I decide to chance it. I look back down the road again and when I still see nothing I jump up to the road and run.

I make it to the top of the hill and look for a place to hide. Off to my right, just at the edge of the woods is the carcass of a big pine tree, probably hit by lightning, half of it still standing. I duck behind the top part that's hanging to the ground. As soon as I look back down the road, I see them. They're just at the spot where I expected to see them before, but they're moving much faster now. Not running, but in a steady trot. It's a good thing I moved or else they might have seen me.

I'm not sure of what I should do now. I look up the road in front of me. It goes down into a shallow hollow, then bends to the right up another small hill about the size of the one I have just run up. Just as I am about to move forward again I see them stop. They're probably 65 to 70 yards away.

Bill motions to the ground. Trapper moves to the edge of the road and sits down. Bill leans forward, bracing himself with his hands just above his knees. Even though I can't see it, I know he's breathing really hard. The cigarettes and whiskey will get you every time, but Bill don't get it, for I no sooner have the thought before I see him fire up again.

It takes seven minutes to smoke a cigarette and I have no doubt Bill will use them all after his unexpected workout. I'm sure he realizes he's barely halfway there if he's headed to the Big Rock, which I'm relatively sure is where he's headed. So before I move again, once more I try to focus on the road ahead of me.

The next two miles are not going to be much different than the previous two. The road will continue to crawl over the hills and hollows like a snake, twisting and turning in different directions. I want to stay just far enough away from them to watch without being seen, but not so far away that I might lose them in case something unforeseen happens. As we get closer to Newcastle Road, Bill may have to detour to keep from being seen.

At the crossroads (Crosston as everyone calls it) is the store where Bill and his catfishing buddy supposedly got a ride, which now I know was a bullshit lie. There's also, to the best of my recollection three houses. One on the east side of the road just before you get up to the store, one across the road up on a hill behind the store and another across Newcastle Road facing the store's front. And where there's houses, there's people, but I'm not sure Bill will take a chance on being seen, especially with a 13-year-old boy held captive with a noose around his neck and a gun to his back. I pray to God that I can get some help at one of these places and get this nightmare stopped. I also pray that I can do it without getting Trapper killed or someone who may try to help me.

There's also another slim possibility of help. Just up the road in front of me, probably no more than a half-mile away is the Oak Grove Baptist Church. I don't really expect to find anyone there. Baptists are maniacs for church on Wednesday nights and most all day on Sundays, but wouldn't think of darkening the door of one on a Saturday. There is, however, off to the right, just before you get to the church, a narrow, almost pig-trail road that will take you down to the creek. At one time years ago, there used to be an old corn mill down there. Part of the dam is still standing. It's a great swimming hole called the Mill Dam. Bill could detour down to the creek at this point and then continue on along its bank to Big Rock. It would slow him down, but would decrease his chance of being seen. If he does, I might have an "ace in the hole." There's an old farmhouse down there, just up from the creek a ways. It belongs to my Great Uncle Mac, my Granny's brother. If Bill heads down that direction, I'll head for Uncle Mac's. If he's there he might be able to help. There's no way we could ever get his car up the pig-trail road, but I know he's got a gun and according to my Granny, he's a crack shot.

Before Bill finishes his cigarette, I need to move on. Using the heavy growth along the edge of the woods as cover, I edge down the hill until I'm out of sight, then return to the road and begin to run.

At the foot of the hill, a wet weather branch has flooded over about an eight-foot section of the road. I jump it, continue on up the hill, then stop and turn back.

This section of the road apparently floods after every big rain and probably stays muddy for days afterwards. Creek gravel has been dumped in it for traction. The force of the run-off water hurling downwards towards the creek has fanned out an array of the gravel along both sides of the stream. When steel balls aren't available, stones from the creeks are the next best ammo for slingshots. I hunker down, hurriedly sort through them and make my selection. I find nine of them I like, all about the size of an average bird's egg. One is slightly larger, an almost perfect replica of a brown thrasher's egg in size and coloring. You could put it in a thrasher's nest and they would never know the difference. I smile when I remember something James told me once, "If you got serious killin' to do, a rock the size of a thrasher's egg is the perfect size to shoot." I drop them in my pants pocket, left-hand front, take another look down the road in the direction of Trapper and Bill, then turn and run as fast as I can up the hill.

For the next quarter mile, I play the same game. Hide, then run when I see them, then hide again.

Bill and Trapper are moving faster. I'm having to run harder to stay ahead. Bill's in better shape than I gave him credit for—a holdover from his wrestling days I surmise. He must be threatening Trapper with a bullet to his brain to make him move fast. Several times when they've stopped a few seconds for a breather, I've seen him hold the gun to Trapper's head. Once he grabbed Trapper by the hair and stuck the barrel of the pistol in his mouth.

I see the church up ahead, less than 50 yards away. I'm tired and feeling really weak, my shoes are heavy with mud. I kick the trunk of a large hickory tree to get some of it off, but it sticks to the soles of my shoes like glue.

I take about five deep breaths and run to the church, not a car in sight. I run up the steps and pull at the door; it's locked tight as a drum.

Trapper and Bill are close behind me. I've got to make a decision fast as to which way I think Bill will go from here—that's the only way I'll be able to stay to their front.

I look up at the sky and then down the pig-trail road towards the creek. The sun is sinking fast, with the gloaming not far away. It will darken faster down along the creek under the cover of the trees and I'm sure Bill will think about that if he considers going that way. I'm not even sure he realizes he has that option. He's nowhere near as familiar with the creek as Trapper and I. Even if he does, Trapper will want to keep him headed towards the crossroads. I can hear him telling Bill now, "That's the fuckin' snakiest part of the creek!" Yeah, I'm sure of it, Trapper will lead him out to Crosston to the crossroads. He'll know it's his only chance or at least think it is, since he isn't aware I'm following.

I'm sure my decision is right as I continue on the Narrows Road, but just to be safe, I only run to a curve in the road, about 35 yards down from the church. If Bill continues to move this way, the curve in the road will hide me until I can move forward at least another 30 to 40 yards. If by some chance he does take the creek route, then I'll have to settle with being behind them again and try to follow as close as possible. Due to the lateness of the day, going by Uncle Mac's is out. Too much time will be lost.

I watch them as they come into sight, they're back to moving at a fast walk. At just about the point where I stopped to get the mud off my shoes, Bill slows Trapper down, then cautiously moves forwards until he's about 30 yards from the church and stops. I see him say something to Trapper then point towards the pig-trail road. I see Trapper shake his head, giving Bill a no, then say something back, all the while making all sorts of gyrations with his tied hands. Bill continues to look all around as he listens to

Trapper talking a mile a minute, then he suddenly jerks the rope tight and pulls Trapper to the opposite side of the road from the church. They move off the road about 20 feet, then continue walking slowly on down towards me.

I was right! He's staying on the Narrows Road. He's skirting the church across the road, using the cover of the woods. He's taking no chance of being seen. I see them only because I know they're there. I watch them until they're almost directly across from the church, then run like hell.

The hide and run game begins again and my empty stomach begins to growl. Even as scared as I am, I'm hungry. My dry, parched mouth craves water. Fear and running has dehydrated my body. As my strength begins to ebb, the guilt about Trapper's predicament returns. *If I feel guilty now, how am I gonna feel if something bad happens to him?* I think to myself.

I imagine the police, using a tag number I give them tracking Bill and his queer lawyer buddy up to the farm. They break down the barn door only to find Trapper's dead body hanging from a noose tied to the rafters, Bill and his buddy gone. All sorts of weird scenarios begin to play back and forth through my head—all of them ending in doom for Trapper.

I begin to ask myself questions: how do I really know Bill is headed for Big Rock? How's his buddy gonna get his car down there? The road down to Big Rock is worse than this one! Maybe the plan was to meet there before they knew it was going to rain? Maybe the buddy will now just wait around and meet Bill on Newcastle Road, maybe alongside the bridge? Questions, questions, questions, but the one that worries me most, the one that has plagued my mind from the beginning—what if for some reason Bill's buddy isn't there? What happens when Bill is backed into a corner? No buddy, no car—what does he do? What do I do? There's only one answer, only one honorable thing to do, and that's to save Trapper. It will be up to me to get him free. I try to think of ways I can do it, but my mind is in too much of a swirl. Maybe it won't come down to that. Maybe I can find help at Crosston. I begin to run as fast as I can.

I run up to the yard of the first house. I've run extra hard to put as much distance between us as possible. I'm guessing them at about a quarter mile or more behind me.

The house sits about 60 feet off the road. It's small, wood-framed and painted white. You can tell that at one time, it was a showplace, a little dollhouse, but now the yard and flower beds are in disarray and the paint on the house is peeling. It sits on the slope of the hill, low to the ground on the front and high off the ground in the back. Hedges and vines along its front have grown high and wild and hold the porch in perennial shade. The metal glider and two metal chairs on it are molded and rusty.

I knock four loud raps on the dilapidated screen door and wait. I count to seven and knock again, this time opening the screen and rapping on the door. I wait again, still nothing. I run off the porch and circle around to the back. The porch is up high, about ten steps up. The ground under the porch is littered with old gardening tools, an old push plow and unused flower pots. An old-fashioned icebox sits just under the porch to my left at the corner. The porch is enclosed with a framed chicken wire fence, about four-feet high, with a gate of the same make and material. I run up the steps and vault the gate. An old calico cat is asleep under a wringer washer sitting next to the door. It bows up and hisses at me and then runs away. I open the screen, rap hard on the door and once again wait…nothing, probably no one home. I vault back over the gate and head back around to the front. I know I've got to get going, I'm wasting time. Trapper and Bill must be getting close, but out of sheer desperation, I try the front door one more time, this time pounding on the door. *No use,* I think to myself when there's still no answer. I turn and cross the porch to leave. I'm just at the porch steps when I hear the creak of the door, and the squeak of the screen.

An old woman stumbles halfway out the door. She could be sixty or maybe a hundred—it's hard to tell. She's small, stooped, wrinkled and pale, but her hair is jet black. She has a walking cane that she's leaning on in her left hand and a smoking Pall Mall cigarette in her right. I know it's a Pall Mall because I can see the red pack poking out of her apron pocket. Just as she begins to speak, she starts to cough. I hear a smoker's crackle from deep in her lungs. I vow to stop smoking again.

"Who the hell are you?" she asks, and before I can answer, "What the hell you want?"

I'm fidgety, I turn my head to check the road, then move up to where she's standing. I can hear her wheezing. Before I can say anything, she fires another question at me.

"Is that you banging on all my doors or is somebody else with you?" she wants to know, as she takes a big draw off the Pall Mall.

"Yes, ma'am, that was me," I tell her. "Is the man of the house here? I really need to speak to him. I really need help."

"You've run me all over this house trying to answer the door, next time stay in one place!" she scolds.

"Yes, ma'am, can I speak with him?"

"Speak with who?"

"Your husband, is he here?"

She has another coughing spell before she tells me.

"Lost him two years ago. Died of consumption, right out there in the front yard. 'Chesterfield' cigarettes and whiskey done him in. Lord I miss him."

I want to tell her she'll probably be seeing him soon, but know it won't be polite. Instead I ask her, "Do you have a gun?"

"A gun? Why the hell would I have a gun? Don't need 'em, don't use 'em."

She sharpens her eyes, then looks closely at my face. "Why? You been fighting?"

"No, ma'am, someone's trying to kill me and my friend."

"If I had a gun I'd shoot you for aggravating me," she tells me, as she moves back inside and closes the screen.

"Is there anyone else here I could speak to?" I ask.

"Git and leave me be," she says and slams the door.

"If anyone else knock, don't answer," I holler at her, but I'm not sure she heard it through the door.

I crouch down low as I move back across the yard, dart behind a big chinaberry tree that grows up close to the road and look for Trapper and Bill. I don't see them. I can only see clear for about 40 yards before the road curves, so as far as I know, they could be right around the bend.

I look across the road to the house up on the hill. The only sign of life is a forlorn-looking old mule in a muddy barbed wire pasture adjacent to a corn crib barn. No matter anyway, not enough time now to go up there. I've wasted too much time with the nutty old woman. What a loon!

I look back down the road, but I still see no signs of Bill and Trapper. I take a deep breath and head towards the store.

Crosston Grocery Store is at the crossroads, about 75 yards away and on the opposite side of the road from the old loon's house.

To be safe, I cross the road now, continue up the hill for about 30 feet, then, using a pine thicket that grows along the base of the hill as my cover, I move down to the store.

It's a little larger than Herman's, but not really a grocery store, just a place to buy bread, milk and gas. They sell a few other things to eat and drink, like candy and dopes, along with a few fishing supplies and bait, but that about gets it.

I have no idea who runs the place, but feel sure that they're probably related to my mother, which by the way brings to mind another problem that I have.

"Don't get sweet on her, she's your kin," my mother will say. "Find someone who's not related." This, by the way, is difficult when your mom is related to about 90% of the county and she considers it incest all the way through fourth cousins.

I've kissed two of my first cousins already and I can tell you, it felt fine to me. Who's to know anyway, if you hide when you do it?

Trapper says it's OK to "do it all," as long as you don't knock them up. "If you do, you'll sire a dummy," he informed me.

That's when it first dawned on me that his mom and dad were closely related.

Just as I reach the front of the store, a green '48 Chevy heading west on Newcastle Road slows for the crossroads, then moves quickly on its way. It isn't a car I recognize.

The store is deader than butchered meat. Not a human in sight, no cars at the pumps. I zip up the steps and push at the door to go inside, but it's locked up tight. There's a handprinted sign taped to the door: Closed for Revival – Open back up Monday 7 A.M. God Bless You. My heart drops to the pit of my stomach.

I remember the revival going on all this week at the Black Creek Church of God. The grand finale is tomorrow—an old-fashioned Bush-Arbor service with dinner on the ground. They'll preach and eat all day. The Bush-Arbor is up in the woods behind the church, not far at all from Trapper's house. He and I have made tentative plans to sneak up there and watch them. See if they have snakes and speak in unknown tongues. Then when they stop to eat, we'll mingle in the crowd and break bread with them. Looks like that's out now.

As I move down the steps, I notice three cane poles lying on the ground. There's more of them lying across a series of brackets mounted over the store's window. The wind must have blown these off. I pick them up and lean them against the building.

I look around the foundation of the store for a water faucet, see nothing, then check out around the gas pumps. There's a water can, but it's bone dry. No faucet around to fill it. They must get their water from a well. There's probably a pump somewhere, but I haven't the time to search.

I run to the edge of Newcastle Road and look across it to the house on the other side. This is probably where the owner of the store lives, but I'm not sure.

I look back down the Narrows Road towards the old loon's house for a sign of Bill and Trapper. When I fail to see them, I dart across Newcastle Road and up towards the house. I'm barely in the driveway when I'm met by a welcoming committee of dogs, two German sheperds and a chow. They're vicious bastards and don't want company. Their barking and growling will attract attention, plus I'm not hankering to get bit, so I chuck this plan and run as fast as I can down the road towards the bridge.

The road slopes gently from the crossroads to the valley of the creek—about 150-yards and you're on the bridge. I'm running along the north side of the road facing traffic, if there was any! Where's all the cars? Surely someone's going somewhere? I strain my ears and listen for a sound of tires on pavement, but hear nothing. Maybe everybody's at the revival?

Along the road to my left is a high road bank, probably about 35-feet high, that falls away about 50 yards from the creek. To my right, it's low and wooded. I run just a short distance, then I cut up the bank to my left and lay prone at its top, facing the store. The trees and bushes screen me. I'll have to let them get back ahead of me here, but not for long—I have a plan.

Bill could have detoured off the road between here and the old loon's house and then picked up the creek, but I'm betting he won't. He's a gutsy fucker and he knows that time is short—the sun is sinking low. The road between here and the creek is already heavily shadowed, the valley of the creek will be worse. *He'll come this way,* and just as I think it, I see them.

They are just at the back of the store, right at the corner of the building. As I watch them, something looks different and then I see what it is. Somewhere along the line since I last saw them, Bill has moved the rope from around Trapper's neck to his waist, I can see it tailing out from under his jacket right into Bill's hand. He's also taken the burlap bindings off Trapper's hands and used a portion of the rope's length to bind Trapper's arms tight to his body. He has zipped his jacket up tight and placed the two empty sleeves in the side pockets, the way someone would do when their hands were cold.

Holding the rope tied to Trapper right at the base of his coat and with the gun pointed to his back, Bill moves him slowly forward alongside the building. Just before the front, he halts him, then moves in front of him and peeks around the corner. He checks out the front of the store, looks out at the pumps, then looks over towards the house across the road. Satisfied that no one's around, he turns back to Trapper. He wraps the rope that he's holding in his left hand around his right-hand wrist, so he can keep the gun at Trapper's back and hold the rope with the same hand. This done, he pushes him around to the front of the building, grabs one of the cane poles that I propped against the wall, holds it across his left shoulder and heads Trapper down Newcastle Road towards the bridge.

I burrow down low in my hideout at the top of the road bank and watch them as they walk fast down the right-hand side of the road.

Bill is a master of deception. Someone passing by will only see a dad and his son headed down to the creek for some late-evening fishing. No one will stop to offer them a ride, because the fishing pole signals where they're headed. They're walking side by side, Bill next to the road and Trapper along the shoulder. As they pass me, I can hear Bill growling commands at Trapper, although the words aren't clear. I let them get about 30 yards to the front of me, then staying low, I move slightly back into the woods, then walking along the crest of the hill, I follow them, using the trees as cover.

As they cross the creek, Bill angles Trapper across the road and comes to a stop at the east end of the bridge. The trail down to the path along creek is off to the left, at the end of the bridge, just in front of them.

Bill leans the cane pole against the bridge, takes off his hat and hangs it on the pole, then using his left-arm coat sleeve, he wipes his brow.

He puts his hat back on, then points up the road in front of them and appears to question Trapper. It looks like he's asking about the road that goes down to Big Rock, but it's only a guess— I'm not really sure.

Then he turns and scopes out the road all the way back to the store, then back along the hill where I lay hiding. His eyes pass right over me.

He unwraps the rope from his right wrist, loops it around his left arm and pulls it up tight, then with the gun right at the back of Trapper's head, Bill pushes him off the road and then downward towards the path that runs along the bank of the creek. I can't believe a car hasn't passed during this entire walk.

I'm midway on the hill where it starts its slope downward, about 50 yards from where they went down on the path. I give them time to reach the creek bed, then moving down across the road, I run towards the bridge as fast as I can. Just before I reach the bridge, I hear the sound of a car behind me.

A car means help! I need to do something! I run to the middle of the road waving my hands for it to stop, but it's coming fast and an asshole is driving it. Stomping the gas pedal to the floor he heads directly at me, swerving in pretense of hitting me, as I lunge to the shoulder of the road. A thought goes through my head that it could be Bill's friend, until another asshole hangs out the passenger door window, gives me the finger and yells, "DUM-EEE!"

I shoot a double bird back at him, zip across the bridge and then on up the road for about a 100 more feet. I exit the road to my left and head down into the woods. The turnoff for the road down to Big Rock is about a football field up the road from where I made my exit. It runs on an angle down to the creek. From where I am, it's a hill and a hollow away.

Once again someone has had this idea before me. The trail, though muddy and wet is clear. I've also been on this trail before, but that's another story. I'll be at Big Rock in half the time it takes Bill and Trapper coming down the creek. My body shakes at the thought of what might be waiting.

— Chapter 11 —
RETRIBUTION

The trail comes out on the narrow dirt road leading down to the creek about midway down to the swimming hole.

I hit the road running even harder than before. The sound of my rapid beating heart pulsates in my ears like the rhythmical beating of a tom-tom. I'm fueled on pure adrenalin.

The road is muddy, full of ruts, potted with water. I look for recent tire marks, but see none. No evidence at all that a car has come this way today.

About two hundred yards down I stop, freeze and listen. As my heart stills, I hear the sounds of the woods, then the far-off cawing of a crow. I can smell the creek from here. There's no other smell like it, so there's no way to describe it. To me it smells like Tom Sawyer and Huck Finn. It brings to mind fishing poles, rafting and eating stolen watermelons. I suddenly have the urge to pee!

Both my brothers who were in the war have told me that when you're really-really scared, your mind starts thinking the craziest things. I think that's happening to me now!

I move to the left off the road, then about thirty feet back into the woods, then forward again, slow and quiet for about another twenty-five yards. I'm just at a small clearing, a spot where the men change their clothing when they swim. From here there's a clear trail on down to where you pull off to park. If someone's here, that's where their car will likely be.

I hold my breath to sharpen my ears for sounds, then listen again… nothing. I wonder why there's no place designated for women to change their clothes. Funny! I've never thought about it before. Then it comes to me! What woman in her right mind would strip off naked down here? Knowing the horny bunch of guys who swim at this place, they'd be an eye behind every bush. I'd probably be in the forefront!

I look down the trail to the parking area, about another twenty or so yards away. I can see about a third of it pretty clearly. I don't see a car. I skirt around the changing area and then crouching low, I move along the edge of the trail, pausing about every twenty-five feet to look and listen.

I reach the area for parking. It's no more than a gutted-out area in the woods, worn bare of vegetation by the countless generations who have come here to swim. It's a small area—more than four cars in it creates problems, so most folks just park along the road. I fall prone and survey it from the mouth of the trail. Nothing…empty as a coal miner's pocket.

I rise to my feet, walk out into the open and look around. I see nothing out of the ordinary, but do notice that shadows are growing long and heavy; the gloaming is right around the corner. *What happens when I can't see?"* I think to myself. I panic for just a moment; a chill runs up my spine! I take three deep breaths to settle myself down. My ears pick up the tinkling sound of the creek and the song of the katydids in the trees as they serenade the end of day. I take another deep breath and return to my task.

I run back through the parking area to the road, look back up in the direction I came, then turn and look on past the parking area to where the road ends, about a hundred feet away. Nothing…no cars… there's no one here.

I follow the short path from the parking area that heads down to the creek. At the edge of the hill I stop, crouch low and survey the shallow valley below me.

For about a hundred feet the bank along this side of the creek is a rumpled formation of limestone. Off the opposite side is a high-banked hill with a heavy growth of trees and bushes, most of them covered with vines. Along here the creek glides slow and straight. It's about thirty-five feet wide, with depths ranging from about three to ten feet. "A perfect turquoise pool built by Mother Nature," was the way Mr. Tyler described it on a field trip over here last year, when I was in the sixth grade.

Mr. Tyler was a substitute teacher we had for a week while Mrs.

Hicks, our regular teacher, was out with a cold. He was young, just out of college and really smart. He took us on three field trips that week. It was in October and he said the weather was too beautiful to sit in a stuffy classroom all day. We loved it and everyone was wishing that Mrs. Hicks' cold would linger on for a while, but then on Friday, his last day, he had to spoil it all by making us write a report. "Pick one of the places we visited this week and write a brief essay on what you remember about it. Don't try to flower it up. I want it in your own words," he sprang on us that Friday morning. "I want to see at least three notebook pages, no double spacing. I want it neatly written with all the words spelled correctly and you can hand it in any time before lunch period," he went on to say.

Trapper and I chose to write about the trip over here and as you would know, we "flowered" it up. In fact, most everything we wrote was Mr. Tyler's words, not ours. He said the two of us reminded him of a Siamese Parrot and gave us a crappy grade. As I look down the hillside, it brings to mind some of the things we said:

At one time, millions of years ago, the limestone formation cropping out of this hillside was probably one gigantic, smooth boulder, but over the eons, erosion from the wind and water, plus turbulence from within the earth has left it serrated, creviced and protuberant. The path of choice that leads down to the creek is almost at the center of the formation. Standing at its peak, I would guess it's about forty-five feet down to the water. For about three quarters of the way down, the hillside is extremely steep. It's riddled with clefts and fissures that over the years have collected soil that now nourishes the random vegetation that grows spasmodically among its ranks—vines and bushes, a few small pines and cedars, a sprinkling of hickory and oak. Once down this steep slope, the scarred and pitted limestone, bare of vegetation, appears almost level as it rolls out into the creek.

With Mr. Tyler's words in mind and staying as low as possible, I move down the hillside. I move cautiously, keeping my eyes cast down the creek to my left towards the bridge, looking and listening for any sign of Bill or Trapper. They've got to be getting close, could be here at any time—I can't let myself be seen.

I loosen the sleeves of my jacket from around my waist and put it back on. Even though I'm now hot and sweaty, the gray of the jacket blends much better with the limestone rocks than my burgundy sweater. I adjust my slingshot hanging around my neck and zip my jacket up to cover it, then staying as flat as I can, I crawl across the last few feet of barren rock to the edge of the creek.

Up to my left there's a small island in the center of the creek, just before the water pools along the rocks. As I look in that direction, it blocks any long-range view, but I can still see fairly clear for about a hundred yards down along the bank. I look hard for any sign of movement, but I see nothing. I listen; all I hear is the sounds of the creek. I would have thought they would have been in sight by now. It's gotta be Trapper, he's slowing them down. He knows he's coming to the end of the line. He's dragging his feet!

The inside of my mouth feels like cotton, so I reach down and cup up a double handful of water and slurp it down. It tastes cold and sweet, my mouth absorbs it like a sponge. I cup up another handful and wipe it over my face. It feels good on my swollen eye and mouth. I ease my handkerchief out and dab at the cut under my lip. It's still hurting a lot, but it's almost stopped bleeding.

I look down the creek again…still nothing…then suddenly my ears perk. I hear a sound—someone's shouting! It sounds like Trapper and it sounded like he was screaming, "No!"

I hurriedly move on down the rocky creek bank to where the rocks begin. They're larger and more crenellated here and they bulge up higher along the hillside.

Keeping low, I climb to the top of the one at the very end, the largest rock of all. It's not really a separate rock, only a portion of the formation that bulges up higher than the rest. At the top it's rough, scabrous surface is almost flat. And, it's big, probably twelve feet wide and about twenty feet in length. It's shaped similar to a giant arrowhead, its point embedded in the hillside and it's notched end protrudes just slightly over the water, about six feet above its surface.

Bending as low as I can, I move along its top to the very back where it plunges into the hillside. The path down to the creek is just off to my right. This is where Bill will have to come up when he and Trapper get down to the rocks. This is probably where he'll stop first.

I move down the path towards the creek. Off to my right, trees and bushes grow thick along the backside of the rock I was just on, hiding it from view until you reach the top of the path. At the bottom of the path I stop and listen, I hear what sounds like voices, but as I look up along the bank of the creek, I see no one in sight.

It's getting darker and creepy. I hear the croaking sound of frogs and the katydids are still playing havoc in the trees. I'm trembling, scared, and have no idea what to do, so I turn and move back up the path to the top of the big rock again.

Contrary to popular belief, this big rock is the prime reason for the swimming hole's name, or at least that's what my dad says. As I move along its top down toward the water, the growth along its backside screens me from the trail below, but still I stay as low as I can for precaution.

About ten feet from the water, almost in the center of the rock, someone has had a big campfire—probably night fishing for catfish, since there's supposed to be some big lunkers in here. They've even spent the time to encircle it with stones, the way you're supposed to do when you build a fire. Had to have lugged them down from the hillside, there's tons of them up there—must have been a lot of work. Could have been dumbass "Boy Scouts, looks like something they would do. There's a pack or whatever they call themselves over at Pinson.

The stones are big and heavy. One of them is kinda pretty, with a vein of what looks like quartz running down the center. I pick it up—ugh! It must weigh at least twenty pounds. It's gotta have been Boy Scouts, no one else would have gone to this trouble.

In the center of the circle, there's still pieces of unburnt limbs and logs, all soggy and wet from the rain. One of them is a stick of oak, burned down to about the size of a baseball bat. I drag it out. If I could get close enough to Bill, I could crush his skull with this, but as I give it a test swing, I find it's way too heavy. After one swing, if I missed, he would have me. I toss it back in the pile, wipe my wet smutty hands on my pants and disregard the idea.

I move to the front of the rock and look down at the water. The late-day shadows color it dark and cold. I squat and listen and think for a moment of happier days here on the creek.

What makes Big Rock my favorite place to swim is the swing. Made from a large woven rope, most likely stolen from Black Creek Mines, it hangs from a tree branch just out in front of me. It's approximately midways of the creek and about twenty-five feet over the surface of the water. You couldn't put a branch in a better place for a swing if you'd planned it. It protrudes from a giant-size cherrybark oak tree that grows at the tip of the small island just before the rocks. The tree according to legend has been here for years and as for the swing, the same. Periodically, someone changes the rope, the last time about two summers ago. I have no idea who, when or how they did it. When I questioned my dad, he said it was probably the elves.

The "rule of thumb," when the swing's not in use, is to leave the end of the rope at the top of the rock for the next person's convenience. As I look now, I see it securely wrapped around the limb of a gnarled old cedar that grows tight to the backside of the rock, just where it's supposed to be. I find it strange how most everyone follows this simple rule, but most everyone does.

I put the swing from my mind and move back across the length of the rock, back to where the path goes down to the creek. But, instead of taking the path again, I continue straight, straight up the side of the hill. I use the large rock formations along the hillside as my screen and the trunks of trees and bushes to pull myself upwards as I move almost belly-flat up to the top.

Just at the cusp of the hill, lying flush to the ridge is a large outcropping rock. It's covered with vine and hidden by bushes. I pray there's no snakes and bury myself in the vines.

I'm up about forty feet from the top of the big rock. Through a break in the bushes, I have a clear view of the creek valley below. Just as I settle, I hear the sound of voices and then I see them, less than fifty yards away. I almost waited too long to conceal myself. I lie very still and watch them come up the creek.

They're moving slowly, Trapper to the front, stopping about every two steps, then waiting for Bill to push him forward before he moves again. Bill's limping, favoring his left leg, the one Trapper bit, the same one he hurt when he fell. He doesn't seem to be too upset with Trapper's pace. He even stops to rest a few moments himself before he moves up to push Trapper forward.

At the foot of the path up to the rocks, Bill moves to the front, wraps a couple more turns of the rope around his left arm and then with his gun up and ready, he slowly moves upward, pulling Trapper along behind him.

At the top, before he moves from cover he stops again. He peers to his left down the length of the rock to the creek, then up the barren rock along the bank where I stopped to drink only minutes ago, then on up the hill towards the parking area and finally back down along the hill where I now hide. I close my eyes and hold my breath as his eyes come my way. When I look up again, his eyes have slid past me.

"Let's go!" I hear him say to Trapper. Then he moves back behind him and pushes him forward, stopping him just to the left of the fire pit, between it and the backside of the rock.

Holding the rope tight, he uses his gun hand to unzip Trapper's coat, then pulls it off his shoulders and throws it aside. He loosens the rope at Trapper's back and unwraps it from around his body, freeing his arms, but leaving it noosed around his waist. "Face down on the rock, hands up behind you," he orders.

Trapper is a pathetic sight. His busted nose has swollen to almost twice its normal size, his face streaked with blood. His hair is hanging wildly down over his eyes. His Christmas sweater is ripped at the neck and at one of the shoulders and both it and his jeans are stained and splattered with mud. The rope burn around his neck is a bloody red welt. I can feel it hurt from here, but even though "torn and tattered," it hasn't weakened his mouth.

"So where's your queer lawyer friend?" He yells back over his shoulder at Bill. "I told you he wouldn't show! Now what'ya gonna do?"

"Shut the fuck up and git down like I told ya," Bill tells him, nudging the back of his head with the barrel of the gun. As he lies down, he says something else that I can't hear, but I do hear Bill give his usual sarcastic chuckle and tell him, "That'll be the fuckin' day!"

Bill pockets his pistol, then leaving the noose around Trapper's waist, he crosses Trapper's arms behind him. He pulls the rope taut and wraps it several times around Trapper's wrists, then cinches it off. He reaches down, bends Trapper's legs up and uses the remainder of the rope to repeat the same process on his ankles. He's hog-tied him again.

Trapper strains to free himself, but it's only for show. He knows he's fighting a losing battle.

"What you gonna do now, big man," Trapper yells to him, "now that your buddy's left you hanging? If you're smart, you'll cut me loose and walk outta here!"

Bill reaches down and picks up Trapper's coat, walks over, wedges it down over his head, then zips it up. "Let's see how smart ya are, asshole," he tells him.

Bill moves across the rock, looks back up towards the parking area, then up to the sky, then back towards the parking area again. He takes off his hat, scratches his head and (I'll swear that it's true) lets a fart that I actually hear.

He looks bedraggled. The long hike after all the booze he's consumed has taken its toll. His leg is really bothering him, he grimaces on every step. His big donkey nose is swollen and red as a beet, making him look less like a donkey and more like Snuffy Smith. He perfectly fits what my dad calls a worthless piece of shit.

Sorry I hit him? Not for a minute! I'm just really scared for Trapper. I wonder what would have happened, if I hadn't bashed his nose? Would we be in the same predicament? Probably? Maybe? Why do I keep thinking about it?

Bill fishes out his Camels and his Zippo and cranks one up. He checks the pack to inventory his supply, then stuffs them and the lighter back in his pocket. He adjusts his hat, then limps down off the big rock and then up towards the parking area.

Going up the steep part of the path presents a few problems for Bill; the gimpy leg and the cigarette in his hand doesn't help. But with the help of some small trees and jutted-up rocks to hang on to, he finally makes it. Just at the top of the hill he stops, takes a final hit off his Camel and flicks it away, then taking his pistol back out of his pocket, heads up the short trail towards the parking area.

I wait until he's completely out of my sight before I move, then cautiously I make my way down the hill. I descend a different route from the way I climbed up, angling more to the left and coming out on the path that leads from the back of the rock to the creek. I'm about halfway down, so staying low, I ease up the path to the top and look up towards the parking area...no sign of Bill...good so far! My heart is racing like a locomotive, drumming through my ears again, my mouth as dry as cotton candy.

Just to my left is Trapper, no more than a dozen feet away. He's managed to remove the coat from over his head and is now lying on his side, trying to cut the rope between his hands and legs by rubbing it on the edge of one of the fire-pit rocks.

"Hey! It's me!" I signal in a high whispery-like voice, just loud enough for him to hear.

I see him freeze for a moment, then he rolls his head towards the sound of my voice.

"You OK?" I ask, as I crane my eyes up the hill for a sign of Bill.

"Duh! Do I look OK? Hurry up and get me untied before that fat pervert gets back."

I dart along the backside edge of the rock and fall to my knees beside him. I pull him up to a kneeling position and begin to fumble at the rope binding his wrists.

"Don't bother with that! Loosen the noose around my waist—it's a simple knot—easy to untie. Hurry!"

He's right of course! A simple noose knot is easy to tie and untie, if you got hands to do it. My dad says it's what the cowboys tied in their ropes when they hung rustlers. Fast and efficient and it don't take a lot of brains to learn how to tie it or untie it.

The knot's at the center of his back. I push the end of the rope up through the one loop holding it, pull the rope from around his waist and unwind it from around his wrists. "Here, get your legs," I tell him, handing him the rope.

Trapper sits back and bends down, pulling at the rope to free himself. I look up towards the parking area. *So far—so good,* I think to myself. *Slick as a whistle.* I'm just starting to smile, when for some reason, I glance up the hill behind us. My heart seems to stop!

Standing in almost the identical spot where I was hiding and aiming his pistol straight at me is Bill. I know he's gonna shoot!

"He's up on the hill behind us! I scream to Trapper, as I throw myself face down to the rock.

At almost the same moment I hear the ting of a ricocheting bullet and the sound of the discharged pistol as it thunders then echoes down the creek.

Only one thing comes to mind–*run-run-run!*

I look back up to the top of the hill. Bill is charging down towards us. His feet slip from under him, he's sliding on his ass.

"Run!" Trapper screams, continuing to free his legs, "I'm right behind you!"

There's only two ways, I can run. If I go down off the rock on the swimming-hole side, I'm wide open; he'll kill me for sure, so I go the other way. I charge straight for Bill, who is now halfway down the hill. He sees me coming and tries to steady himself for a shot, but his feet keep sliding and the trees and bushes on the hillside block his view. We're probably no more than twenty feet apart when I spin to my right and zip down the path along the back of the rock. Halfway down, I turn left and head back up the hill, following the same route I used to come down.

About five feet down from the crest, I fall to my knees behind a midsize black gum tree to catch my breath. I look down for Bill and see him right at the back of the big rock, just at the base of the hill. He's going for Trapper, whose legs are now free, but who, for some reason, is still trapped on top of the rock. "Stay right the fuck where ya are!" I hear Bill scream.

I jump to my feet and move across the side of the hill until I'm directly up behind them. I make a lot of noise, so Bill knows where I am. He and Trapper are at a stand-off and if I know Trapper, he'll risk getting shot before he'll let Bill catch him again. "Hang tight! I'm coming down to help you," I yell down to him.

Bill has his gun aimed at Trapper, but keeps glancing back up the hill at me. Each time he does, Trapper fakes a run.

"Ya try ta run, I'll shoot ya dead," Bill screams at him.

"Fuck you, you pervert!" Trapper screams back. He knows that Bill's in a bind. One, if not both of us are going to get away. Bill knows it, too, so he's playing it close to the vest.

Now that he's here afoot with no one to help him, his chances of being caught have more than doubled, especially if one of us is dead. They'll hunt him extra hard for that. Murder will hang him for sure, so he'll do everything he can to keep Trapper alive short of letting him go. But, darkness is almost on us and that will change it all. If Trapper's not back in hand by then, it'll be the icing on Bill's fucked-up day. He won't let it go any further than that. His vindictiveness will override his caution and no matter the consequence, he'll kill Trapper for retribution.

Was it me, it would be a different matter. In Bill's eyes, I'm the reason for his dilemma. Even knowing he'd spend eternity in Hell's fire, he'd blow me away without hesitation and gladly pay the price.

"Pick up that rope and brang it ta me, right now!" Bill tells Trapper, "I'm tireda screwing with ya."

I move a few more feet down the hill and take refuge in a cleft behind a rotting log. Bill glances back at me again. I'm no more than thirty feet away, too close for comfort, but perfect for my intentions. I take my slingshot from around my neck and dig a couple of the creek rocks out of my pocket. I load one of them into the soft piece of leather that used to be my granny's shoe tongue.

"Do it!" Bill yells at Trapper again or I'm gonna shoot ya right between yore fuckin' eyes."

Trapper moves to his right, his eyes never leaving Bill. He reaches down and picks up the rope and begins to coil it, but instead of walking towards Bill he moves backwards, stopping about two steps from where the rock juts over the water.

If he jumps in the water, he'll never make it. Bill will kill him for sure. He'll also kill him if he throws the rope in. He'll have no way to control him, the game will be over—he won't wait. I'm just about to warn him when he throws the rope.

Instead of throwing it in the water, Trapper attempts to heave it over the heavy growth along the back of the rock. He doesn't make it. The rope hits an upward branch of the old cedar tree and falls back down, then hangs on the very limb where you tie off the swing.

"If you want it, come and get it." Trapper yells, with a look of disappointment on his face.

I don't wait for Bill's reaction!

"Hey, Bill!" I scream. "You too chickenshit to come up here after me?"

I slide the other rock I've been holding in my hand inside my mouth, like I do when I'm hunting for birds. I steady my feet and rise up from behind the rotting log. Just as Bill turns my way, I have him centered in.

I go for his head, but I'm weak and trembly, so my aim is off. The trajectory of the rock is also altered by the ever-present twig of a tree. Instead of hitting his head, it strikes him just at the tip of his left shoulder and then banks to the brim of his hat, hitting it right at the hair line and propelling it down off the side of the rock into the creek.

Bill shrieks in pain, staggers to his right. Grabbing at his shoulder with his gun hand he twirls to face me. His left arm hangs limp to his side; he staggers again and almost sinks to his knees. All the while I'm thinking, what a great shot that would have been if I had been trying to make it and wondering if the padding in the shoulder of his coat saved his shoulder bone?

"Ya no good, lil' rottin', sonna a bitch," he bellows, swinging the pistol around towards me.

Out of the corner of my eye, I see Trapper running up the rock toward the path to the creek, then I fall flat behind the log, just as he pulls the trigger.

The sound of the shot is like a clap of thunder, I have no idea where the bullet goes. Suddenly I hear yelling and I force myself to look.

Trapper is almost to the path, but Bill, instead of coming up after me has sensed his movement and has turned back on him. He's blocking the path and waving the gun in Trapper's face.

"Don't try it! Don't fuckin' try it," he shouts, but Trapper isn't stopping.

Instead of shooting him, Bill swings the gun barrel right at his head. Trapper sees it coming and ducks then veers my way, up towards the hill, but Bill is wise to the move, he throws out his right leg and trips him up. Trapper falls flat, face down on the rock. Bill grabs him by the hair and drags him up. He cries out in pain and kicks at Bill's legs, but Bill avoids the kick, releases Trapper's hair and puts him in a chokehold, then, with no further a-do, drags him back to the center of the rock and throws him face down in the fire pit. He holds the gun to his head, then turning and looking up my way, he barks out a threat, "If I din't shoot ya already, ya gonna git yores next!"

I spit the backup rock into my hand and load it in the pocket of my slinger. It's the thrasher egg, I kiss it for luck, then I answer him back.

"Then why don't you come up and get me, you low-down, yellow cocksucker. You too afraid?"

So much for thinking I might have cracked his shoulder bone, I think as I watch him rub at his shoulder and flex his arm before he gives me a reply.

"I'm gonna have me some fun with yore lil' buddy down here first! Ya kin lay up there un' watch it! Hell, ya got a ringside seat!" he squawks out, thinks it funny, then gives out a two-snorter. "Then I'll be coming after ya!" he lets me know.

I think for a moment on what to do, then decide to follow my usual pattern of negotiation first.

"You better let Trapper go!" I yell down to him. Your buddy ain't gonna show—you hurt him, you're a dead man–I'll see to that. Wait 'til they hear my story, there won't be a lawman in this nation that ain't itching to put a bullet up your ass. Wait 'til the Klan hears what I got to say. They'll gather every Sheet in Alabama and recruit a thousand more the night they burn you and your buddy's ass on a cross.

I pause for a second trying to think of something else, but nothing comes fast to mind.

"Are you OK, Trapper?" I yell down to him.

I hear Bill tell him to keep his mouth shut, but it doesn't faze him at all.

"You forgot to tell him that my dad and brothers will cut his peanut dick and his balls off and make him eat 'em," Trapper yells out as loud and fast as he can.

"Ain't none of this gotta happen, Bill," I holler, "so just let him go. It's gonna be dark soon—come on! Whatta you say?"

Bill rises to his feet, still holding the gun pointed at Trapper's head, making his usual threats about what he'll do if he tries to run. He reaches up to adjust his hat, then remembers it's gone for a swim, so he runs his fingers through his stringy hair instead, then looks up at me and shoots me a bird.

"I say fuck ya—and all yer kin!" he screams. "And the law, and the Klan, and any fuckin' body else ya fergot to mention. I been one step ahead of all of 'em my whole life and I intend ta' stay thet a way—so ya ain't scaring me a-tall! Anyway, ya ain't gonna live long enough to ever testify agin' me, even if ther lucky enough to ketch me. Ya wuz dead the minute ya hit m'nose, ya lil' bastard. Now, ya jist stay where ya are and git all comfy un' watch me introduce Ol' Bob to Mr. Trapperman here…then like I said…I'll be coming fer your ass!"

So much for negotiation! I know what's gotta come next. I rub the "thrasher's egg" rock and kiss it for luck once again, then queasy and scared I begin to slide slowly down the hill.

To keep Bill off Trapper, I've got to hurt him bad. A rock to the head is the best chance I've got, but it's got to be a sure hit so I need to be as close as I can get. The optimum place would be from the foot of the hill at the back of the rock, but I don't dare get that close. Bill could just be using Trapper for bait. At that range he'd kill me for sure, then he'd be home free.

Sliding on my butt, feeling my way with my feet, I inch my way down. My slingshot's loaded, and ready, my eyes locked on Bill, when suddenly everything changes.

I see Bill reaching down for Trapper, grabbing him by the waist of his jeans, attempting to pull him up. He manages to pull him out of the pit, but Trapper clings tight to the rocks around it. "Come on! Git your ass up, we's gonna shuck them pants, see what we got!" I hear Bill tell him. He pulls at him again, moving him away from the pit a little further. Trapper loses hold on all the rocks but one; it's the pretty one I admired, he's dragging it with him.

Bill's full attention is now on Trapper, he's not watching me at all. Maybe I can get down to the top of the rock. Just as I register the thought, Bill drops the gun in his pocket. I scurry downward towards the foot of the hill.

"I'll show ya how to git yore lil' ass up," he shouts as he bends down straddling Trapper, then inserts both hands under his stomach and snatches him upwards.

Trapper comes up, just as Bill planned, but as he does he brings the rock with him, which Bill doesn't foresee. Just before Bill has him upright, he suddenly flips his head backwards, the same move he's always doing to get his hair out of his eyes. Whether planned or from habit I can't say. Nevertheless, the back of his head crashes right into the center of Bill's already busted nose.

Bill squeals like a pig and drops Trapper like a hot potato —but the show's not over. As Trapper drops from Bill's grasp, he uses the momentum of the fall, to slam the twenty-pound stone, with every ounce of his strength right on the top of Bill's left foot. It's gotta be crushed.

Bill hits the deck; he's on his ass, screaming to High Heaven in pain. He's reaching down holding his foot with one hand and rubbing at his nose with the other. Trapper's up like a flash. Grabbing the charred oak limb from the pit, he swings for a homerun, intending Bill's head for the ball, but Bill sees it coming and shies away, throwing up his arms to protect his head, which causes the blow to glance off the underside of his bicep and then into his chest. He falls backside to the rock gasping for breath. Trapper, not satisfied, raises the charred oak limb over his head and sends it crashing down across Bill's chest again. Then while Bill is flat on his back writhing in pain, he kicks him in the balls.

In awe of Trapper's action, I'm frozen in step at the base of the hill, standing just at the back of the rock. Everything's in slow motion again. I see Trapper drop the limb; it seems to float in the air before it finally lands on the rock. I watch him spin around, look down at Bill and smile, then turn, and when he sees me, smile again. I start to speak, but before I can find the words, he's vaulting off the side of the rock, floating to the ground, and running as though stepping in molasses up towards the parking area.

Bill springs back fast, bellowing like a wounded bull. He staggers to his feet, but his crushed foot won't hold his weight. He digs for his gun as he sinks to his knees. His eyes search for Trapper and find him just at the foot of the path. As he swings the gun up to shoot, I snap out of my trance and scream, "Duck, Trapper, duck!"

The shot goes wild. It sparks off a boulder about ten feet to the right of Trapper's head. The sound rattles my eardrums. I set for my shot, but before I can get it off, he turns and levels the gun at me. I panic! My body turns to ice. I flinch back and twist sideways, looking for a place to hide, but there's no place to go.

"Yore dead, you lil' motherfucker," he screams, as he pulls the trigger.

A thousand thoughts go through my mind in a nanosecond— foremost is, I'm dead! But I feel no bullet and have no pain. Then I hear the click, then another and another. I've just been resurrected! The gun has snapped on empty, the fucker's out of shells! I can't believe it! It hasn't crossed my mind the entire day. I should have counted his shots! Duh!

Bill can't believe it either. As he lowers the gun back to his pocket, I guess from force of habit, the last rays of the setting sun reflects the bewilderment on his face.

"Tuff shit!" I tell him as I smile and cock my slinger.

I don't even bother to aim. I do what's called a "Flipper Shot," a way of shooting practiced by some of the old timers who have been shooting slingshots for years. Your aim is by instinct, practice, touch and feel. I snap the stock outward as far as possible, at the same time drawing the leather pocket containing the rock up and over behind my head, then as I release I flip the stock forward. Shooting normal, a rock flies at about two hundred miles per hour—this method makes it a turbojet.

At first I think I've missed him. Out of the corner of my eye I see what I think is my rock sailing off to the right, out over the creek, but at the same moment Bill's head snaps sharply to his left. Then I hear him give a blood-curdling scream as he clutches at his left eye with both his hands. In the fading light, what I thought was my rock was really his eyeball.

The force of the blow must have felt like a freight train when it hit him. He's now flat on the rock, wailing and screaming, holding his eye, trembling all over. As he tries to sit up, blood and a kinda white-looking "goo," seeps out from between his fingers and drips downward over his face. He shakes his head from side to side. "M'eye, m'eye, m'fuckin' eye!" He screams, then falls backwards again on the rock. "Oh, m'God! Ya blinded me," he bellows to the top of his lungs. "I'll fuckin' kill ya, kill ya, kill ya! Oh, m'God…m'eye, m'eye!"

"You better call on someone who knows you," I squawk out to him, enjoying his misery.

I look to my right. Trapper's moving up the rocks toward me.

"He's out of bullets and minus an eye," I holler over at him.

As Trapper nears my side, Bill, still clutching at his face, tries to sit up again, but after a feeble attempt, he falls back and continues to moan.

We walk down the rock and look down at his fat wailing body. He's trying to stop the blood with his coat sleeve. His hands look like bloody claws.

Trapper pulls Bill's arm away from his eye to survey the damage. "Uck! Man! You knocked the shit outta him. Knocked his eye clean out!"

"We probably need to tie something over it so he don't bleed to death," I say.

Trapper thinks for a minute, then pulls at the tear on the shoulder of his sweater. "Get his knife and cut this sleeve off, we can use it," he says. "The sweater's ruined anyway."

I fish the yellow-handled knife from Bill's pocket and cut the sleeve off at the seam. We wrap it over Bill's eye and tie it at the back of his head. He looks like a pirate, celebrating the holidays.

"Put the knife back in his pocket, it's evidence," Trapper tells me. Duh! No shit!" I reply.

Bill, who has given us no trouble while we patched him up, balls up in a fetal position and continues to moan.

"Hey, Bill! Does it hurt?" Trapper asks him and laughs.

"Yeah, Bill, which hurts the worse, your foot or your eye?" I chime in.

"You forgot his balls," Trapper tells me, then laughs again.

"Yeah Bill, with them busted balls, you'll be able to sing tenor in the Kilby Choir until they get around to throwing the switch," I tell him.

"Or maybe, he'll get lucky and get life," Trapper adds. "Then, ol' 'Leroy,' his cellmate, can pork him up the ass every night with his foot-long prong. Nigger's love a big fat ass!"

"That would make them 'soulmates,' not 'cellmates,'" I correct him. We both laugh!

"Ya gotta git me some help," Bill looks up at us and croaks, barely able to speak. He tries to sit up again, but his head is barely off the rock before he falls back. The left side of his face is starting to swell, the marbleized gunk from where his eye used to be, is peeping out from under the bandage. It's the color of a barber's pole. I hear a rattling sound as he labors to breathe.

"Boy! I bet a slug of that ol' pot whiskey would taste good now, huh, Bill?" I say. "Too bad you pigged it all up!"

"M'foot's broke, kin't walk and I thank m'ribs'r cracked," he moans to us like we give a shit. "Go up ta the road un' flag down somebody ta take me ta the hospital, an' tell 'em to hurry."

"Damn, Boogie! Bill wants to be our buddy again," Trapper tells me.

"You think that means he ain't gonna kill us no more?" I ask.

"I don't know? Are you still gonna kill us, Bill?" Trapper looks down and inquires.

"And our mamas and daddies and grannies?" I add.

"Ya'll pay, if'n ya don't!" he croaks up at us again.

"Now look there! He's threatening us again," Trapper says to me. "He's just not to be trusted."

"Sorry, Bill, you're not trustworthy, so we gonna go get help, but unfortunately for you, it's gonna be the law," I tell him.

"And...to make sure you're still here when we get back, we're gonna 'hog-tie' you. Best I remember you're real familiar with that!" Trapper adds.

The very thought of what Trapper has just told him seems to strengthen Bill's vocal cords. "Ain't no son of a bitch gonna ever tie me up!" he screams. Then, with a sudden burst of energy he begins to roll away from us, over and over like a log, down along the top of the rock.

"Look, Trapper! He getting away," I say and laugh.

We follow him along. He stops about three feet from where the rock protrudes out over the water, then lays there face down, his breathing is labored and heavy. Trapper walks over to the old cedar tree and fetches the rope.

Bill doesn't cooperate at all when we tie his hands until I twist his broken foot a little, then it's a cinch. His legs are easy, he gives us no trouble at all, but I tweak his foot again just for the hell of it.

As we stand back and admire our handiwork, I'm pleased, but for some reason, not entirely satisfied. I have a nagging desire to make him suffer more.

"Good thing that ol'cedar caught the rope or we'd of had to tie him with the swing," Trapper says, then looks at me and smiles.

That's when we decide to hang him!

Trapper wants to hang him by the neck, and we seriously consider it, but after weighing all the pros and cons, we decide choking him to death kinda outweighed all the pros.

I'm for hanging him by his crippled left leg and Trapper really goes for it, but we can't figure out a way to tie him high enough on the rope so his head isn't under the water, so that's out.

We finally settle for a noose under the armpits.

The swing-rope elves somehow realize that a rope hanging just to the top of the water from this particular tree will reach only to the edge of the rock, so to provide ample swinging and tie-off capabilities, they always add about an additional fifteen or twenty feet to its length. This gives us plenty of rope to work with.

Trapper unwraps the swing from the limb of the ol' cedar and walks to the edge of the rock. "Come here and help me pull it tight," he tells me. "I wanna be sure where the water line is."

I inform him that you can tell by looking at the rope. "It's cleaner where it hangs in the water," but we agree to check it out just to be sure.

After determining that having Bill's head up about three feet over the water line of the rope when we noose him will do the trick, we drag him over to the edge of the rock.

Bill's still not being cooperative at all. He's screaming and moaning about the pain he's in, making all sorts of promises to us, if we'll "let bygones be bygones" and go get help. One minute he's telling us, if we help him, we'll never see or hear from him again and a minute later making threats about what he's gonna do to us when he's free.

"M'buddy's gonna be here eny minute and ya lil' cocksuckers'r gonna be sorry," he screams. "I got friends thet know I'm over here. They'll come a-lookin' if I ain't back by dark. We'll burn both ya houses down when yore asleep, bar-b-que yore whole damn family," he promises, and on and on and on.

Trapper places the rope around his body, threading it under the arms right at the pits, then pulls the slack through and pulls it tight. I grab the rope and the two of us strain to hoist him up. Trapper comments that he's "dead weight" and we both laugh. Using a combination of push and pull and a little torture, we finally get him high enough for Trapper to noose the rope and pull it tight in the center of his back.

Bill's still berating and begging, sometimes in whispers, sometimes in screams. "Please don't push me in," plays out of his mouth like a "hung up" record.

"Hang on a minute!" Trapper tells me, as he unfastens Bill's overall pocket. He pulls out the Camels and the Zippo, "So they won't get wet," he tells Bill, and laughs. "Ready for one-two-three?" he looks up at me and asks.

I look down off the rock. The water is the color of the darkest of skies. The last rays of the setting sun glitter faintly over its surface.

The gloaming hovers over us just minutes away. "One," I say…

We push him hard! As he falls, it flashes through my mind that he looks like a skydiver, like the ones in the news-reels when they first leave the plane.

His ride isn't very dramatic. About two feet out from the bank, he does a kinda belly-flop, then as the rope becomes taut, it jerks him upward and he begins to skim slowly across the water. At the middle of the creek, his legs start to drag, the momentum of the swing is lost and he sinks downward to almost the tops of his shoulders. As the current of the creek captures his body, it turns him facing to the north, the way that it flows.

He hasn't stopped screaming since his flight off the rock. Loud caterwauling shrieks, mixed with "help me's" and threats, then suddenly he becomes quiet, his head bends downward as though in prayer. Then, turning back up to look our way, he begins to buck, back and forth, back and forth, straining and grunting in an effort to break the rope.

We move off the big rock and walk down along the rocky bank until we're just to the front of his face, then sit and watch him 'til his bucking stops and he's quiet again.

"He might as well give it up," I tell Trapper. "He's never gonna break that rope."

"If he did, he'd drown," he chuckles. "Dumb shit can't swim tied!"

We both laugh.

"Hey! Look out there!" Trapper says, pointing towards the water, "just to the front of Bill. Know what that is?"

"Is that a snake?" I ask, straining my eyes for a better look.

Trapper laughs. "No," he says, "it's the tail end of the rope floating on the water, but it looks just like one."

"Looks like it just swam out of Bill's tussed-up ass," I say.

"Or just gonna swim up in it," he adds and laughs.

"Hey, Bill!" he yells, "Look up! There's a big snake, just in front of you: It's gonna swim right up your ass, eat your insides!"

"That's funny," I say, as we both laugh.

It takes only a few moments, then slowly raising his head Bill looks out along the water with his one good eye. Uncoiled, just to his right is the rope. Drops of water have formed along its oily surface, casting kind of a sparkle as they capture the fading light. The movement of the water beneath it gives an illusion that it's swimming.

"I think it's a diamondback!" Trapper yells out.

Does he see it? I can't tell. One eye, badly hurt, fading light. Maybe? Probably! Or maybe not. Maybe it's just Trapper's suggestion, topped off by his inordinate fear of snakes that does it. Whatever it is drives Bill wild. He's twisting, bucking, wailing to the top of his lungs again, then, just as though someone has clicked his off switch, he suddenly stops, shudders and then hangs there limp.

The gloaming is upon us. The sounds of the creek magnified in its veil. Its darkness invades our mind. Strange noises, heard only at night, begin to fill our ears. Still we sit.

We replay the events of the day from both our perspectives. The things we could have done, should have done and would have done. We reach the mutual decision that we've been lucky, extremely lucky.

I feel very strange, like I'm on the outside looking in. Kinda like the world I woke up in this morning has somehow been replaced. One minute I'm happy and giddy, the next minute I'm sad and want to cry. We talk about missing the party and both of us pretend it doesn't matter. We talk about what our parents are gonna say and do and that matters a lot. We discuss our wounds and try to show them off, but it's too dark to see. We need to go, but both of us dread what's still left to do before the day can end. So we sit silently for a while and smoke Bill's cigarettes.

"How long has it been since he moved or made a sound?" Trapper asks, breaking the silence.

"I don't know, quite a while," I tell him, "maybe thirty minutes?"

"You think he's passed out or just playing possum?"

"Maybe he's dead," I say.

"Don't say that! You're giving me the "heebie-jeebies.""

"His ghost will haunt you forever," I tell him and laugh.

"Hey! How many rocks you got left?" he wants to know.

"Why?"

"Dig 'em out and give me the slinger. I'm gonna stir him up a little, see if I can make him move."

I hand him my slingshot, then stand and dig the rocks from my pocket. "There're seven left," I tell him.

We take turns, not wanting to hit him but, trying to shoot just close enough to him to make him move, but in the darkness it's hard to see. Trapper shoots the last rock. "I think I hit him with that one," he tells me. "I didn't hear it hit the water."

"If you did, he didn't make a sound. You know what that might mean...?"

"Don't say it! It gives me the creeps."

"Let's swim out there and see," I tell him. "Come on, I dare you."

The water's cold as ice, but it feels wonderful on my battered body. We dogpaddle out, Trapper letting me go ahead. He's told me at least fifty times, "If he's dead, I ain't gonna touch him." He'd be telling me now, but he's holding the Zippo in his mouth.

"I touched a dead person once," he confessed, while we were shucking our clothes. It made me feel real creepy," he went on to say.

"So have I, didn't bother me at all," I told him.

"Now I can't even stand to look at someone who's dead," he adds.

"You looked at Bobby Ford."

"I did not."

"Yes, you did—I was standing right beside you when you did it."

"I had my eyes closed."

"Yeah, right!"

"Remember Mrs. Baker, who used to teach our Sunday School class?"

"Sure, she died, so what?" I said.

"She was real young...and pretty..."

"And had great big titties," I add.

"I touched them."

"What?"

"One of her titties, when she was in her casket, when no one was looking. I touched it!"

"You touched her on the titty?"

"That was the one! The one that made me feel creepy."

"We were only about eleven then," I tell him.

"I know, ain't that weird?"

"You need help!"

I tread water just to the front of Bill's body, looking for any sign of life. Trapper's right behind me, breathing on my neck.

"Can you tell if he's breathing?" he whispers.

"Where's the lighter?"

"I got it in my hand."

"Put it back in your mouth, you gonna get it wet."

I move in closer, only inches away from his face. "Hey, Bill," I ask, really loud, how's it hanging?" Trapper's laugh is muffled by the Zippo, but not a single sound from Bill. Trapper mumbles something around the lighter. I think it's, "kann-lo-lee-is-ace," but I'm not certain.

I'm tiring, so like it or not, I grab on to Bill's shoulder for support, then since I'm there, shake him a couple of times. "Bill….Bill, you still hanging in there?" I ask. I don't get his usual "fuck you." Bill ain't talking—in fact, I don't even think he's breathing.

"Gimme the lighter," I say to Trapper, who's hanging on my back.

I stroke the Zippo and hold it tight to the front of Bill's face. It's not a pretty sight. I know he's dead immediately.

Trapper's hanging over my shoulder, taking it all in. "He's dead, ain't he?" he asks.

"As your Grandpa's dick," I reply.

I feel the wind from Trapper sigh along the side of my face, as the air rushes from his lungs…

"God…man…I can't believe it! We killed somebody!"

"We didn't kill him, we ain't killed nobody!" I snap at him.

"We must of, the fucker's dead."

"I think it was the snake," I tell him. We both have to laugh.

"Anyway, he killed hisself," I say, "Don't matter how he died."

"'Cause he fucked with us?" he asks.

"'Cause he fucked with us!" I reply.

"Well, hell, flare up that Zippo and let's look him over again!" he says.

We stand on the rocks and let the air dry our bodies, then begin to dress.

"Doggone it!" Trapper barks.

"What?"

"There's two of Bill's Camels left and no way to light them."

"It was evidence, quit bitching."

I finish dressing, tie up my shoes, then reach into my pocket for my hanky. Creek water is still in my nose. The hanky's wet and dirty. As I unfurl it looking for a clean spot to blow on, my little jingle bell that I had tucked inside falls out and jingles down the rock to Trapper's feet.

"Thanks, but you didn't have to," he says, as he picks it up and shoves it in his pocket.

"What?" I ask.

"Reward me for my heroic action during your escape. Thanks."

"It's the least I can do," I tell him, laughing inside. "Be sure to wear it when we're up on the rock dump."

"What's that mean?"

"It means let's go get Britt and get this thing over. I'm starving to death."

I'm with you there! And, while we're walking, we better think about what we wanna say.

— CHAPTER 12 —

ABSOLUTION

WE'RE JUST AT THE TOP OF REESE HILL, ABOUT A MILE from Black Creek when we finally get a ride. Old man McCombs, the farmer who peddles produce at the commissary on Saturdays picks us up, says he recognized us because we have stolen so many apples off his wagon. He laughs when he says it.

He's in an old, black 1936 Chevy, a two-door Master Deluxe that looks like it's about ready to collapse at any minute. His seats are full of crap, so we ride on the running boards. His top speed is about twenty mile per hour.

As we pass Sarah Humphries' house, I see several cars parked out front, the party's going strong. I think about Darlene and wonder if they're playing the kissing games yet? I imagine some of the creepos there kissing her and her liking it and her choosing one of them to take my place. I almost signal for Mr. McCombs to stop, but I don't.

Mr. McCombs has to swing left on the Trafford Road, so we drop off at the foot of Drugstore Hill and thank him for the ride. We promise not to swipe anymore of his apples. He laughs and says, "I don't believe it," as he pulls away.

As we walk up the hill, I remember my bicycle's at Harleys... "Crap! I should have stopped and got my bike," I say to Trapper.

"Why?"

"Somebody might steal it, dummy!"

"Who'd want that piece of junk?"

We don't have far to walk. Britt's house is just past the middle of the hill, second house down from the filling station. We see no one on the way up.

Just after we knock on the door, the porch light comes on, we move back to the edge of the porch. The door opens; Mrs. Britt looks out at us through the screen.

"Can I help you?" she asks.

"Yes, ma'am," Trapper tells her, "We're here to see Sheriff Britt."

"Are you Camp boys?"

"Yes, ma'am," I say.

"Come up closer to the door so I can see you better," she says, as she unlatches the screen.

As we walk forward, she opens the screen door and studies our faces.

"Goodness Christ Alive! What in the world has happened to you two boys? Have you been fighting?"

"No, ma'am, not with each other," Trapper says. "Is the sheriff here? We really need to see him."

"What's you two boys' names? I'm not sure I recognize you."

"I'm Kerry Smith," I say.

"And I'm Charles Trapp," Trapper adds.

A light comes on in her eyes. "I know you! You've cut my grass before," she says. "You're the ones they call Boogie and Trapper, aren't you?"

"Yes, ma'am," we answer.

"My Lord! Come on in, the sheriff's out back in the utility house. He and Dorcey, Jr. are listening to the *GrandOle Opry* and working on a model airplane. I won't let them play that hillbilly music in the house. Ya'll sit right there on the Chesterfield and I'll go fetch him, it won't take but a minute. Goodness! I can't imagine what's happened to you two boys. We need to get you to the doctor!"

We don't want to dirty her furniture so we sit on the floor and watch her as she whirls through the dining room, out towards the kitchen and then out the back door.

Trapper looks at me and laughs.

"What?"

"You still smell pissy," he says.

"I threw my underwear away when we went in the creek," I tell him. "Must be soaked in my pants. Think she smelled it?"

"I just hope she don't think it's me," he says and laughs.

Mrs. Britt is quite a "looker." A tall stately lady with dark brown hair and kindly eyes and, for the record, about twenty years younger than the sheriff. Everyone jokes that he held his gun on her and made her marry him.

Her parlor, which I'm sure is what she calls it, is very nice. The Chesterfield is big, brown and heavily upholstered, with two chairs to match. The tables are shiny mahogany with lots of lamps and figurines and dollies covering their tops, but it's what I see in the back corner of the room that really catches my eye. I nudge Trapper and point, "Look over in the corner," I say.

His reaction is immediate, "Man! A television," he yelps. "Wow!"

It's a television all right—a big mahogany console with the screen at the top. It has four official-looking control knobs on the front with the brand name, Admiral, in gold lettering scrolled above them.

"Fighting crime must pay well," I say to Trapper. "These things cost as much as a car."

"They're the rage now, if you can afford one," he says.

"Man! I wish we had one."

"They ain't much on them and you can't hardly get anything out here in the boonies," he advises.

"Yeah! But there will be, wait and see!"

I hear a throat being cleared and Britt's familiar "Hup, hup." I see him coming through the dining room headed our way with Dorcey, Jr. right behind him. Britt's tie is off and his usual suit coat has been replaced with a checkered robe.

"I don't know what kinda trouble you two little burr heads have got into, but it better be good, cause you're making me miss 'Red Foley' and 'Uncle Dave Macon' on the *Opry*," he tells us.

"You boys know Jr., don't you?"

Both of us give him a "yes sir" and nod to Jr., even though we really don't know him that well. He's sixteen, goes to school in Birmingham, and has little to do with the Camp boys.

Britt tells us to stay where we are, stands and looks us over for a minute, then sits down on the edge of the Chesterfield.

"Jr., go in the kitchen with your mother, get yourself a Coca Cola or something while I talk with these boys. I'm not sure what they have to say will be fit for your ears. Hup, hup now," he says.

He looks us over again and shakes his head, like he can't believe what he's seeing.

"Now! Before either of you say a thing, here's the rules," he tells us. "Only one of you talks at a time. I'll point when I want the other to talk. Stay with the facts, don't go wandering off somewhere in left field, and no cussing, cause the Missus is real religious and she might hear it, OK?"

We nod our heads yes and he points to me.

We tell him the whole story, taking turns at his direction. He interrupts us occasionally to clarify something or to pull us back into the infield, but for the most part, he just sits and listens, his eyes squinting or opening in bewilderment as he hears our tale. When we're through, he takes us back over parts of it again. Pointing rule still applies.

Britt: "You say Bill picked you up down at Harley's?"

Trapper: "Yes, sir."

Britt: "A little after eleven this morning?"

Me: "Yes, sir."

Britt: "He was drinking whiskey?"

Me: "I smelt it on his breath, but he didn't drink none in front of us, that is, 'til we bought the beer."

Britt: "Boodle's boy, Snakeman, sold you the beer?"

Me: "Yes, sir, but I don't want him to get in no trouble."

Britt: "Ya'll stopped up at Hopewell to visit the dead and he started getting drunk and frisky?"

Trapper: "Yes, sir."

Britt: "Why didn't you tell him to 'screw off' there?"

Trapper: "We wanted the five dollars. We thought maybe he was just joking around."

Britt: "You said you had an altercation over at the falls and he wrecked the car, right?"

Me: "Yes, sir, that's when I hit him in the nose."

Britt: "That's when you finally figured out he wasn't joking?"

Me: "Yes, sir."

Britt: "And, you say the car was stolen?"

Me: "Yes, sir, that's what he told us."

Britt: "He noosed you and tied you up?"

Trapper: "Yes, sir, then Boogie, when he came to!"

Britt: "And he threatened you with sexual violence?"

Trapper: "Yes, sir! He said he was gonna sell us to his buddy. They was gonna cornhole us and make us suck their dicks. Said they'd burn our houses down and kill all our families if we didn't do what they said."

Britt: "Watch your language."

Trapper: "Yes, sir."

Britt: "Did he molest you in any way?"

Trapper: "He just beat the shit out of us is all, just threats on the other stuff."

Britt: "This buddy... he's supposed to be a lawyer...from Birmingham?"

Me: "Yes, sir, that's what Bill said. A 'big shot,' a real rich one, said he had sold him boys before."

Britt: "But you never saw him?"

Me: "No, sir."

Trapper: "No, sir."

Me: "Bill said they killed the boys when he got tired of them; hung 'em. I'll have to whisper, if I tell you what he said they done to them while they were dying."

Britt: "That won't be necessary..."

Britt: "So he drug you noosed, all the way from the falls over to Big Rock?"

Trapper: "Yes, sir, we walked, wasn't a 'soul' on the road. He only drug me when I wouldn't walk."

Britt: "And you had got away, so you followed them?"

Me: "Yes, sir."

Britt: "Why didn't you go for help?"

Me: "He just said he was meeting his buddy down the creek. I didn't know where. I wanted to get his tag number to give to you."

Britt: "Good thinking!"

Me: "Thank you, sir."

Britt: "There was another altercation at Big Rock?"

Trapper: "Yes, sir."

Britt: "Is that the flip you shot him with?"

Me: "Yes, sir."

Britt: "Let me see it."

Britt: "Who whittled this stock?"

Me: "My brother, J.B."

Britt: "Fine piece of work."

Me: "Thank you, sir."

Me: "J.B. said they killed Japs with them during the war."

Britt: "No shit!"

Me: "Yes, sir."

Britt: "This thing's a lethal weapon, so be careful with it, OK?"

Me: "Yes, sir."

Britt: "So, after you two little 'Davids' subdued the 'giant,' you tied him up, is that right?"

Trapper: "Hog-tied him, like he did us, yes, sir."

Britt: "So you had him tied up? Why did you feel a need to noose him to the swing?"

Trapper: "Retribution, sir, showing Britt his neck."

Britt: "Holy shit! Is yours the same way?"

Me: "Mine's burnt, but not like his. I wasn't noosed as long."

Britt: "Why didn't you noose him around the neck when you noosed him?"

Trapper: "We was afraid if he fell off the rocks, it would kill him, sir."

Britt: "But that's what happened anyway."

Trapper: "Sir?"

Britt: "You say he fell off the rocks, you say he's dead."

Trapper: "We said we think he's dead, sir."

Britt: "He just roll off or what?"

Me: "We had to pull him real close to the edge to noose him."

Britt: "And...?"

Me: "I'm not really quite sure, sir. I was feeling real weak…and dizzy…like sorta blacking out, you know? Next thing I know, he's falling in the water."

Trapper: "I think ever' thing we'd been through was just catching up with us, sir, 'cause I was feeling the same way."

Britt: "Why you so convinced he's dead?"

Trapper: "He had some sorta fit out there in the water and after that, he ain't moved or talked."

Me: "We stayed there a pretty long time, hollered at him and everything."

Britt: "You know what? If I'd been you, I'd a pushed him off."

Me: Silence

Trapper: Silence

Britt: "Anything you boys want to add to what you've told me?"

Me: "Nothing I can think of, sir."

Trapper: "Me neither."

Britt: "Change from what you told me?"

Trapper: "No, sir."

Me: "No, sir."

Britt: "So when I go over there, I'm gonna find me a dead man?"

Me: "That's what we think, sir."

Britt: "You know, if you two little burr heads are leading me on a wild goose chase, I'm still gonna be kicking your asses a week from now?"

Trapper & Me: "Yes, sir."

"Junior!" Britt bellows out, "You in the kitchen? Get in here!"

Junior must have been right at the door. "Yes, sir," he snaps too immediately, hurling in towards us.

"Did you gas up the truck today?"

"Daddy! I just washed it this afternoon," Junior whines, knowing it's going to get dirty, because he's been eavesdropping from behind the kitchen door.

"Did ya put gas in it, dammit?"

"Yes, sir."

The truck sorta half-ass belongs to Junior. Britt bought it for his sixteenth birthday, but Britt uses it occasionally to haul off people he's arrested. Mainly, niggers or low-down "white trash" he don't want smelling up his car. It's a pretty truck—a tomato-red Studebaker, with whitewall tires, black fenders and black running boards. Junior likes to flit around town in it, showing it off.

"Where's the keys?" Britt asks him, holding his hand out.

Jr. reluctantly hands them over.

"Now! Here's what I want you to do for me," Britt tells him. Jr. immediately perks up. "Go get your mother's car keys and back her Cadillac out of the garage and stay in it. I'll be out there in a few minutes to tell you what to do. Hup, hup now!"

He turns back to us. "You two boys stay right where you are, I'll be right back."

He walks back towards the kitchen. I hear him talking with Mrs. Britt, but can't understand what they say, then he comes back out and goes into what I surmise is their bedroom, just off the parlor. A few minutes later, I hear what sounds like him talking again, but it's muffled by the door.

"He's talking to someone on his telephone," Trapper whispers.

"You think he's gonna arrest us? Maybe he's calling the county sheriff?"

"For what? We ain't done nothing!"

"Who do you think he's calling?" I wonder.

"Ain't nobody in town got phones, except some of the bosses. Maybe it's one of them?"

"The school principle's got one."

"Why would he call him, dummy?"

"Man! I'm starving," I say, changing the subject.

"Let's hit Mrs. Britt up for some food," Trapper suggests with a grin.

"Yeah, and maybe get her to turn on the television, too!"

We both laugh! It makes our faces hurt.

Britt's gone for about ten minutes. When he returns he's dressed in khaki, both shirt and pants. He's wearing shiny combat boots; his hat is snapped low over his eyes and his .45 rides high at his waist. I see the bulge of his sap in his back pocket.

He heads out the front door with "I'll be right back" to us as he passes. I presume he's headed out to instruct Jr.

He's gone probably five minutes before he returns with new instructions. "You boys come on in here to the dining room."

We arrange the chairs so Trapper and I sit side by side at the far end of the table. Britt brings in a couple of chairs from the kitchen, so I'm presuming eight people, including us, are gonna be here.

I smell coffee perking in the kitchen and think of breakfast. My stomach growls and Trapper laughs. "Maybe we gonna eat," he says.

Britt opens a door of the buffet and extracts a crystal decanter about half-full of an amber-colored liquid, then places it and a shot glass at the opposite end of the table from us. He stands there for a minute, looks around and sighs, then there's a rapping on the door.

"I want you two boys on your best behavior now, you hear? There's somebody here that's gonna want to ask you a few questions before your daddies get here. We'll be right back soon as I fill him in, so hold what you got, OK?"

"Yes, sir," we both answer.

He lumbers to the front door, opens it and slides out the screen. I hear him whine, "I'm sorry," just as the door closes.

"Jr. must be back," Trapper whispers. "He hasn't had time to get our dads."

"They're gonna know soon enough, don't rush it," I tell him.

"Mine's gonna be pissed," he says.

"So is mine."

"Who do you think is out there?"

Before I can tell him, the door opens and I see Jr. headed our way. Britt has exiled him again.

"Hey! What's going on?" he asks in an inquisitive whisper. What happened over at the creek? Why's my dad going over there?"

"How you know he's going over to the creek?" Trapper wants to know.

"I heard ya'll talking, but only got bits and pieces of it," he confesses. "Has something bad happened?"

"We're not supposed to talk about it," I tell him, knowing that Britt is keeping him out of the loop.

"Did my dad say that?"

"That's what the sheriff said," Trapper affirms.

"Then I guess you better not," he says, looking all disappointed and turning to leave.

"Hey, Jr.," Trapper says, stopping him. "We're really thirsty. Any chance of getting something to drink? Maybe a soft drink or something?"

"And something to eat," I add, "like cookies or something," hinting to him that we can be bribed.

"Gee! I don't know if I'm supposed to do that," he says, ignoring our bait. "I guess I could ask the sheriff."

"Never mind!" Trapper tells him.

"Are our dads out there?" I ask him.

"Thought we wasn't supposed to talk about things," he tells me, with a sarcastic smile on his face.

"It'd be OK for you to tell us that," I say.

"Are you two guys under arrest?"

"Heck, no! We're the good guys. Your dad's just holding us for questioning," Trapper tells him. "Ain't that right, Boogie?"

"You sure?"

"Scout's honor!" We both tell him, giving him the sign.

"I ain't gone to get 'em yet. Not 'til the sheriff tells me."

"Then, who's he talking to?" Trapper asks.

"You'll know soon enough," he says, breaking off the conversation and heading for the kitchen.

We sit and wait again; I'm getting hungrier by the minute. Jr. strolls back in, a cold "RC Cola" in his hand. He takes a drink, smacks his lips and sighs, "Man! Is that good." He's just sitting down to drink it in front of us when the front door opens and Britt summons him again.

"Prick," Trapper says when he leaves.

"Royal," I reply.

I'm not totally surprised when I see who follows Britt into the dining room. For several reasons I thought it might be him. Foremost, was the rumor that it was on his order that Britt had banished Bill from Black Creek in the first place; banished him to quell the hottest rumor of them all, a liaison between Bill and Mr. Pat's oldest son, Bert. This should be interesting.

Patterson T. Anderson, superintendent of Black Creek Mining, is the King of Black Creek. It's said that if he likes you, he can't do enough for you and if he don't, well, let's just say you're eventually unemployed. "Mr. Pat," as he's referred to, prides himself on his personal relationship with his "Men," as he calls them. He strolls the operation often and chats with them, asks about the job, the wife, the family. The miners love him.

To me, it's all for show. A "con job," to alter the fact that neither he, nor any of his stuck-up family desire to associate with the commoners, the Camp people. Trapper says he's an Alabama Poly bean counter, a would-be blue blood, who tells everyone how great Black Creek is, and then sends his kids to Birmingham to school. Why ever he's here, you can bet it's in his interest.

He enters the room like Royalty, wearing a checkered, satin-cuffed, smoking jacket over black, sorta silky looking pajamas. He still has his houseshoes on. He hardly looks at us at all.

He's old, like Britt, in his fifties, medium height, doughy plump, and shaped like a dope bottle. His hair is almost total gray and it's thinning, especially on the front. His eyes are large, a weepy looking brown, that he constantly mops with his hanky. He hides them under black horned-rim glasses. His face is saggy and jowled like a bull dog. When he speaks, it's high and squeaky and seems to resonate through his nose, which is a bona fide replica of the one on W.C. Fields.

"Have a seat, Mr. Pat," Britt gushes, pulling out the chair at the head of the table. "Mamma," he yells out towards the kitchen, "is that coffee ready yet?"

Mr. Pat doesn't seem interested in the coffee, as he has already discovered the whiskey and is busy pouring himself a shot.

Just as he turns to look at us, Mamma arrives with the coffee— none for Britt or the two of us, only for him. It's in a dainty little cup with flowers painted on it and a saucer to match. It looks similar to the one my granny keeps in the back of my mother's china cabinet and dares anyone to use. Mrs. Britt beams as she places it on the table in front of Mr. Pat.

"Well I do declare! Mrs. Britt, you honor me," Mr. Pat exclaims, looking up at her with a great big smile on his face.

"Now why in the world would you say that, Patterson?" Mrs. Britt asks, fawning all over him.

"Why? For serving me coffee in fine Victorian china, that's why!"

He picks up the cup and looks at it closely. "Hmm...let's see...ah, ha! Strafford Shire, no less, right? Victorian English? C.F. Bowers, late eighteen hundreds? Right?"

"Now how in the world do you know all that?" She inquires, gushing all over.

Before he answers, Mr. Pat sheds his horn-rims, reaches for his breast pocket hanky and mops his eyes. "I must confess, Mrs. Britt," he says, in a very sober tone. "This china is very familiar to me. My maternal grandmother had this same pattern. As a child, when we would visit her at her home in Atlanta, she would allow me to drink coffee from a cup just like this one. She said coffee wasn't worth drinking unless it was served in a fine porcelain cup. She was right you know!" he adds, taking a sip. "It enhances the flavor immensely."

I look over at Trapper. We both roll our eyes. We've both heard him tell "Peg Leg" Jack, the night watchman up at the Top House that the brew he boils up in a pan over a barrel fire was the best coffee he ever tasted. Ol' Jack serves it up in a tin cup.

"There's sugar and cream, if you'd like," Mrs. Britt volunteers.

"Oh, no, black's fine, thank you," he says.

"Thanks, Mamma," Britt tells her, guiding her towards the kitchen. "We really need to get started here. If there's anything else we need, we'll holler."

As soon as she's gone, Mr. Pat pushes the coffee aside, tosses back the waiting shot, then pours another and looks at us.

"Who else have you two boys told this wild tale to besides us?" he asks.

Neither of us answers.

Britt points at Trapper. "Answer Mr. Pat's question," he tells him.

"We ain't told no one except the sheriff, sir. I guess he must have told you."

Mr. Pat tosses back the second shot and pushes the coffee cup a little further away.

"Me talking to you, don't necessarily mean we believe you, you know...Sheriff Britt's gonna run over there and check it out directly, soon as your daddies get here. I do hope you boys ain't fibbin', gonna be embarrassing to your daddies if you are."

"Then why are you talking to us?" I ask him, but he chooses to ignore it and continues his questions.

"How many folks in town saw the three of you together today?"

Britt points to Trapper.

Trapper thinks for a few moments before he answers. "The onliest ones I can think of right off hand that actually saw us with Bill was Square and Snooks. Can you think of anyone else?" He says, looking at me. I shake my head no.

Mr. Pat looks at Britt inquisitively, "Square and Snooks?"

"Two nigger boys, Mr. Pat. These boys said the two niggers was down at Harley's when Bill picked the two of them up. I don't think it's a problem, never knowed Bill to hang out in the Quarters. They probably don't even know who he is."

"Is that correct?" Mr. Pat asks, finally catching on and pointing to me.

"They saw us talking to him before we got in the car, then Bill chased 'em off the road. Made out like he was gonna run them down. They'll remember that. I don't know where he hangs out or if they know him. He said his buddy hated niggers, only fucked white boys."

"Watch your language," Britt tells me.

"Bill's preference is fat white boys," Trapper adds. "He told me that when we was going down the creek."

I kick him under the table.

"He said the fatter, the better!" Trapper rambles on.

Mr. Pat's face has suddenly gone red; Britt coughs and clears his throat.

Mr. Pat looks at Britt. "This incident with the colored boys disturbs me if what these boys are telling us is true."

"Just how well do you two boys know this vagabond?" he asks, pointing to me.

"Just from when he used to hang out around town's all. He hung mostly around the school and was usually at the picture show on Friday nights. Today was the first time we seen him in about a year."

"Did he come here looking for you two boys in particular or just boys in general?" He asks me.

"I think he was just looking for boys was all…gullible ones."

"Did he today or has he ever mentioned any other young person by name that has or might in the future suffer from his wrath?" He asks, directing it to Trapper.

"He mostly bragged about the women he's screwed. According to him, he's diddled most ever' female in town. As for the boys…he just said he liked 'em fat."

Mr. Pat nods his head towards me. I'm tempted to continue Trapper's Fat Boy routine, but instead I say, "He ain't got no future, he's deader than last year's corn."

"That's still to be verified, young man," he reminds me.

He pours another shot, tosses it down, then looks up at Britt and shakes his head. "Tell me, Dorcey, what possesses these Camp boys? I mean, to think nothing of getting into a car with a man of this caliber…a man with so little degree of worthiness? It escapes me!"

"Greed and ignorance in this case," Britt says, looking hard at us. "But, if what they say is true, they might have done the world a favor today."

"Maybe…maybe," Mr. Pat says, fingering the shot glass and then licking his finger. "But…I'm not sure it's something the world needs to know."

After this comment, everyone is quiet, the silence only broken by the ticking of the clock on the parlor mantle. We all jump when it cuckoos. It does it nine times. I'm surprised it's that late.

"Which of you boys are which?" Mr. Pat looks at us and asks.

"I'm Trapper, Orvil Trapp's son," I volunteer.

"Boogie Smith, Burl Smith's son," Trapper adds, continuing to play the game.

"Two fine boys in most cases," Britt interjects, failing to notice the switching of identities. I look at Trapper and grin.

"Well, if what they say is true and if the repercussions are favorable, then it's a sure bet, I'll remember them when they're of age for the 'pits,'" He tells Britt, still giving us the once-over.

I look over at Trapper. "I's won'ts ta bees da wons what's loads da cole," I tell him.

"An's I's wanna bees da Boss what kiks yo ass whins yo ain't loadin' fas e-nuf," he replies back.

We both have to laugh and so does Britt, until he sees that Mr. Pat doesn't think it's funny.

"You two boys settle down now," he tells us, then looks at Mr. Pat and shakes his head. "I think they might be in shock," he tells him, "I'm gonna have the doc check them out."

"Good idea…and make sure he checks them for the other thing, too," Mr. Pat says.

I hear the rattling of a door knob and the slamming of a screen. Dorcey, Jr.'s back.

"They're here, sirs," he says, rushing into the room, almost saluting. "I got 'em waiting on the front porch."

Britt tells Jr. to put the Caddy back into the garage, then go work on his model plane, he'll call him if he needs him. Then he and Mr. Pat leave for a conference on the porch, so we sit and wait again.

I'm nervous as a cat in heat, dreading seeing my dad. Not fearful of a whipping or anything like that because my dad has never laid a hand on me. If I've ever needed switching, he always leaves it to my mom, who doesn't seem to mind at all. I just dread the look he's gonna give me and the little talk I know we're going to have. I pray there's not going to have to be a trial or some kind of a hearing about this. My dad doesn't handle heavy exposure well. I'll be hearing about this forever.

"I'm gonna quit bitin' my fingernails," Trapper says right out of the blue. He's as worried as I am and has nibbled one down to the quick.

"You say that every time you make one bleed," I tell him.

"Look who's talking, yours are gnawed to the nubs."

"Yeah, but I'm not a marshmallow ass like you are. I don't whine about it all the time. Tell you what! Stick the one that's bleeding up your ass for a second and I guarantee you won't bite it any more tonight."

"Funny, funny!" he says.

The conference on the porch lasts for about twenty minutes before I hear the door finally open. I hold my breath as they all file into the dining room.

In addition to our dads, I'm totally surprised to see my brother, J.B., and Trapper's older brother, Eddie, who is nineteen—help recruited to pull Bill out of the creek crosses my mind. J.B. stops at the dining room door and stares at me until my face begins to burn. Our dads come around the table to where we're sitting and proceed with a ritual of questions that goes something like this:

They want to know: "Are you boys all right?"

We tell them: "Yes, sir."

They: "You look pretty beat up, are you sure?"

We: "We're beat up, but we ain't hurt bad."

They: "Well, thank God for that!"

We: "We already have, sir, we been praying to him all day."

They: "I hope you're not making light of this situation. Ya'll could be in some serious trouble here."

We: "No, sir, we're not, but all we did was try to protect ourselves. It don't seem fair that we'll get in trouble for that."

They: "Why in God's world would you get into a car with an animal like that?"

We: "He said he needed help. You've always told us to follow the Good Book, to help your fellowman."

They: "Britt said, he promised you money, that's why you told him you went off with the varmint. The Good Book teaches charity, there's a difference! I hope you'll remember that in the future."

We: "Yes, sir."

They: "You can be sure, that you and I are gonna have another serious conversation about this once this mess settles down."

We: "Yes, sir."

At this point Britt moves around the table to where we're talking and breaks up the inquisition. "We're ready to go when you guys are," he tells us.

We take three vehicles over to the creek. Britt's Buick, Jr.'s red Studebaker and Trapper's dad's old Chevrolet pickup that he and Eddie had come down to Britt's in.

Trapper and I ride with Britt and Mr. Pat, who we drop off at his house before we follow the others. J.B. drives the Studebaker and our two dads and Eddie wedge into Mr. Trapp's truck.

Britt's Buick is fast. We catch up with them at the foot of Reese Hill, then move to the head of the pack as we descend the other side.

Britt parks the Buick about 50 yards down along the dirt road to the creek, its black color blends into the night. The three of us ride the rest of the way with J.B., Britt in the front and Trapper and I in the truck bed, holding a folded-up sheet and a miner's lamp that Britt dug out of the Buick's trunk. Other than a few slips and slides, we make it down to Big Rock with no problems at all.

The trek down the hillside to the water is made in silence, with the exception of a comment by Britt, who is at the head of the procession shining the light. "Don't nobody fall and break a leg or I'll have to shoot ya," he tells us.

At the bottom of the hill, a spot of light to the middle of the creek confirms our story. Bill is still hanging around.

"Jesus Fucking Christ. Just like they said," Britt tells us all, breaking the silence once again. "J.B., I hope you and Eddie can swim, 'cause you just been elected!"

J.B. and Eddie shuck their clothes and swim out, they pull Bill back towards us as far as the swing will reach, then un-noose him and pull him in the rest of the way to the bank. My dad and Mr. Trapp help them pull him out of the water.

"He's dead, ain't he?" Britt confirms as they deposit him on the rocks.

"Deader than a wedge," Eddie says. "Already gittin' stiff."

"That cold water speeds it up," Britt tells him.

"Did just the opposite to my weenie," Eddie says and laughs. It sets off a chain reaction that continues off and on while they untie him and straighten him out.

It's not an easy job, but with the help of all, with the exception of Trapper and me and Britt who is supervising, we get the body up to the parking area. "Wrap that sheet around him and put him in the back of Orvil's truck," Britt directs; "and Orvil, when we get back to town, go straight to the doctor's office, and pull into the back. Doc's waiting for you."

"Unwrap him and lay him face up on that examining table in there. Doc directs J.B. and Eddie as they lug Bill up on the back porch of his office. He's holding the door open, chewing on his cigar, not looking too happy that he's been called on so late to handle this kind of a job. Mr. Pat is standing alongside him. "That was fast," he comments to Britt as he strolls up to him. "Damn! That's the same thing his wife tells him, Pat," the doc quips and laughs along with everyone else, even Britt.

Doc's about sixty, short and rotund, cocky as hell. He's bald with the exception of a fringe of gray around his ears. His head and nose are always red, rumored to be from all the booze he puts away. He's been the Company doctor here for years, knows everyone. Hands out "Sulphur Drugs" like jelly beans. He mops your throat out even if it ain't hurting, then tells you to stop gagging. He's also, as the rumor mill goes, screwing his nurse who is half his age. She has a great ass and great big tits, which sorta makes him one of mine and Trapper's heroes.

We all trudge up on the porch. "I don't need no big crowd in here while I'm trying to work," Doc tells Britt, stopping us at the door.

"How long's it gonna take?" Britt asks.

"Well, if you just want me to verify he's dead, less than a minute," the Doc tells him. "If you want my best guess from what, maybe an hour. If you want a full-blown autopsy to verify it, probably the rest of the night, but then I'm gonna have to notify the proper authorities for a formal request to do it to make it legal."

Britt pulls at his bottom lip for a moment, then looks at Mr. Pat, who in turn gives him a "let's talk a minute" nod of the head.

"Let me think on it for minute, Doc. Meanwhile, before you get started on the main course, would you mind checking these two boys out to be sure they're all right? They been banged up pretty bad and have been acting kinda strange. They could be in shock. Check it out for the other, too, OK?"

"Put 'em in the examining room with the corpus delicti while I grease up my finger," Doc says, then looks at us and laughs.

"OK," the Doc tells us as he looks closely at Bill's corpse and then drapes the sheet back over it. Strip off them clothes and put 'em on the floor, in the corner over there, so they don't contaminate nothing. Then drag that chair that's over there against the wall out here to the center of the room. One of you'll sit down and the other will stand back quietly, about two paces behind it.

"Does this dead body bother you, boys?" he asks us as we're carrying out his instructions.

"Not really!" We both tell him.

"I didn't figure it did," he says. "I been treating both you boys since you was babies. They ain't two tuffer little nuts in this whole Camp than you two. If that ol' boy laying dead on the table over there had knowed you like I do, he'd a run when he seen you!"

We both laugh!

"Are you sorry he's dead?"

"Kinda," we both tell him.

"What the hell does that mean?" he wants to know. "Either you are or you're not."

"'Cause we might be in trouble if he's dead," Trapper blurts out.

"Just as I figured," Doc says.

"What scared him so bad?" he asks us.

I look at Trapper. "Did you scare poor ol' Bill?"

"All I did was say 'boo,'" he tells me and laughs.

"Don't go playing your little games with me now," Doc tells us.

"Was he afraid of the water? Is that why you pushed him in?"

Trapper looks at me real serious. "You know, Boogie, now that the Doctor has mentioned it, he could have been afraid of water. He certainly was lacking in the personal hygiene department."

"Yeah, Doc!" I say, "He smelled really bad like…what's the word I'm searching for Trapper?"

"Shit?"

"Yeah, Doc, like shit."

Doc laughs! "You boys are something else," he says.

"OK, now! One of you plant your skinny ass in that chair."

He examines us from head to toe and douses us with iodine. It stings like hell's fire and the more we complain the more he mops it on. After he's flooded every crevice of our bodies where there's a scratch or a cut, he makes us open our mouths and mops out our throats, then he makes each of us stand up in the chair and bend over, while he probes at our asses.

"Well, neither of you have been anally penetrated, that's good," he tells us. "I've mopped your mouths just in case. If nothing else, maybe it'll kill some of the bullshit that grows in there."

"You might orta' check Boogie out a little closer, Doc," Trapper tells him. "He's been acting awful 'swishy' lately!"

We all laugh!

"By the way," Doc says, opening a cabinet along the wall and coming out with a big hypodermic needle. "I know you boys won't mind a little old shot. It would be a real shame if them jaws locked up."

"Well, what did you find?" Britt asks the doc when we come back out to the porch. Trapper and I are both rubbing our arms, 'cause the shot hurt like hell.

"The seals are still intact, which I'm sure everyone will be glad to hear," the Doc tells him, still amused at our reaction to having to get a shot.

"That's good! They gonna be OK?"

"Are you kiddin'? Those two little fuckers are tougher than whet leather; they'll sleep like babies tonight!"

"They tell you anything about what happened? Maybe something they didn't tell me or Mr. Pat?"

"They told me nothing at all. I think they've said everything they're gonna say or ever will say about this thing. I can't believe they took a man of that size down. Hell! They're proud of it; you can tell by the way they're acting. They'll talk about it between themselves, but you or anyone else have heard all you're ever gonna hear," Doc tells him, looking over at us, knowing we're listening.

"What the decision on the dead meat? Whatta you want to do?" he goes on to ask Britt.

Britt takes his hat off and scratches his head. "Mr. Pat and I've discussed it. He'd like for you to see what you can do in about a half-hour. Give him a good going-over, then come on down to the house and give us your professional opinion on why the fucker croaked. We'll go from there, OK?"

"Suits me fine. I was just gettin' into my gin when Pat called. I'm looking forward to gittin' back into it."

"All right! Everybody back to my place," Britt tells us, as he herds everyone down the steps.

J.B. and Eddie are the last to leave. As Eddie passes Doc, I hear him say, "That fucker's dead as your dick, Doc, he's already startin' to smell."

Doc just shakes his head, "You know, Eddie, you have a very active imagination, but unless you can get it under control, I'm gonna be forced to commit you. Your mother's already planted the seed, you know?"

"Only kidding, Doc!" Eddie says and laughs.

We're back at Britt's. Trapper and I have been relegated back to the parlor floor, while the rest of them are seated in the dining room drinking Mrs. Britt's coffee (from regular cups) and discussing the "mess." About forty minutes pass before Doc shows up. Trapper and I are almost asleep, but perk up when he comes in and edge closer to the dining room door on the pretense of admiring the coveted television set. Even though their voices are kept low, we hear most of what they say.

Britt: "OK ever-body, let's knock it off and hear what Doc's got to say. You got the floor, Doc."

Doc: "Thanks, Dorcey. Well, …the subject's dead, ain't no doubt about that. I cut his clothes off and looked him over real good. He has a visible injury to his left shoulder, right at the junction of the arm. It's swollen and bruised. His left foot sustained a blow across the top, resulting in the breaking of the cuneiform bones, most all of the metatarsal bones and at least three of the phalanges. In layman's terms, that means the top of the foot and the toes were crushed. His left eye, and I won't even try to describe it medically, has received a blow that has knocked his eyeball clear out of his skull. The eyeball was not with the body. In addition, his two front teeth have been knocked out. I found one of them and the creek rock that apparently did it, in his mouth. This blow, I would say, came after his demise, as there's little blood or bruising. It's my understanding, from what Pat has told me, that one of the boys shot his eye out with a flip. The mouth wound looks like they used him for target practice after he was dead. Aside from these things, he had a few rope burns on his wrist and legs from being tied and that's about it…and, oh, yes! He had a bite mark on his left leg and had recently had a hard lick to his nose which induced bleeding and swelling. And remembering that, I also remember he had a dark bruise across his chest. Looks like he sustained a lick that broke several of his ribs. Musta' hurt like hell."

Britt: "Would any of these wounds or a combination of them all be enough to kill him?"

Doc: "It's hard to say what will kill a man, Dorcey. You need an autopsy for that, but if you want my professional opinion, from twenty-five plus years of practice, the answer would be no! He'd be hurtin' like hell, probably wish he was dead, but none of the blows would have killed him, especially in that length of time. The wound to the eye might would have taken him out later, if he failed to get proper medical attention. That blow's probably what saved the boys' lives. When a man loses an eye it's not just the hurt! It affects him psychologically like you can't believe. The strongest of us turn into blubbering idiots. The only thing I know that's harder for a man to come to terms with than the loss of his eye is the loss of his dick."

Britt: "Then what you think done it, Doc?"

Doc: "More than likely his heart. He's a big, barrel-chested guy, overweight, enamored with alcohol from what Pat tells me. He smoked like a fiend. I can tell that from the teeth he's got left and from the nicotine residue on his fingers. But…that's just a guess, mind you. And, as I said before, you'd need a full-blown autopsy to be sure."

Britt: "Damn, Doc! What you just described about smoking and drinking comes close to home for me and you."

Doc: "I been telling you that for the last ten years, Dorcey, every time I can catch you for a checkup! As for me, hell! I'm already pickled."

Everyone laughs!

Britt: "So you think a combination of everything that happened and then him rolling off in the water caused his old ticker to just stop?"

Doc: "That would be my guess, however, I'm not fully convinced, he just rolled off."

Britt: "Why's that, Doc?"

Doc: "Well…and I'm hesitant to mention it, but something frightened him, terrified him. You can tell it by the expression on his face. Something caused that. Something else happened out there. I asked the boys about it. They laughed it off. Said they just said, 'boo,' to him. Then again, maybe that's what happened, but I feel like I should mention it all the same."

Britt: "You mean he was scared to death?"

Doc: "I think that was part of the equation."

Britt: "Well, I'll be damn! Anything else, Doc?"

Doc: "That's all I can tell you in the length of time I had to look him over."

Britt: "Thanks, Doc, and would you mind sticking around for a little while?"

Doc: "Only if you dig out another glass, so I can partake in some of that whiskey."

Everyone laughs!

The dining room is abuzz with mumbles, everyone talking at the same time about what Doc has said. I hear the buffet door open, then close again, Britt's getting the doc a shot glass. I look at Trapper and whisper, "The doc's a pretty smart ol' bird, huh?"

"I just hope he stays on our side," he whispers back.

Britt: "OK, guys, I'm gonna turn it over to Mr. Pat, he's got a few things he wants to say."

But, before Mr. Pat can say a word the cuckoo clock goes off again, singing its song twelve times, signaling the end of the day. It must have startled everyone again. "Damn, Britt! Go shoot that thing," I hear Doc say, then I hear them all laugh. After this, Mr. Pat begins.

Mr. Pat: "Men, a cur dog came into our town today or I guess now it was yesterday, according to that infernal clock in there. He sneaked in, unbeknownst to anyone. He came to rob us of our most precious commodity, something even more precious than the black diamond underneath these hills and hollows. He came to rob us of our children...and by God, he almost succeeded!"

"Like all mad curs, he also came prepared to kill if things failed to go his way. Dorcey had the Doc bring the evidence that proves it for you to see. He took it straight from the vermin's pockets."

"Could I have that bag, Dorcey? I want these men to see what Doc found."

While Mr. Pat pauses to gather up the bag, I take the opportunity to smile like a Cheshire cat at Trapper and receive one back in return, both of us signaling our cleverness for preserving the evidence.

I hear the rustling of a paper bag and several mumbled gasps coming from the room.

Mr. Pat: "I'm gonna hold these with my handkerchief so as not to tamper with the evidence, Dorcey. I think that will pass procedure.

"First off, and I'll hold it up so you can see it, is a .38 caliber Colt revolver. A snub nose, a belly gun, nickel-plated, no less. It's empty now, but when Bill came here, it was loaded with six bullets, all of which he fired at those two boys in there today in an attempt to kill them—we've all heard their story.

"Next, as a backup weapon, he was armed with this big

yellow-handled knife, which appears to be razor sharp. The boys have told us how he threatened them with it.

"I got to tell you, men! He was armed to kill and it was only by the grace of God that he didn't.

"Also in his pocket was this Zippo lighter. He not only used it to light up his cigarettes, but also to intimidate the boys by threatening to burn them. He also told them he would kill their families—burn your houses while you slept. Nice guy, huh?

"Now, the last thing of any importance I'd like to show you is this wallet. I want you to look at it very closely, especially the gold-lettered initials on the front here…they're kind of faded, but there's no doubt that they read S.R., no doubt at all. Keep that in mind, 'because you'll understand the significance later.

"Yeah, I'll tell you. After looking at this evidence, there's no doubt about what this cur's intentions was, even if we didn't have them boys' story, no doubt at all!

"Now before I move on, because there's a few more things I wanna say. I wanna take just a minute here to say to Burl and Orvil and your two sons here, J.B. and Eddie, just how sorry I am that this tragedy has happened. Being a family man myself, I know how you must feel."

I hear a chorus of "thank you, Mr. Pat" coming from the room.

I look at Trapper; he's rolling his eyes and pumping his fist up and down in reaction to Mr. Pat's performance. I laugh and nod my head in agreement.

Mr. Pat: "Now! I think the best way to continue this discussion is to give you men some information that you probably aren't aware of concerning this vermin who invaded our little town about four years ago.

As most of us already know, he came into town riding on a bus, a replacement for old man Sawyer Ruggles, who had been driving the ol' Blue Goose between here and Birmingham for years.

"As you also know, I'm sure, Sawyer Ruggles was murdered…and then, God help us, violated in a manner too gross to even mention. And, I want to tell you now, Dorcey and I suspected that piece of shit lying dead in Doc's office from almost the beginning.

"After observing his actions around town for awhile, Dorcey here, came to me and said he had a sneaking hunch that this varmint might be involved in old man Ruggles' death. I suggested he notify the proper authorities and if nothing else, advise them of his concerns, which, by the way he did that very day. Nothing came of it! Whether anyone ever bothered to check him out, I can't tell you—anyway we continued to watch him.

"About a year ago, long after he was fired from his bus job, but still continued to hang around our town, both Dorcey and I had had enough, so… (a-hem, a clearing of the throat)… for the good of the town and young boys in it, I decided to take action."

"The first thing we did, since he claimed to live somewhere down in Birmingham, was to contact the 'Bull,' the Birmingham Police Commissioner, who by the way, is a personal friend of mind, as I worked hard to see that he was elected in 1936.

"We gave the Bull a run-down on everything we knew about the piece of shit, including his actions in our town and our suspicions concerning old man Ruggles. The Bull told us he would check him out thoroughly and get back to us, which he did. I'll give you a few of the highlights.

"He does have a Alabama driver's license, issued under the name William Brady—in fact, it's in the wallet here that we took off of him, but he has also used several other aliases from time to time… for example: he did a few bouts of wrestling down at the City Auditorium, mostly fill-ins when the scheduled wrestler was either drunk or just didn't show up. He wrestled as the 'Texas Terror,' he told wrestling officials his name was William Blankenship. He's also used the names, William Bradshaw and even William Penn! Can you believe that?

"These last two names were given to the Birmingham Police when he was arrested for homosexual activities in the Birmingham Courthouse Park.

"Anyway, to make a long story short, after the Bull had filled us in on this character, I told Dorcey to show him the road, ban him from our town. Tell him we don't want him or his kind associating with our youth…and, as I expect most of you know, Dorcey did just that and everything has been fine…until this!

"Now let me tell you this! Dorcey and I didn't just run this bastard out of town and forget about him. No sir! We've kept our eyes and ears on him pretty regular. Last we heard, probably a couple of months ago, he was in California. His showing up here was a complete surprise to both of us.

"Nobody really knows this rascal. Have no idea where he's from or who he really is. The bus company fired him after Dorcey asked them to recheck his references and told them about his antics in our town. Seems as he lied about everything on his application.

"He's constantly on the move, different addresses, and different names—not one friend that Bull or any of his people could find. Everyone they talked to who had ever met him hated him, said he was a 'psycho pervert,' so he ain't gonna be missed…not by anyone. It's been the same down in Birmingham as here. He blows into town and then out and no one really cares when he leaves or whether he ever shows up again.

"Now, here's the way I see the situation: If or when? Now hear me out! If or when what happened here today comes to light, here's what we can expect.

"Remember what happened last year…down in Birmingham? Remember when Bull arrested that Commie Senator from out in Idaho—the one running for Vice President that was cozying up to the Southern Negro Youth Congress, that Negro Commie group? Remember the publicity, the lawyers, the liberal radicals? Hell! It was all the newspapers could talk about. The radio newshounds ate it up.

"Well, let me tell you something. We got Negros involved in our little problem here, too. …Two of them, who not only saw Bill and the two boys talking together and in the car together, but, and this information comes straight from them two boys in there…they—the Negros—were almost run down by the car, courtesy of Bill and as far as they—the Negros—know the boys! I believe the boys told Dorcey, 'you get ten points for a Nigger.' Of course, Bill said it, but you can bet it'll come out just the opposite from the liberal lawyers.

"Yeah! There's no doubt that these two little Negros will be talked to, once this comes out. I can just imagine what they're gonna say. Then, we're gonna have civil rights lawyers and homosexual lawyers out here everywhere, squealing and hollering and stirring things up. They gonna want the boys indicted, maybe for murder, but most definitely manslaughter. They'll ignore the fact that he was a pervert who kidnapped two boys and in the process had a heart attack.

"I can just imagine what some of the 'gossips' in town will tell investigators about those two boys in there, what their enemies will have to say and, as a matter of fact, what yours or my enemies might say when they investigate us, which they'll surely do! Believe me!

"Those lawyers and their investigators will tear this town apart. They'll dig up ever piece of dirt they can find and if they don't find it, they'll invent some. The newspapers and the radio will have a field day!

"Then the laws gonna have to step in—probably indict those boys in there. They'll have them and ever' other young boy in this town in court and on the stand. God only knows what stories some of them might tell. It'll be 'get even' time for sure.

"Orvil, you weren't here then, but Burl, you'll remember it. Remember in '32, when the Union organized? The whole town a war zone, soldiers living in the community house, Marshall Law prevailing? Hell! That was kindergarten in comparison to what this will be.

"Think how this is going to affect the Company—the adverse publicity, the downturn in production that's bound to occur. I gotta tell you, the "big boys" ain't gonna like it. Hell! This could shut down the whole operation here, kill this whole town!

"Just so you know, some of these young 'bean counters' the Company's hiring straight out of college that think they know everything are already asking me lots of questions about the cost of the operations here. Those little fuckers will jump on the bandwagon to close us down, convince the powers to be that they'll be better off without us. We can't let that happen. We've worked too hard to build what we have here…too damn hard to let a piece of scum tear it down!"

For a few moments, there's complete silence in the room, everyone stunned by Mr. Pat's words. I'm pretty shook up myself, now that the possible consequences of today's deeds have been laid out before me.

I look at Trapper; he's started gnawing another nail. He gives me a weak smile. "They can't do nothing to us for protecting ourselves," he tells me, but he doesn't say it very convincingly.

A few seconds later, the mumbling starts again, everyone talking at the same time. I hear a "Mr. Pat's right," and "we can head this thing off if we play our cards right," then a "we gotta think about how this is gonna affect them young boys in there." My spirits are lifting somewhat as Britt settles everyone down. "Hold on boys! Hold on," he tells them.

Britt: "I think the general consensus is that everything you've said is right, Mr. Pat, and that the rest of us are in complete agreement with you. We don't want to see anything happen that's gonna disrupt the town. Whatta you think we orta do?"

Mr. Pat: "Thanks for your support, men…and, Dorcey, to answer your question, let me say, I've thought on this thing long and hard. It's come to me that we should do the Christian thing…what any Christian man would do.

"Orvil, let me ask you a question. Let's say all us in this room decided one hot day to head over to the creek for a swim and let's say you were the first one to get there. Just as you start to dive in, you see a dead cur dog floating in the center of the creek. What would you do?"

Orvil: "Well! After I said, 'Ah, shit!' I'd drag it in and pull it up in the woods somewhere out of sight, then I'd probably throw up!"

Everyone laughs.

Mr. Pat: "Would you tell the rest of us about it when we got there, so as to mess up our swim? I mean, like nobody I know wants to wallow around in water where a dead dog's been a'soaking. You always get water in your ears and your mouth when you swim. Remember that! On the other hand, we all are gonna be hot and sweaty and that water's gonna feel so good. And, hell! Who's to say the creek hadn't already been contaminated anyway! What's at the bottom of it we can't see? Or who pissed in it or took a dump in it or maybe washed their dirty clothes in it? The kind of things we never even think about before we jump in.

"Would you tell us, Orvil, spoil our swim or just keep quiet and let everyone enjoy themselves? What would you do?"

Orvil: "Well, Mr. Pat, let me put it to you this way. I've always kinda gone by the old saying, 'What a man don't know, don't hurt him none.' Too much information just gives a man more shit to worry about. So no! I wouldn't mention it to you fellows, but you can bet your ass I'd laugh ever' time you swallowed some water."

Everyone in the room chuckles at Mr. Trapp's answer. Trapper shakes his head and laughs. "That's my dad," he says.

Mr. Pat: "When you drug that dog up in the woods, would you bury him, Orvil?"

Orvil: "If I had the means, like a spade or a pick, something to dig with in the back of my truck, I would, yes, sir. I think that's the only Christian thing to do. If not, I'd cover it with rocks, or leaves, or something to protect the body best I could. If nothing else, it would help keep the stink down."

Mr. Pat: "Would you think about that dog later, Orvil? Let the thought of it dying dwell on your mind?"

Orvil: "Hell, no! It'd be 'out of sight, out of mind' with me, Mr. Pat. I got enough shit to worry about without getting hung up over a dead dog I don't even know."

Mr. Pat: "How about the rest of you fellows? Anybody here who would do anything different than Orvil?"

I hear rumbling sounds from the room again, then the familiar sound of my dad clearing his throat. "Mr. Pat," he says. "The onliest thing I would add to what Orvil here has said is that wherever I chose for that dog's final resting place, it would be someplace where it would never be stumbled on by anyone…I mean, it might not look Christian if somehow its owner showed up later and somehow, someone, who might of stumbled on the dog's resting place told him the dog was dead and buried and whoever buried it hadn't at least made an effort to locate him, tell him about the fate of his dog."

Britt: "Good thinking, Burl!"

J.B.: "Could I say something, Mr. Pat?"

Mr. Pat: "Go ahead J.B, I been wondering why you're so quiet to-night. You're usually talking a mile a minute."

Everyone chuckles.

J.B.: "Well, first off, I want ever-body here to know that I'm proud of my little brother and of Trapper for what they were able to do to-day. I don't know, nor do I care, how that son of a bitch died. Whether they killed him or he had a heart attack don't mean diddly shit to me. If he weren't dead, I'd kill the fucker myself for what he put those boys through. You can bank on that.

"Secondly, I would like to add something else to what my dad and Orvil has said about the dead dog.

"During the war, when I was fighting the Japs on those islands in the Pacific, let me tell you it was scary. One of the most dangerous times was when you were assigned to 'forward patrol.' Sometimes, in order to survive or to save the life of a buddy, you had to do things you never thought you could or would ever do. Things that neither you nor your buddies ever talked about again, things that you and them will take to the grave. These things were never reported. They never happened if you read the official reports of the missions. We had a 'Pact of Silence' is how I thought of it, to cover this type of situation and nobody I ever know of broke it. I suggest we apply that same philosophy to the saga of the dead dog."

Somebody pick me up off the floor! I can't believe what I just heard my brother say! He's been staring daggers at me all evening and now he says he's proud of me. And, man! I love that 'pact of silence' thing he said. Something else to add to my repertoire. Trapper liked it too! He shot me the OK sign when my brother said it.

Mr. Pat: "J.B., you, like the others here are a very wise man and based on that, I gotta tell you fellows, I think we have just solved our problem. Whatta you think, Dorcey?"

Britt: "Sounds like all the bases are covered to me. I sure as hell can live with it, and just by chance, I happen to have in mind the perfect place for the poor ol' dog's burial. Fits right in with another problem I gotta do something about. One Doc just brought to my attention this week."

Mr. Pat: "Excellent! How about you, Doc?"

Doc: "Hell, Pat! I've been drunk since 6:00 this evening, don't have no idea what you fellows are even talking about."

Everyone laughs.

Mr. Pat: "OK! Then I guess we better get those two boys in here and talk with them, fill them in on what we've decided.

Doc: "Hell, Pat! They been listening to ever' thing we said. The little shits are settin' right outside the door there."

SUNDAY, APRIL 10, 1949
9:00 P.M.

It's a warm, clear, spring night. Probably around 70 degrees. The stars are shining bright in the heavens.

We're in a caravan again, or maybe a better word would be procession, a funeral procession to be specific—Bill's, to nail it down. We're on our way to his internment.

We've just come through the narrow underpass under the dump car tracks on Nigger Quarters Road and are moving at about a 20 MPH pace along the main road of the Quarters. It's unpaved, narrow and rutted, still damp from yesterday's rain, so the dust isn't bad.

Britt, in his black Buick is in the lead. Mr. Pat and Doc are with him. They have all the car windows open so Mr. Pat doesn't gag from Britt's and Doc's cigar smoke. Mr. Trapp's pickup is second, with Eddie and him in the cab and Trapper and me, along with Bill's corpse in the truck bed. We're there to keep it from rolling around or falling out when we hit a bump. J.B. and my Dad are behind us in J.B.'s green '41 Chevy.

I'm "full as a tick." My mom's been feeding me and treating me like a king the whole day. I slept 'til almost noon. It was almost 3 A.M.

when we finally got home and I got in bed. Since the moment I awoke, she's been hovering over me like a hen, either feeding me, rubbing salve or putting cold compresses on me or asking me if I'm thirsty.

For breakfast, which I had at lunchtime, she made me my absolute favorite in the whole world meal, hot "cat's head" biscuits and "saw-mill" gravy. That's gravy made from flour, watered-down milk and "fat-back" grease, for those of you uneducated in southern cuisine and "I love it better than a hog loves slop!" I only ate six of the biscuits, because my mouth is still swollen and the cut under my bottom lip hurts, but the banana pudding she surprised me with at supper, went down like a dream.

Throughout the day I munched on fried chicken, mashed potatoes (with more gravy) and ice cream. I drank lots of iced tea and six Grapicos. My mom said I needed fluids.

She fed me in bed, where she made me stay all day, except when I had to go to the toilet and at supper, when she let me come to the table for the banana pudding. Kid stayed in bed with me and slept most of the day after pigging out on the gravy and biscuits, which he also loves.

Mom wasn't happy about me going back out tonight, but my dad told her it was necessary. I don't know what he's told her about what happened, but so far she's been quiet on the subject. I'm sure she's going to bring it up later.

Granny's dying to hear the story, I know. She's been pampering me, too—helping my mom wait on me and all, then sitting with me, telling me stories when I wasn't asleep. As curious as they both are, I'm surprised they got through the day without asking me about it.

Fanny and Cratham both dipped in for a few minutes to see how I was and to tell me how happy they were that somebody finally beat the shit out of me, because that's what they think happened—Fanny, because she just naturally hates everyone and Cratham, because he's still pissed about the panties on the front of his car and about his keys that are still missing. He and Norman got up about 2:00 yesterday afternoon and discovered that the keys were nowhere to be found. They searched everywhere—the car, the yard and the house. Norman finally had to walk home. Granny said Mr. Williams put the keys back in the switch, after they had searched the car and Cratham hasn't bothered to look in the car again. She said she was sweeping off the porch when she saw him do it. She thinks it funny and hasn't bothered to tell Cratham his keys are in the car, said that would maybe teach him a lesson about drinking. Anyway he's really pissed at me. Didn't believe me at all when I told him I didn't know anything about either the keys or the panties.

Trapper's day has been similar to mine, he says. The one exception is that Jean came over to sit with him for a couple of hours, the lucky "son of a gun." He said she drilled him to tell her what really happened to us, but he maintained the Pact of Silence and stuck with the story that was decided by the group that we would tell.

Since neither of us went to church today, we haven't heard a word about last night's party. We're both on pins and needles about that, both wondering if we still have girlfriends after all the jerks at the party probably put the move on them since we wasn't there. What makes matters worse is that neither of us are going back to school for a few days, so as to make the story that's going to be put out about what happened to us look good. Trapper says if we didn't get "shot out of the saddle" last night, it's sure to happen by the time we get back to school. We both agree that women aren't to be trusted.

Riding on the back of the pickup with Bill's dead body is not really too bad, since we don't have to look at him. J.B. and Eddie wrapped him back up in the sheet and wound electrical tape all around it, then wrapped him in a canvas tarp that used to be Trapper's tent and wrapped rope all around that before they loaded him into the truck.

Eddie bitched and moaned about the smell until Doc suggested that if he continued to be a problem we could just as well bury two bodies tonight. Doc's not in the best of moods. I heard him tell Britt that he looked over the body again today. Since it's Sunday, he kept it at the doctor's office, which was closed. If he has an emergency on weekends, he usually handles them at home anyway. As far as I know, he's still of the same opinion as to why Bill croaked. He also asked Britt about the car Bill was driving. "It's handled,"

Britt told him.

Actually, riding in the bed of the pickup is kinda fun, especially riding through the Quarters on a Sunday night, which is the big night of the week for the Niggers or Colored People as my mom and dad call them. They'd kick my butt if they heard me use the word, *Nigger*. My dad says it's degrading to them, that they don't like it and he doesn't want to hear me using it. Sometimes I slip up and say it, because that's what most all the other guys call them. I also hear it from Granny, who's still hung up over the Civil War, which you better call, The War between the States, when you talk to her about it.

Church is over (that's why we waited so late to perform the ceremony, otherwise, they would have probably thought God and all his chariots were rolling down from heaven); everyone's still all dressed up, strolling around, visiting with one another, gathered up and down the road, or on steps or porches or at one of the several "Jute Joints" constructed out of tin signs and slabs along the Quarters roads. Colored people are much more social than whites. They seem happier, too. God knows why. They always get the shitty end of the stick, be it job or whatever—even I have noticed that.

There is, however, one thing that I have noticed where the Colored have it over the Whites. The water in the Colored' fountains always taste better and it's always colder than the Whites' fountain. Don't ask me why? I'm at a loss to explain. Consequently, since I discovered this, I always drink out of their fountains. Most of the time when I do it is when my mom takes me to Birmingham to shop. People always look at me funny. Once a guy said to me, "I can't believe you're doing that! Drinking out of a Nigger fountain. What if they drank out of ours?" he asked.

"Wouldn't make a shit with me," I told him. "If they want to drink the 'hot piss' that comes out of the White fountains, they're welcome to it."

Just as I said it, I noticed my mom was standing right beside me. I cringed, expecting a backhand to the mouth, but she just laughed, told the guy to mind his own business. Later she told me she'd slap my face if she heard me use words like that again, but she made no comment on where I chose to drink.

I feel the truck stopping. Trapper jumps up and grabs the top of the cab to support himself. I hear the jingle of *my* bell on *his* shoe as he moves. I haven't mentioned him wearing it, even though he keeps shaking it in my face, hoping that I will. It would give him too much pleasure. The doc, however, told him that he thought he needed to examine him again.

I stand up next to Trapper and peer over the top of the cab. Britt's stopped just ahead of us, talking out his window to two guys standing by a car parked along the edge of the road. A wine bottle shaped paper bag is sitting on their car hood.

I don't recognize them at first, not until they start laughing and "jiving" with Britt. I've never seen them so dressed up before.

"Hey! That's Rosie and Freck," I tell Trapper, pointing towards the two of them.

"Jesus! Look at that garb on Rosie," he says and laughs.

Freck has on the normal "Sunday go to meeting" white shirt and tie, with a regular felt hat, but Rosie has gone all the way. He's wearing what in the car lights appears to be, a yellow "Zoot Suit," with a yellow tie, yellow shoes and a big, wide-brimmed, yellow hat that's trimmed out with a yellow feather protruding out of the hat band that must be two feet long. He has four gold teeth in the front of his mouth. I see them shine as the car lights hit them when he laughs.

"No wonder all the gals go for Rosie," I say to Trapper. "Wonder what they're 'jiving' with Britt about?"

"I don't know, but look! Becky must be having a sale," he says, pointing to a house about three houses down on a narrow rutted road off to the right. The house is all lighted up, with lot of cars parked around it.

Becky runs a whore house. She's a friend of mine and Trapper's. We sell her the little bream we catch out of the pond with dough balls. You can catch them as fast as you can bait your hook. We string them up and when we get about fifty, we come over and sell them to Becky for fifty cents. She loves them, doesn't even bother to clean them. Just deep fries them up and eats them whole. They're crunchy like potato chips.

"Probably got some new girls," Trapper suggests.

"More likely 'after church' business," I tell him.

Freck and Rosie are friends of ours, too. Neither of them work at the mine. They mostly just hang around; do odd jobs for the white folks. Rosie mostly washes and polishes cars and runs errands for Mr. Pat, while Freck basically does yard work, mostly for Mr. Pat and the other bosses. He also owns a mule, which he uses to plow up people's gardens in the spring. He does ours every year.

In September they pick cotton. They've been doing it since they were kids; say it's in their blood. Trapper and I always hang close to them when we go to pick, which is only when we're in desperate need of money, only as a last resort. The two of them pick like demons, and since we mostly play around, they throw some in our sacks from time to time for the entertainment we provide them.

Last September, one of the days we decided to pick was so hot that by 11 o'clock the two of us were played out. We were picking for a Mr. Cato, who has a farm over off the Trafford Road. The field we were picking in was just out maybe a hundred yards behind his house. Seeking a shade to hide out and rest, we spotted his barn and promptly cut through the field in that direction.

The barn was much cooler, but the smell left a lot to be desired, so we began to meander around to see what else we could find.

Just adjacent to the barn was another wood-framed building. It had two sections, with doors in the front for each. Both doors had locks in the hasps, but neither was locked. The left side of the building was a tool shed, filled with hoes and plows and harnesses, all kinds of farming stuff, but nothing of real interest. The door to the right is where we hit the jackpot. The inside was shelved all around the walls and sitting on the shelves was, in our determination, the overflow of Mrs. Cato's yearly canning. Fruit jars filled with everything. Peas, corn, green beans, tomatoes, you name it, but the very best of all, and what really caught our eyes were the pickled peaches.

Figuring they would never be missed, we both borrowed a jar of the peaches, dumped them in our cotton sacks and made haste back to the cotton truck, just as the lunch whistle blew.

Just off the back side of the field, down in a shallow hollow, there's a small creek. Rose and Freck headed down there to eat their lunches. Trapper and I tagged along.

The four of us consumed the two jars of peaches for our dessert. They were delicious. We buried the lids under some pine straw and submerged the jars under the water up next to the creek bank, then we skinny dipped in the creek to cool off before going back to work.

When Freck shucked off his clothes, Trapper and I were amazed. "His pecker must be a foot long," Trapper said to Rosie. "No wonders that ol' mare mule of his is so happy."

I thought Rosie would die, he laughed so hard and when he told Freck, he laughed like hell, too. In fact, they laughed about it the rest of the day. Must have given us at least fifty pounds of cotton.

Britt pulls up about another car's length and then stops again. As our headlights hit his car, I see the three of them peering down towards Becky's.

Mr. Trapp pulls on up behind them. Rosie and Freck move over to the truck bed where we're standing.

"Look what da' cat's done drug in," Rosie says, looking at me and Trapper. Freck laughs.

"You better watch it, they love canaries," Trapper tells him and we both laugh.

"So do da' women folks," he says, smiling, showing his gold teeth.

"Hey, Rosie! What's Britt so interested in?" Trapper asks him.

Rosie looks over at Freck. "Thanks I awts' ta tell 'em?" he asks him.

Freck laughs and tells him to "go ahaid."

"Well, fust off, Mr. Britt ax' me if'n Becky wuz a holding a Klan' meetin'? Iz told him 'twas either dat or da Masons, dat 'twas hard to tell since they's one and da same."

We all laugh!

"Din he ax' me if'n Iz' thought it'd be outta orda, since Maser' Pat's da big man, for dem to moves to da fronts of da lines down there and coulds I use my in-fluence to gets dem discounts? Seems Maser' Pat won'ts to change his luck.

This one's a knee-slapper for Freck, and it's contagious. I even hear Mr. Trapp laughing in the cab of the truck.

Rosie hears it, too, and he and Freck move closer to the truck, angling down towards the back. We move with them.

"Mr. Britt say ya'll gonna' blows ups da' whole camp a lookin' faw' some snakes. Said, if'n dat don't gits me un' Freck's, he gonna come back bys and puts a bullet in our haids."

We all laugh again.

Freck points to the bundle behind us. "What's dat ya gots tied ups in dat tarp?" he asks.

"Dynamite" I tell him, "the fuses and caps are already in it so don't shake the truck, it might go off."

Rosie and he move back a step. Trapper and I laugh.

Rosie peers up at us, looking at our faces. "Looks like somebodies, dun' gone un' works you boys over," he says. "Ol' Square ain't done already caught up with ya, has he?"

"For what?" Trapper asks him.

"Well, he done be spoutin' off. He say, you boys tried to run him down, down at da Harley's grocery; dat right? He say, he gonna kick youse' asses."

"Square's been hanging out with Snooks too much. He's starting to imagine things," Trapper says.

Everyone laughs.

Just then, I see Britt pull away and we begin to move forward to follow him.

"Don't spend all your money down at Becky's," I tell them as we pull away.

"Rose da one's gots to worry 'bout dat," Freck hollers. "Dim gals pays me!"

Britt bears to the left, goes up a small hill where the Quarters end, then on down the other side to the railroad crossing. We're at the double tracks, where the coal cars are switched. Up about a hundred yards, off to the right along the side of the hill are the old abandoned coke ovens. That's our destination.

As we continue to follow Britt in that direction, I can't help but think about how snakes, which I abhor, have for the last two days controlled my destiny.

In the past two weeks, three little colored kids have been bitten by rattlesnakes, in and around the old coke ovens—two little girls and a little boy. One of the little girls died, the other two are still in the hospital in Birmingham.

The kids found a great place to play while exploring up in the woods. Started cleaning one of the old ovens out for a playhouse, but it was already occupied. The snakes were nesting there.

Even after one of them was bitten, the other kids kept coming back. It was a great place to play and they didn't realize the danger. After two more of them were bitten, finally Reverend Henry Watson, the colored Baptist minister, and a few of his deacons wised up, checked the place out and have now barred any kids in the Quarters from playing there. They approached the doc about a week ago, when he was treating one of the bitten kids about getting some dynamite to blow the snakes out. Doc told them he would talk with Britt.

Tonight we're going to accommodate them. We're going to blow the snakes to hell and send Bill along for the ride with them. That's our plan and I think it's a good one.

The coke ovens were closed down and abandoned in 1920 when Alabama By-Products Company opened a coke processing plant in Tarrant City, on the outskirts of Birmingham. Since then they have laid in ruin, the forest encompassing them, covering them with de bris and filling in their boundaries with a sturdy growth of assorted trees and bushes. If you didn't know they were there, you would never notice them from the road.

The decision to make this Bill's final resting place was made at the pow-wow last night, then this morning, while everyone was at church, the plan was set into motion.

Britt had the ministers of the three colored churches make an announcement about the plan to dynamite the ovens and kill the snakes. They were told that this would be done after their church services were over tonight. Everyone was warned once again to stay clear of the area. As Sunday morning services were being held, my dad and Mr. Trapp, accompanied by Eddie, J.B. and a few colored men who work at the mine, made a visit to the abandoned ovens.

The ovens are what's called "Bee Hive" constructed and are double-tiered along the hillside about thirty yards up from the road. There's about forty of them. The one the kids were playing in is the third one from the western end, on the lower tier. My dad and Mr. Trapp set charges of dynamite in it and the ovens on both sides of it, then did the same with the three ovens above them on the second tier. The dynamite to blow the six ovens is courtesy of Alabama By-Products Company, provided by Mr. Pat.

After the charges were set, the colored men set up a watch to ensure no one came into the area. They've been guarding the ovens all day.

As our caravan parks along the shoulder of the road, just down the hill from the ovens, two of the men spot us and come walking down the hillside and head our way. Britt jumps out of his car and heads them off, then leads them away from Mr. Trapp's truck, on down the road behind J.B.'s car. Mr. Pat and the doc stroll down to join them, so does J.B. and my dad. As Mr. Trapp and Eddie move their way, Mr. Trapp tells me and Trapper to sit tight and don't move from the truck.

"That goes for you, also, Bill," Trapper quips, as his dad walks away.

We both laugh!

After about a five-minute conference, Britt walks over to the edge of the hill and yells up to a third man still on guard up by the ovens. "Hey, Grover! If a snake ain't eat yore ass, git on down here. These guys are ready to git home, wanna eat some supper!"

"Yasser, Mr. Britt!" Grove hollers back and then I see him stumbling down the hill, shining his flashlight steady at his feet.

Everyone begins to laugh.

"Jesus Christ! If that fucker falls, he'll roll down here and crush us all!" I hear the doc say.

The laughter gets louder.

Grover is huge! Not so much in height, just big around. No one has any idea what he weighs because he won't let them weigh him, even on the cotton scales—says he's allergic to cotton, won't go near a field. Everybody knows that Grover's just allergic to work.

Grover's always got a smile for everyone. When he rolls those big "moon eyes" of his at you and smiles, it can brighten your whole day.

Everyone loves him.

He eats a Baby Ruth candy bar in one bite! And will eat 'em as long as anyone will buy them. A Coca-Cola is one swallow.

He lives with his mother. Her name is Willie. She washes and irons for the white folks.

Just as Grover gets almost to the foot of the hill, the doc hollers out to him. "I'd watch that light, Grover! Snakes are attracted to light. They'll crawl right up to it."

The light immediately goes out.

Everyone is laughing as Grover walks up to the group.

"Man! This bees one place I's ain't sorry ta leaves," I hear him say, the whites of his eyes shining in the dark, plus, "I 'bout ta' starves ta death!"

After another couple of minutes of handshaking and back patting, Grover and the other men head for home. As they walk away, J.B. and Eddie walk back to the truck.

They waste no time. Lowering the tail-gate, they drag the mummy-wrapped body of Bill to the back of the truck. They had tied loops in the rope at both ends of the body when they wrapped it around the tarp. Sliding their arms through these loops and pulling them up over their shoulders, they step back and let Bill's body slide from the truck bed. Telling us to close up the tailgate and stay in the truck, they head up the hill, Bill swinging between them. My dad and Mr. Trapp walk along beside them shining their lights.

It seemed to take forever, but I would guess about twenty minutes pass before I see J.B. and Eddie heading back down the hill in a hurry. They make it to the bottom and head for the truck. Britt leaves the doc and Mr. Pat talking beside his car and walks down to meet them. They're all out of breath and breathing hard.

"Everybody keep your heads down," J.B. tells us. "They gonna blow the ovens any minute now."

"Hey, Doc!" Britt hollers. "Ya'll keep your heads down, they gonna blow 'em any minute."

The doc and Mr. Pat pay Britt no mind, just keep talking.

"Where's Burl and Orvil?" Britt asks J.B.

"They've taking cover up there behind some big boulders, said they'd be safe there. Sent us back down here to warn you it's about the blow any second now."

"Which oven did you put him in?" Britt wants to know.

"The one with the snakes, saw two of the fuckers when we slid the body in," Eddie tells him.

"No shit!" Britt says, and he hardly gets it out of his mouth before the earth starts to tremble.

Th-Womp, Th-Womp, Th-Womp—first the top tier. Th-Womp, Th-Womp, Th-Womp—then the bottom one, all about a half-second apart.

Drop the heaviest dictionary you can find onto a carpet from waist level so as it lands flat. Do it six times as fast as you can. That's what it sounded like. Imagine the glow of a giant firefly. Do it six times as fast as you can. That's what it looked like. Imagine riding in a car with four flat tires over cobblestone. That's what it felt like. Imagine being downwind from the gates of Hell. That's what it smelled like.

Then it's over—all except the debris from the blast.

Pine cones, pine needles, and sweet gum balls, along with other assorted forest debris join a covey of rocks and gravel that rain down on our heads. The rat-a-tat-tat of it hitting the cars sound like a hailstorm.

J.B. races down and opens the trunk of his car and pulls out two large burlap feed bags. He runs back, throws one to Eddie and with their lights jumping, they run up the hill.

"Where ya'll going?" Britt hollers to them.

"Make sure there's no fires," Eddie hollers back.

"Good fuckin' thinkin', but the woods are too wet to burn," Britt mutters, as he walks towards us.

"Hey, Doc! You and Mr. Pat OK?" He hollers out, looking up

their way.

"Soon as I get him out from under the car I'll let you know," Doc yells back. I can hear him laughing.

Trapper and I had laid face down in the bed of the truck and held our hands over our heads, but we're up now taking everything in.

We jump out of the truck to see if Mr. Pat is really under the car. We spot him just as he's standing, the doc's helping him wipe himself off.

"Gracious," he says, really loud and nasally. "I think Burl and Orvil got a mite carried away with that dynamite."

Trapper and I follow Britt as he strolls up towards them.

"They blew the shit outta them ovens, but they done it real quiet," Britt says to Mr. Pat. "I thought it would sound a lot louder."

"It probably vibrated every Negro in the Quarters out of their beds, but it was quiet for that size blast," Mr. Pat agrees.

"More likely their neighbor's bed if he ain't home," Doc says and laughs.

"Goodness! I hope Burl and Orvil found a safe haven, that they're OK," Mr. Pat says to Doc."

"That's what they do down in your coal mine every day, Pat. They blow up shit! That's their job, they know what they're doing, believe me," Doc tells him.

"I hope you two boys have learned a lesson from this experience," Mr. Pat says to us, looking us up and down, still wiping furiously at his tie.

I remain quiet, but Trapper just can't hold it.

"You mean on how to blow stuff up?" he asks Mr. Pat, but before his question is answered Britt reels us in and herds us back towards the truck.

"Don't worry, Mr. Pat," he tells him. "These two little burr heads are gonna get my full attention for the next five years…'til they're eighteen and hopefully out of high school. God willing, I can keep them out of the penitentiary 'til then…then I'm gonna kick 'em out of town, hopefully to college."

Just then we see our dads, J.B. and Eddie, come walking down the hill. We all move up to meet them between Britt's car and the truck.

"Mission accomplished," J.B. says to Britt as they walk up.

"God damn! You boys got a little carried away with that dynamite, didn't ya'?" Britt says, looking at my dad. Rocks and shit pounded us way down here."

My dad looks over his glasses at him, the way he always does me.

"Man who claims he was a big, bad FBI agent, had all kinds of bullets shot at him, orta-not be afraid of a few little ol' rocks, Britt. We'd of really blasted the fuckers, but we run out of powder."

"Well, thank goodness, you're safe!" Mr. Pat interjects.

Everyone is laughing. You can see the tension leaving their bodies—lots of back slapping between them. Trapper and I stand at the edge of the group and listen.

"You should see where them ovens used to be," I hear Eddie say. "Now it's just a mountain of rocks, bricks and dirt."

I hear my dad tell Britt. "Yeah, we probably set the charges a little too strong, but let me tell you something. A week from now, a month from now, or maybe even fifty or a hundred years from now, there's gonna be some curious, crazy, son of a bitch that's gonna be digging in there for some crazy reason. When it happens, and I can guarantee you that it will, they won't even find an eyelash, and by the way, I'll guarantee that too!"

"Yeah, you're probably right," I hear Britt say. "Good fuckin' thinkin'!"

As the jubilant mood ebbs, we all gather together to leave, heading for our separate cars. Britt wants a private talk with me and Trapper. Our dads say OK. He walks us up the road, out of earshot from anyone, then he stops. He turns and looks at us, moving the light cast from his flashlight over our bodies, then he turns it off.

"I just want to take a minute to reacquaint you boys with a few facts," he says to us. "First of all is to remind you that yesterday while rope climbing on them rocky cliffs up by the Devil's Den, both of you fell and hurt yourselves. That's what we've agreed to tell ever-body. I'm sure with your imaginations, you two will have no problem making it believable. Also, I want to remind you that this night never happened, so wipe it from your minds, 'cause we ain't never—ever gonna talk about it again. Will that be a problem?"

"Sir," I say. "You'll never have to be concerned about any problems on this subject from me or Trapper. We never even wanna ever think about this again, believe me."

"Good! I do believe you."

"Also," he goes on to say, "I wanted to remind you boys that I was serious when I said I was gonna keep a close eye on you two…dead serious, so don't forget it. I catch you boys doin' anything serious enough to piss me off, I'm gonna come down hard on you. Real hard! Understand that?"

"Yes, sir," me.

"Yes, sir," Trapper.

He walks up very close to us and puts a hand on each of our shoulders.

"Now, and I don't want you to let this go to your heads, but I gotta tell you boys just how proud of you I am. You are two very—very brave boys. Most young men, given the same set of circumstances, I fear would not have survived. You two, stood up to pure evil and not only survived, but eliminated it, at least as far as that pervert's concerned, so never feel bad about what happened—it was either him or you, a 'life or death' situation. If he'd of lived, he'd of killed you…and probably both your families. He'd have done it if it took him the rest of his life…so never, ever feel bad that he's dead—OK?"

"Yes, sir," me.

"Yes, sir," Trapper.

"That's what I like to hear," he says, giving both our shoulders a shake.

"You two boys are the last of a dying breed," he goes on to tell us. Folks in this country are getting' way too civilized. They want to work with a problem nowadays, rather than eliminate the source. Imagine the kinds of kids this is gonna breed. Fifty years from now the criminals and perverts are gonna control us, because somewhere along the way we forgot how to fight…or lost the will to do it…or maybe both."

"Now," he says, giving both of us a pat on the back. "Get on home and stay out of trouble…OK?"

"Yes, sir," Trapper

"Yes, sir," me.

I wake up at 3:33, according to the clock on the mantle.

I hear my brother, Cratham, rummaging around in the kitchen looking for something to eat before he goes to bed. He's just blown in. He finally found his keys.

I jump out of my bed quietly, so as to not wake Granny or Fanny, tiptoe out of the bedroom and pad into the kitchen.

Cratham's got the mayonnaise out and is trying to spread some of it on a piece of bread, but he's reeling drunk and most of it is going on the table and on the floor.

"Want me to make you a sandwich?" I ask him, going to the Frigidaire and getting out the baloney.

He manages to find a chair and sits down.

"If you'll wash your hands real good," he tells me.

I make him a baloney sandwich and pour him a glass of milk. He wolfs it down and goes to bed.

I know I won't be able to go back to sleep, so I lay on the floor in the living room next to the radio. I turn it on and then down real low. I find WCKY out of Cincinnati and listen to it 'til dawn.

Just before the first rays of the morning sun come through our living room window, I turn the radio off and go light a fire in the kitchen stove. I'm hungry and ready for a new day, but fall asleep before breakfast is done.

— Chapter 13 —
Contrition

Sunday, June 12, 1949

School's out and summer vacation is here again in all its glory.

I feel wonderful! I'm young, strong and extremely happy. Three whole months ahead of me to do nothing in particular, and that's exactly what I plan to do.

I have put the confrontation with Bill behind me, stored it in the far recesses of my mind. The only outward sign of it ever happening is a small scar just under my lower lip, which I guess will remain with me for the rest of my life.

We played our third official baseball game of the season yesterday and won it six to one. I pitched a two-hitter, striking out ten batters and even got a hit myself. Life is good.

Trapper, who only catches when I pitch, otherwise, he plays "pussy" right field, has come up with a new strategy for the heavy hitters of our opposition, in case they tend to present me difficulty. When he shoots me a bird signal, I throw straight at the batter. "Keeps 'em nervous," Trapper said. We call it the "Boogie Trapp." I hit their catcher, who is their best hitter, three times yesterday. He went berserk the last time I hit him and came running out to the mound screaming that he was going to "kick my ass." It took our whole infield to keep him off me. Then, their whole team was off the bench and came running out wanting to fight, but before any licks were thrown, Glenn, our coach along with their coach, broke it up. Their coach said I was purposely throwing at his best hitters, which I of course denied. Glenn said if I hit another batter I was out of the game, so we ditched the "Boogie Trapp" for the last few innings. Trapper said it wasn't our fault that Hugh, their catcher, was so fat and slow he couldn't get out of the way of the ball and kept jabbing him about it the next time he came up to bat.

This morning at church, we decided to go to the afternoon ballgame—Black Creek's men's teams versus the all powerful team from Center Point. We knew that it would be a wipeout. Center Point is in first place in the league and Black Creek in last; mostly due to the fact that Oscar Lowe, our ace pitcher and Rufus Hail our best home-run hitter have not played in a game this year—out and disabled, both, Rufus with the gout and Oscar with an infected ear, from a bite he got in a fight over at Pinson, at the Rock House. Damn near got his ear bit off—it's still all red and swollen.

Anyway, we were right, so in the fifth inning, with Center Point leading 10 to 0, we sidled over to where John Lester (Ha Ya) was selling cold drinks. He ices them down in a big galvanized tub, chips the ice up all around them and sells them at every game. Trapper distracted him by telling him some weird tale about the *Grit Newspaper* going out of business and while John Lester was jabbering and arguing back at Trapper, I stole two RC Colas from his tub (after making sure no one's watching, naturally). Also, just for meanness, I pick up his little notebook that was on the seat of the chair he brings down to sit on. He keeps the ballgame scores in it. It's got a spiral binding with a nub of a pencil stuck in it. I jammed it in my pocket and slid through the cars parked behind the backstop and on out to the road, Trapper right behind me. I gave him an RC and told him to hold it down to his side.

We were both hungry, so we headed towards my house, stopping only to wedge the caps off the RCs with Trapper's pocketknife, which he's carrying with him at all times now.

He needled me about Darlene as we walked. I had to hear for the hundredth time how she had two-timed me with one our buddies, a guy named Lynn, another kid of a local big shot who goes to school in Birmingham. It had happened the night of the wiener roast. Women are so fickle!

Trapper jabbered away.

"Bobbie said they musta kissed a thousand times that night," he told me.

"Who? Her and Albert?" I quip back at him.

"No, Darlene and Lynn, dummy."

"Albert said Bobbie was sucking on his tongue the whole evening, so I don't know when she had time to watch Darlene," I told him.

"He's lying. She only kissed him three times. Twice when they were playing Spin the Bottle and once when they played Go Walking, and she didn't open her mouth on any of 'em," he said.

"Yeah! I bet." I said.

"She swore it to me on a stack of Bibles."

"That's what all women say when they lie," I told him and laughed.

"Darlene was kissing Lynn after church this morning, out by Lynn's mother's car, while everybody was talking and no one was looking. I saw 'em. Looked like she was really putting the tongue to him," he said to me and laughed.

"Up yours," I told him. "Anyway I'm over it, scouting new territory."

"I could talk to Lashie. If she knows I'm not interested in her, she might take you back. Or hey! How about Sarah?" he jibed at me.

"That'll be the day when you have to play Cupid for me, asshole! You gonna die when you find out who's got the hots for me now anyway.

"Who?" he asked, suddenly interested.

"It's secret at this stage," I said and smiled.

"You're lying; I can tell by your lips, they're moving."

"Just remember what I said."

"Asshole."

I laughed.

"Is it the new girl?" he asked.

I laughed again.

"You ain't got a chance with her. She's fourteen."

"Some women like younger men, they tell me, but nevertheless, I didn't say it was her."

"You're such an asshole," he said.

"Prick," I said.

"Dummy," back to me.

"Anyway," he went on, "she's taller than you and you've told everyone that she's kin to you."

"Only about two inches and just third cousins—know what she calls it?" I asked.

"What?"

"Kissin' cousins," I said and laughed again.

"God's gonna punish you for lying and also for taking Ha Ya's notebook. He's probably looking for it everywhere by now," he said, finally changing the subject.

"I'll give it back to him tomorrow, tell him I found it," I said, feeling sort of remorseful that I had taken it.

We went to the back of the house. We still had about half our RCs left that we had saved to wash down food, so we deposited them on the back porch, then being as quiet as church mice, eased open the screen door and slid into the kitchen. I gave Trapper the "button your lip" sign, hoping he'd heed it and not start running his mouth. Music was playing softly from the living room. I peeked that way and saw my mother sitting on the sofa reading the newspaper. No sign of Granny or my dad or Kid.

In the warmer at the top of stove was leftover fried chicken from Sunday dinner earlier today. We helped ourselves—two pieces for Trapper and two pieces for me, with the same amount of biscuits from the plate beside it, then, out the back door with the stealth of a cat. Just as I eased the screen door to the jam, I heard my mother's voice, "Boogie, you boys stay out of that chicken!"

We grabbed the RCs and were on our way down the hill towards Black Creek before we finally began to laugh.

"You're gonna be in trouble, "Trapper told me.

"I know, I know," I said and laughed.

Now I sit daydreaming.

I'm full of chicken and biscuits and RC Cola. We're sitting on what I call, "Meditation Rock," a place down behind my house on Black Creek—a place where I go to think. I consider it my private place even though the other kids in the immediate neighborhood hang out here from time to time. The rock is a huge chunk of limestone, the size of a Crosley convertible that nature at some point elected to dislodge from atop the adjacent hill and plop it downward to the middle of the creek.

There are two ways to get on the rock. You can either wade through the sludge and black-silted water or else, you can climb the old, gnarled, sweet gum tree that grows from the creek bank just across from the rock and then swing down to its top from a limb that protrudes directly over it, about seven feet above its surface. The latter was the way we choose, carefully balancing chicken and biscuits.

Trapper stands and says something to me, but I'm in a daze and don't understand what he says. I look towards him, he's pointing up the creek. I look in that direction and that's when I see it. Actually, in truth, I hear it before I see it—the unmistakable rustic mewing of a catbird. It's perched on the limb of an elderberry bush, one of the many that grow along the banks of the creek and shade the water with the outcropping of their foliage. He's about 35 feet away, on a limb about 10 feet above the center of the creek. On second thought, it could be a she, based on the way it's flitting around and fussing. There's no discernable difference between the sexes in catbirds that I've ever been able to see. Nevertheless, it's a beauty and an inviting target.

"Give me your slingshot," Trapper says to me, reaching to take it from around my neck, "and one of them steel balls I know you got in your pocket."

I give him the slingshot and grapple in my pocket for a steel ball, then hand it to him. "I hope you're not thinking about killing that catbird," I say as I stand up beside him.

"I'm just gonna scare it" he says, as he quickly releases the missile. Trapper shoots a slinger exactly the opposite of me. He uses his right hand as the pocket hand, where I use my left. He misses more than he hits. I'm really not too worried for the bird.

In the shadows of the trees, I can't follow the direction of the shot, so I'm watching the bird and it seems to have survived as I hear the steel ball cut its way through the dense foliage of the elderberry bushes. And then in the blink of an eye, the bird flutters and falls, then spins and spirals down into the creek.

"You just really fucked up," I say to Trapper.

"Whatta you mean?" he asks indignantly.

"Catbirds bring good luck. You just killed yours," I tell him and, "I hope God strikes you dead immediately, 'cause I'm really pissed off that you killed a catbird."

"I don't think I hit him, I think he flew off," he says, looking up the creek.

"You fuckin' killed the bird, trust me," I tell him. It'll be floating by here in a couple of minutes, just watch.

Trapper falls to his knees at the edge of the rock, like he's going to pray, still looking up the creek.

"I don't see no sign of it in the water," he says.

"It's the same color as the water, dummy." I tell him. "Keep your eyes on the water right here in front of you. You'll see it in a minute."

I sit back down and we both watch the water off the left side of the rock where the current is faster.

The bird's on its back as it floats by the rock, so close that either of us could have snagged it. Its wings are spread angel-like; like it's doing a back stroke, except they're not moving.

Just past the rock, there's a slight fall in the creek. The swift current there catches the bird and sweeps it towards the shore, where it's snagged by a limb of a bush and then washed ashore on the edge of a sludge bar along the bank of the creek. Neither of us says a word as we watch its journey.

"I think that was probably the prettiest catbird I ever saw," I finally say to Trapper. "Too bad you had to kill it. I hope it didn't have babies."

Trapper hasn't taken his eyes off the bird and when he turns to look at me, I see they're filled with tears.

"I didn't mean to kill it," he says as he leans over and hangs my slingshot back around my neck, then rubs at his eyes with the backs of his hands. "Anyway, I didn't even aim at it. I was aiming at the limb it was sittin' on, about a foot to the bird's right. It's not my fault your pride and joy slingshot don't shoot true."

Well, that solves the mystery of how he hit it, I think to myself. *He always misses everything he shoots at by at least a foot.*

"You'd been better off if you'd aimed at it," I say to him.

"And that's supposed to mean," he says, standing and looking down towards where the bird lays.

"It means you never hit what you shoot at, dummy. You always miss by a least a foot. Git it? And I might add, no matter whose sling-shot you're shootin' with."

"Shootin' a slingshot is old-fashion, a lost art, no one hardly does it anymore." He says to me. "Why do I care if I'm not a crackerjack shot? Anyway, I don't know why you stick with it. It's so juvenile."

"Saved your skinny ass," I say, then could've kicked my ass a thousand times that I said it.

I stand up and look him in the face, waiting for the retaliation I know is going to come. Trapper's face is all red. I know he's mad with me, but I also know he's madder with himself, upset about the bird. I go for the attack and rub it in.

"You told me no later than yesterday that you would never kill anything again. And just now, for no reason at all, you kill a poor defenseless catbird. Then, you try to cover it up by saying, 'I just meant to scare him.' Bullshit!"

"Uh, hang on just a minute," he tells me, holding his hand in front of my face. "Let's go back just a tad. You saved my skinny ass? Might I remind you that while you're giving me shit for killing a fucking catbird with a fuckin' slingshot, that you fuckin' killed a man with one. Duh?"

"Wounded, not killed," I retort really fast. "There's a big difference, dumbo. And, let me tell you something else," I say, real fast before he can recover. "If I hadn't been a good shot and if you were still fortunate enough to be alive, you'd be blowing shit buggers, painting your nails and talking with a lisp."

"I got away before you ever even shot him," he says to me. "Then, you're standing there wide open like the dumbo that you are. If they'd been another bullet in that gun, you'd be stone dead now."

"I knew there wasn't," I lied.

"How the hell did you know that," he asks, surprise in his eyes.

"Duh! I counted them, stupid. Every time he fired. Do you think I would have gone down there to save your ass if I had known he had another bullet in the gun?"

"You're lying," he says. "You told me afterward when we was just sitting there watching him flounder in the water that you didn't know. I remember the look on your face when that gun clicked. Like a monkey that had just had a banana stuck up his ass. You didn't' know whether to eat shit or go blind for a few seconds, you were so surprised."

"I lied," I tell him, lying again. "Anyway it's a taboo subject. Britt told us not to talk about it."

"He said not with anyone else, not between ourselves," he reminds me.

"Well, I don't want to talk about it," I say.

I move away from him, turn and look down towards the catbird. *I'll bury it before we leave*, I think to myself.

"We've talked about it before," he says, "several times."

"Well, I don't want to talk about it today, so change the subject. Are you gonna bury that bird you killed?" I ask.

"You don't want to talk about it because you realize the same thing I do," he says.

"And that would be" I ask sarcastically.

"That we've really blown it on the 'Big Ten,' dummy, don't pretend you don't know it," he says, sitting back down on the rock, picking up the twigs and leaves gathered on its top and throwing them in the water.

"I thought we just went through them 'here while back' and you said we were OK," I tell him, sitting back down "Buda style," facing him. "We were 6 to 4 to the good you said."

"That was before, 'what you don't want to talk about,'" he says. "Now I think we're teetering on disaster."

"So what are you saying?" I ask him.

"I thought you didn't want to talk about it!?" he sneers sarcastically.

"Fuck you!" I tell him, and shoot him a bird to boot.

"Yeah! Well you're fucked, too!" he says," 'cause we've blown #6 to hell, as far as I'm concerned."

"#6?" I ask, like I'm really surprised.

"Yeah! #6, dummy. That puts us at 5 to 5, and just for your information, there's some we think we're OK on that are questionable."

"You stretch everything," I say. Still, I'm kind worried that he's so concerned about something I hadn't thought to worry about at all.

"Let's go through them again so I know what you're talking about," I say.

I think I need to stop here and back up. Trapper and I, at some point, have come to the conclusion that the Ten Commandments are the Ladder to Heaven. I think it was the same day we smoked two whole packs of Phillip Morris cigarettes and drank at least a half gallon of Muscadine wine, both stolen, but that's a story I won't get into. I've never taken it really seriously; it's just been a game to me—a game we started playing when full of nicotine and wine. We started trying to remember the Ten Commandments and realized we were unable to quote them, even though every Sunday School teacher we ever had, had banged them into our heads since the day we were born. So, a few days later, we got a Bible and looked them up and started playing the game. Simple rule: Honor more of the commandment that you break, you're OK, you're heaven bound, you got no sweat, and, as I stated, the last I heard we were batting 600. I hadn't actually even thought about it until now, it was just a game we play. I'm surprised Trapper is taking it so seriously. I nudge him on, "Go through 'em" I say.

"#1 and #2 we're OK on," he says, "real sound."

"And, those are?" I say.

"Gods before me and carved images, dummy. You know 'em as well as I do!"

"We're a 100% there?"

"Righto!"

"#3, we're in trouble on, but God knows we're working on it, but still it's a negative for us," he goes on.

"And that's?" I ask to piss him off.

"Name in vain" he says and laughs.

"What's so funny?" I say.

"Can you imagine Bill explaining that one when he's trying to get in the Gates?" he says and laughs again.

"You're a sicko, but it's funny," I say and we both crack up.

"#4 and #5, we've got made in the shade, he goes on to say, especially as long as our mothers are alive."

We both laugh again, for it's true. Both our mothers blast our asses out of bed every Sunday morning. You're either dead or you go to church. No exceptions. And we either follow our mothers' instructions or the command to honor comes via a strong slap in the face. So I agree with him. We have no problem there.

"#7 we have no problem on, 'cause we ain't married, but #'s 8, 9 and 10 we're in real trouble on," he goes on to say, especially you on #10, if you know what I mean?"

"I don't know what you're talking about," I say, even though I know what he's talking about.

"Yeah, sure!" he says.

"So liking somebody is right up there on the same sin level as touching a dead woman's titties? Is that what you're saying?" I ask.

"Oh, God! Don't remind me," he says. "Let's just skip it and say we both got problems. OK?"

We both laugh!

"You're not really serious?" I say to him.

"You mean about blowing #6?" He wants to know.

"About saying I killed Bill, dummy, that I broke commandment #6, when you just killed a catbird. Anyway 'we,' note I say 'we,' was defending ourselves and if 'we' killed him, then 'we' are both equally guilty, so don't try to lay the blame on me."

"I'm not laying any blame, I'm just saying that we've got a problem, I think. I think we really probably might of killed him."

"The doc said he died of a heart attack, that's good enough for me," I answer back.

"Maybe so," he says, still looking all worried, "but we could have kinda brought it on. Anyway we gotta do something to square it with God, in case we did."

I don't say anything for a while, still can't believe he's taking this so seriously. We both sit in silence, both of us still looking at the dead catbird washed up on the silt bar along the edge of the creek. Trapper finally breaks the silence. Our conversation went as follows.

Trapper: "We gotta confess what we did to God. Let everything be known."

Me: "Why? He sees everything. That's what all the preachers say. Anyway, Britt would kill us."

Trapper: "Are you a Christian?"

Me: "You know I'm a Christian, we go to the same church every Sunday."

Trapper: "Then you know, same as me, that God said, 'confess your sins.' We're sinners, so we gotta confess."

Me: "The Bible says Jesus died for our sins."

Trapper: "I know, but he couldn't have. I hadn't committed them yet."

Me: "Yeah! I wonder how that works?"

Trapper: "It works like this, dumbo. All sins committed after Jesus died have to be confessed because they hadn't happened yet. That's why God said, 'Confess your sins.'"

Me: "Where did he say that?"

Trapper: "In the Bible."

Me: "Where in the Bible?"

Trapper: "You need to look these things up for yourself and not depend on me."

Me: "But he already knows what we did, why do we have to tell him again?"

Trapper: "God, you're thick! It's like a reminder, you know, keeps him up to date."

Me: "Then why can't we just get down on our knees here and now and say, 'I confess Lord, I did it'! Forgive me."

Trapper: "That won't work. I already thought about that."

Me: "So what's the answer?"

Trapper: "It's simple. God wants us to confess our sins to every-one. Why do you think He went to all that trouble to tell us to confess our sins in the Bible? Since He already knows them, then He must mean for us to confess them to someone else, duh! He knew that we would know that He already knew and that some of us, like me, would figure it out."

Me: "Thanks for explaining it. You've really made it clear."

Trapper: "That's the way it works. When God knows that we've figured out what He wants us to do and hears that we're going to do it, that reminds Him to alert Jesus to move us from the 'not Died For List' to the 'Died For List' so our souls can go to Heaven."

Me: "He'll do all that just because we confess?"

Trapper: "How else do you think He keeps up with it, dumbo? Jesus probably has a whole staff of angels keeping the books. God probably sends Him a trillion reminders a day."

Me: "Man! God must spend all His time doing nothing but listening to confessions."

Trapper: "Exactly, that's why 'He knows everything."

Me: "You're so full of it!"

Trapper: "No! I'm serious, that the way it works."

Me: "God keeps books on all this stuff? Come on, give me a break!"

Trapper: "Oh, you disbeliever!"

Me: "According to the Bible, when God seriously wants to send a message to you, He gives you a sign."

I had been looking at the dead catbird while I was talking to Trapper and just as I uttered my last statement, I thought I saw it move. "Holy shit!" I think.

Trapper: "Yeah! You're right, for once."

Then the catbird flutters and rises to its feet and blows out every feather on its body and shakes itself, like a dog shedding water. I'm seeing it, but I can't believe it

Me: "Jesus Christ, Trapper, look at that!" I scream, pointing to the catbird. "Holy shit!" he says.

Feathers all back in their original position, the catbird flaps its wings two or three times and then gaining altitude soars westward down the creek towards the setting sun. "Holy shit," we both say again.

We decide to confess!

Trapper: "But don't worry! We don't have to do it this very minute. I mean, 'He hasn't given us a time frame."

Me: "That's gotta be a fuckin' sign, unless it was just knocked out or something." Still confused about the bird, I still can't believe what I just saw.

Trapper: "Of course it was a sign, dummy. Now I guess you'll listen to me."

Me: "Whatta you mean, 'we don't have to do it at once'—like not right now?"

Trapper: "I mean as long as we do it before we die. I mean…maybe just a day or two before."

Me: "So we all have to confess before we die?"

Trapper: "Hold on! Let me think about it for a minute."

Me: "Don't forget, we already told Britt."

Trapper: "Yeah, I know."

Me: "And our dads."

Trapper: "I know, I know, and our brothers."

Me: "Don't forget the doc, and Mr. Pat."

Trapper: "That's seven people plus us, right?"

Me: "Right.

Trapper: "That won't work."

Me: "Why?"

Trapper: "'Cause they're in the same boat as us now, they're 'accessories to the facts.'"

Me: "So all of us have to confess it before we die?"

Trapper: "The way I see it, only one of us has to do it."

Me: "Why's that?"

Trapper: "'Cause by now God's got it logged as a 'group sin.' One of us can speak for the group."

Me: "He's got it logged?"

Trapper: "Sure, how else do you think He keeps up with it?"

Me: "What if some of the others have already died before one of us gets around to confessing it?"

Trapper: "Then they'll go on the 'waiting for confession' list and

He'll hold their souls in limbo."

Me: "God's sure got a lot of lists."

Trapper: "Yeah, I know. It must drive Him crazy."

Me: "So when everybody's dead, except one of us, then that person has to confess. right?"

Trapper: "Right, and it'll definitely boil down to one of us, 'cause the others are all old."

Me: "And that person can do it just before he dies and that covers everybody."

Trapper: "It's call 'group coverage,' dummy."

Me: "So, if I'm the last one alive, I have to confess?"

Trapper: "Or me, if you die first."

Me: "What if everyone else is dead and you and me are waiting around for one of us to die and then we was to both die at the same time?"

Trapper: "God won't let that happen."

Me: "Why not?"

Trapper: "'Cause He knows that one of us has to stay alive to confess it. He'd have an 'open entry' in His 'Waiting for Confession' Log forever, dummy."

Me: "Yeah, that's right. I forgot He knows everything,"

Trapper: "Bingo! Now let's decide how we're going to do it, when just one of us is left."

We both sit and think for a while, listening to the sounds of the creek and the calls of the birds as they search for food and play through the surrounding woods. Finally I break the silence.

Me: "If it's me, I'll just tell Mr. Hughes, the barber. In a week the whole world will know."

Trapper: "Good idea, but it won't work."

Me: "Why?"

Trapper: "It's gonna be a long time from now, he'll be dead."

Me: "I got it! Whoever's left can tell the newspaper."

Trapper: "Won't work."

Me: "Why?"

Trapper: "'Cause they never get anything right."

Once again we sit in silence, watching the coal-black water as it slowly slides around the rock. After a few minutes Trapper stands, reaches up and breaks a twig from the limb of the old sweet gum tree, then sits back down, peels the bark from one end and proceeds to rub it over his teeth.

Me: "You're so dumb."

Trapper: "Whatta you mean?"

Me: "You use black gum twigs to brush your teeth, not sweet gum."

Trapper: "That must be what Freck uses."

Me: "Why you say that?"

Trapper: "'Cause his gums are black."

We both laugh.

Trapper: "Man! Nobody's gonna ever believe it when I tell them about that catbird."

Me: "Nobody ever believes what you say anyway, so it won't be unusual."

Trapper: "Wonder why it didn't drown?"

Me: "'Cause it was a catbird, dummy…cat's have nine lives. Use your brain ever' now and then."

Trapper: "It had to be a sign from God. You know, to show us we're on the right track about deciding to confess."

Me: "It'd be nice if He'd give us a hint on how to do it."

Trapper: "If you'd shut up talking and clear your head of all other thoughts, the way I'm doing, He might get the chance. One of us will see it. It'll be just like watching a movie."

All of a sudden our eyes light up!

Trapper: "That's it! That's it. We'll make a movie: Everybody goes to the Picture Shows."

Me: "There ain't gonna be no 'we,' 'goofball.' Only one of us is gonna be left. Anyway, you'd need a book or something before you could make a movie."

Trapper: "You're right! That's the answer. The last one alive will write a book…and then they can make a movie."

Me: "And the one left to tell the story will be the 'star.'"

Trapper: "What will the dead one be?"

Me: "'Supporting Role' if I have to do it, probably—'bit' part if you do."

Trapper: "If I write it, I'll make you the star."

Me: "You want me to say if I have to write it, I'll make you the star, right?"

Trapper: "Well, if I would, wouldn't you?"

Me: "If I knew you would, I would."

Trapper: "But you don't think I would?"

Me: "I know you wouldn't."

Trapper: "Hey, maybe we shouldn't use our real names in the book and on the front cover where it says who wrote it, use one of the fake names in the book; and then maybe find one of the guys in the Camp who'll be an old man then and give him a few bucks to say he wrote it. Yeah, use a fake name for the author. What's that called?"

Me: "Lying."

Trapper: "Man that will really fake everybody off. That way nobody will ever know which one of us wrote it. That'll screw the law up, too, in case they start nosing around. The old guy who claims he wrote it will have to take the blame."

Me: "Good idea! I hadn't even thought about that."

Trapper: "That's because you're a mental retard."

Me: "Wow! This is all sounding great and you're sure this will clear us with God?"

Trapper: "Absolutely! We just have to confess the sin, we don't have to come right out and say we did it."

Me: "Why not?"

Trapper: "'Cause God already knows we did it, dummy. It's the sin he's interested in, not who did the deed."

Me: "I hope He's got a list to remind him of that, too."

Trapper: "Man! I can't wait to do this. I'll be rich and I'll buy me a fancy, "Red" sports car, be a real "cool cat.""

Me: "Sounds like you're planning on being the last one alive."

Trapper: "Duh! How else will I know it gets done?"

Me: "Duh! How will I know you did it?"

Trapper: "We'll make a pact, a promise to each other."

Me: "You promise me shit all the time that you never do."

Trapper: "I know, but this time we'll write it down and we'll make it with God, too."

Me: "I think maybe we need some more time to think about this."

Trapper: "No way! It's gotta be done today...then after we write the pacts, we'll sign them and seal them with blood."

Me: "Yuck! Why do we have to get blood involved in this?"

Trapper: "You know, like Moses and Abraham. They were always killing shit for blood. God takes it serious when there's blood involved."

Me: "Too bad the catbird survived, we could have used his."

Trapper: "Wouldn't have worked anyway, not strong enough. We gotta use our own blood. You know, like we did on the 'Blood Brother' thing."

Me: "I don't have any scabs left I can pick off."

Trapper: "I don't either, so we'll have to cut our fingers with my pocket knife."

Me: "So, why do we have to do all this today?"

Trapper: "I'll tell you later after we get it done. We can use the notebook and pencil you swiped from Ha Ya. God must have been guiding your hands."

Me: "So He's not gonna punish me for copping it now, you're saying?"

Trapper: "Negative, I said that before I realized it was 'Divine Guidance.'"

After about another thirty minutes of arguing about how the pact should be written and what it should say, we finally reach an agreement.

I write mine first, then hand the notebook to Trapper. He looks it over, then flips the page and writes a duplicate of mine. When he's finished we tear both of them from the notebook and hold them side by side to make sure they're identical.

"Should I just sign mine to you and you sign yours to me or should both of us sign both of them?" I ask him.

We argue some more about that, then agree we each should sign both, which we do.

"OK, now," he says, "You have to keep the copy I wrote and I have to keep yours."

We both check our copies to be sure we have the right one.

"And don't forget," he goes on to say. "We gotta keep 'em forever."

"Forever?"

"I mean 'til one or the other of us is dead, dumbo. Now we need to make the pledge and seal it with a handshake."

"What's the pledge?"

"You have to look at me and say…'I swear to you and to God that if I'm the last of the two of us still alive, I will honor the pact we have made here today' and I've gotta say the same thing to you. Then we gotta spit in our hands and shake to seal the deal."

We got through the ritual. As I'm wiping the spit off my hand on my pants leg, I say to Trapper. "I'm surprised we didn't have to burn something as an offering."

"We could have cremated the catbird, if God hadn't felt sorry for it and let it live," he says.

"He knew it was wet and wouldn't burn anyway" I say in jest.

"You're probably right," Trapper says back to me, serious as he can be.

"Shit! I almost forgot, we gotta do the blood thing," he goes on to say.

We have another lengthy discussion about that and it finally boils down to the fact that neither of us want to cut ourselves. So…we decide Trapper will cut me and then I'll cut him. We also decide to cut our forefingers on the right hand because Trapper said they were the ones pushing the pencil.

"Don't cut me deep or I'll lay your finger wide open when I cut you," I tell him as I close my eyes and hold out my finger for him to cut.

I feel the prick of the knife blade then open my eyes to survey the cut.

"Hurry and dab it next to your name on both copies so you leave a print," he says to me as he holds the two copies of the pact side by side up against his chest.

"Damn it! You cut me a lot deeper than I did you," he complains as we go through the same process with him. After he makes his prints, we both check once more to see we have the right copies, then wave them in the air so the blood will dry. After that we both fold up our respective copies and stick them in our pockets and at almost that same moment, our moods begin to change.

Trapper begins to laugh, which is infectious to me.

"Can you believe all the crazy shit we do, he asks me?" Still laughing, but yet for some unexplainable reason, I sense a look of sorrow in his eyes.

"I think what we've just done today tops them all," I say.

"Hey! I bet I can chin myself more than you," he says, as he jumps and grabs the limb of the old sweet gum tree and begins to pull himself up and down. He does ten and then falls flat to the rock on his back out of breath.

I do ten and try like hell for number eleven, but can't make it, then collapse on the rock beside him.

"What we've done is weird" he says, as we lay there. "But why take a chance. It could save lots of souls, especially ours, since we're the ones who thought it up."

"Yeah, you're probably right," I tell him, "but if we haven't committed a sin, we've gone through all this 'hokey pokey' for nothing."

"There's only one way we'll ever know," he says and laughs. "Want to take that chance?"

"And that would be?" I ask.

"If the last one of us alive don't write the book," I think about what he says for awhile, but then decide it's too far in the future to be concerned about, so I make no comment.

"Hey! I gotta go, it's getting' dark," he says, as he grabs the limb and hauls himself up into the tree. I'm right behind him.

We move up the hill, making our own trail through my next-door neighbor, Mr. Reese's garden. At the top of the hill just adjacent to the road, he has about a dozen rows of corn, all full of almost ready to eat roasting ears. As we take a left and walk down the road to the front of my house, I say to Trapper. "In a few more days we'll make a raid on Mr. Reese's corn and build a fire down on the creek and cook it. Whatta you say?"

"Sounds good," he says, "but unfortunately I won't be here."

"Where you gonna be?" I ask.

"That's the reason I said we had to do all this stuff today," he adds.

"Yeah, but you didn't say why."

"'Cause I'm moving or rather maybe I should say, we're moving," he says.

"To where?"

"Back to West Virginia, to Beckley, where my mom and dad's from."

"Why you going up there?"

"My dad's been wanting to move back up there for a long time. My uncle's a foreman in the coal mine up there. He wrote my dad last week, said he had a job for him, so we've moving back up."

As I look at him I can see the gathering of tears in his eyes and can feel the same in mine. I suddenly have a huge lump in my throat and have a problem getting out the next question.

"When ya'll going?"

"Me and Mom and Dad are driving up there tomorrow. Eddie's gonna bring the furniture up soon as we find a house. The rest of the family will come up with him."

"Jean's not moving, is she?"

He grins before he answers. "Naw, she won't ever get Moonie out of Alabama! You know that."

"Well…you'll be coming back down to see her, won't you?"

"I guess," he says, "or hey! You could come up in the summers and visit me."

"Yeah, that would be neat," I say.

We stand there for a few more minutes, tears running down our cheeks.

"Well…I guess this is it," I say.

"Yeah, I gotta go, or Mom's gonna have a posse out looking for me."

We move together and sort of give each other a "half-ass" hug, then Trapper turns and walks away. I see his hand go to his eyes to wipe at the tears while I'm doing the same to mine.

I turn, head across the yard and up on the porch, then turn back and watch him walk up the hill. Just past Margie's house, he turns around and waves at me. He's got the little notebook paper in his hand; I reach into my pocket, pull mine out and wave it at him.

I stand on the porch and watch him until he's almost to the top of the hill, then open the door and move into the house, completely unaware that I will never see him again.

A Very Serious Pact
BETWeen us And GOD.
GOD, we may have killed
somebody but we are not
really sure so just in
case we did this is what
we promise,
1, We promise to confess it
To everybody but we may
wait until the last one of
us is alive.
2, We are going to write a
book and then make a
movie. To show you we
are serious we are going
To seal it in blood,
Signed on July 12, 1949,
Boogie Smith Trapper Trapp

EPILOGUE

I DIDN'T HAVE BREAKFAST...

It's a Saturday morning in early April—April 9th to be exact and the year is 2011. I'm 75 years old. I wake up thankful I'm still alive, and I'm definitely not ready to roll.

I crawl out of bed and look at the digital clock on the TV. It's 6:40 A.M. Strange coincidence I'm sure...then I sit on the edge of the bed and dread once again my task for today.

I turn on TV weather and check the forecast: partly cloudy and rainy the entire day. I stagger to the sliding glass doors of our bedroom and open the blinds to confirm. Miracles never cease! They're right. I hurry to get dressed.

The bad weather follows me all the way to the airport and then on the early morning flight to Birmingham, Alabama. The Southwest pilot never cuts the seat belt lights off. I have a couple of vodkas to settle my nerves.

We land in Birmingham and as soon as I exit the flight and get to a door that goes outside, I check the weather. It's cool out, but not cold, but the sky is forecasting rain, even though none is falling now. I try to remember if it's always rained on April 9th up here, but that's an impossible fact to remember, but it seems to set the stage for my day. *Very similar to sixty plus years ago,* I think to myself.

I hit the Hertz car rental. The car I had reserved, a Hyundai Sonata, which drives better than my Lexus, they say they don't have. I have to settle with a somewhat boxy-looking Chevrolet. "Just think of it as helping America," the rental agent tells me. "Yeah! Sure!" I reply.

Out of the airport, I pick up Interstate 59 East, and cruise to the Huffman Center Point exit, where I turn off and start looking for a Home Depot.

Just on the outskirts of Center Point, I find one. I pull into the parking area and as close to the entrance as possible, exit the car and lock it.

I enter the store and make two purchases. The first one's a breeze, the second one presents a problem. Nevertheless, I leave with what I need in hand.

Upon exiting the store, a light misty rain begins to fall, but it stops about the time I reach my car. The sky still doesn't look too promising but I have a flight back to Florida later today and hopefully better weather by the time I get home.

I throw my purchases in the trunk and continued my journey towards the town of Pinson.

Just outside of Pinson, I take Highway 79 north. We used to call it Blount County Road in the old days. Just across from where I make my turn is the Narrows Road, now smoothly paved and rerouted so it no longer follows the creek.

The falls, whir' that big Oyster Rock is, is now some kind of a state park, the Turkey Creek Nature Preserve, I think they call it. A few years back some environmentalist discovered a couple of what they called, rare specimen darters—some kind of little fish, probably the ones we used to dip up for bait. The state purchased the land and cleaned the area up, so now it's all pristine and beautiful. I visited it a couple of years ago with Wayne (Mr. Big Shot), who now lives in Vero Beach, Florida and who is my oldest and most trusted friend. Both our old bodies creaked and moaned as we traversed the terrain. He wanted to know the purpose of the visit. I told him that since it's so rare that both of us are ever back in Alabama at the same time, it would be fun to visit some of our old haunts and that also I was writing a book. After he finally recovered from his fit of laughter and was able to talk again, we both agreed, that even though beautiful now, the place looked better in the old days when it had more weeds and trees. "So much for progress."

After about a mile further along on #79, I take a left onto a two-lane, paved country road. I remember it as it used to be, unpaved, narrow and potted. It's the road I pleaded with Bill to take all those years ago, the one last chance to take us back to Black Creek through the Quarters. The road the old coke ovens are on. I want to see if I can find them.

As I drive along the winding curves, nothing looks familiar. A few homes here and there, but mostly hills and hollows of Kudzu-covered trees. Where the Quarters used to be is completely unrecognizable now. I only know I'm there when I cross a bridge over a creek that I know has to be Black Creek, because it's the only creek that was ever here. I pull off the road and stand on the wooden bridge looking down at the water. It flows smooth and bright and crystal clear. Of course! It was always clear over here, dummy. It didn't turn black until it passed the 'coal washer' in the White Camp. That portion of the creek has probably cleared up by now, too, but I bet if you look close enough you can still find a trace of sludge and silt.

I look all around me; I'm completely at a loss as to where anything used to be. I know I have passed where the coke ovens were, so I turn the car around and retrace my route. Still, nothing looks familiar. Just about the time that I know I have missed them again, I notice a house sitting off to my left. It's about a hundred yards in front of me, high upon a hill. I didn't notice it before. I continue onward, take a left onto its the paved driveway and proceed up the hill to the front of the house.

I open the door, step out of the car and look around. The house is pristine white, covered with what looks to be asphalt shingles, the kind they don't sell anymore. The owner must have spares because they are spotlessly clean and in magnificent repair.

The house itself is long and low and sits just at the crest of the hill, so that the entrance to the front requires a series of steps with the rear entrance flush to the ground. The front entrance steps lead up to a wide cement porch that covers about half the length of the house. Sitting along the edges of the porch are pots of assorted plants and flowers, all of them neatly maintained like the tree-covered lawn that surrounds the house. On the porch is a green metal glider with two matching chairs. Sitting in the glider is an older-looking black man, with hair as white as mine. He's looking down at me like he isn't expecting company.

I move up the steps and just reach the porch, when he rises to meet me. "May I help you, sir?" he asks. I stand transfixed, the wheels in my brain spinning backwards in time. When they stop, they confirm what I knew at first glance. There couldn't be another head like that in the whole, wide world. I hesitate a few moments more…then blurt it out, "Square?" I ask, "Is that you?"

He cocks his head and looks closely at me. I take off my glasses to give him a better look at my face. That's when he begins to smile. "My God," he says. "It's da Boogieman."

We sit in the glider, two old men, growing up in the same place, but in two different worlds and we laugh and we talk about "the good old days" at Black Creek.

He tells me about his house that he had built in 1958, just after the closing of the Black Creek Mine. He had been given the opportunity to buy this "spot of land" (as he called it) and snapped it up. When his wife died a few years back, he gave it to his oldest daughter and her husband, with one condition: That he could live here for the rest of his life. "And it was a good thing, too," he says, "because they both works, and some bodies got to be around to keep that wild teenage boy and that girl of theirs in line. Home is where the heart is," he tells me, "and you know something, Mr. Boogieman?" he says to me and smiles. "My heart will forever be in Black Creek." I almost cry.

I ask him about Snooks and Freck and about Rosie.

"All dead, with the exception of old Rosie. Last time I hear, he still kicking around. Staying over 'round Pinson with some widder' woman, best I remembers," he says.

"Snooks, he die in 1956. Pulled that knife one too many times. Crazy man shot him four times with a pistol over to Becky's one night."

"Freck, he done wandered off from around here, probably about forty years ago. Wound up somewhere up in north Alabama. My daughter talks with his daughter sometimes. She said he was dead, buried somewhere up around Jasper. Old Snooks, we bury him right over there on the side of the hill, in the old Negro Cemetery when he die. I gots me a trail I walks from time to time, try to keep the old place clean. Nobody else ever go over there anymore."

"Did you bury him next to 'Prince Albert?'" I ask him, which produces a laugh from us both.

Prince Albert, was a name on a tombstone in the Negro Cemetery along the side of the hill, next to the Black Creek. Trapper and I used to see it when we were dilly-dallying around in the woods. We must have spent three months or more scrounging up enough of the red Prince Albert tobacco cans to flatten out and cover his grave. We thought it looked great and so did most of the Black community from what we heard. I know they left them there, but I don't think they ever really knew who did it, or ever even really cared.

As I continue to laugh, it finally dawns on Square. "Now I know!" he says. "You the one put them cans on his grave that time. You and that Trapperman, I 'speck. Still sweep up rusted pieces of them old cans from time to time when I'm cleaning round his grave. Can you believe that after all these years?"

"Innocent until proven guilty," I tell him. He laughs.

"He's dead you know."

"Who? Prince Albert?" I ask.

"No! The Trapperman, I went to his funeral," he says to me.

"You're kidding! You went to the funeral?"

"Last time I seen ol' Rosie. He's the one wanted me to go, to drive him over. One of his daughters' husbands is the one what "backhowed" the grave. She told the Rosie it was for a man named Trapp, who used to live out here when he was a kid. Have no idea how she got all that information. Anyways, the Rosie put two and two together and wanted to go. Even found out that it was only for family, but he said we had an outs for being there, 'cause his son-in-law might need help a covering the grave. So, my daughter drove me and Rosie over there to that cemetery, off'n the Trafford Road where he's buried and we just sorta stood in the background and watched while they prayed and lowered him in. Felt real sorry for his family. Rosie, he cried. Said he remembered all the shit ya'll usta' do to make him and old Freck laugh when ya'll were kids. Rosie did say one thing funny. He say if you'd been there, he was gonna have my daughter fall on the Trapperman's grave and holler, "Daddy, Daddy, please come back, Daddy. He say he knowed that would make you laugh, but he was just kidding when he said it, but it was funny. He talk about you two all the way over there and all the way back. I told him the best thing I could remember about ya'll was that neither one of ya'll could throw a rock 'worth a shit.' Used to run yore little pale asses off them 'dumps' all the time, I told him, with rocks sailing over yore haids. Me and the Rosie both laugh about that 'til our bellies hurt."

I tell Square I remembered it also and after we stop laughing, he says one of the funniest things of all. "Wonder what ever happen to Mr. Gene," he asks.

I tell him that somewhere along the line, I heard he had died. Somewhere in up West Virginia, to the best of my recollection.

"Wonder how long it took the undertaker to cover up that ol' knot I put on his haid," he asks me. That breaks me up!

We both inquire as to what each of us had been doing all these years. I tell him my story, he tells me his. While mine was complicated enough to cause him to scratch his head, his was quite simple and also quite humorous, but only to me. Just after finishing high school, Mr. Pat (as he still referred to him) had pulled some strings that landed him a job at a big cast iron company down in Birmingham. Forty-seven years on the job moved him from sweeping the floors to a foreman in the plant. He says he owes everything to Mr. Pat, "bless his heart." I have to laugh, but only to myself.

He wants to know why I'm here. I tell him to visit my sister and that I only drove through here out of curiosity, that maybe if I have time I will visit Trapper's grave.

I ask him about the coke ovens and he stands and tries to point them out to me but I can never ascertain his directions, so we finally decided to drive down there. They seem to be on the wrong side of the road from where I remembered, but then Square tells me they had changed the route of the road. "No one ever goes up there no more," he tells me. "They're all covered up with trees and the kudzu now. Couldn't git up there if you wanted to." So, I make no attempt to try.

He won't let me drive him back home, said the walk will do him good, so we say our goodbyes until the next time. It's not until I start the car and move on that I remember: I have no idea what his name is, I only ever knew him as Square, and I'll bet it's the same for him, I'm just the Boogieman. Strangely, neither of us even bothered to ask anything different. I almost turn around to go back and ask his name, but then it comes to mind that if it's worked for all these years, why change it now?

In less than five minutes I'm at the intersection of what used to be the Black Creek main road. Just to my right on a tree and vine-covered knoll is where the old Hughes Memorial used to sit. I close my eyes and I can see it now.

I wipe away a tear and take a left. I zoom past where Wayne used to live. The stump of the big oak tree that grew in his yard is still there. I hit the hump in the road that used to be the trip track bridge and though I try not to, glance down to the tree-covered hollow where the commissary used to stand. Too many memories here, too many ghost of the past. I wish I could make this drive blindfolded, but realize if I could, I would still see everything in my mind.

I pass the old school grounds and cruise down Drug Store Hill. It doesn't seem nearly as steep as it used to. I go straight at the Trafford turnoff, then slow down as I cross the Black Creek Bridge, craning my neck, I try to see the water. The best I can tell, it looks clear.

I stay at my same speed and crawl by where Harley's store used to be. The store is long gone now, but their house is still there. Remodeled and beautifully landscaped by their daughter and her husband who live there, both childhood friends of mind. It stands out like a beautiful diamond in the rough.

I'm awakened from my daydreams by the blaring of a horn from a red pickup on my tail. I don't move fast enough, so the driver floors it and zooms past me. I see his hand over the cab of his truck telling me he's one year old. Some things never change in Alabama.

As I accelerate, drops of rain begin to fall. Not enough to use your wipers, just enough to piss you off. Then, no sooner than it starts, it stops. The sky above me is a washed-out gray, but heavier and darker to the west. I hope that patch is heading the other way.

I keep a respectable distance between me and the red pickup as I motor on over the road. Just at the foot of Reese Hill, the truck takes a fast right on the Happy Top cutoff, so I increase my speed until I crest the top of the hill, then I coast the curves down the other side.

About forty years ago, to the best of my recollection, Big Rock was declared off limits. The owners posted all the adjacent land and dozed a large berm to block off the road down to the creek. I was told that they even filled the swimming hole with broken glass. I've heard all types of reasons as to why they did it, but if I had to pick one, it would be for the wild parties that used to be thrown over here at night; the late 50s and the 60s were wild times. Although I was never fond of Big Rock after the incident with Bill, I can remember a few social events I attended over here as early as 1954, my last year of high school. Groups of us guys and our female companions gathered here. We built large fires, then cooked, smoked, drank, and skinny dipped 'til dawn. And, we made enough noise to wake the dead. I think that was the last time I was ever there and I expect it was a prelude to the reason they finally closed it down. But who knows? Or who's still alive to care?

There's still a wide pull-off area just adjacent to where the old road used to turn off to go down to the creek, compliments of the bulldozer operator who bermed the road closed long ago. It's wide enough to accommodate a couple of cars, so I pull in and park, there's no one here but me. I exit the car, lock it, gaze up at the sky and then the territory around me. It's been raining here for the last couple of days. Hopefully it's moving away.

The old road has long since vanished, consumed by the forest that surrounds it. But, as I look around, I see recent tire tracks that go up and over the long berm, so I begin to walk and follow suit. The tracks appear to have been made by either a "dirt bike" or some other type of off-road vehicle that's ridden here regularly, and sure enough, when after a struggle, I finally reach the top of the berm, I can see a well-worn trail. It's running along the hillside, heading down towards the creek.

I take a deep breath, fish out a cigarette, and then with a "flick of the bic," light it up. Then I tally them, something I've been doing at the wife's suggestion for a couple of months: let's see! One before I left for the airport, one before I boarded the plane, one the second I got into the rental car and then maybe another one soon after that, but I'm not sure, so I don't count it. Then, three at Square's, when he got us some coffee and chided me about still smoking. So, counting this one, it makes seven so far today. Not bad! Then, thinking, why at my age do I even bother? I take another drag and begin to walk again.

I'm at about the midpoint of my journey when I begin to smell it, that unmistakable odor of the creek. A smell that must be experienced, not described. As always it makes me think of fishing and swimming and to getting into all kinds of shit and then I remember that I'm past the getting into shit age. Oh, well!

I stop for a few minutes, light up another cigarette, number eight, then think of that faraway day in the past, a day almost like this one, except a little colder and a little more rain. A breeze through the trees ruffles my hair and I think of "Rose" hair oil and laugh, then continue my journey.

The brain is a wonderful thing, if you just listen to it and heed it. If you do, in most cases, from my experience, it will lead you in the right direction. Mine tells me on my first glimpse of the creek that I'm down too far. And so, listening to my brain, I take a left and forge back up along the creek bank on a would-be trail that I finally decide is the old road. I walk no more than twenty yards before I see a cleft in the trees, the area where the swimmers used to park. Although overgrown, it's still recognizable after all these years. I can't believe it!

I edge into the cleft and follow a used-to-be trail down towards the creek and then suddenly I'm there, on the crest of the hill overlooking the rocks, just at the middle, just as I was on that day before, so long ago.

I ease down the incline. It's a lot steeper than I remember, but taking my time, I reach the bottom of the shallow valley and walk out along the rocks to the creek.

I kneel right at its edge, dip my hands in the water and drink. It tastes as clean and pure as always until I suddenly remember Mr. Pat's dead dog story and now I wish I could spit it up. Then I stand and take in the scene.

It could be sixty years ago, were it not for the forest debris that cover the rocks. Back then, the debris was swept aside and the rocks washed clean by the drips of wet bathing suits, otherwise, it looks mostly the same.

I walk along the rocks, up to where they begin and then, with just a slight, concerted effort, climb up to the top of Big Rock, where I stop, sit down and survey the area once again.

The old cherrybark oak and the swing are gone now—no sign of them ever existing. Not even a stump left from where the big tree grew, but on the far side of the island I see where someone, probably kids, have slipped in here and at sometime in the past made a pathetic attempt to duplicate it by hanging a skinny, rotten-looking, little rope from the top limb of a slender hickory tree. It makes me laugh. Then, I close my eyes and listen to the sound of the creek and reminisce.

I remember the day I finally learned what happened to Bill's buddy. The rich guy, the would-be "Klanner," the pervert who was to buy us—the Tulane lawyer from down in Birmingham who liked young boys, and I remember the day my dad finally told me.

It must have been around 1980, about a year before my dad died. I was living in Clearwater, Florida, and had gone up to my parents for a visit. My dad wanted to go fishing, so we threw a couple of rods in his car and headed over to a small lake about six miles away. The lake was down in a pasture, on some property owned by a Mr. Garrett. He and my dad had known each other for years. He usually charged a fee for fishing, but always let my dad fish for free.

"Watch out for them big ol' geese out there, Burl" Mr. Garrett told my Dad. "They'll bite the shit outta you," but neither my dad nor I paid it any mind, too excited to get a line in the water.

It was a beautiful little lake, filled with cattails and lily pads, the perfect place for big, lunker bass and we were rigged up with purple worms, the perfect bait for catching them.

"You fish around the lake to the right and I'll fish the left side," my dad said to me. "We'll meet on the opposite end. If we ain't got our stringers full by that time, we'll retrack each other and meet back here."

I knew why he wanted to fish apart instead of together, so I said, "Sounds good to me."

He's told everyone that he's quit smoking, but he's still slipping around doing it. Trying to hide it from everyone, especially my mother. I could see the smoke every time he fired up.

I fished hard, working the worm every conceivable way I knew how. For my efforts I caught three or four small yearling bass that I didn't even bother to string. Just threw them back to grow bigger for another day.

I must have been about forty feet from the end of the lake when I heard my dad hollering. He was already at the end and I could see his rod bent almost double. "Get over here," he cried, "I've gotta lunker." He was cranking his Zebco as hard as he could to keep the fish out of the cattails.

"Don't give him any slack," I hollered back to him and quickly moved his way.

I was less than thirty feet from him when I saw the goose, a great big white sucker. It was standing maybe ten feet to my dad's rear, watching intently as he was bent over extracting the worm from the mouth of the fish that he had finally managed to get to the bank. "Barely had him hooked," he looked up at me and said, holding the fish by its gills and out so I could see it. It was a bass all right, probably five, maybe six pounds at the most.

That's when the goose attacked like a cobra, biting my dad square in the ass! I probably could have warned him but I didn't, and I'm glad I didn't, because it was funny as hell, something I will never forget. Dad must have jumped about three feet in the air and when he did, he dropped the fish, which immediately flipped back into the water and swam away.

"Holy shit," he cried, looking first for the fish he had lost and then around to see what bit him. All he saw was the ass end of the goose as it scurried back into the trees.

"That fuckin' bastard caused me to lose my fish," my dad said to me, rubbing his ass, as I walked up. "Fuckin' bass must have weighed at least ten pounds." I was laughing so hard I couldn't answer. "You saw it didn't you?" he asked.

"Yeah, it was a lunker," I finally managed to say.

"Damn fucker bit me right on the ass, hurts like hell," he said, still rubbing. "Didn't you see it behind me?"

"I was too busy watching you land the fish," I lied, and couldn't help laughing again.

"Well, my luck's shot for the day, and I'm getting hungry anyway, so what you say we call it quits?"

"Fine with me, "I said, still laughing.

We walked back around the lake and talked, by the time we got there, the bass was up to twelve pounds.

I sat in the shade of a big willow tree that grows just off the lake bank for a last smoke before we loaded up the car to go. I offered one to my dad, and before he could refuse it, I told him he deserved it for what he'd just gone through and assured him I wouldn't tell. He took it, broke off the filtered tip and lighted it up. We sat there for a while and smoked. My dad broke the silence.

"There's something I guess I orta' tell you before I die," he said.

"OK, but I don't think you're gonna be dying any time soon," I remember telling him.

"Never know…anyways, you remember that day a long time ago, with that pervert, Bill…I think that was his name, wasn't it?"

"How could I ever forget it?" I said.

"Well…we never really talked about it."

"If I remember correctly, we weren't supposed to."

"Ya'll said he told you that he was supposed to meet up with another pervert…a lawyer I think it was, and he never showed up… right?"

"That's what he told us."

"Ever wonder why he didn't?"

"Not really…but, I have the feeling you're about to tell me."

"He got killed…head-on collision with a pulp wood truck. Over at Fultondale…just as he was turning off on Newcastle Road. He was a heading your way. It was about three o'clock in the afternoon."

"How do you know that?"

"Britt told me, right before he died. I had gone over to see your Aunt Mertie, in that nursing home over there at Chalkville, was just leaving when he hollered at me. Hell, I didn't even know he was in there. The old fucker looked about a hundred years old. All shriveled up, sittin' there in a wheelchair. Wanted me to roll him outside so he could smoke a cigar…that's when he told me."

"How did he find that out? How did he know it was him?"

"Sheriff down at Fultondale told him. They were friends. Three, four days after all that happened over here, Britt stopped by to see him on his way down to Birmingham…Sheriff told him about a big car wreck they had had over there. Showed him some of the things that they found in the Cadillac that the guy was driving. He told me they made him sick to his stomach.

"What kind of things?"

"Sex pictures of young boys. Even some of them hanging dead. All kinds of ropes and handcuffs, things like that. He had business cards that said he was a lawyer was what capped it off for Britt."

"What was his name?"

"Can't rightly remember, but he had a Mountain Brooke address, Britt said. So no doubt it about it, it was him."

"The hand of God," I remember saying.

"More likely the hand of a drunken pulp truck driver," my dad said. Fucker hardly had a scratch on him, but the pervert was killed outright, according to what the sheriff told Britt. 'Course, I suppose God could of enticed him to the drink. Anyways, thought you might like to know."

"Yeah, thanks Dad," I said.

By the time we got home and my dad relayed the story of the lost bass to my mother, it was up to fifteen pounds and when she rolled her eyes towards me for confirmation, I made my Dad happy by saying it looked larger than that.

A few drops of water and a sudden gust of wind rouse me from my reminiscence. I stand to go, then realize its windblown water from the hillside foliage rather than rain, so I sit back down, fire up number nine and continue to think.

Bill was a mean, miserable, vindictive, cocksucking, son of a bitch and a killer to boot. I've never been sorry, even for a minute, that he's dead. But I have, in the winter years of my life become more remorseful that I contributed to his demise. I know beyond a shadow of doubt that the time I must answer for my actions on that day is not far away. Will St. Peter say he deserved it and pass me through or will he stamp a big reject on my entry request? That's what worries me.

But, then again, God had to have been with us on that day. He had to have been calling the shots. The outcome had to have been in His hands. I remember Trapper saying that He keeps meticulous records. Surely that will give me a basis for appeal.

And with that thought in mind, I rise again, flip my cigarette butt into the water and head back towards the car. At the crest of the hill I turn back and say a silent goodbye to Big Rock for the last time.

Once in the car, I put the pedal to the metal as I head back towards what used to be Black Creek. I feel ancient, apprehensive and depressed, and then I look towards the sky and see a clearing in the east and my mood improves somewhat.

As I take a left onto the Trafford Road, I think of the old community house that used to sit here, and of all the great movies I saw here as a kid. I also remember the taste of young girls' lips and tongues, and the feel of their budding tits, the nights I never watched the movies at all. My mood continues to improve.

As I pass it, I look down towards the baseball field. It's still there, but with a group of soccer nets sitting where the infield used to be. I see a sign, "NORTH/EAST JEFFERSON SOCCER," and my mood begins to deteriorate again. I see no activity, so I assume the kids are all home texting on their cell phones or fuckin' around with their computers. I'm surprised that they ever get enough of the lazy little fuckers out here to kick the ball.

I accelerate my speed and move on. Off to my left less than a mile from the ball field is the new Hughes Memorial Baptist Church, a beautiful, brick tribute to God. Immediately I think of my brother, J.B., and of all the hard work he put in helping to build it before he died. The tears come again and my mood continues to decline.

"Fuck it," I think to myself. I'm having another cigarette, so I crack the window and light up number ten. There's no ashtray in the car so I thump the ashes on the floor. *Fuck 'em*, I think to myself.

Another couple of miles takes me to the turnoff to the cemetery. I make the turn and within five minutes I'm there. Off to my right, just adjacent to the cemetery, I see something added that wasn't there the last time I was here—a large, muddy, fenced-in pen, with an old mule and a gray-nosed donkey, both standing, swatting at flies with their tails, both looking sad and forlorn. There's the semblance of a shed for their protection in case of bad weather, but not a smidgen of grass to graze on. The looks on their faces matches my mood.

There's a new brick church here now, built to replace the old wooden church burned by unknown vandals several years ago. The devil must be stoking the fires, sharpening his knife and salivating, as he waits for their asses to get to hell.

I pull up to the fence surrounding the cemetery, a new addition since I was a kid. Back in those days, the cemetery was all open, the grounds all dirt; covered with stinging nettle and sawgrass. Now it's carpeted in beautiful green grass. I'm sure the inhabitants give a shit.

I exit the car, I'm the only one here. I'm thankful for the first time today for the bad weather. I know how southern people like to visit cemeteries; it seems to strengthen their souls. I walk to the back of the car, open the trunk and pull out the things I need.

First is my old brief case, the one I've had for years. I kept it under the seat in front of me during the flight. Next are the purchases from Home Depot, a small spade, the cheapest I could find, and a sack containing a piece of burlap that was wrapped around the root section of a tree in their garden shop. I paid forty dollars for the tree, gave the clerk a ten dollar bill to cut the burlap off and gave him the tree. I thought I could find some in the store, but to no avail. This was the best I could do. Burlap just seemed apropos for the occasion.

I open the fence gate and walk to my right, lugging my briefcases in one hand the spade and burlap in the other.

Just at the front of the cemetery, almost in the right-hand corner, I see the tombstone, and just in front of it, the graves of my dad; my mother; my brother, Cratham; and my baby sister who died at birth. There are two empty spaces next to the baby's grave waiting for my sister, Fanny, and for me. I get cold chills as I stand there. My space will probably never be used. Tammie will sure as hell plant me in Florida.

Just in front of my families' graves is the grave of my cousin, Bobby, who died when he was twenty-six years old of a brain tumor. Just graduated from jet pilot school down in Pensacola. We were the same age and loved each other like brothers. I kneel down and say, "Hi," to him and tell him I wish he were here with me today.

I meander on up through the graves. I see the tombstones of my great-grandfather and my great-grandmother, my grandfather, and next to him my granny. She died in 1955 the stone says. God! How I've missed her all these years. I close my eyes and I can still see and hear her, "Git in there and eat yore breakfast," I hear her telling me. My eyes cloud up and the tears begin to fall. I'm fuckin' falling apart.

I move on, wiping my eyes, trying to not drop my cargo. Then, believe it or not, I see Moonie's grave, died on December 24, 2006. Dumbfucker died right at Christmas—what a present for Jean. On the stone is an inscription for her, just waiting for the death date. Just the thought of her stirs my blood. I still have yet to see her—I wonder what she must looks like now.

I continue to move forward, toward the back of the cemetery, trying to avoid looking at any other stones. Too many people that I have known are buried here. I don't need the grief.

At the very back, I focus once again on the grave of my brother J.B. Died at forty-nine years old, what a shame. The tears start to flow again. I look at his grave for only a few moments and then turn away and head back down to a newer section where the most current unfortunates lie.

I see Trapper's mother's grave. She died in 1981, came back to Alabama to die. I wonder why? I don't see his dad's grave anywhere. And then I see Eddie's grave, died in 1980. Came back here to die also I guess. He was fifty years old. Killed in car wreck I heard. I didn't realize that this section of the cemetery had been open so long. My eyes move on and then, right next to Eddie's grave is the end of my quest. The reason I came here today.

Charles Edward Trapp is the inscription on the stone; my head begins to swim as I look at it. Right under his name, in big, scripted, sculptured letters is the name, "Trapper," boldly inscribed into the stone. Just under that are the dates: Born March 10, 1936 – Died May 1, 2008, and then under that similarly inscribed, "See you at the Pearly Gates." It's a smaller stone than I thought Trapper would have picked for himself, but with all the flair I knew he would have wanted upon it.

I look all around to make sure I'm still the only person here, then taking the spade; I cut out a section of the grass atop Trapper's grave about the size of a large cookie sheet. I loosen it from the soil and gently, so as not to tear or break it, I carefully sit it to the side. I take the piece of burlap from the bag it's in. It's almost square, probably about three feet in length and width. I spread it next to the cutout and then begin to dig, making sure to dump the dirt carefully on the burlap. I keep the sides of the hole leveled and dig down to a guess-ta-ment of about twenty-four inches, leveling the bottom of the hole as best I can, all the while keeping my eye out for company. No one has yet to show up. The digging is relatively easy due to the still looseness of the soil over the grave and to the rainy weather. I'm thankful for that.

Putting the spade aside, I look at my handiwork. It looks so good, I award myself another smoke. Number eleven, a lucky number and it better be, I think, or else I could get my ass thrown in jail for fuckin' with graves.

I pick up my old briefcase and hold it over the hole. And, as Bill once said, "It's a perfect fit." I look again to make sure I'm alone, then squat down and open it up. Inside is a neatly typed manuscript of the book, tightly bound with a heavy rubber band. Tucked under the rubber band is two old and yellowed pages of 3x5 notebook paper. The contracts we made so long ago. Next to them is the picture of Trapper and myself when we were about twelve years ago, bare-chested, holding our arms around each other's shoulder, grinning like possums. Tears the size of horse turds roll down my cheeks.

I start to close the lid and snap it shut when something else crosses my mind. I reach into my shirt pocket and pull out the remainder of my cigarettes. Fishing out one for hard times I throw the pack with the remaining cigarettes in the case, and then, realizing if Trapper's by some chance in heaven, he probably can't get fire, I toss my lighter in with them. Then, with a sigh, I snap the lid closed and drop the briefcase in the hole.

Burlap has many uses. Bill used it to bind our arms and legs that day and also almost killed Tapper by stuffing his mouth full of it and gagging him. It also rots fast if buried in the soil. Thus, the reason nurseries use it to wrap the root growth of trees and shrubs.

I grab the edge of the burlap where I have carefully piled the dirt, then, hands parallel to the hole I pull it towards me. The burlap falls to the top of the briefcase with the dirt on top of it following suit. I fetch the spade and pat it down, walk across the top a few times and then pat it down again. I spade away the excess dirt and randomly sprinkle it round the cemetery until my filled hole is level to the soil surrounding it. I toss the spade to the side and carefully place the cutout section of grass back in place, in the exact position that I cut it out. I step back and survey my work. You would have to look extremely close to see that it's ever been moved. I walk around the edges of the cut several times, brushing the edges with my feet to blend all the grass together and then I gather several handfuls of leaves and twigs that are lying around and sprinkle them over the grave. Sherlock Holmes would be proud of me.

Looking around again to make sure I'm here alone, I pick up the sack the burlap was in and then the spade. Fuck! I should have buried the sack in the hole, but I guess you can't think of everything, so with that in mind I walk to the edge of the woods surrounding the cemetery, roll up the sack in a tight ball and throw it into the bushes, then with a heavy heave I sling the spade as far as I can down in the woods. *Finders keepers,* I think to myself.

Back at the grave, I reach for the "hard times" cigarette and then remember I have no way to light it. Oh, for Bill's silver Zippo. I hear Trapper's voice from the far reaches of time—it's calling me, dummy.

I look all around me one more time to be sure I'm still alone and then, assuring myself that I am, I bow my head, take three deep breaths, and then I yell to the top of my voice, "Trapper!!!" I scream, "I know you're here, I can feel your presence. I've left you a copy of the fuckin' book I had to write and some cigarettes to smoke while you read it. You'll find a list of the literary agents I have submitted it to stapled to the front cover. So quit hauntin' my ass and start buggin' them, so they'll get off their asses, and maybe one of them will get the fucker published. Now I leave you old friend and in departing, I say these two things to you: First, 'See you at the Pearly Gates,' and last but not least, 'The fuckin' mission is now accomplished, so be there in the red Corvette.'"

Then I turn and head to my car, then back to the airport and then back to Tampa…to wait.

THE END

POSTSCRIPT

ON SUNDAY NIGHT, JUNE 26, 1949, ALL THREE GOATS mysteriously disappeared from Boodles trash dump one day before they were to be slaughtered.

Boodle later related to Sheriff Dorsey Britt that on that night a strange, deep sleep had come over him and his entire family, including his dogs and all of his game chickens.

"Ever' thang on the whole damn hill was 'dead to the world' that night," he told Britt. When we all come to on Monday morning, the goats were all gone. What's more, the dang dogs were all cured of their mange.

"Now, to top it off, I can't get any of my damn roosters to fight anymore" he went on to say.

ACKNOWLEDGMENTS

THE TOWN OF BLACK CREEK DID EXIST, ALTHOUGH IT is named and used fictitiously in this novel. Turkey Creek and the road over to Crosston exist today, but road changes and increased population makes it far different than in the year 1949. References to these areas in the novel are also fictitious and a product of the author's imagination. In all other respects, this book is a work of fiction.

Names, characters, places, and incidents are either the product of the author's imagination or used fictitiously, any resemblance to actual persons, living or dead is entirely coincidental.

The author would like to thank the following people for their assistance in writing of this book:

Chris Wilson, my wife's beautiful friend, who spent countless hours deciphering my terrible handwriting and typing all but three chapters of the first draft—her comments throughout the process were an inspiration.

Deanna Gohn, my awesome niece, who really got the ball rolling by typing the first three chapters.

Evelyn Brewer, Hiram Love, Katie Adkins, Inez and "Buck" Love, Tulie Davis, and others for their "Labor of Love" booklet, *They Called It Bradford*, which I could not have written this book without.

Steve Hunt and Bill Knopke, who were kind enough to read the first draft of the book and give their valuable input. The internet sites of: ClassicCars.com, RemarkableCars.com, HowStuffWorks.com, AntiquesZone.com/G. F.Bowers, Wikipedia.org (Colt Detective Special), and Glossary.com (Gary Miller slingshot).

Also Helen Brewer, BJ and Danny Conn, Staci Moseley, Ellen Henderson, Lorraine Ostrawski, Paula Hunt, Carol Wadsworth, Kimberly Johnson, Alma Jordan, and my two sons, Hal and Mike Brewer, who encouraged me all the way. Also, to stay in good with the Lord, special apologies to all the churches mentioned, they just seemed to fit into the story and I hope there is no offense taken.

CPSIA information can be obtained at www.ICGtesting.com
Printed in the USA
LVOW13s0307091213

364369LV00002B/80/P